IN THE SHADE OF OLIVE TREES

KATE LAACK

PRAISE FOR KATE LAACK

"In the Shade of Olive Trees is a moving novel about finding the joy you deserve after heartbreak. Kate Laack skillfully weaves a wrenching and hopeful story with richly imagined characters while taking you on a beautiful tour through Italy."

— SARAH ECHAVARRE, AUTHOR OF *THREE MORE MONTHS*

"In the Shade of Olive Trees is a stunning debut. Get ready to be swept away to Porto Venere and into Julia's journey to healing, surrounded by sympathetic, secondary characters."

— TIF MARCELO, USA TODAY BESTSELLING AUTHOR OF *IN A BOOK CLUB FAR AWAY*

"Reading this book felt so healing. I'm not sure from what, but I think it may have briefly restored my faith in humanity."

— LIBRARY OF KYLIE

Olive Street Publishing LLC

Middletown, DE

For Mrs. K,
I hope this makes up for not going to
creative writing camp.

For Kiett,
whom I never would have met had I gone to
creative writing camp.

"We look before and after,
And pine for what is not:
Our sincerest laughter
With some pain is fraught;
Our sweetest songs are those that tell of saddest thought."

-Percy Bysshe Shelley

CHAPTER 1

On her wedding night, Julia Brooks sat on her hotel bed drunk on champagne and tried to pinpoint the moment she knew she was about to be left at the altar.

There was the moment in the church when the doors opened and she saw him at the end of the aisle. Whatever she hoped or expected from his reaction at the sight of her and their whole future together, it was not the sad eyes sunken into the ashen face that met hers. He faltered a moment as he stepped down from his place on the dais. Her father hesitated. Then, instead of walking toward him, Will was walking toward Julia. He leaned forward to tuck a stray piece of hair back from her face as he approached, then took her hand and led her from the church, leaving her father perplexed, her guests tittering, and the life she was about to promise to, shattered.

Back in the bridal room, he led her to the blue velvet chaise under the windows.

"Will you sit?" he asked, not unkindly.

In her shock, Julia found she couldn't reply. She had gone

numb. She turned away from him, taking in the whole of the bridal suite, buying time, trying to convince herself that this wasn't a bad dream. The swishing of the taffeta folds of her dress was her only response in the silence. When she returned to face the window, Will was watching her cautiously.

"Just sit with me for a second, okay?" he tried again.

Julia took a step back and tried to organize her thoughts. Had there been signs? A fight not quite resolved, a doubt not quite assuaged, a suspicion not quite absolved? Had she not done enough? Was there something more she could do now? She needed a plan. If she would have known he was having second thoughts, she could have composed the perfect thing to say in this moment. But she had not been prepared for the look on his face in the church, a look that suggested it was already too late. She folded her arms over the delicately beaded bodice of her dress. It was stiff, fitted, ribbed with supports and boning. Like armor, she thought, though powerless to defend against whatever was about to happen. At least refusing to sit might postpone the heartache to come.

"God, you have always been stubborn," Will muttered, brushing past her and beginning to pace the room.

Julia didn't turn to face him. Blood pounded behind her ears as her panic and confusion segued to anger.

"So, that's the problem? I'm too stubborn?" she spat. She realized it sounded foolish even as she said it, but nothing about the present situation made sense. She heard Will's footsteps stop behind her.

"Well, come on Julia, you are. A stubborn, headstrong, opinionated, control freak..."

She spun around to defend herself, but stopped short when she found not malice on his face but the faint traces of a soft smile.

"Which is part of what I loved about you," he finished. He moved back across the room. "Please sit, Jules," he pleaded, voice cracking. He cleared his throat and brushed hastily at tear rimmed eyes. "I'm begging you..."

Without a doubt, she knew then. It wasn't just that he said loved – past tense – it was the pleading. She had heard Will yell, seen him cry, forgiven things he said that he wished to take back, blushed at his whispered innuendos, laughed at his jokes, listened to his practiced sales pitches and shareholder presentations. She knew every rise and fall of his intonation, his voice as familiar to her as her own, and she had never heard him beg. Not when, early on, she had turned down his advances. Not when moving in seemed like a mistake. Not after a particularly nasty fight. Not once. But here he was pleading with her to sit, so that he could explain whatever this was and presumably walk away. With that crack in his voice, something cracked inside her as well.

Her knees trembled, and she reached forward to catch herself on the sofa in the middle of the room. In two quick steps, Will had her by the elbow, lowering her to sit. Then he retrieved her water bottle, made her take a few steadying breaths, took a place beside her, and broke her heart.

It was strange for Julia to feel her world collapse around her. She was aware of every sensation – the pain in her chest, the tightness of her throat, the racing of her heart – yet it felt as if she was watching someone else's tragedy instead of her own. She tried to imagine herself following in the footsteps of the fiery heroines of her favorite romantic comedies, conjuring unnatural poise and control under extreme emotional duress. She listened with steely detachment as Will admitted to his affair. She did not yell or object when he told her to take as much time as she needed to move her things out of the condo they shared. She did not cry or beg when he stood, kissed her cheek, and strode from the room.

3

Left alone, the well of strength Julia had drawn from evaporated. Her dress was suddenly too tight, her makeup too garish. The light streaming through the windows tossed shimmering rainbows along the walls and carpet, beauty she suddenly could not bear to witness. The joyful chorus of the church bells turned to a discordant cacophony. She stood in a rush, wanting as much distance as she could manage between herself and the bridal suite, but when she reached the door, she realized that to storm out would involve facing two hundred, now departing, guests. Trapped, she heaved her first sob of the afternoon, a guttural, wounded sound that Julia was sure she had never made before. A vase on the end table held her bridal bouquet. Seeing it turned her stomach as devastation and rage rose in equal measure. A second sob wracked her chest, and she hurled the vase against the wall.

The shattering of glass from inside the bridal suite set off a flurry of activity. The door burst open revealing two aunts who immediately descended on the room and began fussing over the shards of glass and puddles of water. Her mother followed on their heels, angry tears still fresh on her face. She pulled Julia into a fierce hug, muttering all the while about Will's selfish timing and making a verbal to-do list of things they would need to take care of with the vendors before the evening was over. Her dad stood in the doorway, hands in his pockets, staring past her out the window to the parking lot. Julia turned to see that her brother, Aaron, had caught Will on his way to the car and was now giving him a public dressing down.

From the hallway outside the bridal room, sympathetic relatives called condolences, some wandering towards the doorway attempting to engage her father in a conversational breakdown of the events of the afternoon. Julia glanced toward the door, feeling panic rise in her chest.

"I'll take care of it," he said, stepping into the hall.

A knock just moments later set Julia's nerves on edge. "Go away," she snapped, tears pouring forth again.

"Julia, sweetheart," her mother cut in. "Let's get you out of that dress." She reached for the zipper, but Julia twisted aside.

"Don't touch me," she sobbed, sinking to the floor. "Can't everyone just let me be for a minute? I just need a minute to…"

Another sharp rap on the door interrupted.

"WHAT!?" Julia shrieked. Her lack of control frightened everyone in the room, even her.

Her sister-in-law, Ellie, opened the door and surveyed the scene. At the sight of her best friend, the anger left Julia in a rush, and she curled into a ball on the floor. Her body shook as the tears streamed down her face. She was vaguely aware that Ellie had crossed the room and was on the floor beside her stroking her hair. From what sounded like a great distance, her mother continued giving instructions about flower arrangements and calling the caterer. The door had opened at least twice more, but whether people were coming or going, Julia could not be sure. Only when things had gone perfectly still did she dare turn her face back to the room. It was empty, save Ellie, sitting mere inches away, silent tears streaking her cheeks.

"Get me out of here, Ellie," Julia whispered with a quavering breath.

"C'mon," Ellie said, offering a hand to help Julia stand. "Let's go."

THE CAPTAIN'S suite at the Historic Anderson Hotel was to be set with champagne on ice, rose petals scattered across the bed, and at least a dozen candles around the jacuzzi tub and clustered on each nightstand. Such arrangements were executed by the staff in the minutes immediately following a couple's check-in before they were shown up the grand staircase and through the double doors at the end of the hall. Julia was certain that the concierge need only look at her rumpled dress and tear destroyed makeup to understand that the romantic trappings would not be necessary, but she was relieved to hear Ellie cancel the requests nevertheless.

"You can still bring the champagne," Julia called weakly over her shoulder as they made their way toward the staircase. There was not one, but two bottles on ice by the time they reached the suite.

Julia allowed herself to be coaxed out of her wedding dress and agreed to shower while Ellie ordered food. As she stood under the warm water, she felt any remaining fight drain from her body. She turned off the water, stepping from the shower and wiping steam from the bathroom mirror. Staring into her reflection, she saw only emptiness. There was no joy to be found, not even in the small luxuries around her: an expensive hotel room, room service with her best friend, the knowledge that it was all charged to Will's credit card. The robe in the bathroom linen closet was plush, but it brought her no comfort or satisfaction. There was nothing, she was certain, that could comfort her now. Not even her best friend in the next room.

She tied the robe around her and stepped out of the bathroom to find Ellie stuffing her bridal gown into its garment bag. The sight of it threatened a new wave of tears, and Julia turned away until she heard the zipper close. She drew a deep breath before she faced Ellie.

"You should go," she said as steadily as possible.

Ellie laid the bag on the chair and whirled to face Julia. "What?"

"I mean it, El. You got me here, and I appreciate it; I do.

You're my best friend, so I hope you'll forgive me when I ask you to leave." She moved to the ice bucket to pour herself a glass of champagne, but her hands trembled, and she spilled onto the counter top.

Ellie crossed the room and took the bottle. "Jules, I don't think you should be left alone right now," she said carefully. She filled the glass and handed it to Julia. "You've had your world upended and..."

"And I can't stand the thought of having to sit here and hash through it right now. Even with you." Julia sipped the champagne. She hadn't intended her words to sting, but she saw the hurt flicker across Ellie's face. "I'm sorry, Ellie," she amended. "I just need some space."

"Take all the space you need," Ellie offered quickly. "I'll sleep on the couch. You just shouldn't be alone."

"I am alone," Julia's voice cracked, and she swallowed her emotions along with the rest of the champagne in her glass. "He left me. Alone."

"I'm here," Ellie insisted.

"I know, but tonight, I need you not to be." Julia forced herself to hold Ellie's gaze, silently willing her to understand. After a long moment, she saw her friend's shoulders droop in resignation.

Ellie moved to pick up the overstuffed garment bag where she'd left in on the chair in the corner. "I don't like it," she said. "I don't know how to help you if I'm not here." She paused, but Julia didn't extend an invitation to stay. Ellie sighed. "At least let me get this out of here for you?"

A wave of relief rippled through Julia.

"Thank you."

"You'll need someone to pick you up in the morning. What time is your checkout?"

"I don't know," Julia admitted. She sat down on the edge of the bed. "We had plans to leave early for the airport."

"I'll check with the desk on my way out and send you a text. Do you want me to take that with me too?" Ellie gestured towards the large, black suitcase Julia had packed for the honeymoon.

Julia shrugged. "Leave it. We can deal with it tomorrow."

Alone an hour later, Julia lay across the bed in a champagne induced haze and allowed herself, for the first time, to consider what the future might hold. Gone was the promise and excitement of not just the day, but her whole life ahead. The sun would still rise tomorrow, though the future once imagined for that tomorrow was gone. In its place was pain. Explanations. Separations. Moving and undoing. Uncertainty. Everything that once was good seemed tainted, ruined. Her home. Her marriage. Her future family. Gone. Even her dream vacation through Tuscany and along the Ligurian coast had been taken from her. Will had ruined every good thing for which she had dared to hope, dream, and plan.

Or had he?

With a start, Julia sat up and leapt from the bed. The room spun wildly around her, and she groped for the nightstand to steady herself as she made her way to the large suitcase next to the door. She unzipped the front pocket and found her passport and boarding pass securely tucked into the elastic band of her grey, Moleskine notebook. Maybe not everything was lost. The trip remained. Over this one thing, she still had control.

The honeymoon was her dream vacation, not Will's. She considered that conveniently ignoring his persistent hints about the all-inclusive Caribbean resorts he preferred may have served to drive them apart. Though having to decide between two weeks in Tuscany and the Italian Riviera or in the Caribbean Islands seemed a privileged, first world problem of which one politely lobbied his preference but did not blow up the entire relationship as a result of not getting his way.

When Will relented, Julia assumed it was the first of many marital compromises that would pepper their life together. Though now she was left to wonder if he decided it wouldn't matter because he knew he would never take the trip at all.

But just because he backed out, Julia realized holding the boarding pass, didn't mean that she had to cancel.

She sat on the floor and considered her options, aware the champagne was making it difficult to think logically. Ellie would know what to do, but by the time she came back in the morning it would be too late.

Julia had never been impulsive. She was logical, polished, meticulously organized, and routine driven to a fault. Will had been right; she was a stubborn, headstrong, opinionated, control freak who had planned every moment of their itinerary down to the hour. Somewhere, underneath the fog of the alcohol and the pain of the heartbreak, a tiny voice cried out that to pack up and leave would be reckless and irresponsible. But as she held her notebook, all Julia knew was that doing so was the only thing in hours that had brought her any sense of comfort or control.

The trip was the one part of her future that remained intact. The only good thing she had left to look forward to.

She returned the bundle to the front pocket of her suitcase and walked back to the bed. A plastic card next to the phone on the nightstand listed the number for the front desk. Julia punched the buttons before she had a chance to change her mind. "I'd like to arrange a wakeup call," she announced. "And transportation to the airport."

CHAPTER 2

In the darkened cabin of the plane somewhere over the Atlantic, Julia felt a tinge of panic around the edges of resolve that had brought her this far.

Navigating the complexities of multiple airports and flights had given focus and purpose to her day, and she had ticked off each stage of the journey in her notebook, pleased with the efficiency of her planning.

- *8:30 am - Through security and waiting at the gate.*
- *10:00 am - In route to Boston to make the connecting flight to Florence.*
- *1:30 pm - On the ground at Boston Logan; find lunch at a sandwich cart in the concourse.*

Everything on time, as scheduled. It felt good to be in control of something again. Almost normal.

But not normal.

Julia had been acutely aware, as she left the hotel, that the circumstances of the trip were such that her family would be alarmed to find her missing. Her final consideration before

IN THE SHADE OF OLIVE TREES

she climbed into the cab was who to tell that she was leaving. To text her parents, she was certain, would result in a barrage of questions about not only her emotional state but also the responsibilities she was leaving behind. To rely on a friend was to place an undue burden to have to offer explanations to her family. Ellie was the natural choice, but she felt that, somehow, even Ellie would not understand. Besides, it was early. Best to disturb no one.

Julia scribbled a note on hotel stationary, folded it in thirds, and left it at the front desk to be delivered when Ellie arrived at checkout.

She had set her phone to airplane mode upon takeoff in Chicago, and only thought to check it again hours later before boarding for Florence. She touched the icon on the control screen bringing it back to life. The notifications poured in instantly. Eight from the family text thread. Two calls specifically from her father, who rarely did so without her mom also on the line. A dozen from assorted friends. One from Aaron. Nothing from Ellie.

The boarding call for her flight echoed over the PA system, and Julia hastily replied to her family that she was safe. Their concern may have touched her if she wasn't suddenly consumed with worry and guilt over Ellie's silence. She expected at least a shocked text commenting on her unexpected absence or, assuming that she was not surprised that Julia had run-off, wishes for a safe flight. There was rarely silence between them. She considered calling before she left, trying to make her understand. Guilt twisted in her stomach as Julia thought about sending Ellie away the night before. Then the second call for boarding dragged her attention back to the terminal and the journey ahead of her. She switched her phone back to airplane mode, checked off the final item on her flight itinerary list, and made her way toward the gate instead.

Now, in the quiet, unstructured hours of a transatlantic flight, Julia couldn't keep her thoughts from wandering back to the wreckage of the life she left behind. Her fiancé was gone. She had no place to live. Her future, once intimately entwined with another's, now dangled, directionless. The reality of the situation crashed over her. She was not gallivanting away on a romantic, longed for holiday.

She was running.

Plain and simple.

She felt her throat tighten, and she closed her eyes and forced herself to take a deep breath.

The plane bumped along a patch of turbulence, and she instinctively grabbed the armrest, seeking Will's hand. Her palm met cold plastic, and it took all her willpower to contain the sob in her chest. Do *not* break down in the middle of this plane, she commanded herself. That's what the bathroom was for.

Will's empty seat separated her from the other passenger on the aisle of the row, a willowy woman whose wavy, grey hair was tastefully streaked with blonde. Colorful beads dangled from each ear, and she wrapped herself in an oversized cardigan. She nursed a glass of something amber colored while watching an inflight movie that Julia recognized as an award-winning historical drama she once made Will see with her in the theater. Julia undid her seat belt and stood up awkwardly, catching her row mate's attention. The woman's kind eyes scrunched in the corners as she smiled.

"Excuse me," Julia said with as much calm as she could muster. She shuffled toward the aisle. "I just need to use the restroom."

"Of course," the woman replied, disengaging her earbuds so Julia could navigate past the cord. "It's no problem."

Her voice was lilting and calm and immediately reminded Julia of the popular meditation app she often listened to on her morning commute. She forced herself to return the smile as she slipped past and made her way to the back of the plane. Secure in the solitude of the small, cubicle restroom, however, she dropped any pretense. Gripping the counter, she let her tears fall into the sink, grateful that the roar of the engine would mask the sound of her crying.

A few minutes passed before Julia was able to look up at herself in the mirror. Her brown eyes, normally dancing with flecks of gold, were flat and ringed in red. Her dark hair, swept into a high, messy bun, had begun to slip to one side. She had forgone makeup that morning, a decision she now saw left her looking haggard. Still, she reminded herself, everyone tended to look rumpled at some point on a transatlantic flight. If she could keep her emotions in check, she doubted anyone on the plane could guess the true depths of her distress, a victory considering the circumstances. Once in Italy, no one would be any the wiser either.

Julia found tremendous comfort in that anonymity. No questions. No whispers. No apologies. Nothing like what she had left behind. She wet a paper towel and laid it on the back of her neck, taking deep, steadying breaths. Do *not* think about home, she told herself. She had just one objective from here to her hotel. Hold it together. She wiped her eyes. A couple of hours of sleep before landing would do the most good, she decided.

A soft rapping interrupted her thoughts, and she adjusted her hair before opening the narrow door and coming face to face with the woman from the end of the row. The cardigan hung on her bony shoulders in a carefree yet glamorous sort of way, and she regarded Julia kindly.

"Didn't mean to rush you," she said. "I was concerned maybe you were unwell?"

"It's no problem," replied Julia, unintentionally parroting the woman. "Thank you, I'm fine."

The woman's kind eyes held Julia's a moment before she replied. "Okay," she said, a hint of a frown on her lips. "I'll just sneak by you then."

They did the awkward dance of two strangers trying to exchange places in a small space, and Julia returned to her seat. Before sliding into the row, she opened the overhead compartment, pulled down her backpack, and started to rummage in the front pocket for an Ambien. Things had shifted mid-flight, and the pill bottle was buried somewhere at the bottom. After a moment of digging, she sensed the approach of the woman behind her and turned around apologetically.

"I'm so sorry. Do you mind if I just put this on the middle seat between us? I'd hate to keep you waiting."

The woman gestured back into the row of seats. "Of course."

Julia slid in with her bag, and her companion resumed her position on the aisle where she began scrolling through the list of films. In the bottom of the front pocket, Julia found the small canister and shook out a white capsule. She popped the pill and was taking a long drink from her water bottle when she was startled by the sound of her own name.

"Julia." The woman on the aisle regarded her warmly again.

"Yes. Um..." Julia blinked, unnerved. "I'm sorry. Do we know each other?"

The woman fingered the luggage tag hanging off her side of the backpack.

"Sorry, it was just right here. It's a beautiful name. I've always liked it. It means 'youthful' in..."

"Latin...yeah. My parents liked biblical names that weren't too obvious."

The woman laughed lightly. "Is Julia in the Bible?"

"Exactly. They'd be so pleased you had to ask." Julia rolled her eyes, relaxing slightly. "My brother's name is Aaron. That's a bit more obvious, I guess. It means..." She hesitated as the other woman held up a finger and puzzled.

"Strong. I think. Or maybe a mountain? It's Hebrew. I'm Harriet, Harriet Morris." She extended a hand over the backpack in way of greeting. "It means ruler of the home in German."

"Julia Brooks," she said, offering her hand in return. "You have quite a way with names."

Harriet smiled. "Have you ever seen those little laminated cards that tell you the origin of a name?"

"Of course."

"Well, my husband spent quite a bit of time in the hospital, and I still volunteer there now. One of the things that always gave me solace after a hard day was to go look through the window of the nursery at the new babies. The tradition of the nurses on the floor was to tuck one of those little cards in the end of the boxes, and for some reason, my head just had a knack for remembering them." She shifted to face Julia properly. "So, Julia whose parents like Bible names that don't remind you of Bible names." She leaned in over the arm rest. "What takes you to Florence?"

Julia felt her heartbeat skip, and she squirmed uncomfortably in her seat.

"I've wanted to tour Italy since I was in college and never had the opportunity or the finances to do it until now, so I figured why not?" She picked up her water bottle and took a sip to avoid elaborating further.

Harriet smiled and pulled at a thread on the cuff of her sweater.

"And you decided to do it alone?" She hesitated, kind eyes searching Julia's. Julia forced herself to nod. "Good for you. So many women are afraid to venture out on their own, and then it's too late. They get career focused, or family focused, or married to a man who doesn't want to travel at all. That's my husband Jack. His favorite joke in response to vacation plans was that some husbands were wanderlusty and some husbands were just lusty, and I got the latter."

Julia snorted into her water bottle, surprised to find herself still capable of appreciating a joke.

Harriet regarded her with slight embarrassment. "Sorry, that was too much information." They sat in silence for a moment. "He never held me back from going, but when we knew for sure we only had a limited amount of time together remaining, I decided not to waste any of it apart."

Unsure of what to say, Julia smoothed the blanket over her knees and waited for the sleeping pill to kick in.

"The thing you're wondering about, it's okay to ask it," Harriet continued. "People feel awkward when they realize you've lost a spouse. You start using the past tense or refer to someone as your 'late husband,' and they figure it out and get awkward. But it's not a secret. Jack passed. It's been almost twelve years now."

Julia glanced up. "I'm sorry," she said with sympathy.

"Thank you. Please believe that after twelve years I've found many ways to be okay. Do I still miss him? Of course. You don't fly around the world wearing your dead husband's cardigan unless you still feel inexplicably connected." Harriet pulled the sweater a little tighter around her narrow frame. "He hated flying, but he always wanted me to feel safe and secure; he always wanted me to be warm and comfortable. So, because I can't take him with me, I take his sweater on my solo adventures, but I still have memories of twenty-seven wonderful years spent with him. At some point along the way, I realized it was okay that those two sets of memories were never meant to overlap. It's also okay to enjoy both."

"That sounds very…" Julia hesitated, fidgeting with the zipper on her backpack.

"Counseled," Harriet cut in. "It should sound very counseled. I've had a therapist for all twelve of those years, and she had to drive me to the airport herself to get me on that first flight after Jack passed. Dr. Ellison gets all the credit."

"To Dr. Ellison then," Julia raised her water bottle, and Harriet brought her own glass over the backpack between them in a clumsy toast.

"Cheers," Harriet laughed lightly and finished her drink in one large swig. Julia felt the look of shock cross her face before she could catch herself. Harriet smiled. "Relax. It's apple juice." She lifted and locked the tray to the seat in front of her, crossed her legs and readjusted her cardigan. Then she turned and regarded Julia once again. "So, no husband holding you back from solo travel either then?"

Julia felt the lump rise in her throat and tried to remain impassive.

"Nope, just me," she said, her voice wavering against her will. "Like I said, this was my dream trip."

Harriet considered her quietly for a moment. "And were you always excited about traveling by yourself? So many people go with a partner or group of friends."

A fresh wave of guilt washed over Julia as she thought about Ellie. The choice to leave had been made quickly, but why had she not considered asking Ellie to come? She wondered if she might have agreed to go. She could imagine the two of them sipping wine in a Tuscan vineyard, sunbathing on the rocks of the Vernazzan harbor, sharing a pizza in the shadow of the Duomo. Her heart ached. Her only thought had been to take the trip alone, regain control, hold tight to the only remaining thing that made sense. Julia looked away from Harriet, lost for a reply.

"Forgive me if I'm too forward," Harriet began carefully.

"If Jack was here, he'd warn you it's one of my less endearing qualities, but if I may, how recent was the loss of your partner?"

Julia froze. She was sure her tone lacked conviction, but she had not expected for someone to really recognize, let alone ask directly about, her recent heartbreak.

"I'm not sure what you mean?" she deflected. Her hands trembled as she pulled the blanket tighter around her. "I've never been married, so my husband can't have passed."

Harriet gave her a sad smile. "I always hope when I meet someone as young as you it's not a death. You're too young to be a widow. Heck! I'm too young to be a widow. But death doesn't account for every loss. If you're around it enough, you start to notice the tells. It was your ring finger that gave it away." Harriet nodded at Julia's hands still clutching the water bottle. "Most women don't realize the ring leaves a tan line until they take it off. Then, there's not much they can do about it. When you held up your water bottle it showed."

Julia turned over her hand. There was a thin, lightly colored band of skin around her left ring finger she hadn't noticed.

"I'm... I left the ring..." she sputtered.

Harriet held up her hands quickly. "Forget it, I shouldn't have asked. It's none of my business. You wanted to sleep, and I've kept you. Ignore me. Get some rest." She busied herself with her bag on the floor.

Julia tucked in against the window and pulled the blanket up to her chin. The sleeping pill was working overtime trying to subdue the thoughts buzzing in her head. She hadn't escaped anything. Harriet recognized the truth easily. But why had she bothered to ask? She wasn't wrong, it was forward...too forward. Yet why, Julia wondered, did she now feel compelled to tell her something of the truth?

Out of the corner of her eye, she saw Harriet settle in

with a book and plug her earbuds into her phone. She had one lodged in her ear already when Julia sat up slightly and cleared her throat. Harriet looked up, and Julia was touched by the genuine concern on her face.

"He left," she said plainly. "We were getting married, but he left." Her voice caught, and she looked away hurriedly.

"Julia, I'm sorry," Harriet breathed out in a rush of consolation.

Julia didn't trust herself to meet Harriet's gaze, so she leaned her head on the window, readjusted the blanket, and closed her eyes instead.

A long moment passed.

On the aisle, Harriet closed her book and clicked off her reading light.

In the semi-privacy of the darkened row, Julia hoped she couldn't see her cry.

CHAPTER 3

J ulia woke up groggy and stiff, uncertain of how long
she'd been asleep. The cabin buzzed with conversation,
and light leaked through at the edges of the window
shade. She let the blanket fall away and stretched as
much as the seat would allow. Harriet, she noticed, was not
at the end of the row.

She made her way into the aisle and to the bathroom at
the back of the plane. Even the short walk felt good as her
muscles uncoiled. The bathroom door was locked when she
reached it, and she turned and walked up and down the aisle
a second time to stretch while she waited. The door opened
as she reapproached, and Harriet stepped out in front of her.
She appraised Julia warmly.

"Good morning, or should I say *Buongiorno*. You've woken
up in Italian airspace."

"*Grazie*. It feels good to be here."

"Let me get out of your way." Harriet winked as she shuffled past. Julia noticed she had left the cardigan behind
revealing a smart, elegant, navy-blue sheath dress. Her hair
was twisted back and the colorful, beaded earrings had been

replaced with silver hoops that matched bangles on her wrist and a stack of delicate rings on her right ring finger. For the first time, she noticed a thin gold band on her left hand. "Will you take coffee?" Harriet asked. "The attendants are coming around."

"Yes, thank you." Julia slipped into the bathroom and closed the door behind her. She looked in the mirror. How Harriet managed to look so effortlessly composed after thirteen hours was beyond Julia. Whereas she felt disheveled before her nap, she looked bedraggled now. There was only so much to be done at thirty-thousand feet, however.

She swept her hair into a freshly messy bun and used a packaged face wipe to rub at the dark circles under her eyes. After swilling some mouthwash and applying fresh deodorant, she was at least convinced she wouldn't offend anyone. At the very least, the nap was helping her keep her emotions in check.

Back down the aisle, she paused at Harriet's seat apologetically.

"Sorry to make you get up."

"Hazards of the aisle seat," Harriet chuckled, picking up two cups of coffee so Julia could move the tray table out of the way. When she was back in her seat, Harriet passed her one of the cups. "This one is yours, with these." She handed over a sealed package of breakfast biscuits. "I took a guess you preferred it black?"

Julia smiled. She tore into the biscuits, and dunked one in her cup all the while aware that Harriet was watching her closely.

"Thank you," she said, taking a bite. "Apparently, I'm incredibly easy to read."

Harriet scrunched her nose in an embarrassed grimace.

"I wanted to apologize for last night," she offered. "It wasn't my place to ask the way I did. We don't even know each other, and I was making a lot of assumptions. Besides, I really should have explained more before just ambushing you with a question like that."

"It's okay," Julia broke in between bites of biscuit. "I mean, it *was* forward. You warned me it was going to be forward. I'm not sure why I even told you what I did."

"We don't have to talk about it again," Harriet reassured her quickly. "We don't have to talk at all if you'd rather. I'm afraid I'm that chatty airplane lady you were probably hoping you would avoid sitting with."

Julia looked at the seat next to her. "Well, technically I'm sitting next to my backpack," she shrugged. "So, I think you're okay."

Harriet smiled and sipped her coffee. "In that case, what do you do Julia? When you're not politely tolerating intrusive conversations on airplanes that is?"

"I'm in event management for a hotel chain in Chicago."

"And what type of events do you manage?"

"Mostly corporate."

"Do you travel much for work?"

Julia shook her head and sipped her coffee. "Not particularly. People are usually traveling to our events, not the other way around."

"And do you like what you do?"

Julia shrugged noncommittally. She was good at what she did. Efficient. Organized. Detailed. She rose to a leadership team position quickly, and was often asked for by name with returning corporate clients. Will, she knew, had relished her success. They had climbed the corporate ladder together. Him in finance, her in events. He loved to show her off. Between their professional connections, they had the hot ticket all over town: black tie dinners; fundraising galas; trips out to Martha's Vineyard with his top client. Every other weekend swept up in a climactic scene from a real-life romance novel. It felt like a separate life to her now. She wondered how she would ever convince herself to go back.

"Julia? Where'd you go?" Harriet asked with a hint of concern.

Julia realized she was staring past Harriet into the aisle, and slid her focus back to the conversation. "My job, right, sorry. I like to plan. I like to organize. I like to see all the pieces come together, people having a good time, knowing that I was responsible for the little details that made it something special."

"That's an interview answer," Harriet chuckled, "but I'll let it slide. So, this trip you're on now, I imagine it's a well-orchestrated event?"

"You could say that." Julia pulled her Moleskine book from her backpack. She paged through revealing columns of neatly printed notes and lists. "All my notes on dining recommendations and hidden spots the locals love. I have pages of backup plans if the weather doesn't cooperate or I find myself stuck in an airport or at the wrong train station." She handed the book to Harriet who scanned through the pages, smiling appreciatively at a few of the more detailed entries.

"What are the plus signs?" she asked casually.

Julia's stomach threatened to bring the biscuits back into the conversation. She had forgotten Will's singular addition to the itinerary, plus signs next to the sights and reservations he considered non-negotiable. They were few and far between on the pages as Will had routinely reminded her Italy was not his first choice. Moreover, in his mind every part of the honeymoon should be considered flexible lest a rigid schedule ruin romantic opportunity. Still, there were a handful of experiences that even he admitted were essential. David. The climb up the Duomo. Ponte Vecchio. Each mark

23

on the page was a fresh knife to Julia's heart. She struggled to take a deep breath.

"Those are non-refundable reservations," she lied with a trembling voice. Julia was grateful that, if Harriet noticed, she didn't react.

"Well, you're definitely more prepared than I was the first time I ventured off alone." Harriet closed the book and handed it back to Julia. "Dr. Ellison, my therapist you remember, put me on the plane and told me to follow my heart, and off I went for ten days with little more than a ticket to return home and outfits to cover at least a half a dozen different occasions."

"And what happened?" Julia asked, relieved to have turned the conversation back to Harriet.

"Parts of that trip were very good, and parts of that trip were very bad. But it forced me to take the first steps forward. Even the mistakes have, in time, lost their sting."

Julia ran a hand over the cover of the notebook. "Spontaneity is obviously not my talent," she admitted.

"Can spontaneity be anyone's talent?" Harriet mused. She leaned forward and began to rummage in her bag. "As soon as you decide to practice it, you cease to be spontaneous. If anything, spontaneity is a habit. Lots of people have habits I wish I could pick up but can't seem to stick with. I should drink more water and probably floss."

Julia rolled her eyes. "Everyone should floss more."

Harriet laughed. "Consequently," she continued, pulling something from the bottom of her bag, "I've traveled much more extensively since, and I've learned when to follow the plan and when to be spontaneous." She placed an identical, grey, Moleskine notebook on her lap. "I also take copious notes," she winked.

Julia smiled, relaxing again into their comfortable repartee.

"So have your travels brought you to Italy before?" she asked Harriet, wiping crumbs from her tray table and tucking her notebook back into her backpack.

"Many times. First, I visited all the normal places: Rome, Florence, Milan, Venice; you know the list. Then I came back and got off the beaten path, and that's when it really came alive for me. It's actually most of the travel I do these days, but it's as much for business as pleasure."

"You're in the travel industry then?"

"In a sense. I own a villa that hosts small retreats. We provide, what I like to call, a 'lifestyle experience.' If you want a bus tour or a museum guide, I can arrange those things for you. If you'd rather spend your days privately, you're under no obligation to follow any kind of schedule or spend any amount of time with the whole group. Tours can be so hit or miss, and you shouldn't have to pay good money to do things you're not interested in with people you don't like."

Harriet twisted the stack of rings on her right hand.

"On retreat," she continued, "some people come for a week and never leave the back garden. Others I barely see in between their day trips and sightseeing. There are group meals offered every morning and evening. We also plan a signature full day excursion. Many of the guests choose to participate, but not all. It's really about figuring out what people want and need to get out of their trip."

"Seems a lot like event management," Julia admitted.

"Yes, there's definitely some of that."

"It sounds wonderful. Have I heard of your villa? Are you listed through the major travel sites?"

Harriet shook her head. "I wouldn't think so. I'm a pretty small operation with a relatively niche market. I serve a rather specific clientele."

"Retirees?" Julia guessed. "Women with husbands who won't travel with them?"

"Widows," Harriet offered casually. Julia's face fell. "See, there's that uncomfortable reaction again. So, yes, you could say women with husbands who won't travel with them." She laughed and pulled a business card from in between the pages of the journal. "This is my villa."

Julia took the cream-colored card. The paper was heavy, and the embossed words stood out in deep green.

Olive Haven
- Women's Retreat for Widowed Travelers -
Harriet Morris
hmorris@olivehavenretreats.com

A phone number was stamped on the back.

"I meet the most amazing women. Some have been widowed for years and are just now looking for a way to travel with the security of not being completely alone. Some are looking for the companionship of people with their shared life experience. Some want to tour but don't want to wind up the third, or fifth, or seventh wheel in a group of couples. Some come heartbroken, their loss relatively fresh, seeking solid ground on which to rebuild their happiness."

Julia ran a finger over the raised text. "It actually sounds like an amazing idea."

"Thank you," Harriet smiled. "It's been successful, and I'd like to believe I'm building community as much as providing travel accommodations. I've certainly met plenty of people who have helped me on my own journey." Harriet produced a glossy pamphlet from her bag and passed it to Julia. "I'm located in Porto Venere. Will you make it that way on your travels?"

Julia studied the colored map and sample itinerary on the back of the brochure.

"It looks like I just miss you. After my time in Florence, I take the train to La Spezia, but I won't make it down to Porto Venere."

"Well, it's not a large area," replied Harriet. "The entire Cinque Terre is only about fifteen miles long. You won't be far away."

Static crackled from the cabin speakers as the pilot announced their descent into Florence. Julia reached over quickly and yanked up the window shade. A geometric mosaic in a hundred shades of green glittered like cut gemstones beneath the plane, interrupted abruptly by the red tile roofs of Florence piled against one another along each side of the Arno River.

"Everything you expected?" Harriet asked over her shoulder.

"Even better," Julia breathed.

They set to checking under the seats and in the pockets for stray cords and miscellaneous possessions. The flight attendants moved through the cabin collecting used cups and empty wrappers, and the plane began a gentle bank toward the city.

Julia peeled her eyes from the scenery out the window to look back at Harriet. She hesitated. "Can I ask you a question? It's kind of personal."

"Go ahead," said Harriet, considering her curiously.

"You wear a ring," Julia said. "I just wondered if it was out of habit, or if there was someone new after Jack?"

Harriet looked thoughtfully at her hand.

Julia blushed. "I'm sorry if I shouldn't have asked."

"There was no one after Jack," said Harriet quietly. "He was my great love story, and I never felt I needed another. But that's not to say there weren't opportunities. I started traveling and met all kinds of men. Men who offered to travel with me. Men who offered to wait for me to return to foreign cities. Men who offered security but lacked romance.

Men who offered plenty of romance but lacked security. Just wait," Harriet raised her eyebrows, "you'll find no lack of attention if that's the kind of thing you're looking for on this trip."

Julia felt a nervous jolt. She had not considered that particular implication of solo travel.

"And if I'm not interested in a sordid, international affair?" she asked, her voice rising in panic.

"Why would it have to be sordid?" Harriet smirked, but her kind eyes settled on Julia's. "Relax. I was only teasing. You'll be fine. Florence is incredibly safe."

Julia's heartbeat thundered in reply, but she forced composure. She didn't want Harriet to think she was a coward, or worse, a prude. "You were saying, about Jack?" she asked, prompting the conversation into safer territory.

Harriet nodded. "For myself, I eventually reached a point where I craved a different kind of companionship. Porto Venere is small and close knit among the locals. I set up Olive Haven there because it felt more like home than anywhere else after Jack died. When I began accepting reservations, I focused on giving the women who traveled with me the best possible experience, and they gave me purpose and community. It was one of those first guests who gave me the idea for the band." She twisted the ring on her finger.

"It's not just my wedding band; it's also his. I had them melted down by an Italian goldsmith in Florence and reforged together into a new ring. Olive Haven was a fresh start, and through it I made a re-commitment to myself and what I wanted the rest of my life to look like. This ring is a symbol of what that meant to me. Plus, it was a seemlier way to keep Jack around than wearing the cardigan everywhere." She stared wistfully at her hands. "I didn't realize how naked my hand felt until I put a ring back on my finger."

"That's beautiful," Julia said, watching Harriet spin the band.

They returned to comfortable silence as Julia watched the rooftops of Florence streak past the window. She fidgeted absentmindedly with her own ring finger, her thumb moving back and forth over the light stripe of skin. With thousands of miles and multiple time zones now behind her, she hoped to have found some space to clear her head. But the heartache remained, ever-present, just waiting for a quiet moment to bloom fresh in her chest. She'd been mostly calm on this final stretch of the flight, put at ease with conversation, but her anxiety mounted at the prospect of striking into the city on her own. What had she been thinking? She closed her eyes and sighed heavily.

"Give it a few days in the Mediterranean sun, and the line will fade," Harriet reassured, laying a warm hand over Julia's. "The hole in your heart will take longer. But in the meantime, self-soothing with wine and pasta certainly won't hurt."

Julia smiled weakly.

The ground rushed up to meet the plane, which bounced three times as it touched down, shuddered as it decelerated along the runway, and came to a crawl, taxiing to the terminal. The pilot's voice came to life over the speakers announcing their arrival in Florence. The seatbelt light went off and the cabin burst to life around them.

Julia checked her backpack a final time, tucked the business card and brochure into her notebook, made sure she knew where her wallet and passport were in the front pocket, and took a deep breath.

"I'm so glad to have met you, Harriet," she said warmly. Julia barely knew the woman, yet there was something so comfortable about their time together that she was suddenly sad to consider they may never meet again. She swallowed a growing lump in her throat. "It was the unexpected highlight of my flight."

They stood as the rows in front of them emptied, and Julia shouldered her bag and followed Harriet into the aisle, down the walkway to the terminal, and into the customs area where a security guard was filing people into two lines. They stopped a few feet away.

"Would it be strange if I hugged you goodbye?" Julia asked sheepishly.

"Do you know, I think I'd feel strange if you didn't," Harriet replied, stepping forward. Julia closed the gap between them, and Harriet laid a hand on her hair. "I know we've just met, and I'm probably just a crazy woman on the plane in the stories you'll tell your friends when you get back home," she said gently, "but I think you're going to be okay, and I hope you have an amazing trip."

Julia drew back, tears welling in her eyes. She laughed, embarrassed, and brushed them away quickly. "That's kind of you to say."

"Everyone deserves incredible kindness," Harriet mused, "but people facing incredible heartache deserve it most of all. Now," she said resolutely, "let's get your adventure started. Where do you have to get to in Florence? Do you know where you're going?"

"I'll take a bus to the city center, and then I can walk to my hotel from there."

"Good," Harriet nodded. "You'll want the Vola Bus to the Stazione Santa Maria Novella. You'll find the bus stop to the right out the main doors. It's a small airport. You can't miss it." She smiled warmly as they stepped up to the guard. He gestured Harriet to the right. "*Arrivederci*, Julia Brooks," she said, hesitating for a brief moment.

"*Ciao*, Harriet Morris," Julia replied as she was called forward to the next counter on the left. She handed over her passport, answered the brief questionnaire, and watched the new stamp applied to a fresh page. Another security guard motioned her through a swinging gate and into baggage claim. She turned quickly back to check the other line, but Harriet was already past the counter and gone.

CHAPTER 4

Stazione Santa Maria Novella bustled with midday activity. Every few minutes, a half a dozen buses jockeyed through two lanes, belching tourists onto arrival platforms. Teenagers wielded selfie sticks like swords in front of them, clearing out three-foot circles as they passed through the crowd. Families moved in amorphous groups maneuvering strollers, luggage, and children that threatened to run off, only to be yanked back by a quick hand and sharp word. A dozen languages blended into a general din that was neither unpleasant nor decipherable. On the periphery, street vendors sold maps, sunglasses, plastic molds of the David, and stacks of woven fedoras.

Julia wheeled her suitcase through the crowd and down the sloping boulevard past the calls of the vendors and the sunbathers on the lawn of the Santa Maria Novella Cathedral. With the warmth of the sun on her face and the city sprawling before her, the nerves she had battled began to ebb. She closed her eyes, letting the sounds and smells take over. Mopeds whizzed by on her left; busses filed onto the boulevard on her right. Garlic and sweet cigar smoke wafted on the breeze.

She followed the signs toward Piazza della Republica then turned toward the Arno River, catching a glimpse of the Uffizi Gallery before coming into a small piazza and finding her hotel wedged between a gelateria and a men's tailor. A mustached man wearing a neat three-piece suit greeted her at the desk in heavily accented English and introduced himself as Giuseppe. He checked that Julia's paperwork was in order then led her through the lobby and up the staircase to a second-floor landing with three doors. He opened the one in the middle, stepping to the side so that she could enter ahead of him.

Julia gasped as she crossed the threshold. The room sparkled with afternoon sunshine. Floor to ceiling windows stood open overlooking the piazza below. White linen curtains waved lazily in the afternoon breeze framing each screenless opening. The bed in the center of the room was made up with a clean white duvet and a mountain of jewel tone pillows piled against a dark wooden headboard intricately carved with entwined grapevines. Fresh flowers on both end tables lightly perfumed the air, and in the bathroom, which was done floor to ceiling in white Italian marble, she found a third arrangement to match.

She stepped back into the main room to find Giuseppe waiting patiently at the door. He produced a set of old-fashioned keys from his jacket pocket and set them on the entry table.

"Is everything to your satisfaction, *Signora* Calhoun?" he asked.

Julia had never romanticized taking a man's name. In fact, she'd debated the decision of whether or not to even change her name for months leading up to the wedding. Will was surprisingly traditional over the issue and pressed her to consider what it would mean for their family, their future children, and the shared life they were building. Julia liked her name and had built her reputation on it. But it meant so much to him. The look of pure joy he gave her when she told him that she decided on Calhoun pushed aside any second thoughts she had.

Hearing it used now was a slap in the face, and Julia had to catch her breath before she could respond.

"Please, call me Julia," she forced a smile. "This is beautiful. Thank you, Giuseppe. I'll just get settled in."

He bowed formally and closed the door behind him.

The excitement of moments earlier evaporated. Julia's shoulders drooped, her backpack falling to the floor with a loud thud, the noise masking the sudden sob that escaped her as she covered her face with her hands, sat on the edge of the bed, and cried. It was impossible for her to be there and not think of Will. Alone, the room was luxurious and cheery and welcoming, but she had known just from looking at the pictures on the website, it would be magical and unbelievably romantic with the right person.

She could not unsee it now.

She imagined Will at the window looking down at the piazza, sunlight streaked through his hair. She imagined curling up in the big bed next to him, head on his chest and tangled in the sheets as street musicians played into the night beneath their window. She imagined waking up to find him freshly returned from the cafe down the street with espresso and pastries. He would kiss her good morning, and she would pull him back to bed. Breakfast would be forgotten, but they wouldn't care.

She sunk to the floor next to her backpack, pulling out her notebook and skimming the plans for the afternoon. A historical walking tour of Medici landmarks. Sunset over the Arno River. Dinner somewhere she couldn't pronounce that boasted a Michelin star, a non-negotiable as far as Will's rankings were concerned. She had called in a favor to get the reservation. Something special for the first night of their honeymoon. Julia traced her finger over the small indent Will's pen made next to the address and knew she couldn't face the reality of sitting at the table alone. Tears fell, blotting the ink where they landed on the page.

At a knock on the door, she closed the notebook, pulled herself off the floor, and hastily wiped her eyes with a sleeve. Giuseppe waited in the hall. A bottle of champagne wrapped in a white linen towel sat tucked in one elbow and two flutes dangled from his fingers.

"Compliments of the staff," he smiled, stepping past her and setting the bottle and glasses on the table next to the keys. He turned back to Julia, hesitating before leaving the room. "You're unhappy, *Signora Giulia?*"

"*Si,*" Julia whispered. A solitary tear slipped down her cheek, and she cursed herself for opening the door and letting him see her this way.

"Why?" Giuseppe pressed, his eyebrows knitting in concern.

Julia stepped forward and picked up one of the champagne flutes. For a moment, she could not speak.

"Just one of everything from now on, okay?" she choked, holding out the glass.

Giuseppe's eyes widened. He took the glass from her outstretched hand and rolled the stem between his fingers. He opened his mouth to speak, then closed it again letting out a long sigh heavy with sympathy.

"*Si.* I understand," he said quietly.

The door closed behind him with a soft click, and Julia leaned back against it and shut her eyes. Her breathing slowed as her tears dried in salty streaks down her face. She picked up the bottle and sighed bitterly. Five thousand miles just to find herself with another bottle of champagne in another expensive hotel room…alone. It was *not* what she had in mind when she got on the plane.

She took a swig directly from the bottle. Not champagne, she realized. Italian prosecco. Excellent Italian prosecco. Bright, tangy bubbles burst on her tongue. The sensation stirred inside her the faintest desire to step out and explore. It may not be easy, but she at least had to try. If the complimentary wine at the hotel was the best she'd ever tasted, imagine the culinary wonders that awaited. She could skip her reservation, she decided, but she would still need to eat.

Julia hoisted her suitcase onto the bed and undid the zipper revealing neat stacks of garments. She pulled them out unceremoniously until she found something that interested her, a yellow, floor length dress spattered with pink and violet blossoms. She tossed it on the bed along with a pair of sandals from the front zipper pocket. She appraised the outfit critically. Satisfied, she headed for the shower.

The towels in the armoire were plush and expensive, and Julia tried and failed to avoid thinking about Will coming out of the bathroom with one precariously wrapped around his hips, smelling of lemon soap and aftershave.

The small, marble room filled with steam that amplified the perfume of the flowers then dissipated into the Florentine afternoon through the open window. Standing under the water, Julia tried to relax and banish Will from her mind.

She thought suddenly about Harriet, on her way to Porto Venere by now. By train, or car? Julia realized she hadn't thought to ask. There was a lot she didn't ask, like how Jack had died. But maybe that was too personal? They really just had those few hours on the plane, and it wasn't as if Julia had been looking to elaborate on the details of Will's absence. Maybe Harriet wasn't looking to reveal the details of her most personal tragedy either. Still, she had been so forward, and Julia felt an unexplainable, yet undeniable, kinship with the woman.

She turned off the water and stepped from the shower, wrapping herself in the luxury of the bath towel.

"I can do this," she told her reflection as she stepped past the mirror. She turned to the outfit on the bed and froze.

There was nothing special about the sundress. She had owned it for years, and it lay exactly as she left it. The sandals, too, were not new. Rather, it was her open suitcase that drew her eye. The shuffle through her clothing had unearthed a small package wrapped in lavender tissue paper which now lay on top of the ruffled piles. Julia had forgotten the bundle, a surprise for Will, and she moved to the bed and picked it up with trembling hands. Turning it over slowly, the paper fell away to reveal ivory lace and silk. It slipped through her fingers to the floor, and she felt her heart fall with it. As she reached to retrieve it, she again noticed the light stripe of skin around her left ring finger. Fresh grief consumed her. The effort to get dressed seemed suddenly overwhelming, and all thoughts of leaving the room dissolved.

With a sweep of her arm, the dress and sandals were on the floor. The suitcase followed with a thud a moment later. She crumpled the lingerie in her fist, staring at the delicate fabric where it poked out between her fingers. Another reminder. Will everywhere. Heartsick, she threw it into the wastebasket.

Julia retrieved the wine bottle meaning to carry it to bed. It jostled in her agitation and foam erupted from the open neck spilling down her front. She stood in a puddle of prosecco, bubbles tickling her toes and the bottle sticky in her hand.

"I give up!" Julia burst to the empty room. She let her towel fall away from her body, vaguely aware that in another context, another lifetime, the gesture would have been seductive. She stepped down on it, using her foot to wipe the mess, then carried the sopping heap to the bathroom where she left it on the floor of the shower.

Enough, she decided.

An oversized t-shirt and gym shorts were the least alluring items she had packed, an afterthought, really, in case the occasion called for pure comfort. She pulled them from the pile on the floor, grateful for their lack of romantic intention. Drawing the curtains closed, the room transformed from a sparkling paradise to a shadowed cave in which to withdraw.

Julia threw back the duvet, fell against the pillows, and cried herself to sleep.

WHEN SHE AWOKE HOURS LATER, the room was dark. She fumbled awkwardly for the lights, finding a switch next to the bed that brought to life old fashioned bulbs in wrought iron wall sconces. As her eyes adjusted to the light, Julia assessed her situation. She was by herself, heartbroken, in a foreign country, in the middle of the night, and she was starving. Crying, it seemed, worked up an appetite, and her rumbling stomach refused to be ignored. She had not eaten since breakfast on the plane.

A quick search of the drawers in the room revealed no menus for delivery or room service, and she groaned at the realization that she would have to put herself together and leave to find food. Perhaps if she went back to sleep, she could hold off until morning and face the prospect in the light of day. Her stomach growled again in protest. To sleep would be impossible in this state.

Julia picked up her notebook from the floor and flipped

to her notes on dining around the hotel. The pages stuck together where her tears from earlier had landed, ink bleeding through from one itinerary page to the next. The pages were a mess. So much for preparation. She pulled them apart and left the book open on the bed to dry. Her stomach gurgled again insistently.

She slid into jeans and a sleeveless blouse and raked her fingers through her hair. Glancing at herself in the mirror, she was surprised to find she looked normal. Sleep had eased the red rimming around her eyes, and the tear streaks had rubbed off somewhere on the pillowcase. The empty ache of loneliness remained in her chest, but not on her face. Her anonymity restored, she breathed a sigh of relief.

The lobby of the hotel was quiet as she made her way down the staircase towards the front desk. Giuseppe, Julia noticed, had been replaced by a new concierge, a woman about her own age with dark hair woven elegantly into a knot at the base of her neck. She wore a silk, burgundy blouse with a black pencil skirt, and her gold hoop earrings matched a necklace of braided gold chains draped at various lengths. She seemed to glimmer in the soft light of the chandelier suspended above the desk. Julia felt suddenly self-conscious of her casual attire. It was late, and it had not occurred to her to dress for dinner.

The woman looked up as Julia approached the desk and smiled. Julia relaxed.

"*Buonasera*," she said. "Can I help you, Miss Brooks?"

Julia flinched. Anonymity lost.

"Just Julia, please," she insisted. Despite living as such her entire life, knowing she was to have given up Miss Brooks made it feel just as unfamiliar and jarring as Mrs. Calhoun. "How did you know my name?"

"*Mi dispiace*, Giuseppe asked that I look out for our beautiful American guest tonight. If you didn't come down, I was to go up with more of this." She pulled a silver ice bucket from under the counter, the neck of a prosecco bottle sticking up over the rim. "I told him if you didn't come down, we should probably send something stronger." She winked and retrieved a thin bottle of limoncello, setting it beside the bucket.

Julia offered a weak smile.

"That won't be necessary, though I should apologize for the mess I made earlier. I'm afraid I spilled."

The woman behind the counter waved off the apology.

"It's no *problema*. The bubbles can be aggressive," she chuckled. "I'm Elena, what can I help you with, Julia?"

"Dinner," Julia admitted. "I know it's late, but tell me you have a plate of spaghetti behind that desk you were planning to bring up as well?"

Elena held up empty hands and shrugged. "*Sfortunatamente no*," she replied. "But not to worry, Bianca is still in the kitchen. She will have something." She stepped from around the desk and looped her arm familiarly through Julia's, leading her through the lobby. "This way."

The hotel had no official dining room. Rather, a cluster of tables and chairs sat out in the street to the right of the front door. Elena deposited Julia at a table overlooking the small piazza and disappeared back inside. She returned a moment later with a bottle of sparkling water.

"She says it's too late for the menu," said Elena apologetically, "but she will bring something out, *si*?"

"*Si, grazie*," Julia replied.

"I'll be at the desk if you need anything else." Elena stepped inside, leaving Julia to the night.

A crescent moon rose lazily over the buildings across the way, and Julia watched it slowly break free of the rooftops to join the stars in the black velvet of the sky. She had not made it off the hotel grounds, but she was out in public and sitting alone. It felt like progress. The ache was bearable at least for now, and her tears stayed tucked away. This, she realized, was how one moved on. Agonizingly small baby steps.

Her thoughts drifted to Ellie. She had brought her phone down from the room, intending to let someone know she had arrived safely and hoping to find that Ellie had reached out. Julia couldn't remember the last time they went more than a day without talking. They had been as close as sisters since Aaron brought Ellie home nine years ago.

Julia knew she should call her. It was the middle of the night in Florence, only mid afternoon at home. Ellie would be finishing up at work and headed to her spin class. She would only have a few minutes, but that meant Julia could wrap up the conversation before it threatened her precarious emotional balance.

She was about to place the call when guilt stilled her hand. Ellie had offered to talk back in Chicago, and Julia had sent her home. Ellie would have talked at six in the morning when she was leaving for the airport, and Julia had left a note at the desk and slipped away. Julia briefly considered, however irrationally, that Ellie might actually be upset at her impulsive behavior. It seemed unlikely, but she had to admit that if the tables were turned, and she was the one waiting for Ellie's call from the other side of the world, she would be at least a little hurt that she was being held at arm's length. What good was a best friend if, in the moment you really needed one, you pushed her away?

And yet, Julia knew she wasn't really ready to let someone else into her pain. Though she craved the comfortable camaraderie of her best friend, there was plenty she was *not* ready to discuss.

She let out a heavy sigh, letting her phone clatter back to the table.

Bianca appeared in the doorway, a rotund woman in a

black checkered apron with grey hair wound into a tight bun at the top of her head. She carried a flat dish to Julia's table, and set it in front of her, carefully wiping the edge of the plate before stepping back. A perfect pile of pasta studded with sweet peas and cubes of pancetta lay coiled in the center.

"Carbonara," Julia recognized, already salivating.

Bianca nodded. *"Si, è perfetto."*

"It is perfect," Elena translated, stepping from the doorway behind Bianca.

"Yes, it is," Julia agreed. *"Grazie,* Bianca.*"*

Bianca nodded again. *"Buon appetito."*

The women returned to the lobby leaving Julia to eat in peace.

She eagerly twirled her fork through the pasta and took her first bites of heaven. Salty parmesan, crispy ham, tacky noodles, sugary peas. Euphoria in every bite. Something Harriet said on the plane played at the edges of her memory. Wine and pasta just might fill her broken heart.

The bells of a cathedral began to toll in the distance, echoing over the sleepy city. Julia counted each peel, midnight. A new day. The tiniest flutter of hope trembled in her chest. She had survived the first night. Certainly, that had to be the hardest. There was time for things to get better. She wanted to be here, needed to be here. She would try, really try. She picked up her water glass, raising it to the moon which had climbed directly overhead. She took a deep breath of cool night air.

"To the morning," she whispered.

CHAPTER 5

J ulia slept restlessly, the result of jet lag and a late meal.
As dawn broke golden over Florence, she lay in bed
carefully reviewing her blotchy itinerary notes, plot-
ting a course for a day of sightseeing. She would start
with a walk through the Central Market to the Accademia
Gallery to see the David. The statue had been one of Will's
must-dos, and she hesitated briefly at the plus sign next to
the ticket reservation numbers. Irritation stirred at his
having laid claim to the highlight of her morning. It wasn't
even original, she thought, shaking her head. Everyone in
Florence saw David. It was not special because Will wanted
to see it; Will wanted to see it because it was special. She
would not let him ruin this for her.

She put an X through the middle of his plus sign, trans-
forming it into a starburst. Julia rolled her eyes at the child-
ishness of the gesture, yet felt a rush of satisfaction in erasing
a tiny piece of Will from the page. She made similar marks
next to the other stops she had planned.

The day was hers and hers alone.

She dressed comfortably in a flowing, printed skirt and

navy tank top and packed her small crossbody bag. Phone, keys, wallet, notebook. She locked her passport in the safe and made one final sweep of the room to assure she had everything she needed. Then, nodding confidently at her reflection in the bathroom mirror, she left to join the Florentine morning.

Florence woke slowly. Sunlight spread gradually down the narrow streets and alleys prompting the unhurried opening of shutters and drawing back of curtains. Women draped laundry over balcony rails. Men converged over newspapers and tiny cups of espresso. A flock of pigeons stirred from a cathedral bell tower, made a swirling tour of the city from above, then scattered to the piazzas below to spend the day tormenting tourists for bits of pizza crust and other crumbs.

As she walked toward the market, Julia watched the city unfold around her, aware that a bit of herself was unfolding as well. It was impossible not to feel alive in a place so vibrant. The deep blue of the sky, the red tile roofs, the twang of a mandolin being tuned on a balcony overhead, deep laughter and rich Italian language pouring onto the street from a café on the corner. Last night's meltdown was fresh in her mind, but so was the promise she made herself to make a real effort. It felt easier in the brightness of the day. She wanted to capture the morning in a bottle, hold onto the feelings with both hands.

She arrived in the market early as many of the vendors and shop owners were just opening their stalls, and they smiled, calling *Buongiorno* as she wove through the aisles. She bought a fresh pastry from a bakery cart at the end of a row and an espresso from a barista across the street then found a bench and sat to watch the morning business of the market. Julia marveled that there were people who considered it normal to live constantly surrounded by such history, art, and tradition. It seemed almost counterintuitive to see locals in the market browsing with cloth grocery bags not unlike the ones she carried to Whole Foods. Old-fashioned charm shoulder to shoulder with modern convenience. History in harmony. Were it not for the notable absence on the bench beside her, it was everything Julia had hoped for.

When the bells of the cathedral rang out over the city a short time later, she got up and began a casual stroll toward the museum. As she walked, she stole glances at the Duomo down the side streets. It was splendid in the morning sun, and she fought the almost gravitational pull it had each time it reappeared in her line of sight. There would be time for the Duomo later.

There would be time for everything.

She spent the rest of the morning lost in the rich history of the Gallery admiring renaissance sculptures and paying the requisite reverence to Michelangelo's David. Alone, it was easy to blend in with the other visitors swirling around her, and she managed to catch snippets of three different tours as she tacked alongside the groups bustling between works of art. When she stepped back out into the afternoon sun, she felt the morning had been a success. While Will may have insisted he wanted to see David, he would have hated the repetition of the rest of the museum. Once he had seen one marble statue, Will would have assumed he had seen them all. Seeing his absence as an asset made the visit all the more enjoyable.

She stopped for pizza and a glass of wine at a restaurant across from the University of Florence and watched the traffic filtering in and out of its botanical gardens. Lovers strolled arm and arm through the wrought iron gates; parents corralled children down its gravel pathways, and a group of art students spread out with sketch books to capture leaves and buds and petals with charcoal pencils.

Julia took out her phone and snapped a picture of her meal and the view. She opened a message to Ellie automatically, attaching the picture and a short, chatty message. Her thumb hovered over the button to send. It should be easy. They had sent a million texts. Maybe if she jumped back into the flow of normal conversation, they could skip over the talk of breakups and broken hearts and get back to life as it had been. She wished moving on was that easy, but knew, in reality, it would only take Ellie asking in her genuine, concerned way how Julia was feeling, for the tenuous peace of the morning to shatter. She set her phone to the side, the message unsent.

The lovers had looped back to the entrance and now stood at the corner waiting for traffic to allow them to cross. The man whispered in the woman's ear, and she laughed. He nuzzled his face into her neck. Julia looked away, blinking back tears, imagining how, under different circumstances, she and Will might have shared a similar moment. He loved nothing more than to pull her close in public, snake an arm around her waist, hold her protectively. She missed the gentle, habitual kiss that he would press to her temple after she was tucked in beside him.

She hurried to catch her waiter's attention, anxious for the check. Staying one step ahead of her feelings was the key to remaining in control of the day. As the bells of the Duomo rang out over the city once more, she paid her bill and began the walk back toward the river and Uffizi where she could spend the afternoon lost not in thoughts of home, but in endless galleries of priceless artwork.

Florence provided distractions at every turn. Every street corner seemed to harbor some significant statue. Every bend in the road revealed another piece of history. Trying to take it all in provided little time to think of much else, and by the time she reached the gallery, the couple in the garden was a quickly fading memory.

Her ticket was already arranged, and she fought the bustling midday crowd searching for the reservation desk. At the far end of the entry hall, velvet ropes guided prepaid visitors up to a designated entrance where a man in a black docent's blazer waited to scan the barcode from the confirmation email. He waved Julia forward, and she reached into her bag to retrieve her phone. Her hand landed in the empty space where it should have been, and her heart stopped. She pulled the items from her bag, convinced things must have shifted during the walk. Wallet, keys, notebook...no phone.

The man waved her to the side, gesturing for the next guests to step forward. Embarrassed, Julia shuffled under the rope and out of line. She went through the bag again, confirming what she already knew. The phone wasn't there.

Panic began to set in, and she scanned the crowd for a security guard. Her bag had been checked when she first entered the grounds, but she couldn't remember if she had seen it then or not. If so, she'd somehow lost it on the short walk across the gallery entrance. If not, the last time it was out of her bag had been the restaurant.

Julia felt her heart slide into her stomach. In her rush to leave, she had left the phone on the table. She struggled upstream against the crowd and pushed her way out onto the street. She fought the urge to run, but by the time she reached the restaurant, nerves and the unforgiving afternoon sun left her as sweaty and breathless as if she had sprinted the half mile back to her seat. Her table was empty of guests and, Julia noticed with disappointment, her phone. She walked to her chair and checked the surrounding area. Nothing. Perhaps her waiter picked it up.

Julia spun around quickly in search of a staff member and collided with a crisp, white dress shirt stretched over packed muscle. She stumbled backwards toward the table, only to feel two strong hands grab her shoulders and steady her. She looked up into honey gold eyes.

"Sorry about that," said the man. His accent, Julia noticed, was not Italian. "Are you alright?"

Julia realized she was holding her breath, though over the near stumble or over the man in front of her, she was not sure. She exhaled in a rush and attempted to compose herself. "I'm fine, thank you," she sputtered.

She was acutely aware he was still holding her shoulders, and she glanced sideways at his hands. At the look, he pulled away and rocked back on his heels. The breeze danced over the warm patches where his palms had been, and goosebumps broke out over her arms. "Did you lose something?" he asked. "I was about to leave, but it looked like you were searching for something?"

"My phone," Julia admitted, wondering why it suddenly felt difficult to put more than two words together. "I forgot it. At lunch."

"I see," replied the stranger. "Have you asked the staff?"

"I was about to when..." Julia gestured toward the man.

He smiled sheepishly. "My fault then," he said. "Allow me to make it up to you. Stay here." He pulled out a chair and beckoned her to sit. "I'll be right back."

Julia remained standing. "That's okay. It's no problem, really."

"You don't trust me?" the man asked, feigning offense.

"I don't know anything about you," said Julia. "Except that you almost knocked me to the ground."

"Correction, I believe I kept you on your feet."

"Except for right now when you're asking me to sit?"

The man chuckled. "If you sit, I'll help you find your phone."

"Only if I sit?" Julia asked, glancing skeptically at the chair.

"Well, no," he considered. "But if you're sitting down, you're more likely to stay for a drink with me after."

Julia's pulse, already racing, found another gear. "I don't even know your name," she countered.

"Kev," he offered, holding out his hand.

"Julia." She placed her hand in his. A swarm of butterflies took flight in her stomach, and she pulled her hand back quickly.

"You're American," Kev noted.

"Yes, you're..."

"Australian," he cut in. "Have you been?"

Julia shook her head. "No, but my fiancé has gone on business."

At the mention of a fiancé, Kev glanced around the restaurant uncomfortably. "You're not here alone then?" he asked, as casually as possible.

Julia's hands went clammy, and she cursed herself for breaking the spell of the moment. "I'm just trying to find my phone," she dodged.

"Right," Kev said. "Well then, let me find that waiter."

He disappeared toward the door of the restaurant, and Julia collapsed into the chair, breathing heavily. It had been years since she had been single and making small talk with an attractive man. It felt foreign, forbidden. She felt guilty for even entertaining the notion of flirting, worse for having enjoyed the attention. Adrenaline coursed through her, and she closed her eyes and took a steadying breath. Harriet had told her that romance might find her, but she had not expected to, literally, run into it so soon.

"*Signora?*"

Julia opened her eyes to find her waiter from lunch

standing next to her chair. He pulled her phone from the pocket of his apron.

"Grazie!" Julia exclaimed, relief momentarily over-whelming all other emotions. *"Grazie mille."* She took the phone and put it safely in her bag, looking past the waiter to the front doors of the restaurant. "The man who came and got you, where did he go?" she asked.

"I believe he left, *signora*."

The disappointment that bubbled up made Julia uncom-fortable, and she suddenly desired nothing more than to get as far away from the restaurant as she could. She tipped the waiter, left for the second time that afternoon, and began a hurried walk back toward the museum, replaying the brief encounter in her mind. A staggering realization hit her like a thunderbolt, and she froze in the middle of the sidewalk. It was not so much that she had enjoyed the banter or even that it was so soon after the breakup that bothered her most, though she didn't feel great on either count. There was something deeper, a bigger question she hadn't once considered.

How easy would it be to cheat? Not, she reminded herself, that any of her actions could be defined as adulterous at this point. But Kev had never asked about a boyfriend; he had only made advances. It had been effortless. Too easy. All she had done was bump into him, and there it was, romantic opportunity. She knew that she only entertained the conver-sation because Will was gone. She bumped into plenty of single men every day, but within the confines of a relation-ship, she had never once been tempted to flirt with someone else let alone cheat. But now she could not help but wonder if that was how it had happened for Will? She hadn't asked for the details, but she could imagine it playing out this way. A chance encounter with a beautiful woman. Innocent flirta-tion. An invitation for a drink.

Yet, what drew Julia to a stop in the midst of bustling Florence was not that Will had cheated, but rather how easily the word fiancé had slipped from her own lips, even after their breakup. It had immediately shifted the tone of the conversation. Had it not done the same for Will? Did it not make a difference, or was she never even a thought in his mind? The harsh realization opened fresh wounds in her fragile heart. Gutted, she turned away from the gallery and walked back toward her hotel instead.

THE EVENING LIGHT of Florence threw golden slats across Julia's face where she lay sideways across the bed. She had been there all afternoon, tormented with questions she never wanted the answers to. When? Why? Who? It was torture to imagine a dozen scenarios leading to Will being unfaithful. She knew it would be unbearable to hear the truth of it.

It had not, however, been the complete breakdown of the night before, and she took comfort in the small victory of not having crawled back under the covers and abandoned the rest of the day entirely. Thoughts of Will lingered, but so did the enchantment of Florence. She had already promised herself to go back out for dinner.

For the last hour, she had watched as the street below her window came to life with activity. A maître d' across the way called out house specialties to passersby offering open tables to undecided diners. Two street musicians dueled with a mandolin and accordion. A small crowd applauded enthusiastically at the end of each piece, throwing coins into the open cases at their feet. An old man with a basket of roses went couple to couple pressing stems into men's hands and winking conspiratorially at blushing wives and girlfriends. From the end of the street, a raucous cheer went up from a group gathered around a small TV as the Italian National Team scored against rival France.

Julia stretched on the bed, got up, and went into the bathroom. She washed her face and brushed out her hair, deftly twisting her chestnut waves into a loose braid that hung over her right shoulder. Back in the bedroom, she retrieved the yellow sundress and sandals where they lay on the floor. She stepped into the dress, feeling the soft fabric settle around her, snug in the right places. At the mirror, she applied a swipe of pink lipstick, readjusted her braid, and assessed the look. She almost felt pretty, though admittedly it was hard to feel attractive in a twenty-five-dollar sundress having just been rejected in a bridal gown. Still, it was the most effort she had made in three days, and she was pleased with herself.

She locked her phone in the room safe to avoid another mishap, checked that her wallet and keys were both still in her bag, and headed down to the lobby. She waved to Giuseppe who was back at the front desk, and he blew her a kiss calling, "Ciao, Bella!" as she crossed the entryway and stepped out onto the street.

Golden hour in Florence was unlike anything Julia had seen. The evening sun washed the cream-colored buildings in a soft glow that seemed to resonate from the stones themselves. The red tile roofs flamed against an azure sky, and the deep purple shadows that began to fall along the sideroads were soon studded with bistro lights and flickering candles. Conversation leaked from every open doorway and window, and restaurants spilled tables and chairs out onto their sidewalks to entice hungry diners who couldn't leave the street scene behind them for even one minute.

It was impossible not to see all the romantic possibilities she had lost in Will's absence. She was intentionally avoiding the evening's reservation from her notebook, a restaurant renowned for dishes meant to be shared between two diners.

In front of every restaurant, however, couples sat, heads together, whispering and laughing, and Julia couldn't ignore the reality that she was supposed to be among them. How different it would feel to come down into the magic of twilight, arm threaded through Will's, players in their own Italian love story. Her heart panged.

She put the river to her back and walked a few blocks to the Duomo, seeking the more benign sights of the city. Street vendors near the tourist entrance to the cathedral packed up their carts and street musicians began their evening sets of classic Italian melodies as she stepped into the piazza. The towering facade of the church took her breath away, and she found its solid presence and the bustle of people around her momentarily distracting from the persistent reminders of Will.

She searched the perimeter for a spot to have dinner. A small cafe in the corner, Allegretto's, seemed busy enough to suggest the food was good but not so crowded that she would need to wait. The waiter at the door confirmed an opening on the street was available, and Julia took a seat in clear view of the Duomo and life on the piazza.

The waiter brought warm bread and tart red wine, and Julia immediately tucked into both. A group of children chased a soccer ball into the piazza, kicked it woefully close to a cluster of diners at a nearby restaurant, and after facing a scolding from the waitstaff, disappeared down another side street. A lone violinist leaned against the wall of the church tuning his instrument. Each note resonated off the surrounding stone buildings, and when he started his first concerto, Julia felt the music nestle into her chest, filling her heart. Time stretched on, an everlasting summer evening.

The same old man selling flowers in front of her hotel wandered into the piazza, visiting tables along the edge, presenting white roses to unsuspecting couples in the middle of their dinners, and prompting men into producing coins. Julia watched him progress around the edge of the piazza, his basket emptying as he went. She envied the couples he sold to, wondering about the occasions that brought them to their tables. Anniversaries, honeymoons, birthdays? What a place it would be to be in love. She watched him bow congenially to a young lady, presenting her with a white rose. A memory flashed: white roses in a crystal vase bursting against the bridal room wall. Julia swallowed hard and took a long sip of wine.

By the time the old man reached her corner, he was down to just a few stems. A grey-haired couple a few tables to her left held hands while sharing a plate of spaghetti, and he spent a brief moment in conversation with the husband before gathering the rest of the flowers into a small bouquet and presenting them to the wife. She flushed and leaned across the table to kiss her husband, delighted. The waiter returned with a large plate of pappardelle and more wine, and Julia was grateful for a reason to look away.

The food was delicious. The music swirled around her. Twilight deepened. The magic of the moment was not lost on Julia, and she settled into an uneasy peace. She was not happy, but she was, at least, content.

A group of men, Julia guessed to be about her own age, suddenly burst into the piazza shouting, singing, and haphazardly carrying another man in the air above them. Scattered applause broke out around the square as the group set the man down clumsily, laughing and egging him on toward the tables at the surrounding restaurants. One of the men approached a couple strolling past the church, gesticulated broadly toward the man in the center of the group, and eventually convinced the woman to go with him. He brought her before his friend and, calling to the musicians next to the church, prompted them to dance together. The violinist struck up a lively reel, and the man gingerly took the woman's waist and began to dance. The men around him cheered wildly, and a few broke away from the group to recruit more women to join the revelry.

"*Addio al celibato*," said the waiter, amused, as he returned to collect Julia's plate.

She jumped. "*Scusi?*"

"*Mi dispiace, signorina*. I believe you call it a bachelor party?"

Julia nodded. "Oh, I see. Yes, that's right." She turned back to the spectacle in the square. "So why do they make him dance?"

"I don't know," the waiter shrugged. "Why do they do anything they do at a bachelor party? More wine?"

"*Si, grazie.*"

He cleared her dishes and returned with another glass of red wine.

Three more women had been pressed into service by the friends of the future groom, and he took turns dancing them around the piazza as the musicians took requests from onlookers who tossed coins into their cases. The men whistled and catcalled as the groom-to-be tangoed, then jigged, then two stepped his way around the square. They had captured the attention of the whole piazza, and Julia was so engrossed in the scene, she didn't notice the rest of the men continuing to make their way, table to table, around the perimeter.

"*Ballerai?*" a voice beside her asked enthusiastically.

She turned expecting the waiter but found two friends of the groom instead. They were tall and handsome, eyes sparkling with liquor and mischief. One wore a white button-down dress shirt, damp with sweat; the other sported an Italian soccer jersey.

"*Ballerai?*" The man in the dress shirt held out his hand to her.

Julia smiled shyly. "*Non capisco.*"

"Dance, *signorina!*" a fellow diner called from a few tables over. "They want you to join the dance."

"No, *grazie,*" Julia blushed, staring at the man's outstretched hand.

"*Per favore, signorina, per favore,*" the man in the soccer jersey begged. He dropped to both knees and clasped his hands. The diners around her cheered.

"*Donna più bella,*" the man in the white shirt began again, "*ballerai?*"

"*Balla con lui!*" The grey-haired woman called from the corner.

"Dance with him!" A smattering of encouragement chimed in from the surrounding tables.

Julia was comforted to see her waiter reappear with her check, but before he could make it to the table, the man in the soccer jersey stopped him and took the folder.

"*Signorina,*" he pleaded, "dance with our friend, and we will pay for your dinner." Everyone quieted, anticipating her reply. The man in the white shirt continued to hold out his hand. Her waiter grinned supportively. The same, surprising ripple of adrenaline from her afternoon encounter coursed through her, and the ache she felt to have her own romantic, Italian evening swelled in her chest. Against better judgment, Julia took a deep breath, placed her hand in the man's, and allowed herself to be helped to her feet. The entire piazza cheered as they led her to the middle of the square.

As Julia approached, she got a good look at the groom. He was classically handsome, tall, broad-shouldered, with dark, wavy hair that he styled back from his face and a neatly trimmed goatee. He wore grey pants with a navy dress shirt, both exquisitely tailored. For having been carelessly carried into the piazza by his friends, he still looked impeccable. His brown eyes met hers as she approached, and he gave her a dazzling smile.

"*Buonasera,*" he said in a low voice. The butterflies came to life again in Julia's stomach. "*Parli Italiano?*"

"Not well," Julia admitted.

The man smiled again. "*Americano?*" he asked.

"*Si, signor.*"

"Okay, I see," his rich, Italian accent rolled around the vowels. "I'm Luca." He held out his hand.

"Julia," she replied, her heart leaping to her throat. She placed her hand in his.

"And your husband won't mind the dance?"

Julia shrugged. "No husband," she said, attempting to remain calm. Blood rushed behind her ears.

He regarded her curiously. "My good fortune."

The men of the party bantered with the musicians, tossing another coin in the case which prompted the violinist to draw his bow across the instrument and start a new piece: a beautiful, yet haunting melody.

"Shall we dance?" Luca asked, pulling Julia toward him gently. She reached up and laid a hand lightly on his shoulder, well aware of the one he rested confidently at the small of her back as he drew her in.

They swayed slowly in place, the music not lending itself to the more boisterous displays put on with the other women. Not comfortable making eye contact, Julia watched the piazza spin in a slow circle over Luca's shoulder. She felt him draw her in tighter, and her breath hitched.

"Do you know this song?" he asked softly. They were pressed closely enough that she felt his voice rumble in his chest. She wondered if he felt her heart race in reply.

"I don't," she managed.

He leaned back to look her in the eye as the violinist hung on a sad, suspended note.

"Hold on," he smiled.

Then, the violin was off on a whirling counter melody, upbeat and cheerful. Luca pulled her in close, guiding her expertly through twirls and spins. She held on tightly, chin buried in his shoulder. She smelled his cologne, and beneath that vanilla, and espresso, and something else, something familiar that reminded her of home. Julia's heart soared and her thoughts raced, and a minute later when Luca finished with a perfectly executed dip, she realized she had been holding her breath.

The piazza burst to life with cheers.

Luca returned Julia to her feet, spinning her around a final time.

She would later wonder if it was the magic of Florence, the third glass of wine, or her confused and broken heart that overpowered rational thought in the moment. Whatever it was, it was impulsive, visceral, and almost immediately regrettable. For one brief instant, her better judgment slipped, and she leaned forward, closing the gap between them, and kissed him. She felt him kiss her back—out of shock or desire she would never know. Time on the piazza stopped. Then, almost as quickly, she realized herself and pulled away. He looked embarrassed, though not particularly offended.

"*Czardas*," he said simply.

"I'm sorry?" replied Julia, disoriented.

"The song, *signorina*, now you will know it. It's called *Czardas*."

The rest of the party gathered around, whooping and hollering, elbowing Luca playfully and corralling him toward a side street and their next destination. His hand slipped from Julia's, and she caught his eye as they whisked him away. He smiled a final, perfect smile and disappeared around the corner.

Julia walked back to Allegretto's alone. Her waiter stood next to her empty chair laughing.

"Your dinner - they paid," he said. "Do you need anything more?"

"No. Thank you," she replied, embarrassed by the attention of the other diners as she collected her things. The comfortable intimacy of the piazza suddenly felt oppressive.

She walked quickly across the square and back toward her hotel in a daze, trying hard not to think of Luca's eyes, his smell, his hands firmly in her own, and the way he deftly moved their bodies together through the dance. She tried not to linger on their brief exchanges and the way his accent had played over his words. She fought against the impulse to replay the kiss.

And in trying so hard not to think of Luca, she thought of Will instead. She wondered what he would've thought of the spectacle? Would the men have asked her to dance at all had she been sitting with her husband? Probably not. But if they had, would Will have laughed and encouraged her to join the party or protectively taken her hand and waved the men away? She imagined walking back to the hotel together, buzzing and recalling the scenes of the evening. He would pull her against him into some alcove off the street, and they would sway together, dancing, until dancing turned into kissing.

Because, as it turned out, dancing invariably led to kissing.

The last of the butterflies in her stomach fluttered away leaving the dull, empty ache of shame.

The lobby of the hotel was empty, and she climbed up to her room, sick with regret. Her covers had been turned down, and the lamps on the bedside tables glowed warmly.

She stared at herself in the mirror. Her cheeks were flushed, wisps of hair had pulled from her braid, and her eyes shone. She looked exhilarated, which somehow made it worse.

She slipped out of her dress, and climbed into bed, realizing as she did that it was too big and too empty with just one person. She cracked, tears spilling down her face and onto the duvet.

The answer to the question that haunted her just hours earlier came clear. Yes, it could be that easy. An innocent flirtation had been one thing, but this was something more. A chance encounter. One drink too many. Opportunity. Adrenaline. A kiss. And then? A new, terrible thought came into her mind. She might be a victim of Will's choices, but she was no better than the woman he made them with. One mistake was all it took. Now she was another man's secret. It was all she could do not to be sick.

Curling into a ball under the duvet, she fought impossibly against the desire to replay the dance in her mind, and she prayed that sleep would come quickly.

There was just one detail of the night she had yet to place: that lingering feeling of something familiar, something safe and comfortable, that had pulled at her through the dance. It had been that more than anything, she was sure, that drew her most to Luca in their final, regrettable, moment together. She fixated on the sensation, looking for clues, wondering if while caught up in the dance, she had just imagined the chemistry.

She was just dozing off when it hit her. Familiar as anything else in her world the last three years, the niggling sensation had been the smell of Will's lemon soap.

CHAPTER 6

In the grey light of predawn, Julia found her workout clothes and most comfortable walking shoes and left without so much as a glance at her notebook. She didn't care what she did all day, but she couldn't stand another minute in the room.

She had endured a horrendous night's sleep, wracked with guilt over her actions with Luca and plagued by dreams that roused her every hour to face some new wave of misery. In one, she sat alone in a restaurant, waiting, she was sure, for Will to join her. He approached from behind, wrapping his arms around her waist, and spinning her on the barstool to face him. Only then did she see it was Kev.

She had startled in the dream, jolting awake in bed, only to fall back to sleep and into another in which she watched two lovers strolling through the botanical gardens. They stopped at the corner to wait for traffic to allow them to cross. The man nuzzled his face into the woman's neck. She turned, giggling, and Julia saw it was Ellie. Julia had called out to her, desperate to catch her attention, but Ellie had been too engrossed with her lover to notice. The light changed, and he pulled away revealing his face as he crossed the street. It was Will. Julia woke again in a cold sweat.

She tried to stay awake then, but nodded off despite herself, this time tumbling into Luca's arms not in the piazza but in her bed. She wore ivory lace and silk, and he moved their bodies together, dancing between the sheets. There was no regret between them. She woke up agitated and found she was still flushed as she tied her shoes and pulled her hair back into a ponytail.

Elena was at the desk, and she waved as Julia came down the steps into the lobby.

"*Buongiorno*," she called. "Always our American guests are up early. You won't find much to see yet, *signora*. Italian mornings don't rush themselves."

Julia didn't want company and kept her distance from the counter to avoid being drawn into a conversation.

"I couldn't sleep," she confessed, continuing across the lobby. "I thought some fresh air might help."

Elena nodded. "Piazzale Michelangelo," she called as Julia reached the door. "Across the river. A walk and a climb to clear your head?"

"That sounds like exactly what I need." Julia stopped and turned to face Elena. "How do I get there?"

"Make yourself a coffee," Elena said, gesturing toward a machine on a table across the lobby. "I'll draw you a map."

Ten minutes later, travel-cup in hand, Julia left the hotel and walked back toward the Uffizi Gallery. She regretted not having spent time there, even more so when she thought about the uncomfortable incident with Kev and how easily it could have been avoided. If she felt up to it, she would come back that afternoon, she decided. That currently felt like a big if, however.

Julia was disenchanted with Florence in the early morning light. Gone was the comfortable, old-world charm that had captivated her the previous day. Gone too was the magic of the evening that had inspired her ill-advised romantic notions.

The streets were abandoned, and without the hum of activity and vibrancy of music, language, and life about her, the city showed its age. Trash bins overflowed in alleys, waiting to be collected. Litter lay in the gutter, needing to be swept away before business started for the day. The cracks in the old stone buildings teemed with moss. Paint peeled from the green doors and shutters. Julia considered it all as she walked, disappointed that she let herself get carried away under its spell. Florence was crumbling, and Julia was crumbling with it. Anger blossomed in her chest. She had come all this way for nothing. If she wanted trash bins and littered streets, she could have stayed in Chicago.

Yet, Will made it impossible to stay in Chicago. Her home was gone.

That she found herself in Florence, alone, after a sleepless night was as much his fault as anyone's. If Will was there, she would have been reminded to pick up her phone from the table, could have spent the afternoon in the halls of the Uffizi Gallery, would have shared dinner for two without any knowledge of what was happening at a bachelor party in the Duomo piazza on the other side of the city. If Will was there, she would have no reason to consider kissing another man let alone dream about falling into bed with one. If Will was there, she would be texting pictures and stories with Ellie, laughing over the little mishaps that would become punchlines in the narrative of the trip. Somehow, he was everywhere, and nowhere, and in his absence, she was floundering. She wanted to hate him for it, but despite everything he had done, she couldn't forget everything they had shared.

She crossed the river and followed Elena's map along the

water to the entrance of a park that led up the hill toward Piazzale Michelangelo. It wasn't a steep path, but the exertion felt good nonetheless. Julia took the path at a jog, jostling her coffee, but grateful to feel her mind momentarily clear as her effort and energy went into the climb. When she reached the crest, she found the piazzale empty.

Julia sat on a bench and looked out over the city. The sky was painted in pink and gold. The Apennine Mountains hulked purple and misty in the distance. A peel of church bells echoed. A rooster crowed. Unmoved, she kicked at the stones under the bench and wondered where she would ever find beauty again if she could no longer find it here.

No sooner had she finished the thought, than the sun broke over the mountains. The cathedral caught the light first, its magnificent dome flaming against the water-colored sky. Dingy stone suddenly glowed amber in the dawn. Steam rose off rooftops as the morning dew baked from the tiles. The sun climbed the sky, hitting the river and turning it to molten gold. Like a phoenix rising from ashes, Florence blazed in splendor. The magic came rushing back at once. Julia gasped, overwhelmed with longing to share it with someone.

She pulled out her phone. Will's name caught her attention at the top of her frequent contacts list, and she swallowed hard as she touched it, opening their text thread. For a moment, she contemplated swiping through the conversation, looking for signs of where things went wrong. She stared at the empty textbox for a long time, fighting the urge to say something, anything. There were no words. She closed her eyes, took a deep breath, and willed herself to delete his name. Her finger hovered over the button, yet she couldn't bring herself to do it. There was no way to go back, but for whatever reason, this felt too far forward.

She backed out of the thread, seeking Ellie's name

instead. The fact she had let the silence linger between them now felt foolish. This was, Julia realized, the space she had asked for, and yet, all she could think about was how to re-establish contact, or when Ellie might do the same. But Ellie would wait, Julia knew, until Julia was ready to talk. And that, she was afraid, could be a very long time. Still, she was ready to have her best friend back.

Inspired by the beauty of the new day, she took a picture of the sunrise and attached it to a text.

Julia: Good morning. I'm sorry. I miss you.

It was the middle of the night in Chicago. It could be hours before she might be able to respond, but Julia pushed send before she could overthink it. Baby steps, she reminded herself.

With morning fully broken, Julia began her descent back into the city, angling along the river toward the iconic Ponte Vecchio. Known for its art and jewelry, the shop windows of Ponte Vecchio dazzled with the colors of rich landscapes thick with oil paint and luminous gems set in lustrous Italian gold. Julia browsed from window to window, nose pressed to the glass. She was considering a particularly large diamond in a vintage setting when she heard her phone chime. Surprise and relief flooded her at Ellie's quick reply. Pulling her phone from her bag, Julia thought to call her immediately before it got any later and she went to bed. But as she unlocked the screen, her heart leapt to her throat as she read Will's name instead of Ellie's.

Will: I've been thinking about you.

Julia went very still, nearly letting the phone tumble from her hand.

It was one thing to imagine his presence, wonder at his reactions, then mourn his absence. It was another thing entirely for him to force himself tangibly back into her life. Why would he reach out now? How did he expect her to reply? Why did she feel an overwhelming compulsion to immediately respond? Already, she had opened the message, thumbs poised over the digital keyboard. Three-year old habits, she realized, were not so easily broken.

Julia left Ponte Vecchio in a daze, shuffling back along the river and collapsing onto a park bench. Though she had thought many times about what being together in Italy might look like, she had not considered what Will was actually doing alone at home. She had avoided social media in all forms since the wedding, afraid to spiral into old memories and photographs. But now she opened her feed, and scrolled through the updates she had missed since leaving. There were dozens of supportive messages from friends and a few pointed posts about Will and the wedding. She swiped by in a rush, looking only for him.

A dozen pictures down, she found it. A location check-in and a series of photos. Will in an airport, cargo shorts, a Hawaiian print shirt, sunglasses pushed up on his head, looking happy and relaxed. She swiped. A second picture. He sat in a concourse bar, a margarita glass in front of him, luggage visible on the floor beneath the table. Two carry-ons. A backpack. A woman's tote bag. She swiped again. An airplane selfie. Will's face, clearly framed. To his right, blonde hair and an ear with a diamond stud and two tiny silver loops. A third photo revealed the view from a balcony, two sets of feet propped up on the railing. Pink toe nail polish. Julia didn't need to read the caption or see the face to know the truth. This was the other woman. She stared at the photos in disbelief.

It hadn't occurred to her that Will would also choose to leave town after the wedding. It would've been unfathomable for her to entertain the idea that he would leave with his mistress if Julia hadn't been holding the proof. She looked at his face. He was smiling, really smiling. There was a relaxed, carefree giddiness about it. She hadn't seen him look that way in a long time. Wherever he was, he certainly wasn't heartbroken and confused and struggling like she was. Her anger flared again at the unfairness of it all. He should have to face some kind of consequences for what he had put her through, what he was *still* putting her through.

And yet, he had texted. She remembered him wiping away tears in the bridal suite moments before his confession. Perhaps she still meant something to him.

She imagined him lounging on the beach at one of the tropical resorts he lobbied for, drink in hand, mystery woman splashing in the waves just yards away, but longing for Julia instead. She was ashamed at how much satisfaction she got from the idea. A small part of her still wanted him to want her, and the text had awakened the smallest hope that he did. She hated herself for it, but she couldn't help it.

She was faintly aware of the morning slipping away from her, but she sat and stared at the text for a long time, trying to convince herself to block future messages, arguing with herself that he meant nothing by it and she could, therefore, keep lines of communication open. Deep down, she knew nothing good would come of it if she did. The phone buzzed in her hands, startling Julia so badly she almost fumbled it into the river. It was Ellie. Heart pounding, she answered the call.

"Hello?" she said, her voice small.

"Hey," Ellie's voice was tired, and Julia realized it was almost three in the morning back home. "I just got up for a glass of water and saw your text. I didn't expect to hear from you, so I thought I should probably call."

To hear her best friend's voice was the most comfort Julia had felt in days, and she couldn't respond for the tightness in her throat.

"Julia? Can you hear me? Are you there?"

"Ellie?" It came out as a sob.

"Whoa, Jules, what's going on?"

Julia took a ragged breath and tried to regain her composure. "It's okay. I just..."

"You're freaking me out here. What happened?"

"I'm sorry," she started again. "I'm so sorry, Ellie. That night at the hotel..."

"Yeah," Ellie interrupted with a sharp laugh, "about that."

"I panicked." Julia jumped back in. "I was afraid if I talked it through out loud, I'd lose the nerve to go, and I had to do it, Ellie. I just had to." The words tumbled out, tripping over each other as Julia rushed to explain. "Everything was falling apart, but this was one thing that I wanted so badly that I still had, so I left. And every day I've thought about texting, but I don't know how to talk about this. And when you hadn't texted, I thought maybe you were hurt that I had pushed you away. And..."

"Julia, breathe," Ellie cut her off calmly. "Why would I be upset that you left?"

Julia exhaled in a rush. "I don't know," she admitted. "Maybe because it was impulsive and stupid."

"It was *not*," Ellie insisted. "I mean, impulsive maybe. It *was* entirely unlike you. I mean, I know every part of the trip was planned, and you had the tickets and the suitcase sitting there, so you weren't exactly throwing all caution to the wind. But to see you actually just say 'screw it' and go, that's not stupid. I think it's brilliant."

"It's not brilliant, Ellie," Julia started, trailing off as an elderly couple came hobbling, arm in arm, along the river path past her bench. The old man tipped his hat at Julia as they shuffled by, and she watched them go, longing to trade her broken heart for a distant future in which fifty years of life and love culminated in leisurely, serene morning walks in the park.

"Julia, are you still there?" Ellie asked

Julia tore her gaze from the couple and stared out over the river. "I don't know what I'm doing here Ellie," she confessed quietly.

"What do you mean?"

"Everything I was trying to escape has followed me here, and everything I've found here I'm not ready to face."

"Like what?"

Julia let it all come pouring out, from the first night she had arrived and been called Mrs. Calhoun, to the lingerie she had thrown away. From losing her phone at the restaurant, to losing her better judgment with Luca. From the little reminders she saw of Will everywhere, to the big reminder she had just gotten via his text message and social media posts.

"I'm angry, Ellie, and confused, and heartbroken, and when I somehow manage to put all that aside for a few hours, then I try to figure out how to put my life back together, only to have it all fall apart again." She sighed dramatically. "Other than that, Italy is enchanting."

"Sounds like a lot," Ellie observed dryly.

Julia didn't respond.

"That was supposed to be a joke, Jules," she offered.

"I know," Julia said. "I think I'm incapable of laughter. Am I a terrible person, El?"

"Why?" countered Ellie. "Because you can't laugh?"

"No," Julia groaned, rubbing at the furrow between her eyebrows.

"Okay, so because you kind of flirted with a guy who helped you find your phone, or because you kissed another woman's fiancé, or because you're considering texting your ex?"

"Any of it. All of it."

"I mean, it probably wasn't a great move kissing another

woman's fiancé," said Ellie, gently. "And you definitely should *not* text Will. But no, I don't think you're a terrible person."

Julia sipped the cold remains of her coffee. "All I kept thinking about last night was how quickly that kiss happened, how it might have been the same way for Will."

Ellie sighed on the end of the line. "It's not the same thing if that's what you're worried about. He confessed to a whole relationship with another woman, Jules. This guy, you kissed him at his bachelor party, and then he ended it and left, and you'll never see him again. Ask yourself, if all Will revealed on your wedding day was that he had kissed another woman at his bachelor party, would you be in Italy alone right now?"

Julia hesitated, watching the mahogany sided runabouts streaming back and forth on the water. She dug the toe of her shoe into the dirt under the bench. "No," she finally admitted.

"Right," Ellie reassured her, "because it's not the same thing. You're not the other woman. Do you want to know what I think you should do?"

"Always."

"Give yourself a break."

Julia scoffed. "That's it?"

"You're five thousand miles away; I can only offer so much assistance. C'mon Julia, you had to know this wasn't going to be perfect. Don't overthink it."

Another boat slid past with a couple snuggled up in the back. Italian music played from a speaker somewhere on board, and the captain crooned the lyrics of a love song.

Julia sighed, eyes following the boat downstream. "That's proving rather difficult."

"Well, let me give you some advice," offered Ellie. "Delete the text from Will, forgive yourself for last night, and start looking for whatever it was that convinced you to get on the plane in the first place. That spark, Jules, that's what is going to help you move on."

Julia groaned. "That spark might have been a bottle of champagne."

"So, gorge yourself on pasta and bottles of wine for a while."

"Wine and pasta could fill a broken heart," Julia remembered Harriet's words. Harriet had also said that her first trip had been both very good and very bad. Maybe she wasn't fumbling things as terribly as she thought. Maybe it was all part of the process.

"Sorry, I missed that. What'd you say?"

"Nothing. Something a woman said to me on the plane. I should let you get back to sleep. What time is it there?"

"Almost three thirty. But if you need me…"

"It's okay," insisted Julia. "Just hearing your voice is enough. I have my best friend back."

"You never lost her."

"Good night, Ellie."

"Night Jules, love you."

The call ended, and Julia laid the phone in her lap, tipped her face to the sun, and closed her eyes. For a moment, her heart was full again. Somehow, knowing that someone else was cheering her on made her want to try again to make the best of it. Ellie was right, it was completely unlike Julia to make a big, impulsive decision. Now that she'd done it, she had to learn how to accept the rest of it as it came.

She walked back to her hotel to change, still thinking of their conversation and considering how she would pack everything she wanted to see in Florence into the half of a day she had left before leaving for the coast. The Duomo loomed ahead of her, and despite her resolve to move on, she found the thought of returning to the piazza and visiting the cathedral unsettling. The Uffizi Gallery awaited instead, and then a quiet dinner, a good night's sleep, and tomorrow, a day of train travel to La Spezia and the Cinque Terre.

Lost in thought, she rounded the corner toward her hotel, surprised to find Giuseppe rushing toward her from the doorway.

"*Signora!*" he called, clearly relieved to see her. "It's good that you're here. Elena was not sure how long you would be out."

Julia was alarmed by the urgency in his tone.

"Is everything alright?"

"No, *signora*," he said with a frown. "You have a problem."

CHAPTER 7

Train strikes in Italy, Julia learned, were a routine and scheduled occurrence. It wasn't uncommon to see the strikes announced in the paper before they happened to allow travelers time to make alternative arrangements. Ideally, with some warning, those looking to take the train could schedule around any upcoming service interruptions. But for Julia, whose itinerary depended on her ability to travel by train to La Spezia the next day, the announced strike proved a significant obstacle.

Julia listened with rising panic as Giuseppe explained the situation. They poured over a train schedule in the lobby, considering her options. There would be limited service in the morning for essential travel around the city. She might get as far as a station or two past Florence, but would then likely find herself stranded until the normal schedule resumed the following morning. She could attempt to change her ticket to an earlier train tonight, but had nowhere to stay when she found herself in La Spezia a night early. She could extend in Florence another night but would lose a full day of her time on the coast.

"And your room," Giuseppe added, apologetically, "it is filled tomorrow night. We are *completamente* booked."

Julia leaned over and placed her forehead on the cool marble countertop. She had planned for almost everything, but not a train strike.

"*Mi dispiace.*" Giuseppe laid down the schedule and placed a hand comfortingly on Julia's shoulder. "There are many places to stay on the coast," he assured her, "or here in Florence. I will help you make the calls. What do you think?"

Julia didn't know what to think. Every time she felt ready to start enjoying herself, Florence, it seemed, had other plans for her. She had seen so little of the city, yet the thought of an extra day to explore all that she had missed did *not* excite her. Florence was full of specters and mishaps. Another day, and it seemed something else was destined to go amiss. Whatever spark Ellie expected her to discover, it didn't feel like it was waiting for her here. Maybe getting to La Spezia would be a reset. If she could find a place to stay for the night, she could be back on track in new surroundings. A fresh start. She welcomed the idea.

"I'll call my hotel and see if they have a room tonight," Julia told Giuseppe. "If not, could you help make a few calls and see if something else is available?"

"*Si*, of course. I know people. Not to worry."

"*Grazie.*"

Julia hurried upstairs to her room and retrieved the contact information for her reservation from her notebook. The phone rang a long time before someone answered, and the woman who did seemed hurried and frazzled. Julia wondered how many other guests were making similar calls. She began to explain the situation, but the woman cut her off in rapid Italian. Julia strained to catch recognizable words.

She stepped out onto the landing, thinking to call for Giuseppe, but heard him engaged in conversation in the lobby. Aware she was about to make a fool of herself, Julia pulled a pocket Italian dictionary from her bag and attempted to explain her situation again. The effort was met by silence on the other end of the line. She sat on the edge of the bed and sighed in frustration.

"My train is canceled tomorrow," she tried again in English. "I won't make it. *Una stanza stasera?*" A room tonight. She tried the simple phrase again.

"*No, non è possibile.*"

No. Rejection, it turned out, was a universal language.

Julia thanked the woman anyway. Hanging up the phone, she looked around the room, remembering how it felt to walk in the first afternoon and be swept into the romance of the trip as she had dreamed it with Will. It was still beautiful, but to stay somewhere completely different tonight would feel good, she realized. Anonymity restored again. No shadows of what could have been. Sea breezes to clear her mind. But it all hinged on finding a room and a ticket. The thought stirred up anxiety, moving her to action, and she hurried to pack her bags.

A short while later, she hauled her suitcase and backpack to the lobby and found Giuseppe, still on the phone, scribbling information onto a yellow legal pad. He winked at Julia as she approached the desk and gave her a thumbs up.

"*Si, grazie mille, Marcella! Ciao.*" He tore the page from the notepad and slid it across the counter to Julia. "Your room, *signora*. Marcella is an old family friend; she will take good care of you."

"*Grazie*, Giuseppe," Julia breathed a sigh of relief.

"*Si, prego.* If you can't get the train directly to La Spezia, connect at *Pisa Centrale* or *Viareggio. Capisci?*"

"*Si.*"

Giuseppe smiled and stepped from around the desk. He

placed his hands on Julia's shoulders and kissed her on both cheeks.

"Now you must hurry. The station will be busy. *Ciao, Bella.*"

"*Arrivederci,*" Julia replied affectionately. She wheeled her suitcase out of the lobby and rushed toward the station.

Word of the strike had stirred afternoon travel into a frenzy by the time Julia reached the counter to change her ticket. All around her, travelers shouted into cell phones and pleaded with ticket agents trying to make last minute adjustments to schedules and accommodations. Julia drummed her fingers nervously on the counter while the attendant behind the desk clicked around a large computer screen. His expression betrayed nothing. A whistle blew somewhere in the station, and the attendant looked up and past Julia, then back to his screen. Julia closed her eyes and gritted her teeth. The anxious energy of the station and uncertainty of the afternoon rattled her. She needed him to work faster.

The clacking of the keys stopped, and Julia looked up to find the man staring at her with his arms crossed.

"What?" asked Julia, impatience spilling over.

"*Un biglietto,*" the man replied.

"One ticket?" Julia clarified. "When?"

"*Adesso.*"

"*Adesso?*" Julia glanced at the clock on the wall and then back to the man. "What's *adesso?* When?"

A second whistle blew from the platforms behind her. The man pointed. "Now."

He held out the new ticket, and Julia ripped it from his hand. She pushed her way into the crowd moving onto the platforms and began to search for her train. Julia swept along with the throng as they jostled along the walkways, running when she could, frustrated when the multitude of people made it impossible to do anything but shuffle forward. Her heart raced. Things were out of her control; she was headed to accommodations she knew nothing about, and it all relied on her ability to get on the one train available to her in the next thirty-six hours that may already be pulling from the station. This was not how she operated.

She could *not* afford a setback.

A large, digital schedule in the center of the station announced track assignments and times for the afternoon routes, and she slowed just long enough to see her train listed as departing. She pushed desperately through the crush of travelers coming out at the far end of the station where she found a train official locking the compartment doors. She slammed her ticket into the yellow validation machine, and sprinted the length of the platform, coming to the door of her car just moments after the official.

"Signora, this train is departing."

"I know," Julia gasped. *"Mi dispiace.* I only just changed my ticket. Please. I need to get to La Spezia tonight."

He scowled, but Julia did not stand down.

"Please!" she begged.

Mumbling what she could only assume were curses, he stepped aside and let her board.

The seats in Julia's row faced each other, and she found herself across from a woman engrossed in a *People* magazine. Julia guessed her to be just a few years younger than she was. A spray of freckles played across her nose and cheeks, and her hair, pulled back in a ponytail, was highlighted blonde by the Mediterranean sun.

Julia loaded her suitcase onto the rack overhead and began to slide her backpack in behind it when the zipper caught, opening the pocket and sending a shower of belongings into the aisle. She scrambled, embarrassed, to collect her things from around and under the adjacent seats.

The woman with the magazine picked up her notebook.

"Here you go," she said, revealing an American accent.

"Thanks," Julia set it on the table between them as she repacked her bag, double checked the zipper, and put it carefully onto the luggage rack. Her seatmate watched with friendly curiosity.

"I'm Alex," she said, holding out a hand when Julia finally took her seat.

"Julia," she replied, taking it. "Thanks for your help."

"It's no problem." Alex smiled and returned to her magazine.

Julia watched out the window as the official made one final pass of the train. Her heart continued to race, and she took deep breaths trying to calm down after her dash through the station. She realized she had not eaten all day, and her stomach gurgled its displeasure. That she could be surrounded by such amazing food and somehow forget to eat was a tragedy she promised to remedy as soon as she was settled in La Spezia.

"So, you're American?" asked Alex, dragging Julia's attention away from the window.

"So are you."

"Yes, Kansas City originally, then California." She gestured vaguely at her University of Denver t-shirt. "Denver currently."

"Chicago currently." Julia offered. "Originally from Pennsylvania, outside of Philly."

"Small world."

"Yeah."

They settled into companionable silence as the whistle sounded on the platform, and the train lurched into motion. Julia turned back to the window to watch as they slid from the station, and Florence rose up around them. Winding their way out of the city center, Julia found the Duomo jutting up along the skyline and watched it recede. Her stomach turned in distress as she thought about the last few days. She might forgive herself for Luca, but it would take more than a morning. As for Will and what she had now discovered about his activities since the wedding, she wished there was some way to leave that knowledge behind in Florence. She had enough baggage to haul around on this trip without picking up more of the emotional variety.

The train picked up speed as it reached the outskirts of Florence, and Julia found the swaying of the car did little to soothe her stomach. She watched the Tuscan countryside rush by and tried to steady herself. Her heart continued to drum in her chest.

Her notebook offered a small distraction, and she flipped to her pages on the Cinque Terre. With an extra day to enjoy the coast, her overplanning was about to come in handy. She scanned her notes for the week ahead, considering whether she was better off to explore on foot or spend a day on the water, but she could barely focus. The scenery streaming past the windows continually drew her attention, and her rumbling stomach turned into waves of nausea. The compartment was suddenly uncomfortably warm. She laid her head on the cool window and closed her eyes. The train continued to rock. Julia broke into a sweat. She was finding it difficult to take a deep breath.

"Are you alright? You're really pale."

Julia glanced up to find Alex watching her over the top of her magazine. She closed the notebook.

"I'm not feeling well," she admitted. "Do you remember seeing a bathroom when you got on the train?"

Alex pointed over Julia's shoulder. "In the back."

"Thanks."

Julia stood quickly. Too quickly. A dizzying head rush and the swaying of the train caused her to stumble into the aisle. She attempted to catch her balance, grabbing the back of the chair and taking a few staggering steps toward the back of the train car, but her efforts were in vain. Silver stars popped across her field of vision, and the edges began to go dark. She momentarily panicked, remembering that she had no one to call out to for help. But there was no time to call out even if someone had been there. The ground rushed up to meet her, and Julia's world went black.

WHEN SHE CAME TO, the first thing Julia noticed was that her face hurt. She reached up, touching a hand to her head and causing the dull ache in her nose and forehead to throb deeply. Another moment passed before she remembered feeling sick and getting up from her seat. Then it registered that she was flat on her back on the floor. She opened her eyes and sat up in a hurry, embarrassed to have caused a scene in the middle of the train. A flurry of hands grabbed her shoulders and forced her back down. Julia stared up into a collection of concerned faces.

An older man with salt and pepper hair wearing an orange safety vest leaned over her. *"Signora? Parli italiano?"*

"Un po," Julia replied, indicating a small amount with her thumb and forefinger.

The man frowned and began a rapid conversation with a colleague in a matching vest. They looked back at her with furrowed brows. Julia closed her eyes, imagining what came next. Would they call paramedics? Make her leave the train? Take her to a hospital? Would she even know where she was going if she couldn't understand them? Fear consumed her.

She had no one, and she was in crisis. This, she thought, was why people took vows. Sickness and health. Good times and bad times. Will was supposed to be here. Will was supposed to have promised to stand by her in her moments like this. He was supposed to stumble through the awkward Italian conversations, and make the arrangements, and ensure she was not taken to and forgotten about in a foreign hospital. He was supposed to hold her hand and tell her not to be scared. She felt tears pricking at the corner of her eyes, and she drew a shaking breath, unable to catch them before they fell.

"Scusi? Hai bisogno di un traduttore?" Julia looked up and found Alex standing above her speaking to the men in the vests. The men looked relieved and fired off a flurry of Italian, prompting Alex to hold up her hand. *"Un momento,"* she said. She crouched down beside Julia. "Hi." She folded up a jacket and placed it beneath Julia's head. "Do you know where you are?"

"On the floor of the train," Julia said miserably.

"Good," replied Alex. "Those men in the vests are the train safety officers. They're going to ask you some questions and take your blood pressure. I'm going to translate for you, okay?"

"Sure," answered Julia weakly.

Alex nodded to the men who swooped in with a medical bag. Julia lay still, allowing her blood pressure and temperature to be taken. Alex conversed with the men, narrating their progress.

"Your blood pressure and temperature are normal. They're going to do a finger stick for a blood sugar test. Is that alright?"

"Yes."

"What have you eaten today?"

"Nothing," Julia admitted.

"What?" exclaimed Alex. "How have you not eaten all day? It's almost three o'clock."

"I had an unusual morning."

Sunrise over the city felt like ages ago.

"Good thing you're having such an ordinary afternoon," Alex laughed lightly, returning to the conversation with the train officials.

Julia felt her panic ebb ever so slightly. She didn't know Alex, but she was grateful for an ally nevertheless. Her eyes watered again, this time from relief. Alex looked down and caught her wiping away tears.

"Hey, you're okay," she comforted. "Your blood sugar is low, and you're probably dehydrated. They're going to get you some juice and something to eat. Do you want to try and sit up?"

"Sure."

Alex bent down and helped Julia slowly pull herself up between the seats. Passengers on either side of the aisle smiled sympathetically, and Julia turned away in embarrassment.

The men in the vests returned with a bottle of orange juice, two packages of crackers, and a bag of ice. They handed them to Alex along with a folder of papers, and she nodded as the men went through the documents. She opened the orange juice and handed it to Julia who took a long sip. They watched her cautiously.

"Still doing okay?" Alex asked. "Want to try and get back to your seat?"

"Yes, please," Julia replied, anxious to no longer be the center of attention. She handed the bottle back to Alex, and allowed herself to be helped from the floor by the train officials. They steadied her as she rose, guiding her back down the aisle to her seat. She slid in, and Alex passed her the juice.

"They want you to drink all of that and eat these," she said, handing over the crackers.

"What's the ice for?" Julia asked, looking at the sweating bag in Alex's lap.

"You hit your head when you fell. You might have a bump."

Julia touched the tender spot on her forehead. "My nose too?"

Alex grimaced then nodded.

"Is it broken?"

"I don't think so," Alex reassured. "It's still on straight." She passed the ice pack to Julia.

"What are the papers?" Julia nodded toward the folder.

"An incident report, I'll help you fill it out later. Just relax for a second. Drink your juice."

Julia held the ice to her forehead and took small sips from the bottle. She felt weak but considerably better, whether from the juice or having someone look after her she was not entirely sure. A long moment passed.

"Thanks for your help," she said, finally breaking the silence. "Your Italian is really good."

"Thanks," Alex smiled.

Julia struggled to tear into the cracker bag one handed. "Were you in Florence long?"

Alex shook her head and reached over to help open the package.

"I didn't stay here at all actually. I flew into Rome and spent two nights there. Now I'm headed to meet friends and hike the coast. I've spent today on the train hoping I wouldn't be delayed somewhere because of the strike, but I should be in the clear."

"Your friends are waiting in La Spezia?"

"Not quite. Porto Venere. It's just across the bay."

Julia thought of Harriet.

"Funny. The woman I sat next to on the plane was on her way to Porto Venere. It wasn't even on my itinerary, but every other person I meet is headed there."

Alex smiled. "It's beautiful there."

Another moment passed in silence.

"So are you traveling for business or for fun," Alex asked, prodding the conversation back to life.

"Fun, I suppose," Julia replied.

"You suppose?" Alex raised an eyebrow.

Given that Alex had just saved her from the floor of the train, Julia felt she owed her, at least, a basic explanation. That did not make the words come easier, however.

"I was meant to be traveling with someone," Julia considered her phrasing carefully, "but they backed out at the last minute. The rest of the trip hasn't gone according to plan," she added quietly, holding up the bag of ice and adjusting it on her face.

"I love traveling alone," said Alex. "Trust me. It's really ideal. Like, you got on this train and went without having to hash it out with another person. You can sleep in, go out, do whatever suits you."

"It's less great when you pass out in the middle of the train."

Alex shook her head and opened the second package of crackers, handing it to Julia. "Just wait, this will be a great story you tell at parties someday, and I'll be the random fellow American you met who played hero."

They fell into comfortable conversation. Alex was a graduate student at the University of Denver working on a degree in International Studies. She spoke Italian and French fluently and had spent summer semesters abroad in both countries. Traveling alone was her specialty, she admitted, because her husband, Danny, was a resident at Denver Children's Hospital and unable to take enough time off to vacation. She regaled Julia with the greatest hits of her solo adventures, most of which included hiking, many of which included Italy.

Julia didn't mention Will, though she did allude to

needing some space from home and work. When Alex asked about the last major event Julia had planned, her heart ached to think of her wedding, and she opted instead to explain a recent wine and spirits trade show she had spent six months helping to organize.

They talked about American politics, and Julia proudly confessed to having consulted for the event office that helped manage Barack Obama's acceptance speech in Grant Park. Alex, in turn, impressed Julia by talking about her interest in diplomatic affairs and potential fellowship opportunities post-graduation. She walked Julia through the incident report paperwork, sharing her thoughts about international travel agreements and the benefits and pitfalls of universal healthcare models.

By the time the train pulled into the station two hours later, the women had become fast friends, exchanging contact information and social media accounts. Alex helped Julia unload her luggage from the rack, watching her cautiously.

"Are you feeling any better?" she asked, handing Julia her backpack.

"A little tired and weak," Julia admitted. "But I think I'll be fine."

Truth be told, while the worst of her symptoms had passed, Julia was nervous about venturing off on her own again given the experience on the train. She was enjoying Alex's company and felt considerably better having someone to rely on. They wandered from the station together, and she pulled the yellow notebook page with the address Giuseppe had given her from her backpack.

"When do you go to Porto Venere?" Julia asked.

Alex squinted at her watch. "The ferry won't leave for almost ninety minutes."

"I've got to find my new room," said Julia. "We could walk together for a bit?" she added hopefully.

Alex smiled. "Let's go."

Viale Italia ran all the way from the station to the port, and they walked it in the shade of palm trees and candy-striped awnings, enjoying the cool, salty breeze that rippled through the town. Children in swim trunks and flip flops emerged from a gelateria, faces and fingers sticky with chocolate ice cream. They grinned widely at Alex and Julia as they passed by, before racing off to the next stop on holiday. Near the water, street vendors sold paper cones of fresh fried seafood while seagulls cried overhead waiting to dive for dropped bites. The city was vibrant, but the vibe was unimposing, so different from the grandeur and gravitas of Florence.

Julia relaxed and was relieved to find she felt better the longer they walked. While still a bit shaky, she was otherwise no worse for the wear. With some food and a good night's sleep, she hoped by tomorrow it would just be an unpleasant memory. She would, however, miss Alex's companionship.

They found Marcella's Harbor House Inn two blocks from the pier, a sherbet-colored building with dark blue shutters and brightly colored flower pots on either side of the front door. Julia double checked the address.

"This is me."

"It's cute," Alex nodded. "A great location, right by the water. Not a bad find for a change of plans."

Julia had to agree. Things may not be going as scheduled, but she was lucky that they had worked out as well as they had. Train incident aside.

"You promise you're feeling better?" Alex asked, genuine concern on her face. "I feel a little bad just leaving you all on your own again. You'd be welcome in Porto Venere if you want other people around."

"I thought you said you loved solo travel and getting sick on the train would make a great story?"

"I do, and it will, but I also feel a little responsibility to make sure I'm not leaving you in a bad situation." A blast of a horn from the harbor drew both their attention. "Porto Venere is just across the bay, and there's plenty of room to crash with my friends." Alex said, turning back toward Julia. "You have my number. If something happens, don't hesitate to call."

"Thanks, Alex. I'll be fine," Julia replied more confidently than she felt. She stepped forward quickly, pulling Alex into a tight hug.

"Make sure you eat tonight," said Alex, picking up her duffel bag and turning toward the harbor. "You should not be starving in Italy." She chuckled to herself. "*Ciao*, Julia. Safe travels."

Julia watched her go, grateful for their momentary friendship. She couldn't help but acknowledge how different the trip would have felt with another person along to experience the adventure. Her heart seized in reply. She looked up at the Harbor House Inn, reminding herself that she and Will were never meant to be in this particular place together. She tried to find comfort in that. Whatever happened tonight was completely her own.

The front door was propped open to allow in the fresh sea air, and Julia wheeled her suitcase into the small lobby to find a wisp of a woman with silver hair arranged in a precarious pile on her head. She was wearing a tunic top spangled with shells and fish and smiled widely as Julia crossed to the table that served as a front desk.

"*Buonasera*," she called, warmly. "Welcome in."

"*Grazie*," replied Julia, anxiously creasing the yellow notebook paper in her hands as she approached. "I'm Julia. My concierge in Florence called for a reservation for me? My

plans got a little mixed up because of the strike tomorrow."
She turned over her passport and held her breath as the
woman shuffled some papers around the desk and entered
her information into an old laptop.

"Julia Brooks? *Si*, Giuseppe sent you to us." The woman
beamed.

Julia exhaled with relief.

"Not to worry, Julia. We are glad to have you. I'm
Marcella and welcome to La Spezia."

CHAPTER 8

Her room was simple, just a twin bed under a third story window that looked out over the alley next to the building. The bathroom was tiny, with a shower so small that Julia would have to tuck in her elbows to wash her hair. It was all decorated in blues and whites with prints of the sea and palm trees. Not a single aspect of the room suggested romance or a honeymoon. It was the kind of place Julia might have stayed had she taken the trip in her college years. There was something freeing about a space meant just for her, and she noted with satisfaction how much better she felt here than walking into the fancy room she had planned with Will.

The first priority was to eat, and she consulted her notebook for potential options. Almost all of her recommendations were near the water, and she decided to wander the harbor walk until something caught her eye. Out on the street, she found the city transformed for dinner much differently than Florence. Whereas evening in Florence meant candlelight studded twilight in the shadows of great buildings, evening in La Spezia drew everyone to the water where the sunlight lingered longest. In front of every restaurant, waiters adjusted colorful umbrellas around clusters of tables.

Julia picked a casual spot at the far end of the harbor where she was shown to a table facing the sea. Out along the horizon, the lights of cruise ships glittered in the setting sun. Closer to shore, fishing boats, water taxis, and sailboats docked along a sprawling network of piers. A yacht slid by in the middle ground. Here, life happened on the water just as much as on land.

Her waitress, a young woman, beautifully tan with long, raven hair, brought a chunk of steaming focaccia bread smothered in pesto and took her order, linguine tossed with fresh clams. Julia sipped an iced tea and watched the waves lap at the breakwater. Life felt simpler in the fresh, Mediterranean air. She could imagine herself sitting at a café in the morning sun, watching life unfold on the docks. She could picture herself with a book, feet dangling off the pier into the sea. She could even foresee herself befriending the locals, maybe Marcella or her waitress, as she fell into a comfortable routine of sun-kissed days. Most importantly, she could see herself doing it all without Will in a way that did not immediately move her to despair.

Her dinner came, and Julia ate greedily, soaking up the broth from the bottom of the bowl with the remainder of her bread. She sighed contentedly. A full stomach had remedied any lingering shakiness from earlier on the train, and she was grateful her recovery had not posed more of a hindrance. She couldn't imagine that forgetting to eat would be a problem here as she looked down the harbor walk at the colorful and bustling restaurant fronts. In fact, most of the trouble of the past three days seemed just a bit less intense with her face turned to the sun, infinite blue water ahead of her.

She pulled her phone from her bag, snapped a picture of the harbor in the fading light, and posted her first update since the wedding.

Sunsets are proof that no matter what happens, every day can end beautifully, she wrote, a quote she remembered once seeing on a framed, motivational print. If Will was flaunting his happiness across the internet, she would at least let it be known that she was not holed up in a dark corner crying her eyes out…at least not in this moment. She waited for the photo to upload, closed the app, paid her check, and wandered back to her room at the guest house. She would get a good night's sleep in a bed built for one, make sure she was at full strength in the morning, and then, finally, get things underway as she had imagined.

WHEN JULIA WOKE the next morning, the grey light of dawn had not yet crept into the alley outside her window, and she reached for her phone, disoriented as to the time. Four-thirty. Too early.

She returned it to the bedside table and rolled over to go back to sleep, but before she could doze off, it pinged with a notification. Julia turned, curiosity nudging her awake. The phone pinged again, insistent, and she reached for it to silence the ringer. Picking it up, it was impossible not to glance at the home screen. She froze at the message from Ellie.

"Call me when you see it," she mumbled, reading aloud.

Julia stared at the phone in confusion before realizing the implications of the message. Whatever it was, it must be something public; it must be something big; and it must be something Ellie assumed she was going to need to process out loud. There was only one thing that she knew would prompt such a text.

Her heart began to race.

She swung herself out of bed, suddenly wide awake, and began to pace the room, phone in hand, mustering the courage to face whatever new affront she was about to find. Closing her eyes, she opened her Instagram account, took a deep breath, and stared down at the page. She didn't even need to scroll. It was right at the top staring back.

Not it.

Her.

The woman on Will's arm was gorgeous. Her blonde hair fell in gentle waves past her shoulders and her eyes were the color of the turquoise water sparkling in the tropical sunset. She wore a black and white striped sun hat and a colorfully embroidered coverup that Julia thought she recognized from a celebrity wives' show.

But whatever shock Julia felt at staring into the face of the woman who had stolen her marriage, it was nothing compared to the disgust she felt at the brazen caption beneath the photo. *Sunsets are proof that no matter what happens, everyday can end beautifully. Loving these days in the sun with this beauty.* Julia fought the overwhelming urge to throw the phone out the window.

She opened her messages to reply to Ellie, but saw Will's name first. Before she could stop herself, the thread was open. His message remained unanswered. She had wondered at its intention, wrestled with what to do about it, and now was as confused as ever. *I've been thinking about you.* If it was true, and he was also posting photos on the beach with the woman who had torn them apart, then he was proving himself to be every part the asshole. If it was false, then it was just unnecessarily cruel.

Julia knew Will to be many things— driven, ambitious,

passionate, jealous, intense— but cruel was not one of them. For a brief moment after the text had arrived, she had thought, or maybe hoped beyond reason, that it would provide an invitation to reconnect. She saw now that whatever he had meant by it, she did not want to be any part of it. She fired off a message before it registered what she had done.

Julia: Go to hell.

She stared at the text, feeling the blood drain from her face. Too late to take it back, she deleted the thread in disgust.

She switched back to her contacts and Ellie. She knew what would happen if she made the call. Ellie would tell her she was right to be angry, and Julia would cry. Ellie would attempt to soothe and then worry about Julia being there alone, and Julia would make assurances that she was fine, even as she felt herself fraying at the edges again. She typed out a quick message in the hope to stave off a lengthier conversation.

Julia: Saw it. No words.

The angry tears came hot and fast, falling off her cheeks and hitting the tile floor leaving dark spots on the terracotta. A new and horrid thought occurred to her. Will was winning. She had not anticipated moving on to feel like a competition, and yet here they were, days after the wedding, each seeking closure in their own beautiful, foreign sanctuary, laying the foundations for what would become their new lives apart, and he was doing it better.

It was no longer impossible to hate him. Considering all he had already put her through, the caption was an unnecessarily low blow, and her anger flared. But as much as she wanted to wrap herself in self-righteous indignation and crawl back under the covers, a haunting thought needled her broken heart. That he had copied the post also meant he was still paying attention. He was watching her the same way she was watching him, their stories still intertwined though their futures no longer linked. Even thousands of miles away, even knowing he was with someone else, it still made her ache to think that the life they could have shared was gone, and that he was thinking of it too.

Riding the rollercoaster of heartbreak was trying her resolve and patience. She didn't know how much more she could endure.

She returned to bed, phone still in hand, and reopened the social media post, lingering on the picture for a moment before scrolling down to the comments. She clicked on profile names of people she didn't recognize, scrolling through followers and pictures, seeking out some connection, looking for a name, growing more impatient as she found nothing.

By the time she stumbled onto the profile, the room was light and Julia could hear the rest of the guests stirring in the corridors. Erica Michaelson. She didn't follow Will, too obvious in the midst of the affair Julia assumed, but she followed a client's son whom Julia had once met in Cape Cod. Her feed was full of photo shoots and modeling jobs, except for the most recent posts. Pink toes on a balcony railing. Two cups of coffee. Black and white sun hat and coverup. Will was not in the photos, but the parallels were obvious.

Having the face and name of this woman, Julia realized, gave her another target for her anger, and in that anger, she felt herself stirring to action. If it was a competition, and if Will was paying attention, then she would not go down without putting up at least the illusion of a fight. No one had to know about her tumultuous start. All that mattered was the perception that she too was letting go and moving on with her life.

She picked up her notebook, and opened to her pages on La Spezia, intentionally seeking out what Will had marked as his preferred attraction. The Italian Naval Museum. That's where she would spend her day, and she would make sure everyone knew she was having a fabulous time. She dressed quickly and wheeled her bags to the lobby where Marcella offered her a warm *Buongiorno* and agreed to store the luggage.

"Which way to the museum?" Julia asked, moving toward the door already propped open to the morning traffic.

Marcella gestured toward the water.

"Follow the harbor to the right," she said. "Can't miss it. Enjoy."

Stepping into the bright morning, Julia considered how to best show off La Spezia to other people. She took pictures of everything, the colored shops along the water, the fishermen unloading the overnight catch from their nets, seabirds perched on the dock posts, the terraces of bougainvillea climbing towards the morning sun. There was beauty everywhere, but she reveled in little of it, instead moving from scene to scene intent only on capturing photos for later use.

The museum itself was less photogenic. Historical weaponry and diving equipment sat in thick glass cases labeled with large placards on which descriptions were given in Italian. Wall displays of nautical history provided few opportunities for selfies and trend-worthy images. Still, Julia documented it all, taking special care to pose creatively with a few of the more interesting ship figureheads on display in the second-floor gallery. She left well after lunch time, wandering back along the water, reminding herself to eat, and stopping at a small café for a plate of fruit and cheese and a glass of wine while she sorted through the morning's album.

Julia felt better for having set a task for the day. There was little time to consider emotion and heartache with a project in mind and a deadline to meet. She wanted at least one post up by the time she moved her luggage to her new hotel that afternoon, and she worked to filter and crop images while eating her lunch. She had a drafted caption ready to publish by the time the waiter returned to clear her plate and ask if she would like a second glass of wine. Julia declined, opting instead to celebrate the morning with a stop at the gelateria up the street on her way back to Marcella's. She snapped a photo of the dripping cone, ammunition for a later strike.

At three o'clock, Julia collected her bags from Harbor House, thanked Marcella for her hospitality, and walked back through town toward her original hotel. She knew her new room was a glittering, romantic, swoon worthy suite overlooking the sea, and she steeled herself for the unavoidable discomfort of walking back into a setting poised for honeymoon romance. She would not be blindsided by emotion like she had been in Florence. She would sweep the rose petals from the bed, accept the champagne graciously, and get back to the business of proving to the world that she was fine.

That was the plan.

She walked up to the double doors, thrown open to the harbor. A shapely woman greeted her warmly in rapid Italian, and Julia turned over her passport and watched as the woman entered her information into the computer. A few moments passed, and the woman frowned. She called to a coworker, a man in a linen summer suit, who came over and considered the computer screen. His brow furrowed.

"*Mi dispiace*," the woman said, shaking her head.

"What's wrong?" Julia asked, pulse quickening.

96

The woman spoke again to the man who nodded and looked at Julia with confusion.

"*Signora*, it seems that your reservation has been cancelled," he announced. "Anna said she took your phone call yesterday, and you asked to cancel because of the trains?"

"No, my train was cancelled," groaned Julia, heart sinking. "I was trying to change the reservation. I took an earlier train last night."

The man nodded sympathetically and returned to the conversation with Anna. After some clacking of computer keys and brief exchanges, they turned back to Julia grimly.

"I'm sorry, but we've rebooked your suite. It's been very busy with the train strike." He handed Julia her passport. "You told us to cancel," he added.

"That was obviously not my intention," Julia snapped defensively. She reached up and rubbed her forehead. A headache had started at the bruise from the train. "I'm sorry," she started again. "Do you have anything else available?"

There was more clacking of keys and mumbled conversation.

"*Mi dispiace*," the man replied, shaking his head. "We are full."

"You have to find me something!" Julia insisted, voice rising.

The man stared at her wide eyed. "No, *signora*," he said in a clipped voice, "we do not. You cancelled."

Julia's anxiety mounted as she stowed her passport back in her bag. She sighed. "Do you have any suggestions where I might find a new room," she asked with forced calm. Her voice wobbled, prompting a sympathetic look from Anna, who whispered something to her colleague. He frowned, but his eyes softened.

"You will have better luck away from the water," he reassured her. "There are many rooms, but they fill quickest near the harbor. Try in the city center."

Julia nodded. *"Grazie,"* she said weakly, gathering her luggage and heading back out the double doors.

She walked to the nearest bench overlooking the water and collapsed onto it. Dropping her head into her hands, she drew trembling breaths, willing herself not to cry. Her panic and anger at losing her reservation melted into defeat. It was her own fault the reservation had been cancelled, but somehow it felt like there was something else at work, some bigger force intent on destroying her last remaining shreds of resolve. As if the circumstances of her traveling alone were not enough, the universe seemed determined to deliver obstacles at every turn. Her morning of photo ops and shareable moments was revealed for the charade that it was. This is what the trip had been, one setback after another. The day now offered nothing more than a daunting search for accommodations in a city overrun with stranded travelers.

She thought of Will.

Somewhere, he lounged on a beach with an umbrella drink, toes in the sand, ready to post his next glimpse of paradise, oblivious to Julia's predicament. It wasn't fair. She wondered how he would feel to know she was sitting home-less on a bench in Italy. It hurt to think he wouldn't care. Even if he did care, she realized, it wouldn't change anything. That hurt worse.

Julia pulled out her phone thinking to call Ellie for help seeking out a room online. A low battery warning flashed on the screen. She had spent almost the entire day on her phone; there was barely enough left for a short conversation. Ellie would have to work fast.

She was about to place the call when the blast of a horn startled her. The ferry for Porto Venere pulled into its slip

IN THE SHADE OF OLIVE TREES

just yards away. Julia watched the crew tie off on the dock and begin to help passengers unload.

There was another option. She pulled her notebook from her bag, retrieving Harriet's card. Alex's number was saved in her phone. She looked between the two choices. Closer than Ellie, just a boat ride away, both offered what she needed tonight: a friendly face and a safe place to stay.

She had a sudden, overwhelming desire to reconnect with Harriet, but something kept her from placing the call. Though brokenhearted herself, taking her crisis into a home where widows grieved the loss of their great loves felt somehow selfish. That was *not* Julia's story, nor her heartbreak. Yes, Harriet had offered, but Julia doubted that she had expected a call from the streets of La Spezia after only four days.

Alex, however, might find the change of plans an unexpected and welcome adventure. And once Julia was in Porto Venere, another opportunity to find Harriet may present itself. Decision made, she dialed Alex's number. One nervous moment passed as Julia waited for her to pick up.

"Julia?" Alex's voice burst brightly through the speaker. "You called!"

Julia couldn't help but smile at Alex's exuberance. "I did," she said.

"Is everything okay? Are you sick or just tired of La Spezia and coming to Porto Venere for a real vacation?"

"Actually," Julia admitted. "I've run into a hiccup with my hotel reservation. Well, more than a hiccup really. It's been cancelled."

"Cancelled? Why?"

Julia stood and began to pace a circle around the bench. "It would seem I tripped over a language barrier."

Alex laughed on the other end of the line. "So, then you are coming to Porto Venere?"

"I don't want to impose," Julia hedged. "I just need a place for the night, and then I'll figure out what to do in the morning."

"It's not an imposition," Alex insisted. "There's plenty of room here. You can stay as long as you like. Do you want me to come and pick you up?"

"No need. I'm right next to the ferry. Just tell me where to go when I get there."

"I'll meet you in the harbor. Look for the café with the yellow striped umbrellas. I'll wait for you there."

Awash in relief, Julia sat back down. "Thank you, Alex."

The ferry blared the horn again.

"Don't miss that boat. I'll see you soon."

Julia ended the call, hurried down the pier, and bought her ticket.

As the ferry sped across the bay, she closed her eyes and let the salty sea air wash over her. La Spezia receded behind her, and she was surprised to find herself relieved to have changed course once again. She was exhausted from trying to force the trip along as planned, and she felt better knowing she would not have to soldier on alone, at least for tonight. Tomorrow, she could figure out how to finally get things back under control. She draped herself on the railing to watch the rocky shore drift past, anxious to reach the harbor.

Up ahead, the colorful facade of Porto Venere drew closer. Buildings painted in reds and golds and pinks leaned against each other lazily. Green shutters framed iron balcony rails which hung with drying laundry. A crowded harbor hosted a hundred fishing boats bobbing gently in the surf, and the walkway just beyond was crowded with early diners. On a rocky point jutting into the sea, an imposing stone fortress stood watch over the coastline.

The ferry slowed as it approached the pier, and passengers began to collect their things in preparation to disembark. Julia stepped back from the railing and joined the crowd, nervous excitement building to find Alex.

The boat docked, and she followed the swell of people down the gangplank and onto the pier. Julia wove her way through the crowd and onto the walkway that led past the shoppes and cafes along the water. She scanned the tables anxiously looking for yellow striped umbrellas.

"Over here!" a voice called just behind her. "*Buonasera!*"

Julia spun around to find Alex waving enthusiastically from a table on the edge of a bustling café. She was surprised to find her not in hiking gear, but a navy striped sundress and sandals. Alex stood as Julia approached and kissed her on both cheeks like an old friend. "Welcome to Porto Venere."

"Thank you. I can't believe I'm here." Julia stepped back and surveyed the harbor.

Alex smiled. "You're going to be glad you called. You'll love it, just wait and see. Grab your stuff."

They walked back along the water to the main street into town. Away from the marina, the walk through Porto Venere began to wind uphill. The roads narrowed and darkened; the sounds of the sea faded, replaced with the rumble of her suitcase rolling on cobblestones and music and laughter drifting from the open windows around them. Alex pointed out favorite restaurants and important landmarks as they climbed, but Julia mostly walked in silence, taking it all in. There was something different about Porto Venere; she could feel it. It was friendly, playful, and somehow familiar. Or maybe, Julia realized, it just felt that way because Alex was leading her through it like family instead of a day's old acquaintance.

After a few minutes' walk, the path leveled off and widened into open space above the knot that made up the heart of the city. Small terraced vineyards and lemon groves framed with primeval, dry stacked walls stretched between modest villas overlooking the village below and the sea beyond. Julia looked back over the city mesmerized. From above, the crazy collection of colorful buildings stacked together looked even more fantastical. The harbor glittered in the afternoon sun, and past that, the sea stretched unbroken to the deep blue horizon line.

"It's gorgeous, right?" Alex asked, stopping for Julia to enjoy the view.

"It's amazing," Julia had to agree.

"Wait until you see the view from the house. We're just up ahead."

To the right, a gravel driveway framed by two stone pillars and lined with neatly trimmed hedges wound up a gently sloping lawn. An ancient, gnarled olive tree in the center of the yard dominated the tasteful landscaping. A flagstone path meandered between two gardens up to a white stucco villa with a bright green door and dark wood shutters. Alex wandered up the driveway familiarly, but Julia slowed, gaping at the house in front of her.

"Alex?" she called. "This is where you're staying?"

Alex turned around and laughed. "What? You thought I was backpacking across Europe through youth hostels?"

"Well, kind of," Julia admitted, embarrassed. "You said you were hiking and staying with friends?"

"I am," Alex laughed again. "Friends with a breathtaking Italian villa."

"This is unbelievable," Julia said, coming up the driveway to stand beside her. "Who do you know with a house like this?"

"It's kind of a long story," Alex hedged. She started up the front path.

Julia followed, gazing up at the house in stunned silence.

She stopped at the front steps and turned in a slow circle, surveying the front yard. It was perfect. This was paradise.

She heard the door open behind her.

"You're here," a warm voice called from the entryway.

The hairs on the back of Julia's neck stood up in recognition. Whatever surprise she felt at finding herself in Porto Venere with Alex at a gorgeous villa, it was nothing compared to the realization she already knew the voice behind her. She turned slowly, already certain who she would find.

There on the front step, arm around Alex, stood Harriet.

CHAPTER 9

J ulia and Harriet stared at each other wide eyed, then
Harriet burst into laughter.

"Julia Brooks!" she exclaimed. "You came to Porto
Venere after all."

"Wait," Alex looked between them. "You know each
other?"

Julia nodded in shocked disbelief, waiting for her brain to
accept the reality in front of her. There was Harriet, framed
in the doorway with her hair pulled back in a neat twist,
white button shirt tucked into slim navy trousers. Her kind
eyes locked on Julia's. It was unbelievable.

"So, about that woman I sat with on the plane..." Julia
started.

"You're kidding," Alex grinned. "This is absolutely
perfect."

"Hold on," Julia shook her head, still trying to make sense
of the scene. "How do you know each other? Are you
Harriet's..."

"Daughter? No," Alex interrupted. "I come on retreat with
Harriet every year."

"On retreat?" Julia wondered aloud. "But, you're married. Danny, the doctor."

Alex held up her left hand, and Julia confirmed a thin diamond-studded band around her ring finger. "Danny is my *second* husband."

Julia gawked, and Alex gave Harriet a knowing look.

"I told her," Harriet said. "People get awkward when they find out you've lost a spouse."

"Oh God! I'm sorry," Julia sputtered. "I didn't mean to be insensitive. I'm just...I don't know what to say. I'm stunned by all of this."

"Don't worry. You're not the first one to assume my guests are all blue haired, bucket list fulfilling old ladies," Harriet reassured Julia. "We're full of surprises here, you'll see. That is, assuming you're coming inside?"

Julia stared up at the house. Part of her ached to stay. Olive Haven was beautiful, and that Alex and Harriet would know each other and Julia would somehow find her way to the villa even against her better instinct seemed nothing short of fate. Still, a nagging insecurity lingered. She didn't belong at Olive Haven. She had no idea what it meant to grieve the way these women were grieving, the way Harriet and Alex had grieved.

"I don't know," Julia hesitated. "I mean, I thought I was joining Alex and her hiking friends for the night."

"You are," nodded Alex.

"But I didn't know I'd be here," Julia went on. "I wouldn't want to impose. I don't know that I really...qualify."

Alex raised an eyebrow. "Because you don't have a dead husband?" she asked bluntly.

"Well..." Julia blushed.

"In the strictest sense, no," Harriet conceded. "But in the broader definition of a 'woman without a husband to travel with,' you qualify."

"Plus," added Alex, "you do need somewhere to stay tonight. You can't tell me you're going to find a better place."

"Come inside," insisted Harriet. "Have dinner. Meet everyone. Spend the night. If you want to go back to La Spezia tomorrow, we'll help you find a place. I know you have a tight schedule to follow." She winked.

Julia was tired of making excuses. Uncertainties aside, deep down, she wanted to stay. "Okay," she agreed, carrying her bag up the front steps. "One night."

Harriet led the way into the house, and Julia gaped at the full grandeur of the space. The entryway opened onto the living room which then opened onto the kitchen so that from the front door one could see clear to the back of the house. The walls and upholstery were done in soft neutrals, and the rustic cabinetry, stained deep chestnut, stood in stark contrast to snowy marble countertops veined in pale grey. Around the room, creamy white flowers and silvery olive branches were arranged tastefully in dark green glassware. A stairway curved gently up to the left, railed in twisted wrought iron. It took Julia's breath away.

In the living room, a wall of windows looked out over a manicured terrace garden where an enormous, scrubbed table was set with simple white plates. A garland of bougainvillea took a starring role down the center of the table, and bistro lights hanging from the pergola overhead winked on as the sun dipped below the trees framing the back of the property.

"Wow," Julia breathed, taking it all in. "This is gorgeous."

"Thank you," chimed Harriet. "From May to October I spend most of my time here hosting the retreats. Bernardo, my building and grounds manager, oversees the villa the rest of the time when I'm away on the off-season or other business."

"How did you ever find it?"

"Pure luck. It was one of the very good things that happened early on in my post-Jack travels." Harriet closed the door and turned to survey the entryway proudly. "I met the previous owners, and I fell in love with the property. Four years later when they decided to sell, they sent me the listing, just on a whim. I couldn't resist it." She adjusted a floral arrangement on the entry table. "Make yourself at home. Alex can show you upstairs to the guest rooms. Number six is available."

Julia wheeled her suitcase across the marble tile, stopping next to the stairs in front of Harriet. "Thank you, Harriet. This is amazing."

Harriet patted Julia on the arm. "I'm glad you found us, or rather that Alex found you. Either way, you're welcome. I'm going to make sure dinner is organized. There's a group returning from Riomaggiore in about thirty minutes. We'll eat when they get back."

Harriet went to the kitchen and busied herself with a colander of greens in the sink while Alex helped Julia carry her bags upstairs.

"I'm in room four," Alex noted gesturing towards an open door revealing an unmade bed and athletic clothes scattered across the floor. "This is you in six." She turned into a room on the right just a few paces down the hallway. Julia followed.

The room was simple, yet stylish. A queen sized, four post bed made up with clean white linens took up the majority of the space. Gauzy draping hung between the posts and rustled lightly in the breeze from the open window, which looked out over the front of the house and the enormous olive tree in the yard. There was a small wooden chair in one corner opposite the bed and a matching chest of drawers in the other. It was idyllic. Elegant accommodations in an amazing location. Hesitations about her housemates aside, Julia wondered if she would really be able to convince herself to leave in the morning.

"Do you need anything?" asked Alex.

Julia shook her head. "No, thank you. I think I'll just get cleaned up before dinner."

"Sounds good. Bathroom is through there." She gestured at a door on the wall between the chair and dresser. "If you need anything, just give a shout." She stepped into the hall, closing the door behind her.

Julia set her suitcase on the chair and dropped her backpack on the floor beside it. She briefly considered unpacking some of her things into the dresser, but it felt presumptuous to plan beyond just tonight. Despite the incredible accommodations and a warm welcome from Alex and Harriet, she couldn't shake the feeling that she was an outsider at Olive Haven. Not to mention, abandoning the entire trip as planned was a bit dramatic.

She opened the door next to the chair revealing the bathroom that she shared with the guest in the next room. Across the way she could see her neighbor sprawled on her bed with a thick book.

The other woman looked up at the sound of the door. She wore her sandy brown hair in a neat bob cut, and her blue eyes sparked, electric, even from a distance. Julia waved, suddenly nervous at the prospect of making an introduction.

"Hello," she called, voice echoing through the tiled room between them. "I'm Julia."

The other woman slid from the bed and came toward the bathroom. She stared at Julia for a moment, expressionless, then swung her door closed with a snug thud. Julia flushed with embarrassment. Was it somehow possible to tell she didn't fit in just by looking at her? That was ridiculous, she assured herself. But still, her first interaction was far from comforting.

Discouraged, Julia stared out the window trying not to worry about dinner. An unnerving thought struck her. Certainly, someone would ask about her relationship status at dinner. Would the assumption be made that she was a widow as well, and if so, what was the tasteful way to clarify that no, actually, her adulterous would-have-been husband was very much alive and posting photos with his mistress on the other side of the world? Harriet knew only the vaguest sliver of the truth. Alex knew nothing at all. She could barely imagine telling either of them the full story, let alone sharing with a table full of strangers.

The thought of Will drew her to her phone, and she pulled it from her backpack, sat down on the bed, and instinctively opened social media. She had dozens of comments and messages about her earlier posts in La Spezia, but she ignored them, scrolling to find his feed. It was morning where he was. The sunrise photo overlooked a stripe of white sand where Erica stood, her back to the camera, silhouetted in the morning light. Julia's stomach clenched. He wasn't just sharing, he was flaunting. Yet, inexplicably, her emotions were still jumbled. How could she loathe what he was doing so much and still be jealous of the woman in the photo? She flopped backward on the bed, frustrated with her wavering heart.

The crunch of the gravel driveway from the open window turned her attention. A van pulled to a stop in front of the house, and the doors rolled open. A trio of women clamored out, carrying shopping bags, and chatting merrily. They disappeared up the front walk. A moment later, Julia heard their muffled voices in the entryway below. Her nerves twinged again, thoughts of Will turning to thoughts of awkward introductions.

Realizing she had no idea how formal to dress for dinner, she pushed herself from the bed and began to rummage in her suitcase. She chose wide legged linen pants and a sleeve-less green blouse, dressed in front of the mirror on the back of the door, and brushed out her hair, letting the loose waves fall past her shoulders. In the bathroom, she washed her face and applied fresh mascara and lip gloss. She had just returned her makeup bag to her suitcase when there was a knock on the bedroom door. Julia turned around, startled, just as Alex poked her head around the corner.

"Ready to go down?" Alex asked.

"I think so," Julia looked around the room anxiously.

"Are you okay?" Alex stepped into the room and closed the door partially behind her. "You seem on edge."

"I'm fine," Julia said, voice rising slightly.

Alex raised an eyebrow in silent question.

Julia sank onto the edge of the bed and took a deep breath. "Alex, tell me honestly, is it weird I'm here? I mean, will it be weird with the other women."

Alex laughed. "You're really still worried about the widow thing?"

"It's just," Julia lowered her voice, "I met my neighbor, and she didn't exactly seem thrilled I was here."

"You met Aster?" Alex looked at the bathroom door. "Apparently, she's been holed up in her room away from everyone since she arrived. She actually talked to you?"

"Well, no," admitted Julia.

"Then she obviously can't be upset about your relation-ship status. She was probably just disappointed she now has to share the bathroom."

Julia looked at the bathroom door, unconvinced.

"Besides," Alex continued. "You forget I'm also a widow, and I'm the one who told you to come and stay."

Julia turned back to her in a rush, eyes wide. "About that," Julia started. "Alex, how are you here? On the train...I never would have imagined..."

Alex shook her head. "No one ever imagines," she said. "Why would they? And I don't normally lead the conversation with it. My first husband, Sam, and I were only married for seven months. We met in college and were really young, and we definitely would have waited. But he was sick, and it became a real-life Nicholas Sparks novel."

Julia stared, uncertain how to respond. Alex sat down on the bed beside her.

"I met Harriet while Sam was in the hospital. After he passed, I decided to go to grad school, but before I moved, Harriet invited me to visit her at Olive Haven. I came and ended up having an amazing time. When I got home, I moved to Denver and started school. The next summer I studied abroad in Italy and came up and stayed again. Since then, we've made it an annual tradition."

"And Danny doesn't mind?" Julia asked.

Alex shrugged. "He works crazy hours and can't take the time off, so he probably figures I'm less likely to get in trouble staying at Olive Haven with a group of widowed women than I am by myself. Plus, Danny loves Harriet. Actually, she married us two years ago. Now," she added quickly before Julia could respond. "I feel personally obligated to make sure you eat something." She jumped up from the bed and opened the door to the hall, gesturing Julia through it. "Will you please relax? Let's go to dinner."

Julia and Alex walked downstairs and into the commotion of the kitchen. Behind the island, Harriet was arranging platters of food and opening bottles of wine. A guest with a streak of bubblegum pink through her blonde pixie cut smiled at Julia as she picked up a ceramic salad bowl and headed toward the back garden. Harriet waved them over and handed Julia a stack of cloth napkins and silverware. She headed out to the backyard through the open doors while Alex lingered in the kitchen.

The terrace glowed with the light of hundreds of bulbs suspended overhead and the candlelight of a dozen large, glass-paned lanterns that had been lit around the edge of the lawn. The evening sky, now painted in rich pinks and oranges, matched the bougainvillea and the napkins Julia had been handed. She made her way around the table, carefully setting each place. An extra, unmatched chair had been squeezed in on one long side of the table, and she realized with equal parts guilt and delight that it had been added for her.

Alex came through the double doors, a glass of white wine in each hand. She passed one to Julia.

"Cheers," she said, crystal tinkling as she touched the glasses together.

"Cheers," replied Julia. She sipped the wine. It burst crisp and bright on her tongue.

The rest of the women began to gather around the table, pouring wine and chatting amiably among themselves. When Harriet stepped out a few moments later, they all grew quiet.

"Good evening, everyone," welcomed Harriet. "It's great to see you back and in good spirits. Dinner is ready, so if you'd all take your seats, we'll just have a quick toast and get started."

The women shuffled around in an unspoken game of musical chairs as they reclaimed spots from previous meals. Julia hesitated, waiting to see where everyone landed, but Alex motioned for her to join her near the head of the table where Harriet stood, wine glass in hand.

"If I may," Harriet said, quieting the group again and raising her glass. "To old memories, new friends, and open hearts. Cheers to all!"

They gently touched their glasses around the table, and the cheerful conversations picked up again as bowls of salad, baskets of bread, and plates of pasta were passed. Julia noticed two empty seats, but no one else seemed intrigued or bothered by them.

Twenty minutes into dinner, a man wearing jeans and a plaid shirt came around the side of the house. His dark hair was slicked back revealing grey at his temples which matched the salt and pepper clearly evident in his five o'clock shadow. He knelt next to Harriet's chair, and they shared a brief, whispered conversation. The old woman to Julia's right giggled girlishly.

"Isn't he handsome?" she asked conspiratorially. "I mean, I know I'm at least thirty years his senior, but I can still appreciate a good man when I see one."

Julia looked between the woman and the man, who wrapped up his conversation, and stood to face the table properly.

"Good evening, ladies," he said. His English was good, Julia noted, and his accent added a richness the American pronunciation simply could not compete with. "Enjoy your dinner."

"Thank you, Bernardo," exclaimed Harriet, returning her attention to the meal.

"That's Bernardo?" Julia asked the woman beside her. "The grounds manager?"

"Oh yes, though if I was Harriet, I'd have him managing a few other things as well," she smirked. "I'm Maeve." She held out an arthritic hand.

Julia blushed as she took it. "Julia."

"Don't go bashful on me now. It's a girls' week. I didn't know we were expecting anyone else tonight. Harriet," Maeve cut unapologetically into the conversation happening at the head of the table. "Are you making formal introductions? Your new addition snuck in unannounced."

Chatter quieted, and all eyes turned to Julia. She looked at

Harriet, embarrassed, but Harriet only smiled, kind eyes twinkling in the lights overhead.

"Thank you, Maeve," she said. "This is Julia Brooks. Good fortune brought her to Olive Haven, and she'll be joining us, at least for tonight. Julia, it sounds like you've already met Maeve. Perhaps we could go around the rest of the table?"

On Maeve's right, the woman with the pink streaked pixie cut raised her hand. "I can start," she said. "I'm Margo. I'm from Cambridge, Massachusetts where I'm a medical sales rep."

At the end of the table opposite Harriet, a red headed woman with shockingly green eyes smiled and waved. "Hello," she said. A slight Irish brogue stretched the end of the word. "I'm Elise, Harriet's..." she paused, glancing to the head of the table, "good friend."

Julia looked back and forth between the women, confused by the hesitant introduction.

Harriet rolled her eyes but smiled. She looked at Julia. "Elise is my therapist," she explained.

"Dr Ellison?" Julia asked, turning back to Elise in surprise.

Elise cocked her head toward Julia. "Aye, that's right. But please, just call me Elise while we're here." She gave Harriet a questioning look.

"Julia may have heard about you on the plane," Harriet admitted with a chuckle. "We were seat partners and got to chatting about life and my travels after Jack passed, which you were instrumental in encouraging." She turned back to Julia. "Elise finally agreed to take some time off to see where I disappear to six months of the year."

Elise leaned back in her chair, looked around the terrace, and smiled. "She says 'time off,' but I'm still hoping we might have a session or two so I can write off the travel expenses."

Next to Elise, a tiny woman with a short shock of grey hair and enormous, thick lensed glasses sat wrapped in a beautiful, rainbow pashmina. "I'm Lucy," she said, her voice unexpectedly strong given her stature. "This trip was a gift from my children for my eighty-fifth birthday." Applause broke out among the women. "I'm from San Diego where I lived for sixty wonderful years with my husband George."

The remaining two seats were empty.

"You'll meet the other two sometime this week," Maeve chimed in. "My sister, Aster, hasn't been feeling up to group conversation since we arrived. But she'll come around."

Julia noted the family resemblance with the woman she had seen briefly across the bathroom, but if it wasn't for the high cheek bones and matching blue eyes, it would be hard to believe her reclusive neighbor was related to outspoken Maeve.

"And then there's Beth," Harriet added. "She has private dinner plans this evening but nevertheless brings our total to seven. Julia? Anything you want to share?"

"Oh, um," Julia swallowed hard. "I'm Julia. I'm from Chicago. I actually met Harriet on the plane and then Alex on the train. All roads kind of led to Porto Venere, so thank you for letting me join you." She sat back, relieved to have avoided further questions.

Dinner continued with the women picking up their conversations. The food was exceptionally good, the wine flowed generously, and Julia enjoyed both while catching bits of scattered dialogue. At the far end of the table, Elise talked with Margo about medical supply chains. Lucy listened intently but sat quietly, sipping from a tiny espresso cup. On her left, Alex and Harriet talked about Danny's hospital rounds and what her fellowship could mean for his job opportunities. Maeve recapped the day in Riomaggiore in excruciating detail, peppering Julia with questions about what she knew about the village.

"So, what's the retreat like?" Julia finally managed to ask when Maeve paused for a sip of wine.

"Oh, it's been excellent," Maeve said. "For me anyway. I'd love to tell you my sister is off alone taking advantage of private meditation time, but she's really just locked in her room." She sighed sadly. "It's her loss though. Harriet threw a wonderful welcome banquet, and there are a lot of choices on how to spend your time: hiking, shopping, wine tasting, site seeing, wellness and spirituality work. It's only been a few days, but Harriet can make just about anything happen it seems."

"Not everything," Harriet protested from the end of the table. She winked at Julia.

"Well, I've yet to be disappointed," Maeve assured her. "You were lucky to find your way here tonight," she told Julia. "You won't find a better accommodation on the Ligurian coast."

Dusk settled around them.

When the wine bottles were empty and the candles in the lanterns burned down to stubs, the women gradually began to excuse themselves to their rooms. Lucy left first, escorted by Harriet, and Elise followed shortly behind wishing the rest of the table *"sogni d'oro"* as she stepped inside. Margo stacked the dishes, said her good nights, and carried her wine glass back into the house.

Maeve yawned and stretched. "I should probably check on Aster." She stood from the table. "I'll see you both at breakfast?"

"I'm not sure," Julia admitted.

"You're not leaving us that early?" asked Maeve. "What's the rush?"

"Well, I've got a whole trip planned," replied Julia hesitantly.

"It's too bad you can't stay and join us. Are you meeting other people on your travels?"

"No." Julia shifted uncomfortably. "I'm just by myself."

"Oh, well, I spend plenty of time by myself to know the value of one's own company. Do you enjoy it? Traveling alone?" Julia hesitated long enough for Maeve to frown. "In that case, I imagine I'll see you at breakfast." She smiled and walked away before Julia could answer. "Good night, ladies," she called from the doorway.

"They're a good group," Alex said when it was just the two of them left on the terrace.

"They are," Julia agreed.

They stared off into the darkness beyond the garden.

"Do you really think you'll go back to La Spezia tomorrow?" Alex asked after a moment.

Julia looked up at the house, considering her options. Lights shone in the windows of the upper rooms and lightning bugs blinked in the ivy crawling up the stucco. She heard the faint sounds of the surf washing up on the rocks below, and the laughter of the women upstairs drifted out over the terrace through the open windows. Despite a successful dinner, she could not shake the feeling that, at some point, she would have to address the fact she did not really belong on this retreat. Plus, she did have other plans made.

"I don't know," she said. "I have a whole week scheduled."

"Seriously?" exclaimed Alex. "Come on. One, you don't have a place to stay. Two, if you find one, do you really think it's going to top this?"

"I don't know," Julia said again.

"Three," Alex continued. "We're close enough to the Cinque Terre for you to do anything you still want to do. So, keep the rest of your plans, no problem."

Harriet stepped out on the terrace. "Do either of you need anything?"

"No, thank you, Harriet." Julia replied. "This was a wonderful evening."

"Good," Harriet smiled. "Does that mean I won't be making calls to my hotelier friends in La Spezia tomorrow?"

Julia looked between Harriet and Alex and sighed.

"What is it?" Harriet asked.

The kindness in her voice made Julia unexpectedly choke up as she tried to imagine going back to empty hotel rooms and the shadows of her honeymoon. Still, she was not ready to give up on all her plans. She really hadn't even started them yet.

"Olive Haven is amazing, Harriet," she said finally, her voice trembling. "But I feel like I'm an imposition, and I have all these other plans for my trip, and I don't have a history like the rest of the women. I just..."

Harriet sat down next to Julia. "You don't even know these women's stories yet," she said reassuringly. "Did anyone seem like they didn't want you here tonight?"

"No," Julia conceded.

"Plus," Alex added, "you're also hurting."

Julia froze. "Why would you think that?" she asked quietly.

"I'm just connecting the dots," Alex said, matter-of-factly. "You're reluctantly traveling alone, somehow forgot to eat while in Italy of all places, were inexplicably drawn to staying in a house full of widows..."

"That doesn't mean..." Julia interrupted.

"And," Alex cut back in, "you kept asking for a 'Will' when you came to on the train."

Hot embarrassment bloomed on Julia's cheeks. She didn't remember having spoken his name. She wanted to be upset that Alex had outed her so easily, but was surprised to find she was relieved instead. Worrying about keeping her heartbreak a secret was almost as draining as enduring the heartbreak itself. She took a deep breath, feeling the admission stick in her throat. She forced herself to say the words aloud for the first time.

"Will is my fiancé," she explained quietly. "Ex-fiancé actually. Five days ago, he left me at the altar, but I decided to still take my honeymoon."

"Oh shit!" Alex leaned back in her chair.

"Yeah," Julia said, dropping her head into her hands. "Things have not gone well," she admitted. "In fact, almost nothing has gone as I hoped."

She thought of the wedding, the affair, the text, the picture, the woman, Erica, who had stepped into the future Julia was supposed to have, Florence, Luca. The basic truth of the trip may be out, but she remained acutely aware of the baggage she brought with her. The women on retreat, including Alex and Harriet, had their own heartache and grief to bear. She felt guilty thinking she would infringe on their time together.

She looked up to find Harriet watching her contemplatively.

"So, do you want to talk about it?" asked Alex. "You should let it all out. Recognizing the depths of what you're going through is the only way to know how far to build yourself back up. You taught me that," she pointed at Harriet.

Harriet smiled. "When you were ready for it," she said lightly. "I'm sorry you're hurting," she offered, turning back to Julia. "Nevertheless, the invitation stands. There's no pressure. Get some sleep. See what tomorrow brings."

She patted Julia's hand as she got up from the table, and gestured for Alex to follow into the villa. Julia remained at the table watching the last of the flames flicker into darkness.

Coming to Olive Haven felt like turning a page, but there

was something still holding her back, a tether to the life she could have had that kept drawing her in each time she felt ready to take a step forward. Severing that was going to take more than changing what room she slept in or altering all her plans. But something Alex said had hit home. The first step was recognizing the depths of what she was going through.

Julia thought about the tears she had cried, the despair she had weathered, the anger she had bit back, and the exhaustion she had endured trying to struggle through it. She thought about the mishaps in Florence. The guilt of the kiss. The fear of the train ride. The frustration of the cancellation. She thought about the text, the photos, the woman whose face she now knew, the sunrise photo on the beach. Her mind raced from memory to memory. She was too worn out to cry.

She moved to blow out the candles and collect her wine glass, her gaze falling to her left hand as she reached for the stem. It looked different, almost imperceptibly so, but enough that she stopped to discern what had changed. Shifting it back and forth under the flickering light, the shadows played over her knuckles, and Julia's spirits rose ever so slightly. The pale stripe of skin on her left ring finger had undeniably darkened. This had to be a sign. Maybe things would get better. Maybe Alex and Harriet and Olive Haven could make a difference. Certainly, she had already hit her rock bottom. Now, it was time to start climbing back up.

CHAPTER 10

J ulia had not had a good night's sleep since before the
wedding, and she woke the next morning from a deep
and dreamless slumber after most of the house was
already up and about for the day. Impulsively, she
grabbed her phone. A quick scroll of Will's Instagram feed
revealed no new updates. She didn't want to care what he
was doing, yet she couldn't help but wonder why he was
suddenly too busy to post. How could he torture her by
parroting her caption one day, and then go radio silent the
next? Puzzled, she swung herself out of bed, dressed casually,
and carried her notebook to the kitchen. There she found a
tray of pastries, and after a brief struggle with the espresso
machine, managed to make herself something resembling a
cappuccino. She took her cup and a pastry filled with sweet
cream onto the terrace.

Lucy sat alone facing the gardens and the water. She wore
a house dress in purple paisley, and from behind, her grey
hair was almost translucent with the morning sun streaming
through it. She cut small chunks from a slice of melon

draped in paper thin prosciutto and sipped a glass of orange juice.

Julia cleared her throat to announce her entrance. *"Buongiorno,"* she said.

Lucy smiled. "You slept well?" She brought a forkful of melon to her mouth.

"Very well, yes. The best sleep I've had so far this trip, actually. Where is everyone?"

"Harriet and Alex took Elise on a hike about an hour ago. Margo is out front reading under the olive tree. Bernardo left with Beth and Maeve for the market." Lucy shot a glance at Julia. "If you ask me," she dropped her voice surreptitiously, "Maeve should have left the two of them alone, but I suppose she wanted to get away from Aster, who's still in her room. Everyone hopes to reconvene around lunch time."

Julia shook her head, trying to make sense of Lucy's vague insinuation. "So, it's just you and me left for breakfast then?" she asked. "That is, if you don't mind my joining you?"

Lucy gestured to the seat across from her, and Julia took it. They sat for a moment enjoying the sun and distant sound of the waves on the rocks below. Julia contemplated how to break the silence.

"Why should Maeve have let Beth and Bernardo go to the market alone?" she wondered aloud.

Lucy's eyes glittered with mischief and gossip. "Because," she whispered. "I think Bernardo invited Beth to go as a date, and now Maeve is along to muck it up."

"Beth is dating the groundskeeper?"

"Well, it's only been a few days, but didn't you wonder why she wasn't at dinner last night?"

Julia took a bite of the pastry and shrugged. "Harriet mentioned she had private dinner plans. I assumed she was keeping to herself, taking supper in her room."

Lucy shook her head. "Oh no, that's only Aster. She hasn't

been up for group activities since arriving. But Beth was the first of us to arrive, and that's when she met Bernardo." She raised her eyebrows and fixed Julia with a knowing look.

"But we saw Bernardo last night," Julia objected. "He came to talk to Harriet at dinner."

Lucy shrugged. "Only for a moment. He probably wanted to know if he was allowed to be involved with a guest."

Julia gave a surprised, half-hearted chuckle. "This all sounds very…romantic."

"I wonder what my kids would think if I took an Italian lover." Lucy winked and took another bite of melon.

"You don't think that's the reason your family gave you this trip?" Julia teased.

"I'm always telling them I'm not dead yet, but I don't think they'd be willing to accept I'm still *that* alive. But I could do it, you know, if I wanted to."

"It?" Julia sputtered.

"Take a lover," Lucy insisted. "It just sounds like an awful lot of work, and I get tired." She stared seriously at Julia for a moment before bursting into laughter. Fits of giggles shook her tiny body, and she wiped tears from her eyes.

Julia choked on her coffee. "So, how many kids do you have?" she finally managed, picking at her breakfast.

"Four. Three sons and a daughter, plus eleven grandchildren between them, and three more great grandchildren beyond that."

"And do they all still live in San Diego?" Julia asked around a bite of pastry.

"Two. My middle sons, Allen and Jacob, raised their families there. The youngest, Robert, is in Phoenix."

"And your daughter?"

Lucy looked at her curiously. "But you know that…oh, I forgot you weren't here for early introductions. I'm Harriet's mother."

"Harriet? But you said your kids sent you on this trip for your birthday? Certainly, you could have visited Harriet here before this?"

Lucy shrugged. "I was never a traveler. That was George, Harriet's dad. She takes after him that way. Her husband, Jack, and I used to just sit back and listen while the two of them talked for hours about the places they wanted to go. George eventually convinced me to go along on many of those adventures with him, but given the circumstances, Harriet chose to stay close to home with Jack." She looked past Julia to the gardens, lost in thought. "He would have followed her anywhere while he still could," she added after a moment. "If she would have asked."

Julia looked down at her plate, aware that Harriet may have intentionally kept these details private in their initial meeting.

"He was sick," Lucy went on. "ALS."

"I'm sorry," said Julia quietly. She looked up to find Lucy's eyes shimmering with tears. "And George?"

"George was one of the lucky ones," Lucy said, wistfully. "Peacefully in his sleep. One morning I got up, and he didn't, and that was it."

The finality of Lucy's words hung over the terrace, and Julia finished her coffee, uncertain how to push past the heaviness that had settled on the conversation.

"Anyway," Lucy finally broke the silence. "For my birthday, my kids flew me to Venice. Robert came along and spent five days with me there. Then he put me on a train to Florence where I met Harriet, and she brought me here for the week. Next, I'll be taking a train to Rome to meet Jacob's family."

"That's a wonderful gift," said Julia. "I don't know your sons, but I know just from meeting Harriet that you have an amazing family."

"Thank you, I do." Lucy smiled, closing her eyes and tipping her face toward the sun. After a few minutes, Julia wondered if she'd dozed off. "You know what," Lucy said suddenly, eyes still closed. "I don't think even Harriet would like it if I took an Italian lover."

"Only one way to find out," teased Julia.

Lucy waved a hand, dismissing the idea. "So, what about you?" she asked. "Last night you said all roads led to Porto Venere, but before that you must have been seeing other things? So, what brought you here?"

Julia pushed the crumbs of the pastry around her saucer, considering how much to share. "I started my trip in Florence. That's when I met Harriet on the plane," she began. "The train strike took me to La Spezia a day early, but then my reservation fell through yesterday. So, now I'm here, at least until I figure out what comes next."

"Yes, I know that part," Lucy said, turning her gaze back to Julia, "But what brought you here in the first place?" She leaned forward, elbows on the table.

Julia stared back, pulse quickening. "I'm not sure how much Harriet told you?" she said finally.

"Assume she said nothing," Lucy said. "A story's always better from the source."

Though sharing the truth of the circumstances of her trip was exactly what Julia had dreaded most, she found the privacy of the terrace and her proximity to Lucy now leaning across the table created a comfortable intimacy. Even through Lucy's thick glasses, she saw her kind eyes matched Harriet's, inviting the same confidence she had felt on the plane. She pushed aside her nagging anxiety.

"I was meant to be..." she stopped, clearing her throat. She expected the words to come easier having shared with Alex and Harriet, but the reality was still hard to admit. Her heart continued to pound. "I'm on my honeymoon, but I'm obviously alone, so I'm not really on my honeymoon. He left. On the day of our wedding, with everyone at the church, he decided he couldn't go through with it." She picked up her coffee cup looking for a distraction, but, as it was already empty, she set it down and dropped her head in her hands. Her throat was thick with unshed tears, and she tried to compose herself.

"All the reservations were made in my name for the trip," Julia went on, not looking up. "Being here was really my dream all along, and it felt like the one good thing I had left, so I went." She looked up and took a deep breath. "Anyway, that's what brings me to Italy."

A long silence lingered over the terrace.

"I think that it was very brave of you to still come." Lucy said gently.

"Or stupid," Julia sighed. "Mostly it feels stupid. Florence was hauntingly romantic, and almost nothing went well."

"Well, somehow, you've figured out a way to join up with a group of widows, at least for now, so I think you've managed to take the romance out of things for the time being." Lucy reassured.

"Yeah," Julia chuckled weakly. "Until things heat up between Beth and Bernardo, or you take a lover."

The sound of the front door opening echoed through the house and drew their attention. Margo came through the living room and out onto the patio.

"They're back from the market, and there's trouble," she announced.

The three women listened to the faint sound of raised voices from the other side of the house.

"What happened?" Julia asked.

Margo shrugged. "I'm not sure. I heard them as they were coming up the road. Bernardo and Maeve were together, and Beth looked miserable."

"I told you," Lucy said knowingly. "Maeve went along and messed it up."

"Where's Beth now?" Julia asked Margo.

"They're all out front. Bernardo was making a phone call, and it seemed like Maeve was trying to console Beth."

Lucy rolled her eyes. "Well, I'm not sure what good consoling her is going to do now. If she wouldn't have gone along in the first place, she wouldn't have any consoling to do," she scoffed.

As if on cue, Maeve entered the house. The sound of Bernardo's raised voice was momentarily amplified through the open door then muffled again as Maeve closed it gently behind her and came through to the terrace.

"This isn't good," Maeve said, looking concerned.

"What did you think was going to happen?" Lucy asked in disbelief.

Maeve collapsed into a chair and stared at Lucy in confusion. "What's that supposed to mean?"

"It's just," tried Julia, "you did say he was handsome last night, but if you knew Beth was going on a date…"

"A date?" Maeve blurted. "You think Beth is upset because I interrupted her date with Bernardo?" She looked around at the women's serious faces and burst out laughing. "I could be his mother, so no, I was not headed into the market to interfere with Beth and Bernardo's date. What gave you the impression they were on a date at all?"

Julia looked at Lucy who popped the final piece of melon into her mouth and looked away guiltily.

"They did have dinner together last night," mused Julia.

Maeve squinted at Lucy suspiciously. "Yes, but I talked to Beth when I first arrived. Her husband is only recently deceased. She's far from ready to date, even someone as handsome as Bernardo."

"It wasn't a date," confirmed Margo. "But still, I was surprised to see you tote along."

"I honestly thought they were just going to the market," Maeve confessed. "I thought I'd tag along for the fresh air. But then they went down to the office of a private courier. I lagged behind a bit as it was obvious Beth had some business there. Bernardo had a long exchange with the man, and then Beth got visibly upset. When they came back over, Bernardo said we needed to return to the villa."

"What happened?" Julia prompted.

"It turns out Harriet put Bernardo and Beth in touch weeks ago. Beth intends to spread her husband's ashes while she's here, and Harriet enlisted Bernardo's help to navigate the necessary regulations." She looked pointedly at Lucy as she continued. "Last night wasn't a romantic dinner between the two of them, they were going through Beth's paperwork to make sure everything was in order before picking up the remains from the courier this morning. She had them mailed over two weeks ago."

"So, then why was she upset at the courier's office?" asked Julia.

Maeve shook her head sadly. "The courier didn't have them. They never arrived. Beth is devastated, but Bernardo is furious. He was on the phone the whole walk back trying to get information about what went wrong."

"It'll turn up," Lucy assured. "Harriet will make sure it's found."

"It's going to be her up against the international postal system," Margo replied skeptically.

The front door opened again, and the four women turned to find Harriet ushering Beth into the entryway. Alex and Elise stood framed in the doorway in their hiking gear. Harriet draped an arm around Beth's shoulders, and they leaned together at the base of the stairs engrossed in quiet conversation. Beth looked miserable, nodding morosely along with Harriet's whispered condolences. After a brief moment, she turned, despondent, and headed upstairs.

Harriet came to the terrace followed by Alex and Elise. "Well ladies," Harriet sighed heavily. "I trust no one else suffered hardship this morning?"

"Only Lucy's undo scrutiny," teased Maeve.

"She's kidding," Lucy reassured, shooting Maeve a look.

Alex sat down next to Julia.

"How was the hike?" Julia asked.

"Gorgeous." Alex sighed happily. "The views from the upper ridges are unmatched."

"Spectacular," Elise agreed, taking a seat. "It was fantastic."

"You'll have to show me," said Julia.

Alex smiled. "Anytime. We can go this afternoon, unless you have other plans for the day?"

The conversation with Lucy had left Julia's notebook forgotten, but she reached for it now, scanning over the day's original itinerary.

"Wine tasting at Crestavilla in Manarola." As she read the words, she realized that finally something was going to go as planned. No dragging herself through emotional torture to get dressed. No train strikes. No dinners alone to get carried away with. Just an afternoon of wine in the Mediterranean sun. Days like this were why she had come, and now she would actually have a chance to enjoy one. "I just need to figure out a way to get there."

"That's not a problem," Harriet assured. "We can get you a water taxi. In fact," she looked around the table, "since Bernardo and I will be tied up with phone calls for Beth this afternoon, it will be a bit quiet around here. If anyone else would like to spend the day in the Cinque Terre, Manarola has cliff jumping, bike tours, and numerous cooking classes."

Murmurs of interest went up from the group.

"Good," Harriet smiled. "I'll make the arrangements." She gave Julia's notebook the faintest flicker of a glance. "Don't worry about your bags now," she added to before turning to head inside. "No need to lug them all over Manarola. If you want to head back to La Spezia, there's an evening ferry."

Julia nodded, and Harriet returned to the villa.

As Julia wandered down the hall to her room a few minutes later, she thought back over her conversation with Lucy. Though not entirely sure why she felt compelled to share as much as she had, her apprehension at how she may be received lessened ever so slightly. It was a good morning, a morning of acceptance. And an afternoon in the sun with the best of Ligurian wine, she imagined, would be another step in the right direction.

She changed her clothes, packed the essentials in her bag, and stepped into the bathroom to tie back her hair and put sunscreen on her face. The opposite door to Aster's room was propped open again, and Julia saw that Aster had turned her chair toward the window and was seated looking out over the yard. She crept toward the room, meaning to close the door for privacy.

"Aster?" she said quietly, not wanting to startle her.

Aster whirled around, glaring at Julia.

"I'm sorry," Julia added quickly. "I was just going to close your..."

Before Julia could finish, Aster was up from the chair and to the door. Julia held her gaze, noting not anger, but deep pain and sadness behind her eyes. Aster said nothing, the moment hanging between them, and then she closed the door in Julia's face.

Julia stood in stunned silence. Whatever camaraderie she had found with Lucy and the other women was going to have to make up for what she had not found with Aster. She stared at the door thinking about the depth of heartache that would drive a person to such levels of despair. Her own chest tightened in reply. She thought suddenly of the wedding, the break up, Will's text message, his photos of Erica on the beach. The ache grew unbearable, and she bent over and gripped the countertop. Despite the peace of the morning, there was no avoiding the pain when it came. Closing her eyes, she took steadying breaths, fortifying her resolve to venture out into the afternoon. The moment finally passed, and she looked up at her reflection in the mirror. For the first time it struck her that she and Aster may not be so different after all.

CHAPTER 11

An hour later, the private water taxi pulled away from the dock in Porto Venere and sped along the coastline toward the Cinque Terre. Steep cliffs dotted with precariously perched villas spilled down to the blue water where waves pounded the shore and a few brave swimmers explored tiny, pebbled beaches. Gardens and vineyards, unbelievably terraced down the slopes, stretched lush and green across the rocky landscape.

They passed Riomaggiore. The town sat nestled in the vee of the cliffs, the harbor the point from which the city grew. A wide, sloping launch led up to the central square dotted with overturned fishing boats and colorful umbrellas. From there, a dozen tiny alleys and side streets spider webbed through the buildings and up the hill. Sunbathers dotted the rocks and boulders along the shore. The town was splashed with reds and golds and pinks, all framed against the imposing grey stone cliffs and rich green terraces. Julia couldn't look away, enchanted by the postcard perfect scene.

A train crawled along the wild coastline, its tracks laid into the slope with just enough room for the cars to sneak by the rock face. It was, Julia knew, the train she would have taken from La Spezia had she not lost her reservation. From its windows, she imagined, the passengers had both a breathtaking view of the Mediterranean and the uncomfortable sensation they were about to topple sideways into it. She watched as it was swallowed by a tunnel cut deep in the hillside and was grateful for the sunshine and open air above her.

The boat came around an outcropping of the coast, and the women got their first views of Manarola. It was built up off the water, the buildings at the sea side of the town sitting along the rocky edge. A long slanting walkway led from a docking area below to a town square above. Small crowds were gathered to look out over the deep pools in the harbor into which the bravest swimmers dove from the surrounding cliffs. The lower section of the village sprawled along the primary ridge of the coastline. Behind that perched a small upper section of town surrounded by verdant hillside.

As they pulled into the slip, Alex came up next to Julia at the railing. "We'll be in the lower town by the shops and restaurants," she said. "The winery will be in the upper town on the ridgeline. When you're finished, come find us near the marina. We'll all go back together."

Julia nodded, and they disembarked onto the pier and began the slow ascent to the town square.

The open area above the marina was beautifully mosaiced in pebbles and cut glass, and the buildings around the square leaned lazily on one another, a technicolor array of gift shops and cafes. Julia left the group at the harbor overlook to watch divers plummet into the sea, and she set off into the heart of Manarola. It felt strange to walk alone, both for Will's absence and having left the rest of the women behind, but she tried to put it from her mind, focusing her energy on the walk up the hill and her excitement for the winery. If she had starred reservations as Will had, this afternoon would have ranked near the top of her list.

As she continued into the upper town, the crowds thinned, and she shared the street with mostly locals. Julia stopped and consulted a map of the village that Harriet had provided, then set off up a staircase made of thick fieldstone blocks buried in the hillside. She wound up through the surrounding terraces to a path at the top of the ridge over-looking the entire crevice into which Manarola was wedged. Up ahead, a sign directed her toward rows of trellised grapevines and the Crestavilla winery.

A young woman in dusty denim coveralls met her in front of the main building.

"I'm Julia Brooks." Julia extended a hand in introduction. "I have a 2:00pm tasting scheduled with Mossimmo."

The woman consulted a clipboard then looked back to Julia, confused. "Would it be under a different name, perhaps?"

Julia cringed, and her mouth went dry. "Calhoun."

"*Si, Signora* Calhoun. Mossimmo has a place ready for you and *Signor* Calhoun in the back." She looked up from the list at Julia. "We were expecting two of you."

"Please, just call me Julia," she replied. "Mr. Calhoun won't be joining me. He had an unexpected change of plans, but I found myself still able to make the reservation. I'm hopeful that's not a problem?"

"No problem," confirmed the woman with a nod. "It's just that the Friday afternoon tasting is our couples' event."

"Couples' event?" choked Julia.

"Yes," the woman raised an eyebrow in surprise. "You didn't know? Most couples request it."

"I guess I just got lucky then," Julia said flatly. Her heart sank. She could *not* believe this hadn't come up in her plan-ning, or if it had, perhaps she didn't think twice because it would have made the afternoon that much more special. But that was before.

The woman looked at Julia sympathetically. "*Un momento, per favore,*" she said.

She disappeared into the main building, returning a few minutes later with a giant man in lavender pants and a flowing white shirt. He wore a gold wristwatch, and his loafers were trimmed with gold tassels to match. The top three buttons of his shirt were undone revealing dark curls of chest hair.

"*Signora,*" he stepped forward and took Julia's hand. "Greetings. I am Mossimmo. Lucia tells me that you're joining us alone this afternoon, *si?*"

"Yes," Julia said wearily.

"Seeing as it is our couples' event, would you like to reschedule? We could seat you tomorrow, or if you'd rather return with *Signor* Calhoun at a later time, we would be happy to accommodate."

"*Signor* Calhoun won't be joining me...ever." Julia could not keep the bitterness from her tone. "Is there some reason I can't have my table this afternoon?"

Mossimmo and Lucia exchanged a weighted glance.

"Not at all," he replied. "Right this way."

He led Julia through the main building and out to a large back patio shaded by a pergola. Thick ropes of grapevine climbed its posts and entwined overhead in a thick canopy that shaded a dozen small bistro tables where couples sat holding hands, heads pressed together, rows of glasses sparkling in the sun before them. A single rose adorned every table, and Italian love songs poured from a speaker in the corner. Julia stopped in the doorway, feeling the blood drain from her face. Mossimmo walked to a table on the far side and began to clear the second set of glasses. Julia willed herself to cross the terrace.

"It's very romantic, no?" he said as she approached. Julia thought she heard a touch of sympathy in his voice.

"Yes," she managed.

"If you'd rather..." he paused, waving his hand back to the entrance.

"Thank you, I'm fine," insisted Julia, pulling out her chair and sinking into it. Mossimmo hovered behind her for a moment, then returned to the main building with the extra glasses.

Julia failed miserably to ignore the scenes around her. At the table to her left, a woman's laughter tinkled in response to something her husband whispered in her ear. In front of her, a young couple, college aged, sat with feet, knees, and shoulders touching. Everywhere she looked, a happy couple reveled in the throes of Italian romance. The more she watched, the more the empty chair at her table mocked her, and the more despondent she became.

She stared out at the steeply trellised vineyard rising behind the building and patio. A gleaming streak of silver zigzagged through the vines, a rail on which a train of motorized carts with open sides moved up and down the hillside. She tracked its progress rising up the hill. The woman to her left laughed again. It tweaked her nerves, and it occurred to her that she should get up and leave. Clearly Lucia and Mossimmo, though naïve to the full story, had been trying to spare her this discomfort. To go now, however, would be to forfeit yet another piece of the trip as she had dreamed it, and that made her feel, somehow, worse.

It would be an excruciatingly long afternoon.

"Okay, ladies and gentleman!" Mossimmo announced. He crossed the patio, a bottle of wine cradled in each elbow. "Today we're going to try some of the best *vino* in the Cinque Terre and, of course, our famous Sciacchetrà. But we start with this. *Vino da tavola.* Table wine." He made a circuit of the tables, pouring a glass for each guest. "Crisp, dry, aromatic." He swirled his own glass, indicating they should do the same. "Made from Bosco, Albarola, and Vermentino grapes. You'll taste hay, citrus, green apple, and that touch of salt and minerals from the sea. *Saluti!*" He raised his glass, swirled the wine, buried his nose in the bowl breathing deeply, then took a long sip.

"*Saluti!*" The response echoed around the terrace.

Julia followed along halfheartedly.

The wine flowed. Mossimmo and Lucia brought a steady stream of bottles from the main building, offering samples of Crestavilla's latest vintages and reserve specialties. With each, Mossimmo poured out a tasting portion and offered a toast. The more wine that appeared, the louder and more energetic the conversations around her grew. Self-righteous anger bubbled up in Julia. She should have what these couples shared. The trip was not what she had dreamed, nor had it brought her the control and strength she imagined finding when she decided to leave. Somehow, though thousands of miles away, Will still had the power to haunt her days. Exasperated, she drank deeply and wondered if it would feel better to just fly home. A new bottle came around the terrace, and Julia held up her glass to be filled.

Couples began leaving their tables and venturing out toward the vineyard and surrounding gardens. An old couple stood and began to dance to the music drifting over the patio. The college pair near Julia got up to walk, but now stood by their table awkwardly as the young man fumbled in his pockets. Julia realized what was about to happen a second before the young woman. Her stomach clenched. He dropped to a knee, prompting his girlfriend to squeal and burst into tears. Cheers echoed from all sides.

"*Fantastico!*" Mossimmo shouted. "We will celebrate. Are you ready for the Sciacchetrà?" There was another swell of applause from the group. "*Si?* I will bring it." He disappeared back into the main building.

Julia applauded the newly engaged couple, moving as if she was underwater. Her actions felt slow and clumsy, and the sounds of the vineyard were muted and distorted. She was vaguely aware that there were tears on her cheeks, but she couldn't remember having started to cry. She should leave, she told herself, but she couldn't seem to make herself stand. She watched as Mossimmo returned, circling the grounds and visiting with each couple. The wine and warmth of the terrace washed over her, but left her feeling numb. Julia laid her head on the table and closed her eyes, waiting for the disaster of an afternoon to end.

"*Signora?*"

A voice at her side startled Julia, and she sat up quickly. The patio was empty and quiet. She had fallen asleep.

"Sorry." Julia rubbed her eyes, embarrassed. "I'm not sure what happened."

Lucia set a basket of bread and dipping oil on Julia's table. "Eat something," she offered, pushing the bread towards Julia. "The wine and the heat may have gone to your head a bit."

"I'm so sorry, Lucia." Julia groaned, her cheeks heating in mortification. "I'm terribly embarrassed."

Lucia shook her head. "You were no trouble. Besides," she hesitated, "I think you have had a difficult afternoon."

Julia paused, bread half way to her mouth. "Is it that obvious?"

"*Italia* is the land of love stories," Lucia explained, smiling shyly and taking the seat next to Julia. "They are woven into our art, our music, our history, our DNA. *Italiani* are romancers, which also means we know heartbreak, perhaps better than most."

"That's why you offered to let me reschedule?"

Lucia nodded. "It was something about the way you said the name," she admitted. "You are not happy here." It wasn't a question.

Julia let the silence hang and brushed a tear from her cheek.

"Well then," Lucia announced, standing, "we must give you joy again. Stay here." She walked back to the main building, returning a moment later with Mossimmo who carried a large glass of water.

"*Signora,*" he smiled as he approached. "You missed my Sciacchetrà." He placed the water on the table, and Julia gulped it hurriedly.

"*Mi dispiace,*" Julia offered, coming up for air.

Mossimmo merely smiled. "Come," he said.

He stepped off the back patio, and gestured for her to follow him into the vines. At the base of the first terrace, the motorized carts sat piled with tools and brush wood that had been brought down from the vineyard. Mossimmo spoke briefly to one of the workers unloading the carts, then turned to face Julia. "This is Gianni. He will give you the most breathtaking view of Manarola. You will not be sad on the top of the world."

Gianni hurried the remaining debris off the metal carts and held out a hand. "Your chariot awaits," he grinned.

"I've had entirely too much wine for this," Julia protested.

"You are overwhelmed, not over served." Mossimmo shook his head. "Climb on."

Julia took Gianni's hand and clambered onto the cart.

"Hold on there," Mossimmo directed, pointing to tie down loops on the platform.

"Ready?" called Gianni. "Here we go."

The *trenino* began to climb into the vineyard. Grapevines closed in on both sides of them, and the sweet smell of cut grass and wild flowers mixed with the exhaust from the small engine powering the cars up the hillside. It rose at an impossible angle for a few minutes. Workers in the rows of grapes smiled and waved as they passed. They curved gently to the left and moved along the top of the property.

"You can't beat this view." Gianni made a grand gesture back over the vineyard.

Julia turned to look and gasped.

The crest of the vineyard looked out over the entirety of Manarola. From above, the buildings tumbling down toward the water looked even more precariously stacked than they did from the seaside walkway far below. Heat rippled off their tile roofs in the afternoon sunshine, making the marina appear to shimmer. The pools in the harbor were dark sapphire stains on blue opal water. Farther out, cruise ships bobbed along the horizon line. The entire scene was baked in warmth and golden light that filled Julia's heart.

"It's unbelievable!" Julia yelled over the drone of the engine.

The tiny train banked gently to the left again and began to descend. Halfway down the hill, it cut through a wide row of vines. Small clusters of grapes hung within arm's reach of the carts.

"Try one!" Gianni shouted from his seat next to the engine.

Julia reached out and plucked a tender red grape. She popped it in her mouth. Sour acid burst on her tongue, and she coughed it out.

Gianni laughed at her reaction. "They're not ready yet. They need more time. More sun," he said. "Wait until you try the Sciacchetrà. You'll see what the extra sun can do."

They came out the other side of the row of vines and finished their descent back to the patio. Mossimmo was waiting. Julia couldn't wipe the smile off her face as he helped her from the cart.

"That is better, no?" Mossimmo asked. "Now you will not cry into my best wine."

"You're right," Julia agreed. "That was incredible."

"No," Mossimmo said, with a shake of his head. "That was beautiful. Breathtaking. Idyllic. This," he handed her a tiny tasting glass of amber wine. "This is *incredible*. The Sciacchetrà is made from grapes dried in the sun for one hundred days after harvest, then fermented and pressed for the most intense flavors. You can only find this wine in the Cinque Terre. At Crestavilla, we make it best."

Julia swirled the wine once around the glass, watching the viscous liquid cling to the sides. She took a sip. It was sweet as honey with just the slightest hint of bright citrus and no burn of alcohol to speak of. Mossimmo watched her eagerly.

She smiled softly. "It's perfect."

Mossimmo, Lucia, and Gianni walked Julia back across the terrace and through the main building, lining up in front of Crestavilla to see her off on her descent back into Manarola. As Julia approached Mossimmo to say goodbye, he held out a closed fist before her. When he opened his hand, a single, young grape lay in his palm.

"Oh no," she laughed, shaking her head. "Gianni already got me with this trick."

Mossimmo smiled and popped the grape in his mouth. He watched Julia calmly, betraying nothing of its tartness. "It's not ready yet. But that's not a bad thing. It just needs a little more time," he said. "More sun too," he added, leaning forward to kiss her on both cheeks.

"That's what Gianni said," Julia replied.

"Sun and time," Mossimmo nodded, "improve a great many things." He winked.

"*Grazie*, Mossimmo."

"*Si, signora. Prego.*"

Julia began the walk back to the harbor, mind buzzing

with wine and Mossimmo's final words of wisdom. Her pain and anger had lessened with the ride through the vineyard and the kindness of her hosts, and the cool sea breeze that moved through the town helped her breathe easier. Though she walked alone, something about knowing she was returning to the group of women made Will's obvious absence from the afternoon bearable again.

Traffic in the upper town had increased as locals streamed home for the evening, and she returned polite calls of *Buonasera* as she wound toward the water. Coming down the stone steps to the lower village, she caught sight of Margo's pink hair stepping out of a gelateria, the rest of the women in tow. She noted Lucy bogged down with shopping bags falling behind the group and hurried ahead to catch up.

"Let me help you," Julia said, coming alongside Lucy and offering to take a bag.

Lucy smiled widely. "You're back. Did you have a wonderful afternoon?"

Julia's hesitation was answer enough.

"Well in that case, perhaps it's best that it's over," Lucy added after a moment.

They wandered casually through the crowds streaming in and out of store fronts, Lucy pointing out various novelties and displays they had visited earlier in the day. They caught up with the rest of the women in front of a boutique named 'Regali Unici' where Maeve and Alex stopped to sort through a basket of creatively shaped pastas. Maeve triumphantly held up a cellophane bag tied with black ribbon.

"Are those?" Elise crossed the gift shop, ogling the bag.

"*Peni* Penne!" exclaimed Maeve.

"I thought penne were supposed to be long tubes," Elise said, taking the bag from Maeve.

The group stared at her, then burst into uncontrollable laughter. Julia couldn't help but to laugh along with them. It rolled from her unexpectedly, the first time she had found something truly funny since the wedding.

"Penne yes," Alex said, gasping for breath. "Actually, I guess *peni* too."

Maeve wiped her eyes. "Well, that's likely as close as I'll get to having *peni* these days."

"Personally, I've never enjoyed...cooking...much with *peni* myself," Margo said, nudging Elise while eyeing the bag suspiciously.

Lucy stared at the phallus shaped pasta. "Let's have some," she announced with a wink.

"Penne, or *peni?*" Elise asked, tears of laughter still streaming down her face.

"Either? Both? Believe it or not ladies, I once...*cooked*...with the best of them." The women dissolved into another fit of hysterics while Lucy paid for the pasta. Julia dabbed at her eyes, belly sore from laughter. "Alright ladies, let's see if we can convince Bernardo to make us a feast," Lucy giggled, stepping back from the counter and tucking the pasta into her shopping bag.

"And what will you have served with your *peni* penne?" Alex asked lightly.

"Balls," Lucy said, without irony. "Meatballs."

Fresh laughter erupted as they stepped from the shop into the evening light of the harbor, and they wound their way back to the boat in high spirits. As she stood on the dock with Alex, waiting as the crew helped the rest of the women into the water taxi, Julia turned, looking back over Manarola. The lights of Crestvilla, high on the ridgeline above, winked over a village bathed in the warm, golden light of evening. It was picture perfect. She hadn't been wrong about the day after all. A sliver of happiness *had* found her in Manarola, but it wasn't on her itinerary pages. This feeling, Julia realized, was what she was searching for. Happiness to fill the void that Will's decisions had created in her world. Despite the heartache of the afternoon, she felt something inside her stir back to life now that she had joined the company of the women. There was a joy here she hadn't found on her own.

"We're running a little late," Alex said apologetically. "It's going to be tight if you're still wanting to pack and make the evening ferry back to La Spezia tonight."

Julia's stomach flipped at the notion of leaving, and she turned back to Alex, her mind already made up. Harriet had said there was a time for a plan and a time to be spontaneous. She did not know what her time at Olive Haven might bring, but this still felt like her moment.

"I don't want to go back to La Spezia," Julia said. Despite earlier misgivings, she felt nothing but certainty in the decision. "I'll stay."

"Really?" The excitement was clear in Alex's voice, and it warmed Julia's heart all the more.

"Yeah," Julia nodded, assured. "You were right, something about it just feels like I'm where I was meant to end up."

Alex beamed at Julia's words.

"Ready?" The crew member on the dock held out both hands to help Julia and Alex into the boat.

Julia smiled, placing her hand in his. "I am," she said.

She was hopeful that, for whatever came next, she would be.

CHAPTER 12

The next morning, Julia woke early. Thin threads of
mist hung in the air over the front yard, glittering
in the light of sunrise. Dew sparkled on the lawn,
and the silvery underbellies of the olive leaves glinted as they
dried in the sun. At the scrape of footsteps, she sat up in bed
to see Alex and Harriet heading down the driveway, cups of
coffee in hand. They diverted across the damp lawn leaving
dark prints in the dewy grass and settled in on the bench
under the tree.

As she sat in bed acclimating to the day, Julia impulsively
reached for her phone to check on Will. She scrolled
anxiously to his profile page searching for his latest post. He
still hadn't updated since the sunrise on the beach photo, and
Julia closed the app in disappointment.

Though the glimpses into his new life tore at her, she also
found that knowing for certain his whereabouts was better
than guessing at possibilities. Her mind raced with potential
scenarios as to his silence. Maybe they had a fight? Maybe
they had gone home? Maybe he drank the water and had a
devastating stomach bug? A large part of her hoped he did.

Maybe a monsoon had moved in and they were stranded in the hotel for the day? Her stomach flipped as she unwilfully considered how they may choose to spend an afternoon shut up in their room. She put her phone in the drawer of the bedside table and pushed herself from bed. Best not to linger on such thoughts when the morning held the promise of an exceptionally good day.

Having decided to stay at Olive Haven, Julia had returned to the villa the previous evening intent on being fully present and getting to know the women of the house. It was hard to imagine now that she had been worried about the possible awkwardness of the group dynamic given the differences in their circumstances. Everyone had been nothing but affable. Even Beth, distracted in the midst of the search for her lost package, had come to dinner and warmly introduced herself to Julia.

Beth had, the group learned, spent the day with Harriet and Bernardo tracking her package to a hub in Pontedera, which had allegedly sent it out for delivery. Of course, that Pontedera was not Porto Venere made delivery impossible, so where the box eventually ended up was still in question. Despite her initial distress, she was, Julia thought, remarkably calm and thoughtful about the predicament, and Julia admired her strength in the midst of personal crisis.

The meal had concluded with a round of storytelling from Lucy about Harriet's antics as a teenager, and the reappearance of the *peni* penne, which hadn't made it onto the dinner table as part of the meal, and about which many jokes were made. Julia had gone to bed with cheeks sore from smiling, a feat she would have considered impossible just hours earlier at the winery.

And now the morning had broken clear and bright, and though thoughts of Will remained, and her heart was far from healed, she felt the stirrings of promise in a day that, for the first time, could be entirely untethered from her original plans. Given the time and energy that had gone into it, she was surprised to find that she no longer felt any obligation to maintain her itinerary, though a small part of her did still long for the trip as planned. That version of *as planned*, however, also included the husband and the honeymoon, and was no longer an option. Glancing at the notebook as she left the room, she resolved to no longer fixate on prior perceptions or expectations of what the trip should look like, a near impossible task, she knew, considering the circumstances.

But still, she would try.

The rest of the villa was quiet as she made her way downstairs and through the kitchen. Bernardo watered the gardens at the back of the house, and he waved and set down the hose as she stepped onto the patio.

"*Buongiorno,*" he said. "Is there anything you needed? Harriet is out front."

Julia waved him off. "No, thank you, Bernardo. I saw her with Alex. I'm fine. I just thought I'd sit in the sun this morning."

Bernardo nodded, picked up the hose again, and resumed tending the plants.

Julia took a seat in the sunshine, tipped her head back, and closed her eyes. A cool morning breeze played against her sun warmed face. Birds tittered in the bushes around the edge of the yard, and the surf crashed against the rocks far below the house. Her mind wandered back to Will's whereabouts and when he might reappear on her feed. She shifted in her chair, frustrated that she couldn't find an inner peace to match the tranquility of the scene around her. At the sound of voices from an open window upstairs, she opened her eyes.

She nearly tipped her chair over in surprise to find Margo sitting directly across from her.

"My God, Margo! You scared me. I didn't hear you."

"I'm sorry. I didn't want to disturb you," Margo said. "Did you sleep well?"

"I did, thank you. You?"

Margo shrugged. "Well enough. I like the quiet here and the darkness, but I don't sleep like I used to. I blame age. There's more to grapple with in the middle of the night as you get older: bathroom breaks to take; hot flashes to endure; snoring partners to roll over. Do you know, I had to teach myself how to sleep in a quiet room again after Mona died?"

"Not Will," said Julia. "Sometimes I'd wake up in the middle of the night and have to check that he was still breathing. He sleeps like a dead man." Julia flinched. "Sorry, that was probably insensitive."

Margo tipped her chair back. "Not really. Even in death you can't compare Mona to a dead man. Not every widow loses a husband."

They sat in silence for a moment, Margo running a hand over the pink streak in her hair in a futile effort to tame her bed head. She leaned back in the chair, warming herself in the morning sun.

"Could I ask you a question?" Julia started, then paused. "Actually, I'm not sure I know the right way to ask it."

"However it comes out will be fine," Margo encouraged, her eyes closed. "Ask away."

"What happened to Mona?"

Margo sighed, opening her eyes. "Breast cancer."

"I'm sorry," Julia said softly. "That must have been incredibly difficult."

"It was, yes," replied Margo. "We were together for twenty-four years. We met while living in Boston. Mona was a hospital nurse working mostly in orthopedic surgery. She kept her private life very private from her patients and colleagues." She stared out across the yard, watching a hummingbird flit between the gardens. "It was a bit of a wonder that a physician friend of mine even knew to introduce us. He volunteered with her in a free clinic downtown doing community health education and screenings, and somehow in the midst of the afternoon together, she had let something of her dating history slip."

Margo turned her attention back to the table and Julia. "He called and told me I should make a trip out to the hospital, and that he'd meet me with a new nurse on his team. He made our introduction and suggested perhaps we talk further over a business lunch the next day. When I arrived at the agreed upon restaurant, Mona sat waiting, alone. We had a wonderful time."

She smiled at the passing memory. "It was a perfect setup, although not always a perfect relationship in the early years. It was hard navigating social waters in those days. In certain crowds, with certain friends and even family, plenty of fuss was made about our community and our relationship. Mona was better at it than I was. I tended to take things personally."

"I can't imagine," Julia murmured.

"All I wanted was to follow my heart and live a good life with a loving partner who brought out the best in me. I didn't think it should be so hard. Of course, life throws in its own complications." Margo cocked her head, appraising Julia. "I think you *can* imagine that."

Julia's stomach clenched.

"When we learned we would be able to marry in Massachusetts, I initially pushed back against it. I didn't need a piece of paper to tell me what we were. Though at the same time, as we looked toward retirement, and benefits, and growing old together, there were some practicalities that made sense." She hugged her elbows, drawing herself inward. "It was Mona's idea first. When she proposed, I couldn't say no. We had a small ceremony, threw ourselves a party, and then she got sick."

Footsteps in the kitchen interrupted the conversation as Bernardo came through the doors and out to the table with two cups of espresso.

"For you ladies," he said, setting them down gently. "Help yourself to fruit in the kitchen."

"*Grazie*, Bernardo," they chimed in unison as he returned to the house. A moment later, Maeve and Elise came down the hallway and into the kitchen. They stopped at the counter to scoop fruit into white ceramic bowls.

"You were saying?" Julia asked Margo.

Maeve stepped into the garden.

"I'll tell you later," Margo assured her.

"*Buongiorno*. Another glorious morning in paradise I see. Not that you could convince my sister." Maeve called loudly in the direction of an open window on the second floor.

"Leave her be," Elise chided, coming through the patio doors behind her.

Maeve dropped into an empty chair at the table. "She doesn't need to be let be," she said. "She's always been the brooding one. I suppose that's what happens when you're the politician's wife. She spent her whole life having to toe the line. This trip was supposed to do her some good. Loosen her up."

"Her husband was a politician?" asked Julia.

"Timothy Bailey? Oh yes. Twenty years in the North Carolina State House, and one year as Lieutenant Governor. Quite the man. You've never seen a funeral like Timothy's. Military escort. State officials. Quite the spectacle."

"It was recent then?" asked Margo.

"Almost a year," Maeve said casually. "When Arthur died six months later, I thought we'd be able to lean on each other.

Maybe I could pull Aster out of her shell a little bit. But if anything, she's gotten worse. I thought for certain that a foreign country could do it, but here I sit...alone!" She emphasized the final word, hollering toward the open window again.

"That's not even her window," Elise chuckled, taking a bite of fruit.

"Anyway," said Maeve, cheerfully changing the subject. "Where is everyone heading today? I'm thinking about the park. Bernardo says the Porto Venere Natural Park, that island you see just outside the harbor, is a worthwhile day trip. It's got a beach, a castle, snorkeling. Harriet has a charter boat already arranged."

As if conjured by her name, Harriet came around the side of the house with Alex.

"Good morning, everyone," Harriet looked around the group. "Well, almost everyone. Good sleep all around?"

Julia caught her eye, and Harriet winked. Alex had not been wrong; when she returned to Olive Haven, Harriet had been delighted to learn of Julia's decision to stay.

"For today's agenda, there's a boat to the island available at 10:30. Bernardo will send a picnic lunch. It's also market day in La Spezia. The ferry is your best option for a quick visit, or if you're looking for a more active endeavor, Alex will lead a hike up Mount Castellana. Anyone's welcome. Bernardo will remain at Olive Haven should anyone wish to spend the day here."

The women quickly set about dividing themselves into groups, Maeve ultimately opting to try and convince her sister to join an excursion to the island while Margo offered to wait with Elise to see if Beth or Lucy wanted to join them on the ferry to La Spezia.

Harriet turned to Julia. "And what's on your itinerary for the day?"

"No itinerary," answered Julia. "I thought maybe you would have a suggestion of how to spend a real retreat day."

"Really? Good for you." Harriet smiled warmly. "In that case, perhaps you'd care to join the hike?"

"I'm easily convinced," Julia replied. "As long as that doesn't make me too much of a third wheel for you and Alex."

Alex laughed. "As long as you can keep up with Harriet. She sets the pace."

"Right," Harriet rolled her eyes. "Well then ladies, have a wonderful day. Dinner at the house will be at eight. You all have my number and the number of the villa if you need anything at all."

"You'll be hours away on a cliff," Maeve pointed out.

"True," Harriet conceded. "Probably call Olive Haven first. That's why I keep Bernardo around."

At the sound of his name, Bernardo returned to the back of the house, coiling the hose as he came around the corner. "*Si*, Harriet. Is there something you need?"

"Only a strong espresso," she said, turning toward the house. "How else will I keep up with these two all day?"

AN HOUR LATER, dressed in a royal blue tank top and matching spandex capris, Julia followed Alex and Harriet into Porto Venere to the trailhead toward Campiglia. At Alex's insistence, Julia had borrowed the outfit from the extensive collection spilled across her bedroom floor. Alex wore a similar set swirled in green and yellow. Harriet had laughed when she met them in the entryway, her own sensible cargo hiking shorts and long-sleeved, white, sun shirt drawing far less attention to themselves. 'A matched set' she had called them. Alex had beamed.

Morning traffic was light and jovial. Farmers with their carts headed to the market. Fishermen with their nets and tackle laughed gaily as they wound their way toward their boats in the harbor. Tourists staying in villas along the town's upper ridge wandered to the water toting beach towels and sunhats. A few fellow hikers broke off at various points where dirt paths spindled off the main road and into the surrounding woods and brush.

An old stone church sat near the central square, and its bells pealed a merry melody as the three women moved toward rough steps that had been cut into the hillside leading away from the village. Their chiming needled at something Julia couldn't put a finger on, and she climbed distractedly behind Alex and Harriet for two hundred yards before coming to a flat, graveled trailhead with a loose entrance gate. A red and white placard directed traffic to the right toward *la vista panoramica*.

They went single file onto the trail, Harriet leading the way, followed by Alex. Julia trailed a few yards behind, still pondering the bells, trying to place a nagging memory. She thought back to Florence. The bells had tolled frequently over the city, but she rarely gave them more than a passing thought. Something about this morning was different, but she couldn't discern why.

Julia realized she had slowed down to think, and Alex and Harriet had surged ahead. She rushed to catch up.

"All good?" Alex asked, falling off Harriet's pace to match Julia's slower stride.

"Yeah, great." Julia replied, preoccupied.

Alex looked over, skeptically. "You just seemed eager to hike, and now it seems like maybe you'd rather not tag along?"

Julia adjusted her backpack and shook her head, trying to

clear the plaguing thoughts of the church. "I am excited, really."

"If you say so," replied Alex, unconvinced.

Harriet stopped a hundred yards ahead of them where the trail split, and they caught up with her quickly.

"When I asked Bernardo for that espresso, I didn't imagine that I'd actually be dragging the two of you behind me," she said, raising her eyebrows in silent question.

"Just trying to get Julia out of her own head so she can enjoy the scenery," Alex teased, walking past Harriet and taking the left fork up the hill.

"Is something bothering you?" Harriet asked.

"No," Julia insisted, looking back the way they had come. "I was just thinking about the church. Something about it was unsettlingly familiar."

"You'll have to visit it," Harriet said, starting to walk again. "It's beautifully frescoed inside. Different and softer than the cathedrals in Florence."

Julia followed her onto the path. "I actually didn't make it into any of the churches in Florence," she admitted.

"How is that possible?" Harriet asked with surprise. "There are at least a hundred churches in Florence, and, of course, the Duomo is the center of everything. I'm certain at least one was on your list."

Julia hesitated. She wasn't sure she was ready to start sifting through the rubble of her itinerary. Yet, as she had felt before, something about Harriet invited a confidence that she couldn't help but lean into, at least a little bit. She had, after all, decided to stay.

"You know when you told me that parts of your first trip were very good and parts were very bad?" she asked.

Harriet chuckled. "Oh, yes."

"Well, I ran into a little bit of that myself."

"Really?" Harriet asked. Her tone suggested less of a question and more an intimate understanding, and it made Julia suddenly self-conscious.

"Why do I get the feeling you're not surprised?"

Harriet glanced at Julia over her shoulder. "Because when I first met you, I saw something in you I recognized. A little bit of myself on my first trip," she answered affectionately. She stopped and turned to face Julia properly.

A cool breeze stirred through the woods throwing shifting shadows and sunlight across the path. Goosebumps broke out over Julia's arms.

"How's that?" she asked.

"Brave enough to board the plane. Optimistic enough to believe it might be a first step toward moving forward. Heartbroken enough to lose sight of that courage and optimism from time to time." Harriet fixed Julia with a knowing stare. "Mishaps followed, and then I'd resolve to make it better, and then the cycle would start over."

Julia held Harriet's gaze. "So, what happened to you that first trip?" she asked quietly.

"So much," Harriet chuckled. "Take the flight, for example. My connection in Amsterdam had mechanical issues shortly after takeoff and had to return to the airport. It was very dramatic. Alarms went off in the cabin. Flight attendants gave instructions to passengers in the emergency rows. Eventually, we landed without incident, but it was a harrowing thirty minutes."

Harriet turned and started up the trail again, and Julia hurried to keep up.

"There wasn't another plane available until the next day," she continued. "So, the airline put us up for the night at a drab hotel in a plain, residential section of the city. It was utterly dismal compared to my expectations, and at first, I took it as a sign that the trip was destined to be a disaster."

Julia realized how lucky she had been to find Harbor

House and then Olive Haven. Bad accommodations were not one of her regrets.

"But that night," Harriet went on, "I took my dinner voucher down to the hotel restaurant, and sat at the bar next to a woman, Sophia. We got to talking. She was about my age, traveling for business, and, coincidentally, also a widow. Somewhere between our second and third glass of wine, she asked if I wanted to live?"

Julia stopped walking in surprise. "What kind of question is that?"

"Right? I was nonplussed." Harriet turned back to face her. "Of course, I wanted to live. I'd just escaped what I perceived as a near plane crash. I wanted to be in Rome. I wanted my hotel overlooking the Colosseum. Why would I want to die?

"Then she clarified. She hadn't asked if I wanted to die. She asked if I wanted to live, like really live, not just go through the motions of life numb to it. When her husband passed, she explained, she was no longer afraid to die. Her faith convinced her that to die would be to see him again. But to live, seek joy, find love again, that was hard and scary. It was so much easier to just shut down, numb, disconnect. Deciding she wanted to live again was a pivotal moment in processing the loss of her husband. It turned out it was for me as well."

Julia came up next to Harriet, and they set off again, side by side.

"So, after you met Sophia that first night, did your trip change?" she asked.

Harriet chuckled. "Oh, Sophia probably encouraged my pendulum to swing a little too far in the other direction. I'd like to tell you I abandoned my inhibitions, but I probably abandoned some of my common sense as well. As I'm sure you've discovered, it's not difficult to find opportunity and romance here."

Julia caught the look Harriet threw her and guilt twisted in her stomach as she thought of Luca and the kiss. She looked away shyly, trying to force the memory away.

"Too easy," she confirmed quietly.

"I won't ask if you don't," Harriet gently teased. "But whatever happened, don't beat yourself up. Sometimes, doing the best you can means forgiving yourself a lot."

Alex sat waiting at another fork in the trail ahead, and they stopped as they reached her, rummaging in their packs for water and snacks. They spent a moment eating granola bars and catching their breath in the shade before beginning the climb up Mount Castellana.

"You wanna take the lead?" Alex asked Julia.

"I'm not sure which way to go." Julia felt the weight of her admission in the larger context of her trip, of her life.

"It's not hard if you don't overthink it," Alex assured her. "We'll make sure you don't wander off a cliff."

Harriet rolled her eyes and picked up her backpack. "Go forward," she said. "The best thing to do when you're not sure which way to go is to just move forward."

Julia led the hike for the next forty-five minutes, pushed along by Alex and Harriet. They periodically crossed above the tree line, glimpsing the sparkling Mediterranean on their left. Red tile roofs scattered across the hillside below, and train tracks cut like a jagged scar on the rocks. Alex occasionally pointed out markers on trees and boulders along the path, and Julia continued along the trail to the right, wandering higher up the slope.

The fresh air heightened Julia's senses, and without the distraction of conversation, her mind raced from Will, to Florence, to romantic reminders of a lost future, to Kev, to Luca, to regret. Her legs and lungs burned as she increased her pace up the hill. The pain in her chest, however, had little to do with the physical effort.

She heard Alex and Harriet sharing sporadic exchanges and laughter behind her. She marveled that tremendous tragedy had not hardened them, but rather shaped them, somehow, into warm, open hearted lovers of life. Harriet was living through Olive Haven, Julia realized. Really living, like Sophia had suggested. Taking risks, embracing change, forming community and building new relationships. And it was hard to imagine Alex as anything but the outgoing, free spirit that she was here in Italy. Perhaps they had always been this way, and moving on had really just been a matter of finding a way back to themselves.

If that was the case, Julia wondered who it was *she* needed to find her way back to in order to move on. She remembered what Ellie had told her, to find the spark again, the thing that had gotten her onto the plane. Something deep inside her had known that she wanted, or maybe needed, this trip as a marker of a tiny bit of her future plan that she could still hold on to. But she was miles off course, nowhere near where she had planned to be. As the sea breeze pulled at the loose strands of her ponytail, and she found herself simultaneously washed in warm, Ligurian sunshine and cool, briny air, Julia had to admit that whether she had imagined it this way or not, it was a pretty good place to be.

She stopped at the next fork in the trail and waited for Alex and Harriet to join her.

"For not knowing the way, you set a pretty strong pace," said Alex, shucking off her pack.

"There weren't that many options," Julia admitted.

Harriet smiled. "We rarely have as many options as we think we do."

"You're not talking about the hike," Julia said.

Harriet shrugged. "Life is a hike."

"Life is a highway," Alex exclaimed.

"And here I thought life was like a box of chocolates," Julia laughed.

Alex unclipped a set of hiking poles from her bag, handing one to Julia. "In case you want something for the climb," she said.

She showed Julia how to adjust the length and lock the telescoping parts in place. Harriet produced a similar set from her own pack and positioned herself in between them, one in each hand, testing the height.

"I'll take the lead again for a bit if it's alright with everyone," Alex said when they were repacked and ready.

"Off you go," Harriet smiled. "We'll be just behind you."

Alex took the right fork moving away from the coast just visible through the breaks in the tree line.

Harriet gestured up the path that Alex had taken, and Julia set off in front of her.

"Can I ask you something?" Harriet asked after a few minutes of silence. "Why did you decide to take this trip alone?"

"I wasn't sure who I'd bring." Julia admitted, then sighed, considering. "Actually, that's not true. I would have taken Ellie, my sister-in-law, but I didn't give myself time to think about it." She thought guiltily back to the night in the hotel room, asking Ellie to leave, feeling like it would be impossible to explain her emotions to another person. "I guess I thought that time alone was what I needed to try and figure things out."

"I did the exact same thing," Harriet said. "Lots of people think time alone during a crisis is what they need to reset, but I've learned that most of the time what people really want is to be surrounded by people who understand them. My brief evening with Sophia was the first time I felt like I was seen after Jack died. She understood the hurt; she understood how hard it was to think about what life looked like moving on." Harriet drew even with Julia. "You don't want to talk about your story with the women on retreat. You said as much when you arrived. You were worried you didn't share their same stories."

Julia thought of Margo on the terrace that morning, Beth's lost package, Alex being a widow while still in college, Aster refusing to come out of her room. "I don't," she said, glancing at Harriet.

"But don't you think, of all people, we might still be able to understand what you're going through?" Harriet asked quietly. "You don't think I understand what it feels like to face down life's incomprehensible moments? You don't think Alex understands being blindsided by the unexpected?"

Julia couldn't deny her logic, but stayed quiet.

"That said, I won't tell you not to take time to yourself, Julia. I run a retreat. Of all people, I understand the need to get away from it all. In fact, I encourage you to spend time alone. Sometimes the best thing we can do is just sit quietly with our feelings, get right into the middle of them. But it's hard, exhausting work. It can be so painful."

Harriet stopped in a shaded patch of trail and pulled her water bottle from her bag. She took a long drink before continuing. Julia caught her breath.

"That's what I love about being on a retreat," Harriet went on. "You can take that time and space when you want it, but there is also a community just steps away to help you bear the burden when you need to be uplifted." She repacked her backpack and laid a hand gently on Julia's shoulder. "Don't shy away from your story. You're its heroine, even if you don't feel it yet." Smiling, she set off up the trail again.

They crossed out of the tree line and wound up a dirt path that switched back and forth up the side of gradually sloping Mount Castellana. Julia followed Harriet in silence, thinking over her brief time with the women in the house. Harriet was only partially correct. She *had* worried that her story was not like the other women's. Yet, when presented with the opportunity, she had shared openly with Harriet on the plane, and to Lucy the previous morning. Had she had the time with Margo, she may have felt comfortable enough to confide then, as well.

It wasn't the act of sharing, she realized that bothered her, but rather that to tell the story was to admit to its reality. She couldn't hide behind anonymity or pretend she was anything but heartsick once the truth of her circumstances was known. Sharing was incredibly vulnerable, and that vulnerability gave Julia pause. She didn't want to turn her broken heart over to just anyone, though she couldn't deny the women of Olive Haven were quickly earning her trust.

Still, the camaraderie alone wouldn't be enough. There was work, she recognized, that she would need to do on her own. There had been plenty of feelings in Florence, heartbreak, regret, confidence, assurance, remorse, even momentary euphoria. She had sat with very little of it. She had run from it, wallowed in it, attempted to force it in other directions, and given into its immediate effect, but to just be was not something she had innately embraced.

"How would you start?" Julia asked Harriet, finally breaking the silence. "When women come on your retreat and want to take meaningful time alone, what do you recommend?"

"That's easy," said Harriet. "The bench beneath the olive tree."

"I saw you and Alex out there this morning."

Harriet nodded. "It was one of the first things I added to the grounds after purchasing the house. While I was remodeling the villa and getting things ready for that first retreat season, I would go out to that bench every morning and just be. Sometimes I'd sit and listen to the world wake up. Sometimes I'd talk to Jack."

"Lucy told me he was sick." Julia offered, her voice quiet with sympathy.

Harriet nodded. "There were so many conflicting emotions when he passed. Grief, obviously. Also, relief that he wasn't suffering. In some ways, I had already said goodbye to Jack months before he passed." She sighed, gazing up to the blue sky above them. "When things started to deteriorate, well, we weren't partners the way we had once been. If you want the reality of it, I had started thinking about what my life would look like after he passed while he was still sick."

She paused, the weight of her truth hanging between them. "When the time came, however, it was much harder to take those next steps than it had been to daydream about them."

"What helped the most?" asked Julia. "You obviously decided to keep going and traveling after that first trip. So, what eventually helped you figure it all out?"

"No one thing," Harriet replied, still moving up the hill. "But I kept reminding myself, and I eventually came to believe, that doing the hard thing, living life through the pain, was better than the alternative. I saw things that helped me believe that: beautiful sunsets over the beach in Barcelona; a perfect double rainbow over the clover green fields of Ireland. I also met people who allowed me to see good in the world again." She turned and faced Julia. "I continue to meet people who allow me to see good in the world around me."

"You mean like Alex?" Julia deflected, glancing up the hillside to find Alex stopped at a rock in a bend three switchbacks up. She waved. Harriet turned to follow Julia's gaze, then continued on up the trail.

"Yes, like Alex." Harriet said, affection clear in her tone. "It was probably something more like fate that brought the two of us together. Tragic fate, albeit," she added quietly.

"Jack and I never had children. We'd tried, briefly. A baby would have been a miracle, but after his diagnosis, we decided it would just be us. We didn't know how long he'd have. It turns out, our miracle was twelve unexpected years together."

Julia was uncertain how to respond and let birdsong and the whispering breeze fill the lull in the conversation.

"After he passed," Harriet continued, "I wanted to keep volunteering at the hospital where he'd received much of his care. A lot of people questioned why, and I wasn't really sure myself. But then one day, there was Alex sitting alone at a cafeteria table wearing a look I recognized having worn myself." She glanced up the trail to where Alex sat waiting. "But she was so much younger than I had been, and it broke my heart."

"Were you instant friends?" Julia prodded.

"Given the circumstances," said Harriet, "Alex wasn't much in the mood to be making friends. But she was a special kid. What she was doing for Sam and his family was extraordinary. I'd met lots of people in the hospital, had talked to lots of families about grief, shared lots of stories, but there was something different about Alex. I felt protective, maternal even. I couldn't help but check in on her and Sam when I was there." Harriet glanced back up the hill, and Julia thought she saw her brush away tears. "You never know when someone's going to touch your life in an irrevocable way," she added, her voice even.

They'd reached the final switchback and were level with the spot Alex had stopped. Harriet slowed her pace, buying time to finish the story.

"I wasn't at the hospital the day Sam passed away, but she called me, and I went. I found her sitting in the chapel alone.

Her family had gotten on the first flight from Kansas City but wouldn't be there for a couple of hours." Harriet watched her feet, lost in the memory. "We sat together and cried. I held her as she trembled with grief and stayed until her parents arrived. On the way home, I wondered if that afternoon was the final act in our fledgling friendship, if maybe our paths had crossed so that I could help bridge those few hours she was alone." She hesitated.

Julia realized she was holding her breath. "But obviously not," she prompted.

"No," said Harriet thoughtfully. "A few weeks passed when I didn't hear from her at all, and then suddenly, she started calling every day."

"She was lucky to have you there at that moment," Julia offered. "It obviously brought you that much closer together."

Harriet stopped and turned, and Julia could see the emotion in her eyes. "I was honored that she called that day," she said. "It's a privilege to be allowed to share people's stories, Julia, especially the tragedies. For someone to let you see their heart, even when that heart is broken, it's a remarkable thing to share." She held Julia's gaze an extra moment before turning back up the trail and closing the gap to where Alex sat waiting.

Julia hesitated before following. She envied Harriet and Alex. She wished there had been someone she could have called in the moment her world fell apart who would have come and just been with her. Her parents, brother, friends, even Ellie, were all, similarly, wrapped up in the moment in some way. They also had relationships with Will, also felt betrayed and heartbroken, also needed to process and rationalize what was happening. What wouldn't she have given for a neutral third party to just sit and be with her while she cried? She doubted a single person there would say in hindsight they were privileged to share in her heartbreak.

Up ahead, Harriet leaned her poles against the side of the hill, took off her pack, and sat down next to Alex. Julia watched the two women waiting for her, realizing with a nervous jolt that they were offering to fill that space for her now. The whole purpose of Olive Haven was to be that community, but just as it had taken Alex making the call to Harriet, Julia now recognized she would have to be the one to reach out and accept the invitation before her. Embrace her story? She wasn't even sure how to find the words to *tell* it. But she knew it was time to just move forward. She closed the gap between them.

"About time," Alex teased. "Find something interesting to talk about?"

"You," admitted Harriet.

Alex rolled her eyes but smiled. "I am interesting," she muttered. "Julia, maybe you should take the lead back. I can't have Harriet spilling all my secrets from here to La Spezia."

Julia swallowed hard. Her heart hammered and her palms grew damp. "Actually," she said, gripping the walking stick for support and resolve. "I was wondering if we could walk together for a stretch? There's something I want to talk with both of you about."

Harriet and Alex shared a look.

"Of course," offered Harriet warmly. "What's on your mind?"

Julia looked between them and took a deep breath.

"Will."

CHAPTER 13

T he climb up Mount Castellana evened out from the series of steep switchbacks to a gradually sloping trail that traversed the sun-drenched hillside. Tall grasses, reeds, and wildflowers grew in abundance along the slope, alive with gliding butterflies and buzzing bees that flitted between the vibrant blossoms. The crashing surf and screaming gulls of the seaside below had been replaced by a whisper of the breeze through the meadow, the crunch of gravel underfoot, and the occasional songbird.

Julia, Alex, and Harriet continued up the path three abreast. They walked the first short stretch in silence, Julia searching for the words to begin.

"Will and I met three years ago in a hotel bar," she started. "Cliched, isn't it? Though maybe not when you consider I work in hotels, so hotel bars are kind of like my office break room. Anyway, I'd stayed late to finish up the details of a large convention coming in that weekend and stopped for a quick drink with a colleague, and there he was at the opposite end of the bar, sipping a gin and tonic and reading the *Wall Street Journal*."

Julia swallowed hard. She could instantly picture him there, shirt sleeves rolled up, gold watch glinting in the dim light of the bar. Their eyes had met briefly as he glanced over the top of his newspaper and her stomach had done a backflip.

"I meet a lot of people 'just passing through' in my line of work," she continued, "and as a general rule, I don't look to make connections with people who are in town for just a few days. So, when he approached as we were getting ready to leave, I politely declined the offer to stay for a night cap and didn't give the interaction a second thought." She sighed. "But then, there he was again the next morning, sitting in the hotel lobby, reading *The New York Times* with two cups of coffee on the table next to him."

"Sounds pretentious," Alex muttered.

Julia laughed half-heartedly and shook her head. "Not really. The papers are around the bar and lobby for free. Lots of people grab them to flip through while they wait."

"And that second coffee was for you," Harriet prompted the story back on track.

"Right," said Julia. "He said he understood his advances probably made him look like an out-of-towner in search of a fling. Therefore, I should be relieved to learn that he was actually from Chicago. It happened that he'd purchased a condo, but his apartment lease had expired before the work had finished on the new building. He had put his belongings in storage and had taken up residence in the hotel until it was ready. Given these new circumstances, could he take me to lunch?"

A group of hikers approached from the opposite direction, and Alex and Harriet slid in behind Julia on the path to pass by single file. Julia nodded politely and muttered greetings to the group as they went by. The interruption in the story tested her resolve to keep telling it, but before she could change her mind, the group had passed and Alex hurried up next to her again.

"And?" Alex prodded expectantly.

Julia took a deep breath. "I'm normally quicker with excuses, but he was so smooth. He was in wealth management and had a knack for sweet-talking his clients, working a room, making a grand gesture. He has the good looks to go with it. Golden, wavy hair. Deep blue eyes. Perfect smile." His face swam in her mind, familiar as her own, and she cleared the tightness from her throat before continuing. "He immediately made his presence known when he entered the room. He was dynamic, and it was exciting. Even that morning as we talked in the lobby, I could feel the eyes on us. When Will was there, people noticed. Which is probably why I ended up falling for him as fast and as hard as I did. When I was with him, people noticed me too."

Julia paused, taking in the scene as they crested the hill. Down the other side, fields stretched to a scrubby brush line that eventually gave way to neat rows of grape vines and fruit trees. Beyond the terraced rows, a smattering of villas dotted the landscape, increasing in density as they approached La Spezia perched along the deep blue coast line in the distance. It should be impossible to be anxious with a view like this, yet her pulse quickened thinking of the admissions yet to come. Reluctantly, she picked up the story again.

"By the time his condo was finished, he was already talking about my moving in with him someday. It would be a year before I did, but that's how fast we fell and how intense those feelings were. That whole first year was a fairytale.

"But when we moved in together, things changed a bit. It wasn't all fancy dates and Saturday nights. It was Tuesday morning when we were out of coffee and I had reminded him three times to pick some up on the way home the night before. It was Thursday evening when I thought I'd be helpful by doing the laundry and accidentally dyed his white undershirts pink by missing my red pajamas stuck to the top of the washer drum."

Julia hesitated, waiting for the pain of the memories to subside.

Alex smiled encouragingly. "That's real life."

"Right," Julia nodded. "And if anything, I loved it more than the fairytale. Dancing in the kitchen. Sleepy Saturday mornings in bed. Sharing a bottle of wine after a long day. Things were great most of the time." Julia sighed heavily. "Will struggled. There were parts of our real lives that, once revealed, weren't quite how they once appeared."

"That's very normal," reassured Harriet.

"I know," Julia continued. "But things got tough for a while. Will travelled with clients often. Living apart, the phone calls and Facetime just felt like normal parts of our separate routines. In a shared space, I felt his absences more keenly. There were times when he was gone that I even considered finding my own apartment again, just to try and recapture some of the original excitement, reclaim my loneliness as independence."

A long silence settled over the women. Julia had not told anyone, not even Ellie, that she had once entertained the idea of finding her own place again. They had talked about her loneliness and Will's travel schedule, and Julia had spent long weekends tucked up in Ellie and Aaron's guestroom when the empty condo was too much to bear. Why hadn't she given more weight to the fact that it never really felt like her own home? She steeled herself to continue.

"But there was probably a bigger red flag than being lonely in the condo," she admitted quietly. "Will started to get insecure about the number of men I met through work. Like the fact that we met in the hotel bar suddenly struck him as a liability because if he'd picked me up that way, what's to say other men wouldn't try. I'd remind him that he tried and failed to win me in the bar, and he'd point out that he had ended up with me anyway." Julia felt her bitterness rise. "He would spend his time away worrying who I might be getting on with, while the irony was, he would be the one who eventually had the affair."

On the trail beside her, Alex sucked in a sharp breath, and Julia glanced over to find her clenching her jaw in disgust. Julia's heart warmed at her care and concern.

"Don't misunderstand," Julia went on. "There was a lot that still worked well. We did love each other, so I reassured him when he needed it and never harbored any suspicions. Life went on. The night he proposed he had just returned from five days in Maui. It was Christmas, but he burst into the condo, tanned, smelling like sunscreen and lemons. He always smelled like lemons. He used this lemon soap. He said it smelled like summer." She cleared her throat, trying not to dwell on the memories. "He was wearing this ridiculous Hawaiian print shirt and flip flops, even though it was five degrees outside. He shouted 'Mele Kalikimaka,' as he raced to the couch, scooped me up, and swung me around the room. I thought he was drunk. He was frenetic."

Julia's stomach twisted as scenes from that night came rushing back. She stopped on the trail, and closed her eyes.

"He set me back on the couch, and dropped to his knees in front of me, confessing that every night, sitting on his balcony watching the sunset, all he could think about was me." She forced herself to continue, eyes still closed. "It was more than just missing me, he said. He imagined me there at sunset on the beach, tanned, happy and laughing while walking in the surf. He imagined he would take my hand, drop to a knee, and ask me to marry him." Her voice caught, and she hesitated before going on. "I laughed and told him it sounded great, and he should book our flights. But he looked at me seriously, and told me he wasn't willing to wait."

Julia opened her eyes to Alex and Harriet a few yards ahead watching her thoughtfully. Harriet's kind eyes were sad as she offered a small, sympathetic smile.

Julia took a deep breath. "He pulled out a postcard from the pocket of his cargo shorts," she said quietly, "a picture of a beautiful sunset in golds and pinks, palm trees silhouetted against the sky. I turned it over. On the back he'd written, 'Will you marry me?' When I looked back at him, he was waiting with the ring."

She looked away, hastily wiping the tears that threatened to fall.

"Hearing it out loud, knowing how it ends, it doesn't sound like a great love story. Harriet, to hear you talk about Jack, and Alex, what you did for Sam, I don't think I had anything close to that." She started slowly down the trail, closing the space between them. "I probably should have had my suspicions before we ever got to the church. The fact that he was always a little paranoid that I'd meet some traveling stranger when I was at work struck me as his own insecurity. In hindsight, it was probably a fear based on his awareness of the people *he* could meet while he was traveling. Or maybe it was guilt over the person he did meet."

Julia took a deep breath and blew it out dramatically, and Harriet reached for her hand as she approached. She squeezed it consolingly as they started back down the hill together.

"I've never felt as foolish as I did sitting in my bridal gown listening to my fiancé tell me that there had been someone else." Julia hesitated, pushing past another wave of emotion. She could put herself back in that moment so clearly, and she grimaced to remember the pain of it. "My world shattered. Everything I thought we shared and would share evaporated. It was like I didn't even know him anymore. And even then," she stopped, unable to finish the admission.

"Even then, what?" Harriet prompted gently.

Julia slowed her pace and held her breath; this next part hurt most. It was the reason, she was sure, her emotions were still as fresh and easily jumbled as they were. It was the reason she could *not* block his number. It was the reason she still cared if he cared.

"Even then," she said, with a heavy sigh, "I might have stayed and tried to figure it out if he would have given any indication that he wanted the same."

Harriet and Alex shared a look.

"Oh, Julia…" Harriet started.

Julia shook her head and held up a hand. "It doesn't matter now. Given everything since the wedding, it's feeling more like I never knew him at all."

Silence settled over the trio again. Julia had gotten through the nuts and bolts of the relationship in a rush of adrenaline, and her pounding heart had slowed, but there was a dull ache at her temples.

"What's happened since the wedding?" Alex pressed after a moment.

Julia swung her backpack around so she could reach the front pocket and pulled out her phone. She opened her social media feed and clicked onto Will's profile. She hesitated a moment before she turned the screen, checking for any recent updates. Nothing new had been posted. She handed the phone to Alex.

"Erica happened," she said.

Alex and Harriet stopped on the path to scroll through the feed.

"You have got to be kidding me!" Alex burst. "I can't believe he's posting this."

"Yeah." Julia nodded grimly. "And I've been living for the updates," she added embarrassed.

"Well, you need to stop that immediately," Alex asserted.

"This is the woman he had the affair with?" asked Harriet.

"I don't know for sure," Julia admitted. "But I hope it is."

"Why's that?" Alex passed the phone back to Julia.

"If it's her, then at least they have some history, albeit deceptive, adulterous history. Still, I think I'd feel worse if it's not her, and he's moved on and headed to some tropical island with someone he's just now decided to date." Julia closed the app. "But that's not all, when I saw the first set of photos," she continued, "it wasn't actually the fact that he was traveling with a woman that upset me the most. I mean, she does upset me, but she's probably not controlling what he posts on his Instagram."

"What was it then?" asked Harriet.

"Two things," Julia replied. "The first was that he looked happy. I'm supposed to get the vacation while he sits home and reconsiders his life choices. It makes me mad to hurt the way I did, the way I do, and to see him, seemingly, unbroken over it. He may have been the one to call off the wedding, but we both should have to struggle with the implications for a while. It seemed so obvious that he'd go back to her that it never even crossed my mind that he would actually do it. So, to see him there, beaming, with her…" she trailed off, taking another deep breath.

"If it would make you feel better," Alex offered lightheartedly, "we could take a picture right here for you to post in retaliation."

Julia raised an eyebrow.

"You don't think it's the same?" Alex feigned insult. "You are also traveling through a foreign country with another woman. Multiple women actually."

Julia managed a laugh.

"It might not move him to soul crushing jealousy," Harriet admitted, "but isn't it better to capture your own moments of joy however you find them?"

Julia thought back to her photo blitz in La Spezia, seeking beauty for the sake of capturing it and sharing with others instead of really experiencing any of it herself. It was not, she realized, any more fulfilling than the days that she had spent floundering in Florence.

"Now that you mention it..." She spun around on the trail, holding up her phone and capturing her face with Harriet and Alex in the frame behind her. It was a wonderful photo.

"You said there were two things, Julia? What was the other?" Harriet asked as they began to walk again.

Julia's brow furrowed. "His outfit," she said simply. "It's what he wore the night he proposed."

"Shit!" Alex cringed. "That's brutal."

"Yeah," agreed Julia.

They continued down the hill, the path flattening out and cutting across a wide field of tall grasses, rippling in the wind like waves. Julia trailed a hand through the waist high stalks as they walked the narrow lane single file.

"Okay, new question," said Harriet.

"Shoot," Julia replied.

"Afterwards, at what point did you think taking the honeymoon was a good idea? You told me why you took it alone, but why take it at all?"

"I don't know that I ever thought about it as a *good* idea," Julia admitted. "Sitting in my hotel room, thinking about what was going to come next, finishing a bottle of champagne alone, I realized it was what I had left. After months of planning a wedding, years invested into a relationship, countless hours spent crafting the perfect itinerary, all that remained were the plane tickets and the reservations in my notebook. It was something I could control. An escape hatch from the difficult conversations, and responsibilities, and aftermath of the wedding."

"And is that how you feel about it now?" Harriet asked.

Julia considered her question. "I don't know," she finally answered. "Maybe taking this trip was just my way of hanging on to something that doesn't exist anymore."

"Which is why you joined us," Alex offered.

Julia chuckled. "That's true. This was entirely off script."

"Off script is probably the best place to be right now, in my opinion," said Harriet. "Tell me something, how hard do you think it would be to just ignore whatever Will is doing on social media?"

"Almost impossible," Julia confessed.

Harriet nodded understandingly. "Well then, maybe turn off your phone, or block his Instagram. Dwelling on what he's doing is only ruining the time that you have here to do what you want to do. There's nothing you can do about it while you're here anyway. That's drama to figure out when you get home."

Julia's shoulders drooped. "I'm already dreading it."

"That's human," Harriet offered. "We always find more than enough time to dwell on the hard things. It's joy and fun and adventure and friendship that get shortchanged. It *will* be hard at times, but as much as you can help it, don't waste your time here on anything other than *la dolce vita.*"

Julia let a comfortable silence fall as she deliberately tried to let go of the fixation that had taken hold since she first saw Will's pictures. It would be impossible to let all thoughts of them drift away, but if she was really going to find the way forward, she knew that she would have to find a way to stop letting Will's days dictate her feelings about her own. It would be hard, but she wanted to start.

They crossed the field and reached a footpath that snaked

through a wood dappled in sunlight. The coast behind them had completely disappeared, and the one in front of them had yet to materialize through the trees. Without the conversation to fill the void left by the pounding of the surf and the whistle of the wind through open fields, it felt as if the world had been put on mute. Then, as if on cue, Harriet's cell phone rang causing all three women to jump.

Harriet pulled the phone from her bag.

"It's Bernardo. *Ciao!*" she answered. She plugged a finger into the ear not pressed to the phone, though Julia wondered which part of the silence she was trying to block out. "Hold on. I can't hear you. We're in the...just a second." She lowered her phone to her shoulder. "Help me with this," she said to Alex, holding out her hiking poles, and sliding off her backpack. "I'm going to go up ahead a bit to see if I can catch a better connection."

Alex caught her bag, and Harriet hurried away, cell phone in the air, looking for a signal.

"I told her that holding it up in the air doesn't move it close enough to anything to make a difference," Alex said, watching her go. She started retracting the poles and packing them back into Harriet's bag. "So, when it comes to not stalking your ex online," she said casually, not looking up at Julia. "I recommend a replacement."

"What do you mean?"

"Like every time you think about wanting to check in on Will, you do ten sit ups instead."

"So, a punishment?" Julia questioned.

"Not when you have killer revenge breakup abs," Alex smiled. She stood up, sliding her arms into Harriet's backpack so that she carried it in front of her. "Or pick something that feels like a reward. A reward for *not* stalking his whereabouts. Like a glass of wine."

"Could be a good way to get drunk first thing in the morning," Julia replied with a chuckle.

Alex shrugged. "It doesn't have to be a glass of wine," she said. "But if you pick something, it works. Trust me."

"You've used it," Julia said. It wasn't a question.

"Yes," Alex looked away, "when Sam died."

Julia didn't know how to respond so she waited for an explanation.

"I could spend hours on his page going through old photos, reading the messages his friends had left in memoriam, searching out our tags and memories together. At first, I thought it was helping, but after a little while, I had to figure out a way to start moving on. So, I swapped habits."

"What did you do instead?" Julia asked.

Alex paused, kicking a rock away from the walking path. "I called Harriet," she replied with a gentle smile.

Julia stopped and turned to Alex. "Well, that's going to be awkward here," she said.

"You can't have that one anyway," Alex laughed. "It's mine. But whenever you can, shift your focus."

"I'll try," Julia promised.

Harriet reappeared wearing a look of triumph. She hurried back down the path toward them, and Alex slid her backpack off her shoulders and held it out to her. She talked in excited bursts as she approached. "We've got to get into La Spezia; Bernardo's sending a van." She smiled widely. "They've found Beth's package!"

CHAPTER 14

J ulia, Alex, and Harriet found Bernardo's driver waiting
for them on the southernmost outskirts of La Spezia.
The red and green passenger van was easy to spot in
the beach parking lot wedged between a row of mopeds
and a sleek, Italian sports car.

"Feel free to stay in La Spezia and take the ferry back to
Porto Venere later this evening," Harriet said as they
approached the vehicle. "No reason you have to give up the
rest of your day."

But when they reached the van, they were surprised to
find Beth not with Bernardo, but with Elise, Margo and Lucy
looking every part the tourists in bright floral prints, large
sunglasses, and floppy sun hats.

"We're going to Pisa!" Lucy announced jovially in
response to Harriet's questioning look.

"Bernardo didn't mention Pisa," Harriet said, confused.

"Bernardo wasn't thrilled about it," Lucy admitted. "But
Pietro assured him it was really no problem to make a quick
stop to drop us off."

"Pietro?" Harriet asked.

The van driver spun around in his seat. "Pietro!" he said, tipping his fedora in introduction.

"A pleasure," said Harriet, lacking enthusiasm. "And how is it that half of my retreat is now headed to Pisa this afternoon?"

Pietro smiled and ran a hand over his white goatee. "Pisa. It is one of the best cities in all of Italy," he said nonchalantly. "Why would you not want to go?"

"Oh, I see," said Harriet. "Let me guess, you're from Pisa?"

"*Si, signora,*" Pietro's grin widened.

Harriet turned to Alex and Julia. "Well, I guess your choices are La Spezia or Pisa, then."

"I'm with you," Alex said, looking to Julia.

Julia had intentionally skipped over Pisa in her planning. Despite the infamous leaning tower, those she knew who had visited the city were otherwise underwhelmed. It seemed far more desirable to spend the day along the coast. However, as she looked into the enthusiastic faces of the women peering at her from the van, only Beth, sitting on the far side of the back seat staring out the window in the opposite direction, looked morose at the prospect of losing a day along the water.

"I'm off script, right?" she shrugged at Harriet. "Why not?"

"Fine," Harriet said resignedly. "Everyone in."

They piled into the van and headed south toward Pisa. The coastal views of La Spezia gave way to Tuscan farmland. To their left, columns of grapevines and golden plains of wheat stretched to the hills that rolled along the horizon. To their right, the fertile fields and vineyards turned to sandy scrub as they moved toward the sea. Pietro peppered the women with facts and trivia as they ventured south along the coast.

"You know," he called to the backseat. "The name Pisa means 'marsh,' which is under the whole city. You build on the marsh, your tower leans. Your tower leans, you become a world-famous tourist attraction. Oh! Here's one more thing." He accelerated and passed a car, tapping the horn as he did so. "The tower, it leaned after just two stories, and they kept building! Who does this? Just keep going pretending that nothing bad is happening?"

"Rich, ego driven men, that's who," said Margo, shaking her head.

"It does stand to reason they couldn't give up on their giant, yet slightly crooked phallus," quipped Alex.

The backseat erupted in laughter.

"I thought it was built as part of a church complex?" Lucy asked.

Pietro nodded. "Yes, *signora*. The Cathedral of Pisa. It is the bell tower."

"That just confirms it's a phallus," Margo smirked. "Who'd know more about it than the church? Cover the statues with fig leaves to protect the modesty of the populace, build a giant homage to the male anatomy next to your cathedral instead."

Alex snorted. "Turns out it's about size *and* angle!"

The women burst into laughter once more, and Julia was relieved to see even Beth caught up in the moment of levity. She was, Julia marveled, astonishingly good at taking things how they came, and Julia envied her that.

"I don't think that's what they were doing," said Lucy defensively, hands folded tightly in her lap.

Margo's eyes widened. "Does she of the *peni* penne have a soft spot for the church?" she asked, surprised.

"I wouldn't call it a soft spot," Lucy replied. "Though I did consider the convent for a stretch in my twenties."

Harriet spun around in the front seat. "Mom!" she exclaimed. "You married Dad when you were twenty-one."

"I did," Lucy admitted. "But he wasn't always a picnic."

180

Harriet rolled her eyes. "You would have left dad to join a convent?"

"Probably not," Lucy hesitated. "But having considered it briefly before I met your father, you better believe there were moments, especially early on, when I thought about making different choices."

"What would you have done in a convent?" Harriet teased.

"Probably prayed a lot," said Lucy seriously. "Gone to mass. Cleaned the floors of the cathedral. Stared out the windows at the phallus shaped bell towers and thought about making different choices."

Elise and Alex snorted and turned away, looking out the windows to hide another fit of giggles. Julia caught Harriet's eye, and smirked, shaking her head in amusement.

"I could have been a teacher," Lucy insisted.

Harriet rubbed her forehead. "Mom, you were a teacher."

"Well sure," said Lucy. "But I could have been one of those scary teachers who hit kids with a ruler."

"I had one of those teachers," Margo chimed in. "You don't strike me as the type who could have done it."

"Oh, she could have done it," assured Harriet.

Lucy huffed indignantly. "I never hit any of you kids!"

"Only because we were faster than the wooden spoon," Harriet laughed.

The conversation died away and traffic increased as they approached Pisa. The women snapped photos from the windows as farmland and meadows gave way to urban sprawl.

"I will drop you off near the train station," said Pietro. "Who is staying with me to go to Pontedera?"

"I'll stay with Beth," Harriet said. "Alex will come to help translate if necessary. Ladies, follow the Walking Street, on your left away from the station. It will take you all the way to the tower."

Pietro eased over three lanes of traffic, ignoring the honking and gesturing of his fellow drivers. He pulled up next to the curb and jumped out of the van to open the side doors.

"Okay, ladies!" he shouted over the traffic. "*Divertiti! Ciao!*"

Julia, Elise, Lucy, and Margo climbed out onto the bustling sidewalk, and set off to the left of the station dodging hawkers selling tour tickets and other travelers trying to get their bearings in the bustling intersection. The road transitioned to a series of roundabouts, and they spiraled off each one trying to keep in the general direction Harriet suggested. A large piazza a few blocks from the station gave them a chance to reorient to their position in the city, and past a towering bronze statue to the right of the square, they found the entrance to *Corso Italia*, the Walking Street.

The Walking Street wound its way crookedly through Pisa toward the Arno River, and Julia had to remind herself that, while they should stick together, she wasn't actually responsible for babysitting the other three women as they scattered off in different directions. Modern shops sat next to boutiques of local artisans; street performers played on the sidewalks in front of the storefronts; and every twenty yards, the flow of pedestrians had to scatter around a collection of tables and chairs that a restaurant had spread in the street outside its front door.

Energy hummed along the walkway, and Julia felt exhilarated to be in a city she hadn't planned on seeing. There was no expectation here, only possibility. She explored, meandering from storefront to storefront, stopping in front of a jewelry store window display of earrings, rings and pendants set in vibrant Italian gold. She was admiring a particularly striking diamond tennis bracelet when she felt a presence to her right and turned to find Lucy, nose pressed to the glass, beside her.

"Which is your favorite?" she asked Lucy.

Lucy pointed at an elegantly set emerald pendant in the front of the display. "That one," she said definitively. "I don't have pierced ears, and my fingers don't accommodate rings the way they once did." She held up her hands revealing swollen, arthritic knuckles. Julia noticed a thin, diamond studded gold band on her left hand.

"You still wear your wedding band though," Julia observed, nodding toward her hand.

"I do," said Lucy, reaching for her left ring finger. "It's hard to stop feeling married after sixty years. My finger would feel naked without it."

Julia absentmindedly rubbed her thumb over her own ring finger. "I can imagine," she said. "I still catch myself worried that I lost mine from time to time. Maybe I should replace it with something like Harriet did?"

Lucy considered a moment, moving to the next window and another display of jewelry. "You could," she agreed. "Harriet didn't replace that ring immediately though. Besides, I warned her when she did it that it was really going to cut down on the attention she got from men." She laughed lightly. "Of course, Harriet didn't care, but," she gave Julia a knowing glance, "you might."

Julia felt an anxious jolt at the idea of new romantic inclinations. "Right now, it seems safer to swear off men for a while. The whole marriage thing didn't work out like I'd planned."

"The whole *wedding* thing didn't work out like you planned," corrected Lucy. "Take it from someone with sixty years of experience, the wedding doesn't say much about what the marriage will be. When you do decades of life together with someone, very little of it actually goes according to plan. Life has a way of taking away your happiness one moment, and giving it back the next. Finding the right person to ride that roller coaster with, it's incomparable to anything else you'll have or do. You weren't wrong to want it. You'll want it again, I'm sure."

They turned from the window to watch life stream past them on the street. Vendors pushed carts of souvenir knick-knacks from tourist to tourist. A guitarist on a bench in front of a bakery picked a busy melody. A mime strolled past, beholden to the tug of an invisible rope.

"So, what's your greatest take away from sixty years of wedded bliss?" Julia asked, not taking her eyes from the scene.

Lucy looked at her skeptically. "When people ask that, they're looking for an easy answer or a sound bite. 'Never go to bed angry,' or, 'be each other's best friend.'"

"Well, give me the truth then," Julia pressed.

Lucy turned back to the jewelry case, thoughtfully examining herself in the mirror of the window. "We are a reflection of who we love," she said. "George was braver than I am, and he brought out my courage. He wanted to adventure, and he brought out my own curiosity. He helped me build a home and life that was safe and comfortable, and I walked through life confident and secure because of it. I was blessed. Experience the opposite in a partner, become the opposite yourself."

Julia took a deep breath, wondering what Will had reflected into her world. Ambition? Drive? At the time, she had felt like she was, in fact, a better version of herself, but in light of the breakup, it was hard to remember what made her feel that way.

"That's very wise," she said quietly.

Lucy smiled, turning to face Julia and dropping her voice conspiratorially. "My second piece of advice, marry a good lover."

"Do you know what Lucy?" Julia laughed. "I'm beginning to understand why your kids don't want to think about the idea of you having an exotic affair. I do believe you'd do it if the opportunity presented itself."

"So maybe I wear the ring for my kids' sanity."

Elise and Margo found Julia and Lucy in front of the jewelry store, and they set off again, continuing down Corso Italia past American staples Victoria's Secret and Old Navy and Italian classics Armani and Gucci. They stopped to watch two street performers complete a levitation act on woven mats that appeared to hover like magic carpets. Margo bought a cream fedora with a bright pink band that perfectly matched the streak through her blonde hair. They all bought gelato.

Julia walked next to Lucy, licking at the creamy ice cream and trying to remember what she would have been doing instead if she had followed her itinerary. It could not, she was certain, have been more enjoyable than an afternoon of uninhibited wandering through Pisa. She felt physically lighter from having shared with Alex and Harriet earlier, and her mind was clear. The laughter of the women was sweeter than the silence of solitude, and it further buoyed her already soaring spirits.

The Arno River brought the Walking Street to an end, and they crossed over to the other side, beginning to follow signs for the Cathedral of Pisa and the Leaning Tower. They opted to detour briefly through the *Orto e Museo Botanico*, a verdant oasis of miniature palms, cropped hedges, and lily pad strewn ponds. A steamy greenhouse in the corner of the garden housed at least two dozen herbs planted in long rows on waist high work tables. The humid air was heavily fragranced with every scent of an Italian kitchen, and they wandered through bushy basil plants, long stalks of thyme, spikes of rosemary, and leafy puffs of parsley, stopping to smell each distinct aroma.

It seemed impossible to Julia that she might have missed this.

Out the other side of the greenhouse, they found the back wall of the gardens crawling with ivy and bougainvillea. Beyond that, they caught the first glimpses of the cathedral with its leaning tower, and they wound back through the gravel walking paths out the side gate and headed purposefully toward the famous edifice.

The open, green space around the cathedral teemed with people picnicking in the sunshine and posing in awkward positions for photographs that, through the lens of the camera, appeared to show them holding up the tower. The women made their way across the piazza to the fences surrounding its base. They stared up at its crooked height, white marble stark against the deep blue sky.

A tour group passed by, the guide speaking loudly into a portable amplifier.

"The tower took over two centuries to build, and was twice halted because of military conflict," he announced. "After the second pause in construction, the fourth, fifth, and sixth stories were added, and the tower shifted from leaning to the north to leaning instead to the south. The tower continued to tilt despite numerous attempts at stabilizing the structure, and only in 2008 were engineers finally able to anchor the building in a way that the lean stopped increasing for the first time since its construction."

The women waited for the last of the tour to cross in front of them, then took turns taking the obligatory photos with the tower in the background.

"After five minutes, there's not much to it, is there?" said Lucy. "It leans, but nothing else happens."

"You're difficult to impress at eighty-five," laughed Julia.

"I'm not eighty-five until tomorrow," Lucy said proudly. "Are *you* impressed?"

Julia shrugged, tilting her head to the side to better study the building. "I'm impressed it's still standing. It's been crooked and shifting for a long time, and somehow, it's still here."

"I've never been straight a day in my life," Margo said. "I'm still standing."

The women laughed loudly, drawing attention from other tourists.

"I'm going into the cathedral," Lucy announced. "Anyone else?"

Elise agreed to join Lucy, and they left Julia and Margo staring up at the tower.

"It *is* a bit anticlimactic," admitted Margo when they'd gone.

"Not you too," said Julia. "C'mon, it's part of the Field of Miracles!" She read from a tourist placard along the fence. "The tower should have been destroyed during World War II when American troops in Pisa were ordered to destroy all Nazi military bases in the region, including the tower which had been used to host German forces. However, the Allied forces were so taken with the structure, they never called in the artillery." She continued on from another section. "Most engineers believed the tower would collapse after the lean extended beyond five degrees, but soil stabilization work in the eighties and nineties helped extend the life of the tower, even as it leaned at a precarious five and a half degrees. Today the Leaning Tower of Pisa is considered one of the Seven Wonders of the World."

"It's been lucky, that's for sure," Margo agreed, then

paused. "That's the real wonder of the world, isn't it? Some things escape disaster over and over again, and other times you beg for a miracle and nothing happens?"

Julia noted the change in her tone. "Is something wrong?" she asked gently.

"Of course not." Margo forced a smile. "Let's get out of the sun."

They turned away from the tower, and walked in silence across the grassy piazza known as the Field of Miracles. The lawn was dotted with families resting in the shade and teenagers sunning on picnic blankets. They found a seat in the shadow of the cathedral, and Margo laid back with her hands behind her head, sunglasses covering her eyes. Julia hugged her legs into her chest and rested her chin on her knees.

"Margo?" Julia asked after a few minutes.

Margo's eyes were closed behind her sunglasses, and for a moment Julia thought she was dozing in the sun. "Hmm?"

"Will you tell me the rest of Mona's story?"

Margo pushed back her sunglasses and propped herself up on her elbows. "What do you want to know?"

"Well, you got as far as the wedding this morning. I assume it was the happiest day of your life?"

A young couple strolled by, arms around each other, looking for a place to claim in the shade. Margo watched them pass, preoccupied, before turning back to Julia. "Questions like that remind me of how different moments in my own relationship were from other women's," she said finally. "When we announced we were getting married, I asked my dad to walk me down the aisle, and he agreed. But that morning, as I was getting ready, he told me, 'You know Margie, we could have done this for real a long time ago if you'd have fallen in love with someone else.'"

Julia gasped.

"My dad loved Mona. He had never said a bad word against her. Even after he said it, he laughed, and took my hand and acted as if it was just a joke. But it obviously didn't come from nothing, so I had to wonder how he really felt."

"That must have been incredibly painful." Julia said quietly.

Margo lowered herself back onto her back. "It's not our job to take responsibility for how other people respond to our lives," she said. "But that's a hard lesson to remember, especially on your wedding day."

A long, quiet moment passed between them. Across the field, a group of girls chased the small, white butterflies that flitted between the purple clovers studding the lawn. Julia was so caught up in watching their pursuit, she jumped when Margo continued.

"We found out Mona was sick six months after the wedding. As a nurse, she was diligent with her screenings and tests, and we hoped they had caught it early enough, but it was aggressive." She sighed and rolled onto her side to face Julia. "All the practical reasons to be married were suddenly laid bare. She was on my insurance. I had oversight over her medical care. Her retirement accounts, bank accounts, were all protected as marital property. It made managing the crisis the tiniest bit easier. There were fewer hurdles to clear; nobody gave it a second thought."

She looked past Julia and watched a young family playing frisbee. "Nobody," she said quietly, "except my father, who once offered the pearl of wisdom that, 'If I would have married *someone else*, we probably wouldn't have had to worry about breast cancer.'"

"Margo, that's awful," Julia lamented, shocked. "Why would he say that?"

Margo pulled at blades of grass absentmindedly. "In a strange way, I think he was grasping at anything that would ease his own pain, as if his pain was my fault because of the partner I'd chosen. While I know that doesn't make sense, I tell you again, we can't control how other people respond to our lives. For two and a half years she tried to fight and keep going."

"Two and a half years of asking for a miracle?" Julia asked quietly.

"Of course," said Margo, her voice thick with emotion. "Everyday." She sat up and looked at the tower leaning at the other end of the piazza. Dozens of tourists swarmed at its base. "A tower that has no business standing, inexplicably lasts hundreds of years, while a perfectly stable life comes to pieces in a heartbeat right before your eyes."

Julia's heart broke for Margo, and her own wedding day came to mind. Though Will had not turned out to be the man she thought he was, not once had anyone suggested that they should not, or could not, be together. Her father, in the moment before they walked down the aisle, had wiped tears from his eyes and confessed his pride. He never would have disparaged Will, though in the aftermath that followed, he may have wished he had. Her chest tightened.

"I'm so sorry, Margo," Julia offered quietly. "I wish you would have gotten your miracle."

Margo looked at Julia with a sad smile. "Mona needed the miracle; I already had mine. It was her. Love is a miracle, Julia. If you find it, even for an instant, then someday you'll come to accept that heartache is just part of the gift."

Julia thought of Will and looked away, avoiding Margo's gaze as her throat tightened.

"Julia?"

"I'm sorry." Julia brushed the tears from her eyes. "It's just particularly hard to hear that right now."

"Because of your engagement?"

Julia's head snapped back up. "How did you know?"

Margo bit her bottom lip. "Lucy told me, well, she told everyone actually, yesterday in Manarola."

"*What?*" Julia burst, surprise flashing to anger then to embarrassment.

"Don't be upset," Margo soothed. "I know it wasn't her story to tell. She actually didn't tell much of a story at all, just the fact of it. She is a terrible gossip. I mean the rumor she made up about Beth and Bernardo, c'mon? I think she thought you might not stay, or that if you did, she was protecting you, making sure no one would ask or say something to make you uncomfortable. Though I'm afraid I may have done just that."

Lost for a response, Julia allowed herself to be distracted by a new tour forming up on the road at the edge of the lawn. It was, she noticed, mostly couples. The pairs streamed in, some from the field where they'd been waiting, others from the main gate having arrived just in time for their reservation. A few singles lingered, out of place, at the front and back of the group, college students in colorful spandex with bulky backpacks and older visitors leaning on walking sticks, expensive cameras hanging from their necks. Julia knew how they must feel to mingle on the edges, not quite part of the group.

"It's the thing I worried most about when I got to Olive Haven," Julia admitted with a sigh, "that I didn't share the life experience that bonded the rest of you together."

Margo shook her head, the gentle reassurance settling Julia. "Grief is a universal experience. We find it in a host of ways, and learn to cope with our own through the experiences and stories of others."

"Maybe," Julia considered, "but what about love? To hear you talk about Mona, to think of everything you must have gone through just to be together, Will and I never had to endure anything like that. We struggled, same as any couple, but nothing was ever really stacked against us. Yet, we still couldn't make it."

"If that's the case," Margo said, a comforting smile playing at the corners of her mouth, "then you should draw strength from knowing that while the heartbreak you feel might be the worst you've ever known, there's still a love story out there for you that's better than you've ever imagined, one that you'll fight for even when the odds are stacked against you."

Julia felt the now familiar lump slide into her throat, then her phone vibrated inside her bag, interrupting the moment. She pulled it out and looked at the text notification from Alex.

"They're on their way back," she said, clearing the emotion from her voice. "We should find the others."

They stood up, brushing grass from their clothes and making their way to the entrance of the church. A steady stream of visitors came down the stairs, and they looked for Elise's fiery hair among the crowd.

"Check inside," Margo said. "I'll walk back towards the baptistry to see if they headed that way." She joined the traffic flowing away from the church doors.

The bells began to chime over the courtyard, the same, simple tune that had rung out in Porto Venere that morning. Déjà vu washed over Julia again, and she looked up at the bell tower. All at once, the memory clicked into place.

Ellie's Ford Explorer rolled into the parking lot of St. James Episcopal Church. Julia's veil, already secure in her updo, whipped in the breeze as she climbed from the backseat. She pulled the garment bag with her gown from the trunk; Ellie grabbed her tote bag and shoe box, and they walked up to the front doors of the church. All the while, the bells chimed in the background, the very same melody.

Julia stood, frozen, on the walkway staring up at the

double doors, struggling to breathe, remembering everything that happened next. Walking down the aisle, turning around, breaking apart in the bridal suite. It had been one week, almost to the hour.

A sudden nervous fluttering in her stomach was similar to the butterflies she had felt before she had started down the aisle with her father. But Will wasn't here, and the church wasn't full of guests, and she wasn't in a gown, and there weren't vows to be made. Still, her mind raced as she climbed the steps and walked through the open doors of the cathedral.

The vestibule was mainly empty, just people entering and exiting the sanctuary, and she walked straight through to the second set of double doors that opened at the start of the aisle. She thought back to that afternoon, getting ready with her bridesmaids, the photographer circling the room capturing every moment from every angle, her mother's cool hands zipping the back of her dress, the murmuring of guests quieting as they settled into their seats and the procession started. She could still hear the groaning of old church pews as everyone stood when she came around the corner.

Her breath caught, and for a moment, she stood paralyzed at the back of the cathedral.

A walk down the aisle is not long, but few walks are as significant. Julia had felt it standing in the back of the church with her father, and she felt it again now as she hesitated at the entrance to the sanctuary.

One week ago, she had started this walk and never finished it. Will had taken that from her. Something inside her stirred, nudging her towards the front of the church. It was innate. Aisles were meant to be walked, and she had never gotten to finish hers.

Julia's heart hammered as she stepped into the space, moving between the rows of pews, her pace methodical and even. Stately Corinthian columns stood as sentinels on either side, solid guests to watch over her progress. Past them, she caught glimpses of rich oil paintings, colorful frescos, marble sculptures, and banks of candles. Sunlight streamed, sparkling with dust, from windows set high in the towering vaults of the ceiling, creating the illusion that glitter rained from the heavens. She slowed as she reached the middle of the aisle, remembering, hurting, willing herself forward.

She tipped her head back and stared up at the brightly colored ceiling. The truth of what she had told Margo ripped through her. Her and Will's was not a great love story. She had not overcome tragedy like Alex, nor stood by an ailing partner for over a decade like Harriet, nor faced scrutiny for whom she loved like Margo. Perhaps not every romance was destined to be an epic, but she at least hoped for more than infidelity and insecurity. She was not sure how to move on, but when in doubt, move forward, Harriet had said. Taking a deep breath, Julia began to walk toward the front of the church. She felt strength in every step.

At the front of the church, she took a seat in a pew, taking off her backpack and pulling out her trusted grey notebook. She turned to the day's original plan. It was, she saw from the number of blue plus signs on the page, the day Will had been looking forward to most. A trip to Monterosso al Mare. A plus next to a catamaran ride. A plus next to snorkeling. A plus next to dinner on the beach. All things he could do in the islands. All things she was not sad to have missed.

Closing the book, she pulled the elastic band tight around it and ran a hand over the cover. She had boarded the plane wanting to hold onto a small piece of the old future she had dreamed of with Will, but she realized now that what she needed was a chance to begin the new future she would have without him. She looked around the church, thinking of Olive Haven and the women waiting outside. They were all looking for their second chances as well. Perhaps they would find them together.

She reached for her phone, opening her Instagram feed and posting the photo from the morning's hike without a caption. Simple, genuine joy. It had found her unexpectedly once again. Smiling, she strode back up the center aisle and into the bright afternoon.

Margo had found Elise and Lucy, and they were waiting in the courtyard outside the cathedral. The four women left through the gate in the old Pisani walls and stepped back into modern life. *Via Bonanno Pisano* took them directly to the Arno past a series of old city walls and guard towers. The bridge over the river ran parallel to the train tracks, and they followed them back toward the central station. Near the drop-off where they were to meet Harriet and Pietro, they stopped for a second gelato. Then, finding a seat along the edge of a fountain in the center of the station piazza, they waited for the van while watching people bustle in and out of the train station, wheeling suitcases over the black and white patterned cobblestones.

"There they are." Lucy pointed as the red and green van spiraled through the roundabout, spitting out in front of the station.

Pietro jumped from the driver's seat and whipped open the side doors. *"Buonasera!"* he called from the curb. *"Andiamo!"*

They slid off the edge of the fountain, hurrying into the van. Pietro slid the doors shut, returned to the driver's side, and eased them back into traffic. Julia settled in next to Alex.

"How was it?" Alex asked.

"Still standing."

"Hmm," Alex responded, eyeing Julia curiously. "You or the tower?"

"Both," chuckled Julia. "How did it go in Pontedera? Did you find it?"

Alex turned to the seat behind them, prompting Julia to follow suit. Beth sat with her arms around a well taped and slightly battered cardboard box.

"Pontedera is nothing special," Beth said. "But it's the best day of the trip so far."

Julia smiled. That it was, she thought. That it was.

CHAPTER 15

Despite the buoyant mood at Olive Haven that evening and Maeve's assurance that her sister had, in fact, left her room that afternoon to join her at the beach, Aster once again refused to come down for dinner. The rest of the women crowded around the table, enjoying homemade pizzas, hand stretched by Bernardo and fired in the villa's outdoor brick oven. The wine and conversation flowed easily, and Julia felt perfectly at ease. She was as comfortable now around this table of days' old acquaintances as she was with her friends at home. Travel worked strange wonders on time and intimacy.

Crisis did too.

The dinner dishes were removed from the table and replaced by platters of delicately rolled cannoli that Bernardo insisted were his grandmother's secret recipe. The curls of shell were perfectly crispy; the cream inside was sweet and airy, and whether an old family recipe or not, they all agreed they had never tasted better.

In truth, Julia found that everything tasted better here. Be it the fresher ingredients, the time and tradition, or the influ-

KATE LAACK

ence of the surroundings, the meals on the back terrace of Olive Haven were unrivaled by even the nicest Italian restaurants and caterers Julia knew in Chicago. Of course, she expected the original to be best, but to experience the dinners here was true perfection.

Bernardo served espresso and brought more wine. The bistro lights flickered on, bathing the patio in warm, golden light as the twilight deepened to indigo and stars came out overhead. When they were pleasantly full and conversation gave way to contented, companionable silence, Harriet produced a stack of white folded papers and a bundle of Sharpie markers from a box on the ground.

"I wanted to give you all a few days to think about this," she started. "Your last night here will be the Festival of Lights. There will be processions through the streets, and the entire hillside will be lit up with luminaries. I think you'll find it magical." She began handing out folded papers. "As part of the celebration, people write their hopes, wishes, regrets, griefs, prayers, on these paper boats and send them into the harbor bearing a candle." Harriet took one of the papers and pulled at two of its creased points, revealing how the origami boat opened with a wide, flat bottom. She picked up a tea light from the table and set it in the vessel. "When the candle burns down, the boat burns up until it's swallowed by the water. Whatever is written on it is given to the sky and sea as an offering." She removed the candle and folded the boat closed. "So, if you choose, on your final night in Porto Venere, you'll have a chance to launch a boat. As I said, I wanted to give you all a few days to think about it so that your experience is as meaningful as possible." Harriet looked around the table as she handed out the papers. Her gaze locked with Julia's for a moment, and she winked.

Julia looked at the clean white paper in front of her, wondering how she would ever capture all the feelings tied to Will. The day had left her hopeful for a future in which she had moved on, but she wasn't sure how to express what she wished for in that future either. The task seemed enormous, and she closed her eyes, wondering how to begin.

She felt a presence at her shoulder as someone reached over for her dishes. Opening her eyes, she found Alex refilling her wine glass.

"What are you doing?" Julia asked.

"Making sure you're not thinking too hard over here," said Alex. She held her own glass and gestured toward Julia's. "Come on."

Julia picked up the glass but didn't drink. "I honestly can't take another sip," she said. "I'm stuffed."

"You should put on your boat that you regret that one of your meals in Italy was orange juice and crackers on the train."

Julia rolled her eyes. "I'm about to write, 'I regret sitting next to Alex on the train at all.'"

"No, you don't," Alex smiled. "I brought you here."

Julia wasn't the only person struggling for ideas, however. A full day, large meal, and plenty of wine left the other women lacking for inspiration, and one by one they took their papers and filtered off the patio to their rooms. Only Lucy, seemingly brimming with ideas for her own vessel and determined to see the clock roll to midnight on her 85th birthday, appeared undaunted by the assignment. Julia wished her and Harriet good night and retired upstairs.

As she padded down the hallway, her curiosity piqued at the quiet bedtime sounds coming from behind the doors on either side. Soft music from one. Snoring already behind another. Outside Alex's room she heard muffled voices, one notably distorted by distance or the phone speaker. Danny, Julia realized. She returned to her own room and closed the door.

She changed into her pajamas, and went into the bathroom to brush her teeth. The light of Aster's room shone under the opposite door, and Julia saw the shadow of feet cross back and forth in rhythmic intervals. She was pacing. Maeve had come down to dinner relaxed and carefree from their day on the island; Julia wondered how the very same day could leave Aster so agitated.

Back in her room, she flopped onto the bed, reaching instinctively for her phone on the bedside table. She thought better of looking for Will, remembering what Alex had said on the hike, but the screen came to life before she could stop herself revealing a new notification.

Ellie: Saw your photo online. Where are you?

As supportive as Ellie had been of Julia's need to take the trip, Julia wondered what Ellie would say when she found out that Julia had gone rogue with a group of widows. She texted a hasty reply explaining the changed plans and giving a general description of Olive Haven. The response came almost immediately.

Ellie: You're where?! Why?

A string of emojis followed, and Julia could all but hear Ellie's stunned laughter echoing in the room. There was too much to explain via text. Ellie was just going to have to trust that Julia knew what she was doing.

Julia: I know it sounds weird, but for some reason, I think this is what I need. Don't worry.

She closed out of her messages, and stared at the home screen. Despite her resolve to move forward, curiosity over Will still nagged at her. One peek, she told herself, and then she would go to bed.

Her thumb hovered over the home button when she was startled by a sharp knock on her door. She got up and opened it, finding Alex in the hallway, one hand on her hip, the other holding her own phone to her ear. Alex glanced down at the phone in Julia's hand. She pointed at it, then drew a finger across her throat.

"How did you know?" Julia asked quietly.

Alex smirked and leaned the phone away from her mouth. "My spidey-senses were tingling." She pushed her phone back up. "No, I'm sorry, Babe," she said into the receiver. "I said my spidey-senses were tingling... No, not like that..." She blushed slightly and rolled her eyes. "I had to talk to Julia for a second."

Julia was surprised that her name required no additional explanation.

"No, keep talking," Alex went on. "She's going to bed. Right?" she implored.

Julia returned the phone to the nightstand and closed the drawer, holding up her hands in surrender.

"Good night, Alex. Good night, Danny," she said, closing the door as Alex retreated down the hallway. She moved to shut the bathroom door assuring Aster had privacy when she decided to get ready for bed. The shadows of feet crossed back and forth and then back again. Julia watched them pass, curious about her neighbor and sad for her suffering.

Returning to her room, she turned off her lights, settled under the covers, and dreamed of the sea and gelato.

The next morning, Julia woke before the rest of the house, dressed quietly in black yoga pants and a tunic top, and slipped out the front door. The sun had yet to burn off the early fog, and the edges of the dark form of the olive tree were fuzzy in the misty blanket that covered the yard. Barefoot, she made her way across the grass and to the tree. The spot in front of the bench was worn down to the dirt, and as she stepped onto it, she felt an overwhelming connection to the dozens, maybe hundreds, of women who had come to this very spot, under this very tree. She wondered at how many tears had watered this patch of ground.

Taking a seat on the bench, Julia wondered how she was supposed to begin. Harriet told her to just 'sit and be.' She took in the morning around her. Birds chirped overhead. A bicycle wheeled by on the road out front, invisible in the fog but for the reflectors on the wheel spokes. Faintly, from the back of the house, she heard the slightest murmur of voices.

Closing her eyes, Julia allowed her mind to wander, expecting as she did that it would wander to Will. Instead, it drifted to Erica. She wondered what she would ever say to her if she had the chance. Would Will be so bold to allow her to move into the condo before Julia was even moved out? Would she be there when Julia eventually went to collect her things? The thought prompted one part anger, one part anxiety. Watching her from a distance was one thing, but she could *not* imagine having to see her, up close, taking over Julia's place in the home she had made. She shifted on the bench, trying to push away the discomfort, then realized that this kind of emotion was exactly what Harriet had told her to 'sit and be' with. She took a few steadying breaths. Life would move on, and she would have to be ready to move with it.

Ever so gently, she probed at her broken heart, seeking the base emotions. Loneliness. Disappointment. Distrust. Insecurity. The last bit surprised her. She had never considered herself insecure. Certainly not before Will. In their relationship, it had always been his doubts that she was trying to assuage. He brought the jealousy. He brought the insecurity. She never felt it herself, until now. He was the person with which she had been most vulnerable, most herself, most open, and most committed, and she had reassured him of that over, and over, and over again, only to have him throw it all back in her face the way he worried she might do to him. We are a reflection of who we love Lucy said, and now she was Will's mirror.

Anger, she realized suddenly. There was plenty of anger there too.

She wanted to hate him. She thought it might be easier if she did. She sat on the bench and tried. But there was too much history. She could hate what he did, what he was putting her through, but despite those things, she could remember the best of what they had as well. They had built a life; they had plans and dreams for their future; they supported each other in their work and personal endeavors; they laughed; they challenged; they loved each other. It was that, more than anything, that kept bringing him to mind. She may have realized it was not a great love story, but it was a love story, nevertheless. It had not lacked for genuine feelings.

Footsteps on the driveway stole her attention, and Julia opened her eyes to find the sun had crested the ridge, and the fog, though burning off, was now a trillion flecks of gold glitter suspended in the morning air. It sparkled all around her and seemed to shimmer in a halo around Bernardo. He wore khaki pants and a denim shirt and was walking up the driveway with an enormous bouquet of hydrangeas in his arms. Julia waved to him, and he broke off the path to cross under the sprawling branches of the tree.

"*Buongiorno.* You're awake early, *signorina.* You are enjoying our tree?"

Mist had settled on his dark hair and glimmered in the shifting light of the morning.

"Yes," Julia looked up into the dappled sunlight peeking through the leaves. "It's lovely." She looked back to Bernardo. "Where do you find such amazing flowers at this time of the day?"

He adjusted some of the stems in his arms so as not to crush the petals. "For these, I fortunately have an inside source. My wife." He smiled at Julia's surprised expression.

"I didn't know you were married. Lucy thought you were dating Beth."

Bernardo laughed. "*Signora* Lucy is marvelous, but also mistaken. My wife and I have a small farm a mile down the road. It's nothing compared to Olive Haven, but it's home for us and our two girls." He pulled a photo from his wallet revealing a dark haired, petite woman holding hands with a toddler. Bernardo stood next to her with his arm around an older girl in a school uniform. "Millie and Annabelle," he said, pointing to the young girls, "and my wife, Clara."

"You have a beautiful family," Julia said, feeling suddenly and unexpectedly emotional. "Do they ever visit Olive Haven?"

"Sometimes," Bernardo admitted. "When they are going into town and walking by or at the harvest time they will stop. They will be at the festival this week. You may even meet them there."

"I'd like that," said Julia, smiling. "I honestly thought you lived on the grounds somewhere, like you came with the house."

Bernardo patted the trunk of the olive tree. "No, the only thing Harriet got with the house was this tree...this tree and a lot of work. You should have seen her when she first came to Porto Venere after buying the house. The first time we met her, she told us: 'possibilities are made from nerves and dreams.' She had plenty of both. But as the months went by, she did it, like magic. She made Olive Haven a reality right in front of everyone's eyes."

The front door opened, and Harriet came down the steps. She smiled at Bernardo and Julia as she approached the tree. "For a retreat, it's awfully difficult to find a place to sit and be alone, isn't it?" she laughed to Julia, coming next to the bench.

"Oh, I think I got at least a minute or two."

"My fault," confessed Bernardo. "Harriet, the fresh flowers you asked for."

"*Grazie*, Bernardo. There are vases for them already filled with water in the garden."

Julia followed Harriet and Bernardo around the side of the villa to the back terrace. Sometime after they had all gone to bed, Harriet had transformed the garden in honor of Lucy's birthday festivities. Colorful dahlia blossoms strung together as garlands were draped from all sides of the pergola. The table had been covered in a thick, cream cloth flecked with gold, and each place was set with antique China plates, etched with delicate olive branches around the rim. At the head of the table, the chair had been swathed in white linen, bows of gold ribbon holding the draping in place on the top rung of the chair back. A small, impeccably wrapped package sat on the plate in front of the seat of honor.

Paper thin *crespelle* rolled with fresh jam and ricotta cheese were folded neatly and heaped, steaming, on two large platters. Harriet covered them with silver domes as Bernardo arranged the hydrangeas in large pillar vases down the center of the table. The rest of the mist burned off as they made their finishing touches, and by the time the women began joining them, the sky overhead was clear and blue. Julia couldn't imagine a more perfect morning.

A commotion in the entryway announced the birthday girl's arrival at breakfast. Maeve belted 'Happy Birthday' in a quavering voice that echoed through the house and onto the patio. She followed Lucy, who was wrapped in a knit shawl and still rubbing sleep from her eyes, onto the terrace. Maeve pulled out her chair dramatically and dropped into her own seat next to Julia as she hit a final, unnecessarily garish, note.

"Oh, enough already!" Lucy insisted emphatically. She sounded exasperated but looked wholly pleased with the situation. "You're not here to indulge a, now, eight-five-year-old woman's ego."

"Then what are we here for today?" Maeve asked.

Harriet smiled warmly. "As always, the day is yours to do with as you wish, though there is a tour arranged for the Gulf of Poets that I highly recommend for those of you interested in the local history. The surrounding landscapes and views are said to have inspired Lord Byron, the Shelley's, DH Lawrence, even Virginia Woolf."

"The Shelley's? Like Mary Shelley of *Frankenstein?*" asked Elise.

"That's the one," Harriet confirmed.

Elise looked around the garden. "I haven't seen anything around here that would inspire something like that." she said. "It's idyllic."

"You have yet to see Aster first thing in the morning," Maeve chortled. "That'd inspire a monster for sure."

Breakfast continued as a lively affair. Harriet brought in multiple phone calls for Lucy from her family, and Bernardo led another chorus of "Happy Birthday" in Italian when he brought her an espresso topped in whipped cream and a plate of pastries studded with birthday candles. Only when Harriet insisted that anyone wanting to tour that afternoon was going to have to leave presently or literally miss the boat, did the party break up, sending Julia, Alex, Maeve, and Lucy scrambling to get ready while the rest of the house begged off to enjoy a quieter day at the villa.

Julia quickly donned a sundress and sandals, threw her water bottle into her backpack, and gave her phone only a passing thought before leaving it safely in the end table drawer. At the last minute, she carefully tucked the paper boat into her notebook and stowed it in the front pocket of her bag, just in case inspiration struck.

When she returned downstairs, she found Maeve and Alex already in the entryway waiting with Bernardo. A large wicker basket sat on the floor between them, three books stacked on top. Julia glanced at the pile as she reached the bottom of the stairs.

Bernardo smiled, reaching down to hand her the first volume. "For your time with the poets," he said.

Julia read the title embossed in gold on the cover. The complete collection of Percy Shelley.

"Perfect," she smiled.

"Ah! *La regina del compleanno.*" Bernardo announced, looking over Julia's shoulder.

She turned to find Lucy coming down the stairs in a flowing, jewel toned tunic over white linen pants. A pendant looking remarkably like the green emerald from the jeweler in Pisa hung from her neck, and she had finished the look with an oversized straw sun hat.

"*Fantastica,*" Bernardo said, offering his hand as she stepped into the entryway. He raised it gently to his lips before letting go.

"I told you," Lucy said, "no more fussing."

"But when you come down the stairs looking so radiant..." Bernardo teased.

Lucy rolled her eyes and headed out the front door. "Well, if I can't look good at eighty-five," she tossed over her shoulder as she left, "what's the point?"

Bernardo shuttled them to the harbor to avoid having to haul the books and basket down the hill himself. Waiting in a slip was their charter for the day, a vintage, wooden runabout. The sleek mahogany hull had been waxed and buffed to a gleaming shine that glistened in the morning sun. The skipper stood on the dock in white dress pants cuffed at the ankle, a striped navy polo shirt, and boat shoes. As they approached, a woman in a red and white shirt dress sat up from where she'd been reclining in the sun on the back seat of the vessel.

Bernardo approached the boat and confirmed their reservation.

"*Si, si,*" the captain replied. "I am Captain Marco Francolli. Please, just call me Marco. This is my daughter, Giovanna. She will be your guide for the day."

Marco helped the women aboard along with the basket. Giovanna smiled as she saw the books. She picked up the top one and rifled through the pages.

"Do you know him?" she asked the women as they settled in. "Percy Shelley?"

"Some," Julia admitted. "Um, 'Ozymandias'?"

"Yes," Giovanna smiled.

"'To a Skylark'," offered Alex.

"Also, yes. How about this? 'As the sunrise to the night, as the north wind to the clouds, as the earthquake's fiery flight, ruining mountain solitudes, everlasting Italy. Be those hopes and fears on thee,'" she read.

"That's Shelley?" asked Julia.

Giovanna nodded. "It's called 'To Italy,' and it's one of the many works that we have from these romantic poets who spent so much time in this part of the country, and from whom the gulf now takes its name."

The boat slid back away from the dock, and Bernardo waved them off from the shore. They headed into the bay, the island of Palmaria directly in front of them. Like much of the surrounding coastline, its rocky shore gave way to steep cliff faces, but unique to the island, they could see numerous caves hollowed out along the water. Giovanna explained the island's national park status, with help from Maeve who had spent time there just a day earlier. Already the small dock was crowded with water taxis and tourists, and Marco, promising better views and less chaos further along, motored past without stopping.

The boat bounced on the waves, and the women laughed and squealed as salt spray misted their faces. Julia wondered vaguely at what her original plans may have contained, but in the face of another unexpected, yet joyous, adventure, it was impossible to feel like she was missing anything. She was grateful for having found her way to this moment.

Beyond Palmaria was the heavily wooded island of Tino. Smaller than its neighbor, the island boasted a military light-house on the top of predominant cliff face. A small port on one side of the island sat empty, and Giovanna explained that tourists were only permitted to visit one day a year on the feast of San Venerio, which, unfortunately, it was not. Marco made a slow orbit of the island so they could take in the lush vegetation on all sides, and more interestingly, the hints of ancient Roman ruins just visible through the foliage.

A stone's throw away, the final island in the chain was Tinneto, a seemingly large rock bereft of vegetation or archi-tecture. Julia wondered why anyone even considered Tinneto remarkable, though Giovanna explained, with some enthusiasm, that it was home to a distinctive species of lizard found only on the tiny island. As they rounded the shoreline, however, the women saw Tinneto wasn't without other merit. Rising up out of the sea, a few yards off the coast, was a beautifully rendered, marble statue of the Virgin Mary.

Past the sculpture, Marco revved the engine and the boat sped off toward the distant coastline. The women shrieked and laughed as the wind whipped at their hair and pulled tears from their eyes. All around them, the turquoise water was dotted with sailboats, jet skis, fishing boats and water taxis. The sunlight sparkled like glitter scattered across the gulf, and seagulls and seabirds circled wildly overhead.

It was impossible for Julia to dwell on her heartbreak or attempt to untangle the complicated feelings of her morning while racing across the bay. Her heart soared as adrenaline coursed through her. She had found brief moments of comfort, and strength, and joy in her time at Olive Haven, and now she could add exhilaration. She couldn't imagine the romantic poets ever experiencing the water in quite this way, but it wasn't hard to fathom how the surroundings might inspire bursts of artistic inspiration.

Forty minutes later, windswept, tear streaked, and with bellies sore from laughter, the women relaxed as Marco navigated through the tidy marina at Lerici. To their right, an ancient castle sat preserved on an overcropping above the town. Ahead and to the left, white sand beaches and a bustling harbor walk. As was now commonplace, brightly colored shops and apartments were piled together near the water and climbed up the hillside behind. Giovanna gave some history on the town as Marco docked.

"We'll stop here for lunch and exploring," she said. "There's a picnic area above the harbor." They disembarked on the pier and began to weave their way along the dock and toward the walking path leading up to the lookout. "Lerici is where most of the poets referenced in the gulf's namesake spent their time," Giovanna explained as they walked. "Here, and neighboring San Terenzo. It was the Shelley's who had property nearby, and they invited Lord Byron to stay with them. Eventually he would come and stay of his own accord as well.

Percy Shelley has a less known poem, 'Lines Written in the Bay of Lerici.'" Giovanna began to recite from memory. "'I sat and saw the vessels glide over the ocean bright and wide like spirit-winged chariots sent o'er some serenest element...'"

"That's very beautiful," said Maeve.

"Well, that part is," Giovanna admitted. "The rest of the poem is about heartbreak and grief. But to experience heartbreak and grief in such a beautiful setting is quite a juxtaposition for poetry."

"Or life," Alex said quietly, passing Julia.

They reached the castle overlook and unpacked sandwiches, fresh melon, and bottles of water from Bernardo's basket. Giovanna read them poetry as they ate. The sea breeze and verses of the romantic masters washed over them in turns, and Julia again wondered how she ever imagined herself anywhere but here. As they finished, Alex and Lucy wandered up toward *Castello di Lerici*, while Maeve propped her feet up on the stone wall and closed her eyes. Julia sat with Giovanna looking out over the water. She picked another book off the stack and flipped through its pages.

"You like Byron?" Giovanna asked.

Julia shrugged. "Not enough to recite him from memory. But it's lovely to read."

She continued to turn through the book, stopping to read bits of romantic verse here and there. It was an idyllic way to spend an afternoon, she thought. A picnic, sea breezes, a view of the coast, Will stretched on a picnic blanket, poetry book open in his lap. The thoughts arrived uninvited, and Julia sighed, frustrated to find him so easily come to mind in quiet moments. She chose a page of the book at random to distract herself and read.

Halfway down the page she stopped, struck by the undoubtedly somber nature of the verse. She read aloud under her breath.

"'Though my many faults defaced me, could no other arm be found, than the one which once embraced me, to inflict a cureless wound? Yet, oh yet, thyself deceive not; love may sink by slow decay, but by sudden wrench, believe not hearts can thus be torn away. Still, thine own its life retaineth, still must mine, though bleeding, beat; and the undying thought which paineth is – that we no more may meet."'

Goosebumps broke out over Julia's arms. "Giovanna," she called. "What can you tell me about this poem?" Julia passed her the book, watching as she scanned the page.

"'Fare Thee Well'," Giovanna replied. "It's a very beautiful poem, but sad. He may have written it here. It was a lament to his wife who left him after just a year of marriage. After their separation, he left England and never went back. Much of his time away was spent here, but he eventually bought property in Venice also."

"His final goodbye," Julia realized, aloud. She jumped to the final stanza. "'Fare thee well! thus disunited, torn from every nearer tie. Seared in heart, and lone, and blighted more than this I scarce can die.'" She looked up. "He's heartbroken just like Shelley."

Giovanna nodded. "They wrote what they knew. Poetry is at its best when it resonates, and grief is part of the human experience. Like all people, they had to cope. So, they came here, wrote, healed."

Julia stared at the page. Margo had said the same thing just yesterday: grief was universal. It seemed healing heartbreak with Mediterranean life was nearly universal as well.

"Did it work for Byron?" Julia asked, wondering what chance she stood if a great, romantic poet had not been able to move on here.

Giovanna laughed. "Well, he stayed for a number of years, and he wrote prolifically, so it certainly didn't hurt."

Julia smiled, turning the page. The next poem was just four lines. "'A year ago, you swore, fond she! To love, to honour, and so forth: Such was the vow you pledged to me, and here's exactly what 'tis worth,'" she read.

"He sent her that with the signature on their divorce papers," Giovanna explained.

"Really makes you consider the meaning of 'poetic justice,'" Julia laughed halfheartedly. She stared down at the lines again, moved by their blunt simplicity. She could still hear the hurt behind the words, but there was something else too, a feistiness, a fighting spirit. They had bite. She opened the front pocket of her backpack and took out a Sharpie and her folded paper boat. Giovanna watched her curiously.

"You like this poem?" she asked with confusion.

"Like you said, good poetry resonates." On the inside flap, where it could eventually be consumed by the candle flame, Julia inscribed the four lines of Byron's poem.

"Does it remind you of someone?"

"Yes," Julia admitted.

"Well, you might take comfort to know that Byron probably has you beat," said Giovanna. "He married his wife Annabella after being rumored to have fathered a child with his half-sister Agatha. The marriage lasted less than a year, during which time he had another daughter, and after which they separated in disgrace. It's sad, but it's not a love story."

Julia stared at the lines she had written, unsure how to respond.

Marco appeared at the top of the lookout steps, and Giovanna waved him over. He looked at the book in Julia's hands as he approached. "Byron?"

"Yes," answered Julia. "Do you have a favorite?"

Marco gave a wry smile. "'Don Juan.' It has a little bit of everything, love, loss, trickery, pirates."

"A long poem for a different afternoon," Giovanna said, chuckling as they began to pack up the picnic lunch.

Alex and Elise returned from the castle.

"What'd we miss?" said Alex, surveying the group.

"A poetry reading," Giovanna smiled at Julia.

"A history lesson," Julia smiled back.

"And speaking of history," Giovanna said, "rumor has it

that Byron used to swim the bay between Porto Venere and San Terenzo to visit friends. We will anchor off Byron's Grotto on the way back for anyone who would like to take a dip."

"Didn't Byron drown attempting that swim?" Maeve asked, rejoining the conversation.

"That was Percy Shelley," Marco corrected, "and he was not swimming. His boat capsized. I'll be much more careful," he said, smiling and picked up the basket. "Shall we ladies?"

The women followed Marco from the lookout, clambering down the steps, eager to get back to the water.

Julia stayed behind for a moment, repacking her bag. The poem had captured just a small fragment of what it felt like to move on, but she craved something more. Byron had packed up his entire life and started over. Had she not done some of the same in taking the trip? As she looked at her notebook, she realized she had not truly left everything behind. Taking the honeymoon was simultaneously running away from and chasing a life that no longer existed. Only in the last few days was she really trying to chart her own path forward.

She tucked the boat in the band of the notebook, meaning to return both to her backpack, when it suddenly occurred to her that she didn't need to wait until the festival to release some of the feelings about her original trip. She could leave something right here, just as the poets had. She slid the boat from under the elastic and moved it to the front pocket of her bag. She ran her hand over the cover of the notebook thinking about the time and effort and dreaming that had gone into the plans. The past few days had shown her, it was okay to want something more than what was here. She could not sink it in the harbor with her boat, but she could leave it behind, definitively.

She saw a trash can on the far end of the picnic area; she

shouldered her bag and started toward it. Her palms grew sweaty as she drew near, and she hesitated. It was silly, she realized. It was just a notebook. All the reservations and information were still in her email. It was not as if she was actually changing anything. But it still felt important. It felt like moving on.

She wasn't entirely sure she was ready.

"Julia!" Alex called. "Are you coming?"

Julia turned to find her friend watching, concerned, at the top of the steps. She smiled. "Right behind you," she assured her.

Alex disappeared down the stairs.

Alone again, but not really alone.

She could see the women below jostling toward the pier, laughing and talking. Her heart swelled. Baby steps, she remembered. Taking a deep breath, she let the book clatter into the can.

CHAPTER 16

Another perfect evening of wining and dining at Olive Haven gave way to another perfect morning. Julia woke up eager to embark on Harriet's signature day, and in the early morning light, as the women piled into the van that would take them to the harbor and their charter, there was a palpable, shared excitement. They loaded onto a water taxi and headed west down the coastline toward the colored frescos of the Cinque Terre.

The only one who seemed unmoved by the event was Aster. Still shut in her room that morning, Julia heard Maeve through the bathroom door as she was getting ready, pleading with her sister to attend the tour. Aster refused to come down, and when Maeve came through the kitchen a few minutes later, her exasperation was apparent. As their boat slid through the calm, Ligurian waters, Julia found Maeve against the deck rail watching Manarola pass by.

"I'm sorry your sister wouldn't join us," she said sympathetically.

"I'm sorry you have to share a bathroom with her," Maeve

answered pointedly. There was humor in her tone, but bitterness, Julia noted, as well.

"Is she this way at home, too?"

Maeve shrugged, her gaze still transfixed on the passing scenery. "When Timothy died, she changed. When Arthur died, it got worse. Arthur and Timothy were best friends. Close as brothers. For a long time, the four of us were inseparable. She got married and then had her daughter. Arthur and I got married and started our family. Timothy got elected, and we saw them less. Honestly, I thought now that everyone was grown up and Timothy and Arthur were gone, we would become best friends again. But that hasn't happened yet."

She looked sadly out over the water as Corniglia came into view, and Julia let silence hang between them. She thought of Ellie. She was the closest thing Julia had to a sister, and Julia couldn't imagine navigating months of worrying over her moods, silences, and grief, hoping they would still have a relationship when she came out of it, trying daily to make things okay. Julia often felt badly for Aster's pain, seeing the light under the door and wondering what depths of despair she must be enduring. Now she felt sorrow for Maeve.

The pier at Corniglia sat at the base of a cliff, three hundred and eighty-two bricked steps below the first road into town. Compared to the picturesque marinas and harbors of the rest of the Cinque Terre, Corniglia barely felt like a seaside village. There was no formal dock or port, just a sloping concrete ramp that led into the water and a few boats anchored off the shore. At less than two hundred and fifty residents, the smallest of the Cinque Terre villages lacked the obvious appeal of sun kissed days on the beach or harbor walk.

As they approached the rocky shoreline, Julia thought

Corniglia looked cold. Perched high above the water in the crux of a ridgeline, the town was well protected from the relentless pounding of the waves but otherwise exposed to the wind and uninviting to the sea wary traveler. Even the colors of the town seemed less vibrant than its neighboring villages, no doubt a casualty of being aloft in the constant grit of salty sea air.

"What do you think?" Julia asked.

"Of what?" Maeve replied.

"The village. I think it looks crabby." Julia thought again of Aster.

"How can a village look crabby?"

"Every other town is full of life," answered Julia. "The harbors are teeming with people. There's music, and noise, and busyness, and vibrance." She looked up at Corniglia. "It's just holed-up in that dip of the cliff. You can visit it if you *want*, but it's not making any effort for you."

The boat came to rest against the concrete ramp, and the crew helped each woman ashore. Julia joined Alex near the front of the group, and, when everyone had disembarked, they followed the ramp to a sloping walkway that zigzagged away from the water before meeting up with the staircase that climbed to the top.

Harriet's voice stopped them before they could begin the climb. "Welcome to Corniglia," she said. "The oldest and smallest of the Cinque Terre villages, we'll start here for a quieter morning and work our way into some livelier festivities later in the day. It's almost four-hundred steps to the top of the cliff, though a bus will start running in about an hour for those who would prefer not to walk. In the meantime, if you would follow me this way, please."

She led them along a path that wound to the left against the hillside, descending back toward the water. They walked a brief stretch toward a cavernous opening in the rock face ahead of them.

"What is that?" Julia asked Alex.

"A tunnel," she replied simply.

"I can see that. But a tunnel to where?" Julia pressed.

"I don't know. Harriet's never brought me here. But it ought to be good."

They reached the entrance to the tunnel, nine feet tall in the middle, with walls and a floor of smooth concrete. Julia thought it looked secure enough despite disappearing almost immediately into the pitch blackness of the mountain.

Harriet faced the group. "At the end of this tunnel," she announced, "is one of Corniglia's fabled, hidden gems. A beach. Guvano. A setting that is both beautiful and..." she paused, considering her words, "liberating, as many sunbathers often choose to forego more traditional swimming attire when sheltered in its reclusive location."

"A nude beach?" laughed Margo.

"You're kidding!" exclaimed Alex, grinning. "Honestly Harriet, of all the places we've been together, I never imagined you leading me onto a nude beach."

"How do you think her mother feels?" chortled Lucy.

Harriet shrugged nonchalantly. "I'm not saying anyone has to take her clothes off or that you even have to come at all. It's a fifteen-minute walk through that winding, unlit tunnel to get there. I'm just here to provide the experiences." She turned and moved into the entrance of the tunnel, turning on a flashlight to illuminate the darkness just a few feet in front of her. She faced them again, half shadowed. "If we go now, we're more likely to have the beach to ourselves before the afternoon rush. If you'd rather stay, feel free to wait here for us or wander ahead into Corniglia. The stairs take you to the main road, which leads into the city center.

We'll plan to meet in front of St. Peter's church at eleven o'clock. So, who's with me?"

Julia looked at Alex who nodded and laughed. "Why not?" she said.

"I'm in!" burst Maeve. "Lucy?"

"It'd be irresponsible not to supervise my own child under such circumstances." Lucy smirked at Harriet.

Harriet rolled her eyes. "Beth, Margo, Elise?" she asked.

The three women shared a look.

"I'm honestly more worried about the walk through the tunnel than taking off my top," admitted Elise.

"And I wouldn't leave just one woman to wander by herself," said Margo. "So, if Beth is in?"

Beth looked up and sighed, then nodded slowly. "Let's get on with it."

Harriet passed out flashlights, and they wandered into the tunnel. The thin beams threw sharp shadows across the concrete, revealing graffiti and water staining. Soon the entrance was just a pinprick of light. The exit remained lost around a bend in the tunnel ahead. Minus the feeble beams from the flashlights, the blackness engulfed them. Somewhere ahead in the darkness, there was a scurrying of tiny feet on cement. Someone in the back shrieked, and the flashlight beams swung wildly around the tunnel walls while women giggled in nervousness. A few minutes later, the beating of wings caused them all to momentarily scatter, ducking with hands over their heads, shouts of panic and uproarious, anxious laughter echoing in the enclosed space. When they found each other in the center of the tunnel again, they clutched at one another's hands and moved forward as a collective body.

Julia's heart raced. She hated being scared and was not keen on enclosed, dark spaces, but she also had to admit the walk was exhilarating. Adrenaline coursed through her, and she gripped the hand next to her so tightly she could feel both pulses coursing through her fingers. The tunnel curved to the left, revealing a sunlit opening closer than she had expected. In another minute, they had reached the end and stepped back into the light.

Guvano was a crescent shaped beach of dark pebbles and coarse sand sloping gently into the clearest water Julia had seen on the entire trip. The small, natural cove was well protected from the surf that pounded other parts of the coast, and the result was undisturbed, turquoise water lapping peacefully at the shore. It faded into deep blue, but even thirty feet out, Julia could see large rocks and silvery schools of fish near the bottom.

The beach was deserted save for three large beach umbrellas staked out at the far end, and a single, clothed, man. He waved towards the women, and Julia saw it was Bernardo. Harriet set off across the sand toward him, and the rest of the group, anxious to get away from the tunnel and take in the scene, hurried after her. As they approached, Julia saw he not only had towels and beach umbrellas, but also fruit, pastries, prosecco and orange juice.

"*Saluti* ladies!" Bernardo called. "You all made it."

"I think I would have preferred your way," Beth replied shakily, nodding toward the dinghy tied up in the shallows.

Bernardo smiled. "But that's not the experience, and the experience only gets better from here." He handed out flutes of prosecco and nodded to Harriet. "I'll return by eleven to pack up the supplies, unless you need something in the meantime?"

"Thank you, Bernardo," Harriet replied. "This is all we need."

"You'll kindly remember to fly the yellow flag when the beach is clear for my landing?" Bernardo nodded to a stake in the sand next to the umbrella.

"Clear for his landing?" Beth asked.

"I think he means we're clothed," Julia laughed.

"*Si, grazie,*" Bernardo smiled, his cheeks betraying the slightest tinge of embarrassment.

They watched as he returned to the boat, wound up the line, fired up the motor, and disappeared around the bend of the coastline.

Harriet turned to the group. She raised her glass, using it to gesture to the beauty around them. "Ladies," she smiled, "have at it!"

They claimed towels and staked out spots in the sand. Beth nervously chose a place against the cliff face at the back of the beach where she sat protectively with her backpack and read a book. Still fully clothed, Elise and Margo ventured toward the water. A few minutes after submerging, however, they were hooting and hollering, waving their bathing suits above their heads. Alex lay topless on her stomach, trying to even out her racerback tan lines. Harriet sat with Lucy under the umbrellas helping to apply sunscreen.

Julia wandered a bit farther down the beach where Maeve was laying out her towel.

"Mind if I join you?" Julia asked.

Maeve looked up. "Have you ever been to a nude beach before?" she asked in reply.

"No," Julia admitted. "Have you?"

"Yes," Maeve smirked. "The first rule is that when the beach is wide open like this, you never set up your towel right next to someone."

Julia blushed. "I'm sorry. I didn't know," she said, flustered, glancing around to find another spot to call her own.

"Relax," Maeve laughed. "I'm kidding. Join me."

Julia hesitated.

"Really," Maeve reassured her. "It's fine."

Reluctantly, Julia spread out her towel and sat down next to Maeve.

"You've really never been to a nude beach?" Maeve asked.

"You really have been?" Julia responded.

Maeve looked out at the water. "Not with Aster, mind you," Maeve replied. "I know I said we were best of friends, but she has always been a prude." Maeve looked at Julia and smiled mischievously. There was no malice in her tone, and Julia was relieved to find Maeve's mood improving.

"Arthur was a bit of a wild child," Maeve went on, "which is amazing when you consider he was best friends with Timothy. Tim was all business. I'll tell you how we met." She turned and sat cross-legged facing Julia and smoothed the edges of her towel. "Arthur and Timothy showed up one summer to work at the law firm where Aster was a clerk. We knew Timothy from high school. *Everyone* knew Timothy in high school. He was your quintessential hometown hero, though Arthur Kennedy stole a fair bit of his thunder when they showed up in town together." A smile played at the corners of her mouth. "Timothy had gotten so serious, law school being the gateway to the life and career he imagined in politics. Aster was better suited for that life. She's the older sister, the driven one."

Julia couldn't stop the memories of the hours she had spent listening to Will practice presentations, entertaining clients, encouraging him over his career. He had always reciprocated, but she wondered if Maeve would have considered him serious like Timothy.

"So anyway, one day I'm working as a teller in the local bank, and this guy walks in to ask about cashing some traveler's cheques. He's tall, dark, handsome, in a neatly tailored blue suit. Clearly older than me, and yet, clearly interested." She adjusted her coverup around her shoulders. "We start talking about his recent trip to the south of France and his plans when he gets out of law school. He mentions he's just passing through town for the summer, filling an intern position. Honestly, when he left the bank that afternoon, I figured I'd never see him again, save a chance meeting somewhere around town. Then two days later, he walks back up to my counter and asks if I'd join him for dinner that night."

A cheer went up from the water as Lucy crossed the beach and splashed into the waves, joining Elise and Margo.

Maeve chuckled as she continued. "Now I was nineteen, but my parents weren't keen to let me date, particularly with an out-of-town stranger who was passing through on a return trip from the south of France. But it just so happened that Aster had also been asked to dinner that same night, and somehow in making out the details of the evening, we came to realize our dinners actually overlapped, a double date. My mystery man wasn't a mystery at all, but rather intimately connected to Raleigh's favorite son. My parents were thrilled and eagerly agreed."

The women in the water hollered again, but Julia hugged her legs to her chest and rested her chin on her knees, giving Maeve her undivided attention.

"Fast forward five months later. Aster and I would make the five hour drive up to Georgetown to see them at law school. Timothy was consumed by school work, insisting Aster put any other plans on hold while he finished papers, prepared briefs, and edited the law review. I'd find Arthur in the middle of work, and instantly convince him to abandon it for a whirlwind adventure. We'd run into Baltimore, or take off to the coast, or meet friends in a downtown dive bar, or stay in bed all day." Maeve smirked. "Aster and Timothy were the traditionalists, certainly not exploring any sexual chemistry between them." She tipped down her sunglasses and looked over the frames at Julia. "That wasn't a problem for Arthur and me."

Julia laughed, now certain that Maeve would consider Will, and possibly Julia herself, serious and boring. "So, on one of those adventures he took you to a nude beach?"

"Oh yes, that," Maeve exclaimed. "On the night he proposed, Arthur took me to Colonial Beach. It was one of those spring days that holds all the promise of summer, but it was too early for the beach going crowds yet. He built a driftwood fire and dropped to a knee as the sun dropped over the water. That was that. We sat in the sand as the beach grew dark, and as the stars came out, I suggested we go for a swim."

"Wasn't it cold?" asked Julia, surprised.

"Freezing," Maeve confirmed. "But it seemed exotic and daring, and I was so giddy that I didn't care about throwing caution to the wind or the temperature. We threw off our clothes, laughing the whole way into the water. We held each other in the waves, out of a desire for each other's warmth or each other's body, it didn't really matter." Maeve paused.

"And then?" Julia pressed, eyes wide with expectation.

"And then a spotlight came down the beach and a coast guard patrol showed up and called us back to shore."

Julia's mouth fell open with a laugh. "You're kidding!"

"I wish." Maeve laughed. "My parents were furious. Even Arthur seemed embarrassed."

Julia shook her head in disbelief. "I would have been mortified. My...ex..." she stumbled over the word, "used to freak out if we got a parking ticket downtown."

Maeve shrugged. "You can't take life so seriously."

"That's a great story, but that wasn't a true nude beach," said Julia. "It doesn't count if you were just naked on a normal beach and got caught doing it."

"Oh, well, we got to a real nude beach eventually," Maeve admitted. "After we were married, we returned to the south of France on our honeymoon, and nude beaches were par for the course. Though they were far less exciting than being chased out of the water the night of our engagement."

Julia shook her head, laughing.

"Don't laugh," said Maeve. "My husband and I enjoyed each other, and we enjoyed life together. I used to look at my sister and how serious she was with her husband and wonder how anyone was happy in a marriage that looked so different from mine? Arthur and Timothy were best friends and complete opposites."

They turned, sitting shoulder to shoulder and looking out at the water. Julia thought about Arthur and Maeve. There was a carefree, easiness about the way Maeve told her story that Julia envied. She and Will had traveled with his clients, but there were always dinners to attend, sales to coordinate, deals to be made. He had admired and encouraged her work as well, but it was always just that, work. There had been black tie events, exclusive invitations, even a private jet once, but she tried to remember the last time they really had fun together, let alone spontaneously. Why had it never bothered her that they had not vacationed or explored? They did *not* adventure. Perhaps, she realized, it was part of the reason she had held onto this trip so tightly when it was finally time to plan something just for them.

"Will almost proposed on a beach at sunset," Julia admitted, still staring straight ahead.

"Almost?" Maeve asked.

"Well, he'd been in Hawaii while I was in Chicago. He came back and proposed with a postcard of the beach at sunset."

"Oh," said Maeve, looking at Julia. "Feels a bit stiff." When Julia didn't return the glance, she turned back toward the water. "I like my story better."

Julia chuckled. "I do, too."

"So, I take it Will would never have ever taken you to a

nude beach?" Maeve asked.

"Probably not," Julia admitted. "He could be insecure."

"Would you have gone yourself?" Maeve asked, mischievously.

"When we were together? Never. Not if I thought it would upset him."

"And now?"

Julia sighed heavily. "Now it doesn't matter."

"Why not?"

"Because he's in some tropical paradise with someone else."

Maeve's eyebrows knitted in confusion. "What does that have to do with anything? If that's the case, you can't possibly upset him. Remember the woman you were, the one before Will. Strong and independent, I'm sure." She took off her sunglasses and looked at Julia. "Would that woman have gone to a nude beach?" she asked earnestly.

Julia turned to face her. "I don't know," she admitted. "I feel like I barely know her anymore."

"Sure, you do," insisted Maeve. "She's you, and you're here, aren't you?" She arched an eyebrow knowingly.

"So, you're saying?"

"C'mon, let's go!" Maeve laughed. She stood up, and pulled off her swimsuit coverup.

"Go where?" Julia asked, skeptically.

"In the water!" Maeve announced.

Julia hesitated. "Naked?" she balked at the idea.

"Naked, clothed, topless, bottomless. Why do I care? But for me," Maeve turned her back to Julia and undid the top of her swimsuit, "this sure beats Colonial Beach in April." She ran toward the water, eliciting cheers from Margo, Elise, and Lucy, still bobbing in the waves. "Live a little, Julia!" she called back over her shoulder. "It's freeing...literally!" She splashed, laughing, into the waves.

"Well, go on," Alex called from down the beach, grinning as she turned onto her back.

Julia looked around at the otherwise empty stretch of sand. A nude beach; it was not the way she had imagined finding the way back to herself. Still, the day had brought her here. Julia glanced at the otherwise empty stretch of sand. Then she stood, threw caution to the wind, pulled on the string of her bikini top to loosen it, and followed Maeve into the water.

NINETY MINUTES LATER, the women toweled off in the sun, bathing suits securely fastened once again, and salt stiffening their hair. Bernardo reappeared with the boat to pack up the umbrellas and breakfast picnic, and the whole group reconvened at the mouth of the tunnel for the nerve wracking walk back to the road toward Corniglia. Unlike their trip to the beach, however, they were no longer alone, now joined by a stream of beachgoers navigating the tunnel in the opposite direction. They passed clusters of cell phones and flashlights every few minutes, and nervous laughter and excited energy echoed ahead and behind them.

Emerging in the sunlight on the other end, they picked their way back down the path to the base of the zigzagging staircase that led to the city center high above. Harriet again suggested the bus to anyone who didn't want to make the climb, though not even Lucy accepted the offer. They gamely began the ascent.

Less than a third of the way to the top, the stairs met up with the walkway leading from the train station. Tucked tightly against the rock, with no view of the town to speak of, visitors arriving to Corniglia were let off at the platform and made to walk with their luggage up the road and the staircase into town. Fortunately for the group, few were carrying much more than a small bag, though Beth continued to haul the backpack in which her husband's urn was securely packed.

They climbed in near silence, everyone focused on the brick paved steps and reaching the top.

Lucy, walking with Harriet, occasionally offered words of encouragement laced with sarcasm. "C'mon everyone," she called from the back of the pack. "Almost there. Remember, the more tired and relieved we are at the top, the better Harriet's plans are going to look when we get there."

They crossed *Via Stazione*, took a small side road marked with a red bullseye pointing them toward the city center, wound through a maze of quiet shuttered buildings, and came out in a pebbled courtyard in front of *Chiesa di San Pietro*. Saint Peter's church. The low stone wall around the edge provided a spot to sit and recoup in the shade.

Julia took a long drink of water, and took stock of the morning. She was in a beautiful place, with good people, enjoying a great view, and had unexpectedly spent part of her morning bathing topless in the Mediterranean. It was not, she thought, how she ever would have planned it, but abandoning the plan had been the best decision she ever made. Being liberated from expectation had changed her entire trip, and it was leaving a lasting impression.

When they all assembled and caught their breath, Harriet led the way to the marked path that stretched through the winding streets of the village past souvenir shops just opening and restaurants setting up their chairs and tables on the sidewalks for the early lunch crowd. The entire trip took just minutes, and soon they were on the edge of town, looking out at the most jaw dropping panorama Julia had ever seen.

Whereas each village featured areas of terraced vineyards

and orchards clinging to the side of the surrounding cliffs, the green expanse between Corniglia and neighboring Vernazza was patchworked as far as one could see down the coast with grapevines, olive trees, lemon groves, and vegetable gardens: a dozen shades of green all stitched together with dry stacked stone walls. Below, the Mediterranean stretched from aquamarine in the shallows to deep cerulean at the horizon. A slice of Guvano beach revealed tiny colored dots and squares, where umbrellas and towels now populated the sand. Far off in the distance, the silhouette of a cruise ship. In the foreground, the clean white sails of a passing schooner billowed in the sea breeze.

"Some say this stretch between Corniglia and Vernazza is the most beautiful in the entire Cinque Terre," said Harriet as they set off onto the path. "The walk is about an hour. Enjoy the scenery. Share a conversation. Breathe in some fresh air."

The trail was narrow, and they mostly walked single file to pass by the hikers coming from the opposite direction. Julia walked with Beth in front of her and Alex behind her, and they proceeded up a gentle slope climbing away from Corniglia. They crested the ridge and followed the gravel trail framed by brush and rock to their right, and a rough, split rail fence guarding from the sheer cliff that dropped down to the expanse of emerald and sapphire on their left.

"Watch your step!" called Harriet as they came to the first set of narrow stairs that worked around the natural stone of the cliff.

Further ahead, the trail widened, and in the shade of the surrounding orange trees, a local man sat pressing fresh juice from the fruit hanging overhead.

Julia looked back at Alex. "Did Harriet plant him here?"

Alex laughed. "I wouldn't put anything past Harriet, but I'm guessing not. Some places are just naturally this idyllic."

They stopped for a refreshment, watching the man casually pluck the round, sun ripened fruit just inches above him, cut the sphere in half and load each piece into the press. His movements were deft, and a constant stream of juice poured from the spout on the front of the device. A young girl filled paper cups and offered them to the women. It was the best orange juice Julia had ever tasted.

They rested in the surrounding grove, claiming patches of shade to recline. Julia looked up, recognizing the silvery underbellies of the leaves winking in the sunlight. Olive trees.

Beth, Julia noticed, had moved off to the side on her own, her red backpack at her feet, arms crossed, brow furrowed, leaning against the trunk of a large tree. She stared off at the Mediterranean. While Julia had reveled in the morning, she couldn't imagine what it felt like for Beth, and she hesitated, wondering what solace she could even offer. She approached the tree cautiously, realizing that just sitting with Beth might be all the comfort she would need. "How are you doing?" she asked softly, coming into the shade.

"Julia, hi," she said, attention shifting. She said it kindly, but Julia felt her forced cheerfulness, and the smile didn't reach her eyes. "I'm fine, thank you."

Julia sat down on the smooth curve of an exposed root, and waited, hoping to offer the kindness of a willing audience without prying. A long, silent moment passed. Beth looked up at the tree sadly, tears brimming.

"It's a big day," she finally offered. "I've always known that if Anthony went first, I'd be making this trip. But there's a big difference between knowing you'll have to do something and actually doing it."

"Was it unexpected?" Julia asked, keeping her gaze locked onto the surrounding scenery.

"A heart attack. One in three deaths come from heart disease. Did you know that? My mother died of a seizure disorder. My father died in an accident. My husband was the one in three. So maybe it shouldn't have surprised me."

"I'm sorry." Julia said. "Did you...do you...have a family?"

"Two sons," Beth said. "They're fanatical about their health now, worried they'll take after their dad."

"They didn't want to come on the trip?"

Beth sighed sadly. "They have families and jobs, and, to be honest, they're angry at Anthony for not taking care of himself as well as he should have and then leaving us behind." She stopped, then added quietly, guiltily, "I'm angry, too."

"You don't seem angry to me," Julia reassured her.

Beth looked over at her. "You don't seem angry to me either," she said. "And yet, from what I've heard, you would have good reason to be as well."

Julia felt the familiar pit settle in her stomach. "I've been angry," Julia confessed, "but it comes and goes unexpectedly for me. Sometimes the strangest thing sends me into a tailspin."

"Then you understand how it is," Beth said. She paused, smiling slightly to herself. "You know, when Anthony's ashes didn't show up at the carrier in Porto Venere the other day, I blamed him as if he had missed his flight or something. In case it wasn't bad enough that he had died in the first place, now he was going to ruin my vacation on top of it."

"For what it's worth," Julia offered, "I've admired your strength in the face of adversity all week. I know it's difficult; I haven't handled all of my emotions as gracefully as I would like on this trip."

Beth looked down at her hands. "Well, thank you," she said quietly. "Though, if it makes you feel better, I did plenty of wallowing behind closed doors."

They watched a line of hikers file past. Murmured conversations punctuated by brief bursts of laughter filtered up through the trees. To their left, Alex had laid her head in

Harriet's lap and was dozing. To their right, Lucy and Elise picked small yellow wild flowers poking up through the dirt.

"If you don't mind my asking," Julia broke the silence. "Why did he want to be brought here?"

Beth looked wistfully out over the water. "Anthony loved Italy. He romanticized it. His grandmother was a first-generation immigrant. She taught him the language when he was little. He talked of retiring here, though when the time came, the arrival of our grandchildren had something to say about that. If he couldn't spend his life here, then he wanted to spend his eternity here. 'Find me the *best* view in the world.' That's what he told me."

"Did you come here together?"

"Three times. I've always enjoyed it."

Julia smiled sympathetically. "So even though you were angry, you brought him home?"

"Of course." Beth looked over, eyes brimming once again. "That's what we do for the people we love."

Julia hesitated as Beth dabbed away tears. "Do you think it will help?" she asked quietly. "Knowing that his final wish is granted, will it be enough to help put aside your anger and move on?"

Beth looked at her curiously. "No," she said plainly.

Julia stared back, surprised. "Why not?"

"If it was that easy," Beth sighed. "I would have dumped him out a long time ago." She nudged the backpack with her toe, smiling sadly. "Okay, maybe not, but still, bringing him here was about fulfilling his wishes and making sure he rested in peace. My peace will come later."

"How?" Julia asked.

"Same as yours will," Beth held Julia's gaze. "Forgiveness."

Julia was stunned into silence. She had thought about keeping tabs on Will's activity, competing with his updates, responding to his text messages. She had wondered at his motives, loathed his behavior, longed for his presence. She had tried to fill his absence with wine, food, social media, tears, friends, Olive Haven, even, however briefly, other men. She did it all in the name of moving on. But not once, had she ever considered forgiving him.

She wasn't certain she even knew how.

Back on the trail, Harriet called for the group to gather, and Beth picked up her backpack. "Are you ready?" she asked Julia.

"Not at all," Julia answered quietly, distractedly.

Beth gave her a knowing look. "Then let's hike," she said calmly. "There's time for the rest of it later."

They joined the other women and set off west along the coast. A quick bend in the trail revealed the first glimpse of Vernazza's tower-tipped peninsula reaching out into the turquoise water. Straight off the point and across the bay, the coast slashed left across the horizon, and the colorful buildings of Monterosso al Mare sat sandwiched between the deep, green, forested hills behind and a white sand beach that stretched between the village and the sea.

Julia hardly noticed, lost in thoughts of Will, home, and how she would ever bring herself to forgive what he had done. She had only just convinced herself not to check in on him three times a day.

Alex came up alongside her. "You seem preoccupied all of a sudden."

Julia looked up. "Just lost in thought," she said.

"Well, get unlost," Alex said, throwing an arm over her shoulders, "because you aren't going to want to miss this. If I had to choose one place to show off the entire Cinque Terre, it would be Vernazza." She nodded toward the very first of the yellow and pink buildings ahead on the trail. "Wait until you see it," she smiled. "It's pure magic."

CHAPTER 17

Vernazza sat below the walking trail so that the women saw the entire sprawl of the town before descending into its winding streets and back alleys. A single, main road led down from a train station at the top but was closed to car traffic. It crawled with pedestrians, tiny as ants from above, who darted in and out of shops and restaurants streaming back and forth to the water. The village met the sea at a natural harbor where a large outcropping of rock jutted out in a semi-circle enclosing an area two hundred yards wide. Locals and tourists alike waded in the shallows off the pebbled beach while boats and buoys bobbed in the deeper water.

The castle ruins, watchtower, and fort sat overlooking the entire scene. Perched on the cliff on the east end of the village, the watch tower was originally constructed as a lookout for pirates, though had long ago been retired to a tourist attraction. The fort below housed a restaurant, its multi-leveled outdoor seating suspended over the water affording some of the best dining views in the region.

As they came into the village, the women stopped at the

tower and paid the required Euro to the local volunteer at the door. They climbed a narrow interior stairwell, tightly wound around the center column of the tower, and came out in the open air on the crenelated parapet.

Looking out over the village, Julia felt the small comforts she had come to expect, once again, help to steady her racing mind. The laughter of the women, the cool, salty tang of the breeze, the warmth of the sun on her face. In just days it had become familiar and grounding, and reminders of Will aside, she felt herself settle back into the joy of the afternoon.

Immediately below them, waitstaff opened umbrellas and set tables on the restaurant balconies in anticipation of the lunch crowd. Harriet pointed out the cluster of tables on the topmost, private balcony and announced that was where they would be stopping to eat. In response, the women eagerly rushed back down the tower steps, anxious for shade, rest, and the promise of a world class meal.

The path from the castle ruins led past villas and restaurants on the outskirts of the town, down into a series of steps and cobblestoned back roads tucked between tightly packed houses. Laundry drying in the breeze snapped from heavily laden wash lines strung across the narrow alleys, and window boxes spilled flowers, livening the shadows. A tabby cat darted ten feet ahead of them, stopping on doorsteps and around corners to turn back and inspect their progress.

They snaked back and forth down the gently sloping lanes until they came out in a mob of people on *Via Roma*, the town's main street. To the right, people filed in and out of a focacceria, a butcher shop, a gelateria, and a fresh market. To the left, the buildings abruptly gave way to a large stone piazza overlooking the water. The women squeezed through the stream of traffic, turned left, and arrived a moment later at the Vernazza harbor.

Julia was certain she could stay on the harbor piazza for

years and never fully capture everything that made Vernazza, Vernazza. Alex was right, it was magic. A palpable energy buzzed around the piazza and shimmered out over the water of the crescent shaped harbor. For a moment, it was impossible to do anything but spin in a slow circle, ridiculous grin plastered on her face, and take it all in.

On the west side of the piazza, a church watched over the proceedings of the afternoon. Its cream stucco was peeling to reveal the aged, moss-covered stones underneath. As she stared, its bell tower chimed the hour, and for the first time on the trip, Julia's heart beat along harmoniously with the sound.

Vernazza was alive, and it was impossible not to feel alive in it. Every love story here must end happily ever after, Julia thought. She simply could *not* feel heartbroken here. Her worries of Will went out with the tide.

Harriet allowed the women a moment to revel in the scenery before motioning them to the elevated harbor walk and yet another stone staircase that climbed to the ruins of Vernazza's fort housing its signature restaurant.

The maître d, Magnus, met them at the entrance, greeted Harriet familiarly with an affectionate kiss on the cheek, and implored the group to follow him through the restaurant. Out the back doors, he led them up to the top balcony where the tables had already been laid with an abundance of appetizers. As they settled into place, Magnus introduced the dishes: anchovies three ways, steamed mussels, pan fried rings of calamari, caprese, charcuterie, and a steaming bowl of something including tentacles that Julia was surprised to hear called a 'salad.' Magnus brought bottles of sparkling water and liters of wine, and the women tucked in.

Perhaps it was the scenery. Perhaps it was because the events of the morning and the subsequent hike had left her hungrier than she'd been all week. The anchovies, pan seared, pickled, and sauteed in lemon and butter, went down bones and all—a magnificent, balanced, bite. The mussels and calamari, pulled fresh from the Mediterranean that morning, were tender and flavorful. Even the tentacles, which Magnus came back to clarify was octopus and part of a 'warm seafood salad' specific to Vernazza, became less daunting when smothered in butter and taken with the fresh basil and crusty bread served on the side.

By the time the appetizers were finished, Julia couldn't fathom taking another bite. Then the pasta dishes came out, and she found herself coerced to fill another plate. Tightly rolled trofie smothered in pesto from the Vernazzan hillside. Thin ribbons of pasta dyed midnight black with squid ink and tossed with prawns poached in butter. Tagliatelle with Bolognese. Spaghetti with clams. All handmade. All fresh from the sea. All paired with house wine.

When Magnus returned an hour later to inquire as to whether Harriet would like the fish course brought out, the women begged off. The only thing harder to imagine than taking another bite, Julia thought, was how they'd all make the walk to Monterosso with full stomachs. But fortunately, Harriet seemed content to linger, and though the dishes were cleared, they made no move to get up and leave.

"Well," asked Alex across the table, "was I right, or was I right? Is Vernazza not magical?"

Julia sipped her wine and breathed in the Mediterranean air. Vernazza smelled of salt, basil, wet stone, and cut grass. It was heaven. "It's perfect," she admitted.

"It's my favorite place to spend a day," Harriet agreed.

"If I would have gotten here sooner," Julia said. "I might not have left."

"Which would have been our loss," Harriet replied warmly.

"Besides, Harriet does it best," Alex agreed.

The women raised their glasses.

"To Harriet," Margo called. Glassware tinkled around the table. They drank deeply. "How did you manage to get this whole thing arranged?" Margo asked, setting down her glass. "The star treatment is impressive."

"Good point," said Alex, head snapping to Harriet. "You've never brought me here like this before."

Harriet's smile turned shy. "Magnus is a personal friend. He generously agrees to arrange it once a summer."

Lucy smirked. "A personal friend? Seems like you two were pretty comfortable with each other."

"I'm not discussing this with you, Mom. You know I haven't dated in years."

Lucy rolled her eyes and shook her head. Julia realized one small, unspoken detail of Harriet's past travels falling into place, and caught her eye. Harriet shrugged almost imperceptibly and settled back into her chair.

"Oh my God! Harriet!" Alex exclaimed, nudging her playfully.

Harriet stifled a grin. "It was a long time before I knew you."

"I don't need to know," Alex laughed. "Honestly, I never imagined talking about something like this with you."

When Magnus came back to the table to ask if anyone would like dessert, Maeve and Margo snorted into their water glasses. Another thirty minutes of heckling Harriet, including a final visit from Magnus during which he announced the restaurant would be closing to transition to dinner service, but the women were welcome to stay and siesta in the sun on the balcony, and the group was finally convinced to give up their perch over the town and start the trek to Monterosso al Mare.

They took the steps back to the harbor walk and started up Via Roma away from the water and toward the hills.

There was plenty of afternoon walking traffic to guide them to the popular azure trail leading west, and they passed the train station, a pirate bar, and the afternoon market carts before reaching the trailhead at the top of the village. Like the trail from Corniglia, the path was dusty and narrow, cut into the hillside where travel would have otherwise been impossible and overgrown in places by the wild greenery that cascaded down the cliffs on all sides. Hydrangea bushes taller than Lucy drooped over the trail as they climbed out of Vernazza. Butterflies, hummingbirds, and honeybees joined the flow of traffic in both directions buzzing from blossom to blossom.

For much of the first section of trail, they walked single file, pressed tight against the rock to make space for the hikers heading east to Vernazza. Walking alone, Julia imagined what the day might have looked like if things had played out differently. She didn't wonder what it would have been like to be there with Will. She wondered instead how things might have been had she not found these women, had Harriet never spoken up on the plane, had she not been on Alex's train out of Florence, had she kept her reservation in La Spezia. She laughed at herself for having worried that she would not be welcomed here. She pictured them relaxing in the waves on the beach that morning, sharing a five-star meal overlooking the village, trekking together along the coastal ridge. Staring at the backs of the bobbing heads in front of her, she couldn't remember feeling more accepted anywhere.

As the path leveled out, and the tangles of trees gave way to open expanses and panoramic vistas of the sea, they crowded together with those going the other way, everyone clamoring for a first or last glimpse at Vernazza from the famous overlook west of the village. Julia had always assumed the postcards she had seen of the town from this angle were heavily filtered and edited to enhance the natural beauty of the area. However, in the afternoon Mediterranean sunshine, she was surprised and pleased to find it looked exactly like the photos.

Vernazza disappeared behind a bend in the coastline, and Monterosso drew nearer ahead of them. The largest of the villages, Monterosso was framed in front by a white sand beach stretching the entire length of its shore. Though it seemed impossible that such views were becoming commonplace, Julia noted expectantly that this harbor front also consisted of colorful shop fronts and a stuccoed church tower rising above the rooftops. On the hillside above the town, a hermitage and columbarium looked out over the sea.

The final stretch of path turned into a boardwalk that came out level with the beach, wrapping around the sand and depositing the women in yet another piazza ringed with restaurants and overlooking the water. Before they could set off to explore, however, there was the business of Anthony's ashes. Beth had been quiet as they approached the city, and she now gazed at the Punta Mesco, an overlook above the village, an unreadable mix of emotions on her face.

"We can come with you," Harriet said quietly, laying a hand on her shoulder. "Or we'll wait for you at the harbor and you can meet up with us again when you're ready."

"I don't know," said Beth. "I can't imagine climbing up there myself, and I can't imagine having an audience as I say goodbye."

"We'll come with you as far as you want us," Harriet assured her. "You tell us when you're ready to go on alone."

At the far end of the beach, they found a road that switched back and forth, eventually meeting up with another walking trail that took them past an enormous sculpture of a man built into the side of the cliff. He appeared to be falling forward, head down, legs buckling, as if someone from above was driving him to his knees.

"*Il gigante*," Harriet pointed out as they filed by.

The procession continued in silence.

They reached the columbarium, it's white marble walls holding the interred remains of hundreds of Monterossan citizens dating back five generations. There, the path ran out at a grassy hill that sloped up to Punta Mesco. Dotted with trees, the women walked toward the summit through dappled sunshine.

Julia watched Beth, wondering what one thought in the moments before saying goodbye for the last time. She hoped that the moment brought her some sense of closure. Closure, she thought, might prompt the forgiveness Beth needed. Closure, Julia realized, was something she was still seeking as well.

Beth stopped next to a twisted olive trunk three hundred yards from the summit. "I'll go on from here," she said, turning back to the women.

Harriet nodded, and the group crowded into the shade of the trees and watched as Beth proceeded farther out on the peninsula with Anthony tucked in her red backpack.

They watched as Beth reached the top of the hill, unpacked a small canister from her bag, and stood facing the water. Julia held her breath. A moment later, a dusty cloud appeared in front of Beth drifting out and away from the point. She stood watching it float on the breeze, then returned the container to her backpack and headed back down the hill toward the group.

Julia was unsure what she expected, but Beth looked almost unaffected. Eyes dry. Face calm.

"How was it?" Harriet asked gently as she approached.

Beth's brow furrowed. "Is it wrong that I expected to feel more?" she asked guiltily. "I thought there'd be this poignant moment. That I'd feel him with me. I know it's what he wanted, and I'm not sorry I brought him here, but I just feel…"

"Relieved?" Harriet asked.

"Lighter?" offered Alex.

"Empty," Beth said, heaving an unexpected sob as she did so. She covered her eyes, and the tears unspilled in the previous moment, now poured forth.

Harriet pulled her into a tight embrace. "You're not empty," she reassured her. "You're tired. Cried out. Numb. You have a heart full of love, and a mind full of memories. That's not empty."

Empty, Julia realized, might actually be an easier way to be. It was the remembering that hurt. If only memories were shed as easily as tears. Moving on would be as easy as a few good cries.

The rest of the women crowded around, all reassuring Beth she did the right thing and that Anthony was watching over her now, proud of her devotion. Beth hugged them each in turn, coming last to Julia, whom she held an extra moment.

"I'm sorry," Julia whispered.

"I'm not," Beth sighed, her voice stronger. "He's at peace, free, finally. And now, I can work on the same for myself and my sons. I hope you find some as well."

"How will you start?" Julia asked, drawing back. "Maybe I should follow your lead?"

"We just continue to live, and hope each day brings us a little closer to being whole." Beth looked down the hill back toward Monterosso al Mare wistfully. "It's amazing to think that the people who live here do anything other than sit on the beach and eat gelato all day," she mused. "Every village is different, and yet somehow every village boils down to sea views, restaurants, and gelato. It's like a recipe for Italian life." She took a deep, trembling breath, smiled, and looked back at Julia. "So, we've had two of the three, today. Who wants ice cream?"

~

THE REMAINDER of the afternoon in Monterosso was a blur of beaches, ice cream, cobblestone streets, and shopping. Harriet played tour guide from stop to stop showing off the finest local artisans, wine makers, shopkeepers, and hidden gems of the village.

In a tiny, sweltering art studio off the beach walk, they watched stained glass being set in beautiful, intricate, mosaics of blues and greens. At a road side table next to an ancient millstone, they tasted oils and vinegars on tiny silver spoons. An enormous Italian man holding a violin that looked comically tiny in his massive hands invited them into a crumbling church to listen to his string quartet rehearse Vivaldi.

Wandering on her own during a brief break in the activities, Julia found herself again in front of a jewelry store window, longingly staring at the Italian gold settings.

"Thinking of a souvenir?" Alex asked, coming up beside her.

"I don't know," admitted Julia. "They're beautiful, and I just gave back my best piece."

"So why don't you pick something out?"

Julia considered, eyes not meeting Alex's. "The truth?" she asked, embarrassed. "I've never bought myself jewelry before. I mean, I have, but not like this. Good jewelry. 'Real' jewelry. I'm trying to decide if doing it now would make me feel better, or worse."

"A piece to remind you of the trip, Olive Haven, everything you overcame to get here. That's positive."

"But a piece to remind me of the honeymoon..." Julia's thumb brushed over the empty spot on her ring finger.

"It's not the honeymoon anymore," Alex insisted. "You made it yours. Celebrate that."

Julia sighed, remembering with some satisfaction the moment the notebook had fallen from her hand. "So, you think I should get jewelry?"

"Get whatever you want," Alex looked through the glass at the display. "If it was jewelry, what would you buy?"

"I'm not sure," Julia admitted. They were all beautiful, but nothing stood out as meaningful.

"You'll know it when you see it," Alex said. "Having something tangible to remind you that you're moving on can help, even in just the tiniest way. A step forward."

"Did you?" Julia finally turned to meet Alex's eyes.

Alex nodded.

"What was yours?" Julia asked.

Alex turned her arm revealing a small ampersand tattooed at her wrist.

"And?" Julia asked.

"Yes," Alex said with a smile. "Have you ever heard of 'yes and?' In improv or acting you're not allowed to say no, only to accept what is offered and build upon it further."

"So, Sam died..."

"Yes, and," Alex cut in, "I kept on living."

"Yes, and you met Danny."

"And Harriet."

"And me," Julia said, a lump forming in her throat. "I get it. Thank you, Alex."

Alex pulled Julia into a hug. "Yes, *and* now you're probably stuck with me. I have no interest in a forever goodbye at the end of the trip." Her voice was thick with emotion.

"Me either," Julia assured her. She looked back at the jewelry display. "It's not here," she said with certainty. But she would find it, she thought, assuredly. She had already found so much else here.

～

BY THE TIME the sun began to sink toward the horizon and Harriet led the women back toward the main beach where they met their boat back to Porto Venere, they were sun tanned, salt sprayed, and enchanted by the day.

They returned to Olive Haven as the sky faded to lavender then violet. The now familiar villa looked and felt like home as they came up the driveway after a long day of touring. Julia climbed the curved staircase to her room, looking forward to cleaning up before dinner and the conversations that would flow late into the night. She kicked off her shoes, tossed her backpack on the chair, and went to the bathroom door to start the shower. Locked.

Surprised, Julia walked back around the bed to the night-stand where she picked up her phone automatically, forgetting any misgivings about accidentally scrolling to Will. The motion triggered the screen and revealed seventeen notifications. The first eight were panicked texts from Ellie. Julia went very still. A sharp pressure formed in her chest. For a moment she couldn't breathe. Couldn't speak.

Her bedroom door was open to the hallway.

"Alex," she called in as even a voice as she could muster.

Alex appeared in the doorway. Her sweaty hair clung to her forehead, and she had yet to change out of her dusty walking clothes. When she saw Julia, her brow furrowed instantly in concern. "What's wrong?" she asked.

Julia held out her phone, unlocked but undisturbed from the home screen. "What is this?" she asked, her voice hitching slightly.

"I warned you not to look," Alex exclaimed, taking a step closer, her hand reaching for the phone.

"I didn't," Julia said, shaking her head. "I mean, I wasn't thinking about it...just...look, please."

Alex took the phone and swiped up, revealing the full set of notifications and messages. Julia watched her eyes dart along the screen. After a moment, Alex lowered the phone, extending it half-heartedly back to Julia.

"My best guess," she said cautiously, "is that if you open your social media, you'll likely find that Will has shared some news."

Julia's heart hammered. Her pulse pounded behind her ears, and her body became insufferably warm all over. "You're guessing or you know?"

"Well, I didn't look if that's what you're asking."

"What is it?" Julia asked it quietly, though her nerves screamed.

Alex looked back at the phone but didn't reply.

"Alex," Julia pleaded. "Is he getting married?" The idea struck her as ludicrous even as she said the words, yet given the circumstances, anything seemed possible.

Julia watched Alex visibly relax.

"No," Alex said assuredly. "He's not getting married."

"Then what?"

Alex didn't meet Julia's eyes.

"Alex?"

Alex raised the cell phone again, and Julia watched as she opened her social media feed and scrolled through the recent updates. She glanced up nervously at Julia.

"Tell me," Julia said quietly.

"Just look," Alex said, turning the phone around.

"I don't want to see it," said Julia, quickly looking away.

"You think I want to tell you?" Alex asked. The pain was clear in her voice. "Okay," she said, coming farther into the room and guiding Julia to the edge of the bed. They sat down. Alex held the phone face down on her lap, still open to whatever Will had posted. She took a deep breath. "I'll tell you, and then we'll go pour a glass of wine and do whatever it is you need to do to process."

"Just tell me," Julia said, closing her eyes.

Alex looked down at the phone screen again.

"She's pregnant," she said, finally. The words hit Julia like bullets.

"What?" she breathed incredulously.

Alex held up the phone. There on the beach was Will and Erica. His arms wrapped around her waist, hands resting on her stomach where they were posed in the shape of a heart at her belly button. The start of a baby bump was clearly evident between the pieces of her royal blue bikini. Julia did not need to read the caption to know it was true. Her stomach heaved, and she jumped from the bed, afraid she was going to be sick.

"Julia?" Alex stood up immediately.

"I need some air," Julia managed, stumbling into her sandals.

"Julia?" Alex tried again.

"I can't breathe." Julia said through gasps, tears blurring the doorway then the hallway in front of her.

"Harriet!" Alex called as she trailed Julia down the stairs to the front entry.

Julia threw open the door and staggered onto the porch. The last rays of evening sun bathed the front yard in gold, a scene that would have been breathtakingly beautiful if Julia had breath left to take, but she was already emptied out, gutted. In moments of crisis, Harriet had said, most people think they want to be alone, but they really want to be surrounded by people who understand them. She knew that Alex wanted to help, that everyone would sit around and talk for hours if it meant seeing her through this. But how could anyone understand this? She didn't even understand this. For this, she needed to be alone.

"Julia?" Harriet's voice echoed from the kitchen. Alex intercepted her in the entryway, phone still in hand, hastily trying to explain.

Julia didn't wait for Alex to finish. She stepped off the porch into the golden evening and took off down the driveway.

CHAPTER 18

Whom she reached the road, Julia kicked at the stones, hugged her arms to herself and began to cry. The tears fell fast and hard, dripping into the dust where she stood.

She turned and began to walk slowly down the hill toward the village. Mopeds and bicycles zipped past her, throwing dust out behind them. It drifted and glittered in the evening sunbeams. She walked for a few minutes before she heard a voice behind her.

"Julia?" Harriet called. "Julia!"

Julia took a shaking breath and turned around, tears still streaming down her face. Harriet had stopped a few paces behind her, but now stepped forward, arms open. Julia hesitated a moment before closing the gap between them and collapsed against her, crying onto her shoulder. They stayed that way for a long moment. Harriet pulled back, reaching up to brush the tears from each cheek.

"Come with me," she said. She took Julia by the hand, and they walked silently back to Olive Haven, up the driveway, and across the lawn to the bench beneath the ancient olive tree. They sat down. Julia dropped her head into her hands, fresh tears pouring forth.

A long moment passed.

"Olive trees carried so much cultural and spiritual significance in Mediterranean life that people just started using the fruit as a name," Harriet said casually, breaking the silence. "And of course, it's a biblical name that doesn't sound like a name from the Bible, so you probably could have ended up an Olive."

Julia looked up. "What?" she asked through sobs, her brow furrowed in confusion.

"I actually don't think the name Olive is in there," Harriet admitted, "but the tree is. I mean that dove came back with an olive branch from somewhere." She stopped and looked at Julia who dropped her head back into her hands.

She was *not* in the mood for metaphors. There wasn't a metaphor for adulterous, ex-fiancé announces his mistress's pregnancy the week after his would-have-been wedding. It just was what it was. Devastating.

Harriet continued, unabashed. "Well, ever since then we've been talking about olive trees and reconciliation and friendship and compromise and peace. But do you want to know what I thought about the first time I saw this tree?" She ran a hand lovingly over the bark. "I thought about Jack."

Julia didn't look up. She didn't want another story of love and loss. She didn't want to hear about the great love of Harriet's life. She got it. Jack and Harriet had a wonderful relationship. She and Will did *not*. End of story. No need to pile it on.

Harriet sighed. "This tree is 800 years old if you believe Bernardo. It's been the constant on this property for centuries. Seasons changed. Owners changed. The whole world changed around it, and the tree just kept on growing. When the house was built, they had to work around it. You don't dig up an 800-year-old olive tree." She surveyed the yard. "Now I have this beautiful house, these perfect gardens, a paradise, but when you walk up the driveway, what's the first thing you notice? This tree. You can't ignore it. It demands your attention. It sets the tone for everything around it. I named the house after it."

The women sat in silence, leaves rustling above them. Harriet turned to Julia.

"If we're lucky," she went on, "we get a handful of people in our lives who help define us. We find them, we become rooted in them, and we are better because of them. My marriage to Jack is an 800-year-old olive tree in my life, Julia. Everything was oriented around it. Seasons changed. The world changed. But there it was. Solid. Secure. When he passed, I thought, at some point, that would dissipate into the background of my story, but it never did. You can't dig up an 800-year-old olive tree."

Julia leaned back, the trunk of the tree solid behind her. She closed her eyes, silent tears still leaking down her cheeks. "Are you telling me that Will was my 800-year-old tree? And because I can't cut him out of my life, I just have to accept he'll always be there, tormenting me, mocking me, forcing my attention..." she broke down bitterly, dropping her head back into her hands.

"No," Harriet said patiently. "I know it doesn't feel this way now, Julia, but this is a passing storm. It's not the end. Give it time, and one day you'll realize there's an 800-year-old olive tree in your front yard bearing witness to your whole life, and it won't be Will."

"How do you know?" Julia asked, a muffled sob.

"When Jack died, I cried a lot. I went to therapy. I questioned everything." She folded her hands, and leaned forward, elbows on her knees. "The thing about grieving a husband is that while part of you mourns the absence and all the time you didn't get together, you also have the memories of what was to comfort you. They're with you all the time. They can sustain you. You don't doubt them. They're solid. You make wedding vows, until death do us part, and then when the time comes, it's heartbreaking, but in a tragically romantic way, you've also kept your promise. You signed up for that finale together."

She laid a hand tenderly on Julia's back.

"You're not tethered to something like that, Julia. The thing you can't look past right now is a tragedy. It's heartbreak. But it's not solid; it's not secure."

Julia turned to look at Harriet, her face wet with tears.

"You're lost in the grief of what-could-have-beens," Harriet continued. "You doubt everything you thought you had, everything you thought you knew. You didn't sign up for this. Will made a choice to leave. But before he ever left, he made a choice to walk away from what you had, or at least what you thought you had. You lived the illusion until he told you the truth, and the illusion is what you lost as well." She brushed the back of her hand across Julia's cheeks, wiping at tears. "You can't compare your grief about that, to the grief of the women you've met this week, and I doubt a single one of them would trade their pain for yours."

Julia took a deep breath. "I can't believe he didn't tell me." Her voiced wobbled. "He told me there had been someone else, told me he had broken it off months ago. Why not tell me this? How could he just leave this out?"

"Do you want to give him the benefit of the doubt?" Harriet asked earnestly.

"What? No," Julia wailed.

Harriet crossed her legs and leaned back against the tree. "Let me play devil's advocate then. What if he didn't know? Maybe he did leave this woman months ago, only to reconnect with her after calling off the wedding and learning then that she was pregnant."

"That's a stretch," said Julia with a scoff, rolling her eyes.

"Maybe," Harriet shrugged. "So, let's not give him the benefit of the doubt. In that case, would telling you at the church have made any difference?"

Julia froze. "What do you mean?"

"Not to put too fine a point on it, but he stopped your wedding, as you came down the aisle, to let you know he couldn't marry you because he'd had an affair." Julia flinched, but Harriet continued, undeterred. "In that moment, would knowing he also got that woman pregnant have changed anything? And since he didn't tell you then, after you left the church, when would have been the appropriate time to call and let you know?"

"Why are you defending him?" Julia moaned.

"I'm not defending him," Harriet assured her. "The thing is, Will did something to hurt you. It's a terrible thing that you didn't deserve, and your hurt and anger is real and justified. However, in the moment he told you, would it have somehow been better if he piled it all on? Does it change anything?"

"I wouldn't have been blindsided." Julia offered.

Harriet reached over and took Julia's hand. "Grief will blindside you no matter how prepared you think you are, Julia. I had twelve years to prepare for Jack to leave, and it's been twelve years since. Even now I find there are moments where the pain takes my breath away. It comes in waves you can't escape."

"So, what can I do?" Julia asked softly.

"Who says there's anything to do?"

"Well, I can't just stay here forever. What happens when I go home?"

"The truth?" Harriet's eyes were kind, but her tone was direct. "You want to know what happens when you go home? You'll have to face this...head on. You're going to go to the condo with boxes and bags, and you're going to pack up your things. You're going to have to see Will. Maybe not then and there, but one day, there he'll be on the train, or at the grocery store, or walking his dog with his new baby. In the moment, you'll believe these things will destroy you. But then they'll pass, and the more time that passes, the more you'll realize that it doesn't hold your attention quite as much, and you'll start to rebuild."

Julia looked up through the branches, catching glimpses of an evening sky water colored in pinks and purples. She heaved a sigh. "I'm not ready for it," she admitted.

"You never will be," Harriet said quietly. "And yet, you're going to find a way to do it regardless. I've seen you come back to life the past few days, Julia. You forget I saw you on the plane that first night, caught you crying in the bathroom. You found something here, same as I did."

"What?"

"The will to live."

Julia stared at Harriet, confused.

"I was never going to..."

Harriet shook her head.

"That's not what I mean. I mean *really* live, remember? Experience beauty, seek joy, revel a bit. Isn't that what you want? Didn't you have it here, at least for a moment? Don't let Will take that from you again."

Footsteps on the driveway behind them turned both their attention. Alex came down from the house, two glasses of wine in hand.

"It looks like you've got someone else coming to offer

counsel," said Harriet, standing up. She laid a hand gently on Julia's shoulder. "One day, you may realize that though misguided in his methods and timing, Will actually did you a favor. But that day isn't going to be today, and no one expects you to be okay right now."

Alex stopped a few paces from the bench and exchanged glances with Harriet who touched her arm affectionately before starting up toward the villa.

"Want some company?" she asked. She walked to the bench and held out a wine glass. Julia took it gratefully. "You know, I don't even like olives, but I love this tree."

"So does Harriet," said Julia. "It reminds her of Jack because it's permanent and holds her attention."

Alex watched an ant climb along the trunk.

"Huh, well I guess that makes sense," she replied.

"Will certainly knows how to get my attention," Julia muttered.

"But he's not permanent," Alex said gently.

"No, he's not," Julia agreed with a heavy sigh. She bent over, elbows on her knees. "When I started this trip, I felt Will everywhere," she said. "I could imagine what it would be like to have him here. It followed me around Florence. Even when I thought I had out run it, something would happen, and he'd come rushing back at me." She sipped her wine, lost in thought. "I thought the hardest part about losing him was seeing him missing from all the little parts of life we were supposed to do together." She choked back fresh tears. "But now I realize that's not the worst of it." She hesitated.

"What is?" prompted Alex.

"It's that he's out there," she paused, waving her hand to the world beyond, "living the life *we* were supposed to share with someone else. I'm not just imagining him missing from the scene; he's in the scene with someone else. My possibilities are someone else's reality. She is going to step into the life I was making, and I'm just supposed to figure out how to start over." Her voice wavered, and she swallowed hard.

Alex nodded thoughtfully. "Yep," she took a drink. "Starting over sucks."

"That's all you're going to say?"

Alex shrugged. "It's the truth. Take it from someone who knows."

"How did you do it?" Julia asked earnestly.

Alex's brow furrowed, and she stared at the ground. "Mine was different. When I married Sam, I knew I'd be his forever, but I also knew he wouldn't be forever for me. We were twenty-two. He wanted a wedding, and I knew I could give that to him, but I also knew he couldn't give me a life together." She turned to Julia. "When you say the vows," she continued thoughtfully, "you know you're promising the good and the bad, the sickness and the health. But truthfully, with Sam, I knew that I was really just signing up for the worst of it. He was already sick. The prognosis was already bad." Alex took a shaky breath. "I loved him, and he's always going to be part of my story, but it wasn't like what Jack and Harriet promised. He was never going to be permanent."

"But with Danny..." Julia's voice trailed off.

Alex took a deep breath. "Danny and I could promise whole futures to each other," she offered. "It felt different from the very beginning, and if I lost Danny now, that would feel different too. There's so much hope wrapped up in what we want for our lives. I get it; to lose all those possibilities would hurt the most."

The sun sank behind the villa throwing long shadows across the yard. Despite the balminess of the summer evening, Julia hugged her arms to herself, rubbing away goosebumps.

"How did you know you were ready, to move on I mean?" she asked after a long moment.

"I didn't," Alex looked at Julia seriously. "I took baby steps. Like calling Harriet instead of spending hours on social media. Going back to work. Applying to grad school. I almost backed out that summer before I moved. It's part of what prompted Harriet to invite me here."

Julia sighed and fidgeted with her wine glass. "I might have skipped a few baby steps by jumping on a plane and going straight to international travel."

Alex nodded. "I mean, I think you're a total badass for packing up and leaving, but you did miss all the good breakup parts."

"*Good* breakup parts?" Julia scoffed.

"Maybe good is the wrong word. Indulgent? Self-care? Like, you live in your pajamas and watch your favorite sad movies, and eat your weight in Ben and Jerry's, and get together with your girl friends to bad mouth your ex. Did you get to call him horrible names yet? Because I don't even know the guy, but I'd be all for going back to that stage and helping you through it."

Julia rolled her eyes. "This isn't a romantic comedy,"

"No, it's a tragedy," Alex confirmed. "You deserved to treat it as such, and you jumped on a plane and tried to make everything fine."

Julia felt the truth of the words hit home. She had sought control, tried to follow the plan, forced herself ahead even when things had gone awry. She thought about Florence, how she had been insistent it would be the next stop, the next sight, the next checkmark on the list that would make things better. When she left, she was certain La Spezia would make the difference. When it hadn't, she had turned to Alex. Finding Olive Haven had brought brighter days, but even here, Harriet had pushed her to sit and be with her feelings, and she had done very little of it. The pain wouldn't be denied any further.

They sat on the bench in silence sipping their wine and watching the evening shadows deepen.

"What do I do now?" Julia asked quietly.

"Do?" Alex replied.

"About Will."

"Julia, there's nothing to *do* about Will. He's where he is with who he wants to be with."

Julia grimaced.

"I'm sorry," said Alex. "But it's the truth. What you do now has everything to do with you, and I can't answer that for you." She finished her wine, stood, and looked up through the leaves of the tree. "I want you to find your answer though. We all do."

They were quiet for a long moment.

"You know what I do love about olive trees?" Alex smiled at the branches overhead.

"What?" Julia asked, following Alex's gaze.

"The shade. Haven't you noticed? It's the best place to rest." She squeezed Julia's shoulder and turned back toward the house.

Julia sat beneath the tree a long time, thinking about Will, the baby, the illusion of the past five months, the wedding that was never going to happen. It was over, she realized, long before she ever walked down that aisle. Yet, for some, unknown, cruel and selfish reason, he had let her live the lie until the very last moment. It tore new holes in her heart, and sobs wracked her chest.

She thought of the places she had pictured him in Florence, recognizing now it was all a charade; he was never going to be there. She remembered, foolishly, how much she had worried over Luca, the dance, and the kiss. At the time, she had compared herself to Will and his affair. It seemed ridiculous given the recent revelation. At least now, she felt easily compelled to forgive herself for the transgression. It brought her just a shred of comfort.

Forgiving Will, however, seemed even more impossible now than it had this afternoon.

The yard grew dark. Crickets chirped in the background. Fireflies rose out of the grass. Her sobs turned to silent tears rolling down her cheeks.

Julia left the bench and turned back toward the house. The windows glowed cheerfully. It was a perfect summer evening, in a perfect Italian paradise, after a perfect day of Mediterranean living, but it wasn't enough. It couldn't erase the truth with which she now wrestled. It couldn't hold together the pieces of a broken life.

From the back of the house, the murmur of voices and a burst of laughter punctuated the stillness of the scene. Part of Julia longed to join the women, dive into a meal and conversation. If she stepped onto the terrace, they would offer to sit and talk, help her through it, ask the right questions and offer sympathy in the right places. It would be comforting, but it could no longer fill the hole. It wouldn't erase the hurt that now demanded to be felt.

She crossed the yard, walked through the front door, and went quietly up to her room. Closing the door behind her, she collapsed on the bed, burying her face in the duvet, letting the tears leak out again. She startled when, a moment later, a voice echoed through the bathroom. She sat up quickly, brushing the tears from her face. Across the bathroom, Aster stood in the doorway of her bedroom, staring through to where Julia lay on the bed.

For all Julia had wondered about her reclusive neighbor, she had no interest in making new friends tonight. She pushed herself from the bed and moved to the door. The women stared at each other across the darkened space between them.

"I'm sorry we haven't met sooner, I'm Aster," she began.

Julia stared at her blankly. She felt nothing, no curiosity, no compassion, no obligation to return the greeting. Given her absence all week, Julia thought, Aster, of all people, should understand. Numb, she lowered her eyes, reached over, and, with a thud, closed her door between them.

CHAPTER 19

Despite it being their final full day in Porto Venere, and despite Alex insisting it was a festival day and not to be missed, Julia begged off the group tour the next morning. She lay in bed listening to the chatter and laughter of the women gathering in front of the house to walk into town for the morning ceremonies and tried to capture an ounce of their joy. Just a day ago she felt so close to it. This morning, however, her head hurt and her heart ached.

Alex had been right to suggest that leaving as quickly as she did, robbed her of a deserved breakdown. Today, she embraced the opportunity to wallow. She spent a long night dissecting the intricacies of her relationship, looking for signs, remembering when things were good and uncomplicated. In light of the past twelve hours, it was hard to believe they ever had been. The insecurities Will had expressed, the reassurances she had given him, the time spent apart while he traveled, it all felt heavier. She replayed every fight, every disagreement, wondering which was the moment he decided to give it all up.

Somewhere around two in the morning, she started scrolling through photos. For hours she swiped through pictures from birthdays, trips, events. She analyzed the scrunch of his eyes, the stretch of his smile, waiting to see something different, a hint that things were not as they had once been. She stared at herself. She looked happy. She tried to remember how it felt to be in love, certain and secure. As the earliest morning light illuminated her window, she deleted the first of the photos. Dozens followed. She ached to watch them disappear, tears falling as each one vanished from the screen.

Her future was gone, and her past disappeared too.

Now, as she listened to the voices of the group fading down the driveway, she lay, staring out the window, exhausted. The birds chirped, and the leaves of the olive tree rustled in the wind. Bernardo whistled through the yard, watering the gardens. It sounded like a glorious morning, but Julia ignored it all. Pulling the blanket over her head, she drifted into an uneasy sleep.

When she woke sometime later, she felt weak and empty, as if she had endured a long night of illness. The yard was quiet, and she wasn't sure how much time had passed. She lay still, listening for any sign of movement or conversation in the house. Her empty stomach grumbled in reply. Ignoring it, she rolled over to stare out the window. Part of her wished she had never left the hotel in Chicago. Another part wished she never had to go back.

She wouldn't go to the festival, she decided. There was so much more satisfaction in unapologetic self-pity. She may not even get out of bed.

After fifteen minutes, however, her rumbling stomach refused to be disregarded, and she got up, wrapped herself in a robe, and made her way through the empty house to the kitchen. On the counter she found a note in Harriet's neat, loopy cursive.

Good morning!
Please find breakfast and lunch prepared for you in the
refrigerator. We will be
back at 6:00 before the Festival of Lights.
If you're up to it, I hope you'll consider joining us.

The clock on the stove showed it was already 12:30, so Julia passed over the breakfast platter of pastries and berries and found a container of creamy risotto with instructions for reheating taped to the lid. After brief consideration, she returned the dish to the refrigerator. She opened the freezer, found a cardboard tub of chocolate gelato, and took it out onto the terrace. She stretched out, legs propped up on a second chair, and ate the ice cream while warming herself in the early afternoon sun.

She let her mind wander back to Will, raw emotion threatening to upend the fragile peace of the terrace. She opened up her social media feed, scrolled to his pictures from his trip, and studied his expression. His eyes matched the turquoise water, and they crinkled where his genuine grin reached them in the corners. His sandy hair was bleached by the sun and lightly tousled in a carefree way he rarely wore at home. He looked lighter, she thought. Lighter than she'd seen him in some time. Lighter than he looked in so many of the photos she had deleted. She realized that while she'd imagined Will with her on the trip, she'd never imagined him like this: free, relaxed, casual. Her Will was brooding, intense, passionate. Harriet's words from the night before drifted into her thoughts. Someday there would be someone else. Perhaps he had done her a favor.

Julia closed the app, returned the ice cream container to

the freezer, and padded upstairs to her room. She washed her face, put up her hair, and found her favorite navy-blue shorts and a white cotton t-shirt. She debated crawling back under the covers, but the ice cream had revived her spirits slightly, and sunshine streamed through the window invitingly. After a moment, she decided to go down to the olive tree. Having already resolved to sit and be with her feelings today, Harriet's favorite spot seemed as good a place as any.

As she approached the bench, however, she found it already occupied.

"Hello?" Julia asked cautiously.

Aster peered around the base of the trunk. Julia froze. She was dressed in black leggings, a black, v-neck t-shirt, and wrapped in a flowery silk kimono; her gold earrings and bracelet shimmered in the filtered sunlight beneath the tree. Her bob cut was expertly straightened and styled, and her blue eyes and sharp cheekbones made her look both dramatic and refined despite not a trace of makeup on her face. If Julia hadn't known better from their previous interactions, she would have guessed her to be completely put together and at ease.

"Julia," Aster said, surprised. "Maeve mentioned you may be staying back today."

"Yeah... I," Julia hesitated. "I wasn't really feeling up to the festivities."

Aster looked away bashfully. "You may have noticed that I haven't really been feeling up to this entire trip. So, you're in good company."

"I'm sorry about last night," Julia said awkwardly. "It wasn't my proudest moment."

Aster shook her head. "I'm afraid I wasn't the epitome of welcoming this week either."

"Well, I guess we're even then," Julia smiled weakly. "I'm sorry to have bothered you." She turned toward the house.

"Would you care to join me?" Aster blurted, her pitch rising slightly.

Julia turned back to find that Aster had slid to one side of the bench to make room for her. She gestured toward the empty space, and her hand trembled. Julia wasn't certain she wanted company, but her curiosity was stronger than her need for solitude.

"Why not," she said, moving to the end of the bench.

"I'm glad to have a chance to meet you," Aster said after Julia had settled in. "I'm sorry to have been so standoffish. It's been difficult..." she trailed off, staring across the lawn.

Julia followed her gaze, uncertain how to respond. "I'm sorry about Timothy and Arthur," she finally offered. "Maeve told me. To lose them both so close together, I can't imagine what that was like. It sounded like the four of you were very close."

Something passed over Aster's face. "Like you wouldn't imagine. This trip, to be here alone with Maeve, I'm not sure why I thought it was a good idea." She looked sadly down at her hands.

"I've been wondering about that for myself this morning," Julia admitted.

Aster looked up. "Yes, Maeve's told me about your honeymoon gone wrong."

"As of yesterday," Julia took a deep breath, "I would call it a honeymoon gone wrong, gone right, and then gone wrong again."

"Well, it sounds like we both need cheering up, so why don't you start by telling me what went right?"

Julia leaned back, looking out at the beauty around her. "Not the honeymoon part," she admitted, "but this part. Finding my way here. It felt right. Hearing the stories of the group, having them play a part in mine, it was nice to have the company."

"You think that part helped?" Aster pursed her lips. "Telling the stories?"

Julia nodded slowly. "I do," she said. "It was nice to share; for much of the week, it made things easier. You're lucky you had your sister here with you. Even without joining the group, you still had somebody."

"Yes," Aster said quietly. "But having her here makes my story untellable." The yard seemed to still. "I was hoping to run into you this morning," she went on. "From what Maeve has told me, I know of all the people on this trip, you are the one who needs to hear my story the most, and I thought this would be the moment to do it with the rest of the women away. But now that you're sitting in front of me, I don't think I can ask you to bear the burden after all." She pushed herself up from the bench and turned toward the house.

Julia's curiosity flared and she reached out a hand to stop Aster's retreat. "Aster," she said softly. "I understand you barely know me, but if you think it would help, I'm a willing audience if you want one."

Aster looked at Julia sadly. "You don't know what you're agreeing to," she said.

"Maybe not," Julia admitted. "But I'm here, nevertheless."

Aster waited a long moment. The silence was heavy all around them. "I want you to know," she said finally, "I'm not proud of any of this. Saying it out loud, well, it puts it into the world in a way that I won't be able to control anymore. Yet, perhaps against reason, I'm going to tell you because you walked into this trip as the person most apt to hear it."

Julia waited with bated breath, and Aster crossed her legs and settled the kimono around herself back on the other end of the bench. She picked nervously at the edges of a well-manicured, lavender fingernail.

"Everyone knew Timothy Bailey when we were in high school. He was the classic, all-American, hometown hero.

Traditional good looks. Captain of the baseball team. His family had old money and was well-connected in all the important social circles. So, no one was more surprised than me the day he walked up before third period and asked if I wanted to go for a milkshake after school." She glanced at Julia. "I wasn't the most popular," she explained. "I wasn't the best looking. I was an honor student and played clarinet in the band. I thought it was a joke that someone had put him up to."

"But," she shrugged and held up her hands as if the reality of the moment still surprised her, "when I walked out the front doors that afternoon, there he was, leaning up against his car. We went to the restaurant, and he ordered two malts. We sat in a booth, and he tried to make small talk, but I was still skeptical and made it difficult on him."

She sighed. "It didn't take all that long for him to admit that he needed a French tutor, and I was top of the class. I wasn't surprised, but somehow it still hurt. Some part of me wanted to believe that I was worth more than that to him." She took a steadying breath.

"So, you tutored him?" Julia guessed.

Aster looked at her, surprised. "I most certainly did *not*," she said with indignation. "That's how people expect the story to go though, isn't it? Somewhere over a milkshake and a French textbook we fell in love and the rest was history." She shook her head. "It wasn't that way for us. I told him I would tutor him if he could show me he was able to at least translate a simple phrase. I scribbled it across a napkin and waited. He stared at it for a long time, got this lopsided grin on his face, and told me I'd just proven why he needed a tutor. Then he sat there waiting for me to agree with him. I did agree, but it wasn't going to be me. So, he found another tutor, and his French did improve, but I think it always bothered him that I'd turned him down first. Even then, Timothy was used to getting his own way."

Aster clasped her hands, pinning them between her knees. "When we graduated, I stayed home to start a secretarial position at the law office where my father worked. Timothy would come home from college on some weekends and over the holidays, but we saw each other only in group settings. I dated occasionally, but nothing serious, and he occasionally brought a girl along to an event, but nothing serious. A good stretch passed where I lost track of him all together. Then one summer, who walked into the law office as intern clerks?" A flicker of a smile pulled at the corner of her mouth. "Timothy Bailey along with his best friend from law school Arthur Kennedy.

Timothy saw me and that lopsided grin spread across his face. He walked over, kissed my hand, and in perfect French said, '*C'est trop beau pour être vrai.*' I couldn't help but melt a little because it was the same simple phrase he'd been helpless to translate years earlier."

She hesitated and leaned back against the tree. Already, Julia had a million questions, but dared not interject lest it stall the momentum of the story.

"When he asked me to dinner there was only one caveat," Aster continued, "that Arthur came along on a double date. I agreed, though I didn't know at the time it would be Maeve. I didn't even know that Maeve and Arthur had met. So, the four of us went to dinner. Arthur was charming and charismatic, and it was clear Maeve was smitten. Timothy was kind, asked thoughtful questions, and took the check at the end of the night. He drove us home and kissed me softly on the cheek in front of my parent's house while Maeve and Arthur made out in the backseat of the car."

She rolled her eyes at the memory, and Julia stifled a laugh.

"The four of us became inseparable, and when their internship ended at the end of the summer, Maeve and I would drive to Georgetown together on the weekends to visit them at law school. After ten months, Arthur and Maeve were engaged. Timothy proposed three months later. It surprised no one. My parents were thrilled. And I was thrilled too," she hesitated, "mostly."

Julia glanced over to find Aster turned away, worrying at the edging of her robe.

"Like all relationships we had our ups and downs. Timothy was so serious. He felt the pressure of his parent's expectations. He had aspirations to edit the law review and entertained the idea of entering politics someday. Many weekends, by the time I got there, he was so burned out from the week that we would grab a quick bite to eat and then go sit somewhere quiet to work a crossword puzzle or read the paper side by side. We were already an old married couple months before our wedding."

Aster glanced at the ground, her focus on the dirt beneath their feet. "The opposite was true for Arthur and Maeve." Her tone shifted, and Julia was surprised at the bitterness behind her words. "They were always running around somewhere on an adventure. They'd jump in the car and go up to Baltimore for a change of scenery, or drive out to the coast and look at the stars, or find a party around campus to enjoy, and when Maeve told me about the physical excitement of their relationship, well, Timothy was a consummate gentleman, which came with clearly defined physical boundaries. I respected him for it, but to see Maeve's cheeks flush when she talked about how passionate Arthur was, it was hard to imagine Timothy ever reaching that level of abandon."

Not bitterness, Julia realized, jealousy.

Aster took a deep breath. "We were married less than a month apart. Timothy and I went first. Two weeks before the wedding, I went alone to Georgetown to finalize the last-minute details. It was April. Timothy was already stressed about finals and applying to the law review and transitioning to his summer internship. We were supposed to look at apartments together. We'd put it off too long and now faced being married without a place to live. We had fought about it a number of times, including that weekend. So, on Saturday afternoon, when Timothy got called to interview with the editorial board and rushed off to campus without so much as an apology for abandoning the appointments I'd made to look at apartments, I eagerly took up Arthur's offer to take his place."

She stopped and swallowed hard. Her face had gone pale. On the other end of the bench, Julia tried to slow her racing heart.

"Arthur was fun. He made a game out of it. Most of the landlords assumed he was Timothy, and he did his best impressions of Timothy's serious tone and no-nonsense attitude. I instantly saw what Maeve was attracted to; I'd always seen it. After the last appointment, he took me out for a drink. Then one drink became two. I told him about the first milkshakes Timothy had asked me to in high school, about how terrible his French had been, how much I missed the confident, flirtatious swagger he used to carry. I told him I admired how much life there was in his relationship with Maeve." Aster looked up, regret in her eyes. "I even told him I envied their passion."

Julia forced herself to remain impassive.

"Arthur flattered me with compliments, praising how I tolerated Timothy's brooding moods. He even confessed to wishing Maeve demonstrated some of the seriousness about their relationship that I displayed with Timothy." She frowned, her gaze going distant with the memory. "What I interpreted as their enviable, free-spirited adventures,

Arthur sometimes worried lacked deeper substance. It was as if they stopped moving, they would lack the inertia to hold the relationship together."

Aster paused and closed her eyes. For a moment, Julia thought she may not continue, but she started again without making eye contact.

"It was already twilight by the time we left the bar. The street lights were just winking on, and the evening was warm for early springtime. Arthur offered me his arm as we walked under the cherry blossoms. The world seemed brighter, more alive. At the end of the road, he stopped and looked at me. His hand brushed my cheek." Her voice broke, and she cleared her throat, failing to push the emotion from her tone as she continued. "He took a deep breath and admitted that it wasn't the first time he'd imagined things could have played out differently. If Timothy hadn't asked for that date first, he might have gotten the nerve to do it himself, and part of the reason he'd chosen Maeve was it allowed him more time to be close to me, to know me better through Maeve's eyes. It was more romance in five minutes than I'd felt from Timothy in five months, and when he leaned down to kiss me, I kissed him back despite myself."

Aster paused again and met Julia's eyes.

"Are you sure you want to hear this?" she asked.

Julia's stomach turned to water. She could guess at what came next. Innocent flirtation. One drink too many. Opportunity. And then… She had wondered just days earlier if this was how it played out for Will. She swallowed hard and nodded.

Aster looked away with a sigh. "Arthur took me back to his room," Her voice was small, barely a whisper now. "Everything inside me screamed that I was destroying my life and Maeve's, yet when we touched, I couldn't stop myself. I was set to be married to his best friend, and in that brief space and time, we pretended none of it mattered." Her hands trembled on her lap, and she hugged her elbows to keep them still.

"Of course, it did matter. When it was over and we lay sweaty and tangled in his sheets, we both realized that we weren't going to blow up the lives of the other people we loved over a single moment of passion. We got up and dressed, and he nervously took me back to Timothy. When we got there, Timothy met us, apologizing for blowing off the appointments, anxious to hear about the apartments, and Arthur and I looked at each other and knew we'd never speak of what passed between us again."

Julia realized she was holding her breath, and she exhaled in a rush. "Aster, I…" she began, but Aster shook her head.

"Please, let me get the rest of this out," she begged. Tears had begun spilling down her cheeks. "After we got married, I quickly learned that while loving and tender, passion was not a word I'd readily apply to intimacy with my husband. Nevertheless, the first weeks of our marriage were relatively calm and even joyful. I buried the memories of what had transpired that night with Arthur the best I could, but it was impossible to get away from him entirely. He was always there with Maeve."

She wiped her eyes. "I learned I was pregnant a week before their wedding, and while it was technically possible that Timothy was the father, I knew it was Arthur's. Though I wasn't sure what either of us gained by sharing the news, I thought he deserved to know my suspicions. When I told him, he didn't even question it. He knew in his heart the baby was his, too."

Aster looked up at Julia, but glanced away hurriedly when their eyes met. She sucked in a breath. "When Arthur offered to call off the wedding, I allowed myself to entertain what it would look like to have that passion in my life forever." She breathed a heavy sigh, dropping her head into her hands. "It was the worst kind of selfishness to think of not only destroying my marriage but to take my sister's from her before it even started, and I emphatically turned him down. Still, as I stood at the altar, waiting to stand by her side as she said her vows, I couldn't help but wonder if there was any possibility he might still choose me."

She choked back a sob. "Then there he was at the front of the church in his suit. I willed him to look at me, to catch my eye, to give anything away about how he was feeling, but he wouldn't. Maeve came down the aisle; they said their vows and exchanged their rings, and it was done." She paused, tears spilling over. "He had chosen for both of us, and he had made the nobler choice, but that didn't stop my heart from breaking."

Julia shifted uncomfortably. Part of her wanted to reach out and take Aster's hand in comfort, another part wanted to run from the bench before she had to hear another word. Still, Aster continued, her words all but lost in her tears.

"At the reception, he asked for a dance. I noted how carefully he took my waist, how much space he left between us. The band played 'You Made Me Love You,' and it felt like a scene from a movie. He told me I had been right; we couldn't destroy the people we love. He said we weren't even sure the baby was his, and you don't blow up marriages based on a hunch, no matter how strong. He begged me to keep the secret with him, to bury our night together deep in the past for good. What could I do but agree?"

She paused, forcing herself to take deep, trembling breaths, regaining her composure.

"When our little girl, Andrea, was born, three weeks early, but a healthy seven pounds, I called it a blessing with the rest of the nurses. And when I looked into her hazel eyes, closer to Arthur's green than I could ignore, I pretended to see the streaks of brown as Timothy's instead. I worried in those early days what would happen when Timothy and I had other children if they looked nothing like their older sister, but it never came to pass."

"And then what happened?" Julia managed to squeak.

Aster looked at her sadly. "Arthur and I never spoke of it again. We lived our lives with a bomb underfoot that could have upended our families and marriages at any moment. When Timothy died, I mourned. We had a whole life together, memories of holidays and birthdays, three grand-children, a vacation home in Myrtle Beach. It was a good life full of care and stability and companionship. But there was part of me that also relaxed for the first time in forty-three years because I knew that I'd protected him from the hurt."

She looked up, trying to hold back a fresh wave of tears. "Arthur died six months later, and it shook me harder than anyone understood. It was too late to explain I'd just lost the father of my child, and while he took the secret to his grave, it's still here with me. I look at my daughter and I see him there, and it hurts me to know that she never knew him as her dad. I look at my sister and the family she raised with Arthur and sometimes think, however selfishly, that it could have been mine."

Aster stopped, dropped her face back into her hands, and sobbed. Julia sat rooted to the spot, face wet with tears, stomach churning. Her already fragile heart broke fresh for Maeve, the ache taking her breath away. Minutes passed, and Aster's sobs calmed to heavy sniffles. She looked at Julia with red-rimmed eyes.

"When Maeve came to the room and told me what you learned about your ex last night," she said quietly, "the guilt was overwhelming. I'm the other woman in your story, Julia. Some part of me, however small, once wished the heartache you feel now on my own sister."

"But you didn't go through with it," Julia said. "At the end of it all, you protected your marriages."

"Did we?" Aster asked sadly. "What is protection if the thing you're keeping safe is an illusion? Only now, with both of them gone, do I feel like I'm living in my true story, and it's a story of heartbreak. Maeve thinks, you thought, I was sequestered in my room every night to avoid the heartbreak of talking about Timothy. But really, I sit alone in my room to avoid the heartbreak of listening to Maeve talk about Arthur."

The two women looked at each other for a long moment.

"You should be mad about what happened to you," Aster said finally. "And you can hate me for being a shadow of the same woman who put you here. But I had to tell you so that you knew that if it had played out differently, had your fiancé kept quiet and the other woman gone away, that you would have lived life in a precarious balance."

Julia stood up from the bench. She'd endured Aster's story without questioning or interrupting, but she could not bear to sit here now and listen to her speak of what might have been with Will.

"Even if you didn't realize it," Aster continued, "there would have always been something just below the surface that threatened to rip you apart. You deserve to build a life on stronger stuff than that. Maeve deserved to build a life on stronger stuff than that, and I spent over forty years trying to make sure she had it, and I'll go to my own grave pretending that she did."

Julia couldn't meet Aster's gaze. "I think I'm going to go to my room for a while," she whispered.

"I understand," Aster replied, defeated.

Julia took a few steps toward the house, but her legs felt like lead, and she struggled to leave the moment behind her. "I just have one question," she said, turning back to the tree.

"Ask me anything," said Aster warily.

"The phrase you asked Timothy to translate, the one he later used to ask you on a date, what did it mean?"

Fresh tears glistened in the corners of Aster's eyes. "It's too good to be true."

CHAPTER 20

J ulia went to her room, collapsed on the bed, and cried harder than she had since the wedding. Waves of emotion crashed over her, and she buried her face in the duvet and sobbed until she was out of tears. Just yesterday she craved the kind of love story Maeve professed to share with Arthur. Today, she realized how close she was to having it in ways Maeve would never understand. At that moment, she knew what Harriet and Alex had said the night before was true. Will had done her a favor. A soul-crushing, heartbreaking favor.

She found her phone and dialed Ellie. It rang twice before she picked up. "Julia! Is everything okay?"

Hearing the concern in Ellie's voice brought a lump to Julia's throat, and it took her a moment to respond.

"Julia? Are you there?"

"Hey, Ellie," she managed.

"Hey sweetie, I'm glad you called. Hold on." Julia heard a muffled conversation between Ellie and Aaron in the background, then footsteps and a door being closed.

"I was worried when I didn't hear from you last night. I

IN THE SHADE OF OLIVE TREES

didn't want you to find out alone." The sympathy in Ellie's voice was almost too much to bear. "It's terrible. He's a total dick. I can't believe he's out there on social media just flaunting..."

"Ellie," Julia cut in.

"I'm sorry. I'll stop. How are you doing?"

Julia hesitated, hugging a pillow to her chest. "I don't know," she admitted. "I'm processing. I'm trying to figure out what it looks like to come home and move on."

"No one is expecting you to just move on," Ellie reassured her.

"I know," Julia said, tearing up. "Honestly, it might be easier to just stay here forever, but I can't, and I just..." She held the pillow over her face for a moment, smothering a sob.

"Julia?" The concern in Ellie's voice was palpable from five thousand miles away.

Julia took a deep breath and ran the tassel on the corner of the pillow through her fingers. "I don't want to love him anymore, Ellie," she whispered, a single tear spilling down her cheek. "How do I stop loving him?"

Ellie let out a long, heavy sigh. "There's time for that. We'll figure it out. You don't have to have the problems of the universe figured out by the time you get home." She waited for Julia's sniffles to subside. "Just because he stopped loving you doesn't mean anyone expects you to let it go just as easily."

Julia pushed herself from the bed and walked a slow circle of the room. "But shouldn't it be easy, especially given this? What is left to hold on to?"

"The memories," said Ellie, gently. "It wasn't all bad."

Julia turned and paced the opposite direction. "You don't think everything we had was a lie?"

Ellie hesitated. "Not all of it," she said finally. "But the part where you were going to live happily ever after, that part was, whether he stopped the wedding or not."

Julia thought back to the moment it all ended and let out a sharp, sarcastic laugh. "Do you know, he had the audacity to cry right before he told me?"

"Huh?"

"Will," Julia groaned. "At the church, in the bridal suite, he wiped away actual tears. I thought it was for me, us."

"In the moment, it probably was," Ellie offered.

Julia shook her head slowly. "I don't think so, El. I think it was for him. I think it was relief that it was all finally over. The truth was out." Harriet's words echoed through Julia's mind. "Maybe he did me a favor," she said quietly.

"I wouldn't go that far," Ellie protested.

"Why not?" asked Julia, flopping back onto the bed. "Can you imagine if we were married right now and this came out?"

"No," admitted Ellie.

Julia rubbed her forehead. "I deserved better than this, Ellie."

"You're right."

"I want something better than this."

"I know."

A long moment passed.

"Do you want to hear something funny?" Julia asked.

Ellie let out a chuckle in surprise. "You actually find things funny again?"

"I have here," Julia assured her. "Ellie, I came here thinking it was all I had to hold on to, a second chance at happiness. I don't think that's true anymore."

"You don't?"

"No," Julia said, looking wistfully out the window. "I don't need a second chance at happiness, I need a first chance. I've yet to experience the kind of love that lasts a lifetime. I still have a first time for that."

"That's not funny, Jules," Ellie replied, voice trembling. "That's beautiful. No one deserves it more than you."

"But it still hurts," Julia said, choking up. It was one thing to know what to want, another thing to put all the pain aside to go after it.

"Yeah," said Ellie with a sniffle. "It's going to hurt."

Companionable silence settled between them again, and Julia felt calmer just knowing Ellie waited in the faint static on the other end of the line. They had not shared this moment in the hotel the night of the wedding, but she was grateful to share it now.

"You know what?" Ellie said. "You sound better than I expected, more grounded. I don't know what's going on over there at that old ladies' retreat, but whatever it is, I think it's rubbing off on you."

"They're not all old," insisted Julia with a chuckle.

"Maybe not, but Aaron only just stopped Google-stalking the villa. He's finally convinced you're not going to wind up in a ditch somewhere missing a kidney."

Julia laughed weakly.

"You *can* laugh again," Ellie said, sounding surprised.

"I told you," Julia insisted, standing and moving to the window, "they've been really amazing. It feels like where I was supposed to wind up."

"Then don't give up that feeling," Ellie encouraged. "Whatever you've been doing, keep doing it. The spark, Jules. Remember? I don't know how or why, but I think, somehow, you found it there."

The afternoon sun glinted off the silvery backs of the olive leaves, and Julia saw Aster slumped against the trunk of the tree, shoulders rounded in sorrow. Given all the time, grace, and perspective the women had extended to her this week, Julia suddenly saw that in the face of Aster's incredible heartache, it was up to her to extend the same incredible kindness.

"Listen Ellie, I'm going to have to let you go. It's the Festival of Lights tonight. They illuminate the hillside above the village with hundreds of torches and send wishes on candlelit boats out into the sea, and I've got a few things to still get ready."

"It sounds beautiful," Ellie said.

"I'm looking forward to it," replied Julia, realizing as she said it that she actually was.

"Well, call me later if you need to talk again, okay? And we'll be at the airport to pick you up in just a couple days.

"I'll see you soon."

"Love you."

"*Ciao.*"

Julia set the phone on the bed, raced downstairs and out the front door. "Aster!" she called across the front lawn.

Aster peered around the trunk of the tree, clearly surprised.

Julia reached the tree and caught her breath. "May I?" She gestured to the bench.

"Please," Aster said, sliding over to make room.

"I kissed a man on my first night in Italy," Julia blurted. "Luca. We danced in the piazza beside the Duomo, and I got caught up in the moment and kissed him." She continued in a rush. "He was engaged. It was his bachelor party. I have no idea if he'll tell his fiancé or not, and if he does what will happen. I'll never meet him again, but I walked around for days utterly mortified that I'd made such a foolish mistake, and worrying that I'd ruined the life of a stranger."

Aster stared at her, wide eyed, in confusion. "Why are you telling me this?"

"Because if that's how I felt about an errant kiss with a

stranger, I can't fathom how you've kept what you have for the last forty-five years with your sister." She slid closer to Aster on the bench. "I'm going to keep your secret, Aster. The only thing it can do now is hurt people. There's no chance left at a life together for you and Arthur, and there's no chance at a relationship between Andrea and her father. The only thing left are the memories."

Her throat tightened, and she looked up into the leaves of the tree, fighting emotion.

"All week I've been thinking that the worst kind of heartache is the loss of the possibilities of what could have been. I know that you mourn that for Arthur too. But I realize now there's a worse heartbreak to suffer, and it would be to live a whole life believing what you had was unshakeable, only to find out everything was a lie." She looked at Aster seriously. "To take away Maeve's memories of what her life was with her husband, to taint the only thing that's left of the decades they shared together, how would she come back from it? Everything that she knew would become an illusion, including her relationship with her sister."

Aster looked away. "I know that," she said quietly.

"But you can't keep doing this, the distancing, the staying in your room." Julia shook her head. "Maeve believes you're mourning Timothy, but that's part of the lie too."

Aster nodded slowly. "You're right," she said. "Maeve deserves a sister who's not so busy mourning the death of a man who is not her husband that she misses out on a relationship with the woman who was his wife."

Julia sighed. "I can't tell you how to build back the bond between you, but I do think I know how you can start." She held out her paper boat. "Go to the Festival of Lights with me tonight."

Aster recoiled from the offer. "But it's the last night in

Porto Venere," she hedged. "I'd just be the tagalong with everyone now."

"Don't worry about that," Julia insisted, pushing the paper toward her. "Maeve wants you there. She's wanted you here all week. It could be your fresh start." She turned the boat over in her hands, opening the fold to reveal the lines of poetry she'd inscribed inside. "On these boats, we're supposed to write our hopes and wishes and dreams and secrets. Our stories are two halves of the same whole. Let's send them off together and try to take a new step forward."

Aster reached for the boat tentatively. "I don't know," she replied.

Julia shrugged. "I can't tell you what to do, and as I said, I'm not going to tell anyone your secret. But if you don't find some way to move yourself past it, it's going to become just like this tree." She placed a hand affectionately on the trunk.

"Gnarled and unseemly?" asked Aster.

"No," Julia said with a small chuckle. "The thing that draws all your attention whether you want it to or not."

Aster stared at Julia, and tears welled in her eyes again. She ran her fingers along the creases of the boat. "You may never meet the woman who stole your wedding from you," she said, "so, on behalf of someone who once wished to do the same to someone else, I want to apologize for the heartbreak you've experienced. I'm so sorry for what you've been through."

Julia reached over and squeezed her hand. "And you may never have the chance to hear it from the person you threatened to hurt most, but for what it's worth from me, I forgive you."

WHEN THE REST of the women returned to the house that evening, Julia and Aster met them at the door, ready to join the festivities. While everyone was surprised to find Aster out of her room, Maeve nearly bowled her over with a hug, enthusiastically previewing all the best sights they found that morning to watch for on their way back through town. They walked upstairs together. Maeve draped an arm over Aster's shoulders, and for a moment, Julia could envision the two sisters, years younger, walking arm in arm through the Georgetown campus on their way to see the men they loved.

Alex passed Julia in the entry on her way upstairs to change. "So, you found what you were looking for today?"

"I'm working on it," Julia reassured her. "It's been a much better day than I expected."

"And Aster?" Alex raised an eyebrow. "She just came out of nowhere today, huh?"

Julia shrugged. "Yeah, how about that?"

"How about that," Harriet said, giving Julia a significant look as she passed through the entry.

Alex bounded upstairs with the rest of the group to change, and Julia followed Harriet into the living room.

"It's good to see you up and about," Harriet said when they were alone.

"Thanks to you," Julia replied. "Really, Harriet, I don't know how to thank you for everything this week. Last night..." she looked away and swallowed hard. "If I would have been alone, the trip might have wrecked me."

Harriet shook her head. "You would have figured it out. Remember what I said about my first trip? I made plenty of mistakes. If anything, I may have kept you from making a few more along the way." She pulled the cork from a bottle of wine and poured two glasses, setting one in front of Julia. "But if there's one thing to take from this week, I hope it's resilience. You've been surrounded by it all week. These women, they've all overcome something. You have too. It's just good to see you starting to find your way again. As for Aster, well, there you worked magic."

Julia shrugged. "She needed what we all needed: incredible kindness."

Harriet raised her glass, and Julia touched hers to it.

"The thing about kindness is that it takes someone kind to show it. It doesn't just exist on its own. Whatever you did, it was the right thing," Harriet said, smiling. She took a sip of the wine before setting her glass aside. "Now, perhaps you'd show me some of the same and help me set out this antipasto before we go back to the festival?"

They went to work in the kitchen, arranging trays of meats and cheese, tortellini, pepperoncini, olives, artichokes, and anchovies. Harriet opened more bottles of wine and set out plates and glasses.

Margo was the first to arrive downstairs wearing a stunning silk blouse that matched the pink streak in her hair. She speared an olive, winked at Julia, and accepted a glass of wine from Harriet whom she followed onto the terrace.

Elise came down next in a kelly green sundress that brushed the floor as she walked and was printed with large white flower blossoms. "You must have had quite the day," she said as she worked her way around the island filling a plate.

"It's been quite a *trip*," Julia admitted.

"Wait until you see the harbor tonight," she said excitedly. "We saw them setting it up this afternoon. It will be exquisite." She walked outside to join Harriet and Margo.

One by one, the rest of the women trickled back into the kitchen, Beth in a rose-colored pants suit; Maeve in a nautical striped dress, followed by Aster in a beautiful, brocade jacket; Lucy draped in her rainbow pashmina; and Alex in a fitted black cocktail dress with gold accents. Soon they had all filled plates and assembled on the terrace, breaking into comfortable conversations about the best parts of the week. Each woman checked in with Aster, anxious to make a connection in the short time remaining together.

Julia rushed upstairs to dress. The inky blue, satin wrap dress, an admitted splurge she had justified as being for the honeymoon, was laid out on the bed waiting for her. She tried to imagine wearing it under different circumstances. When she had pulled it from her suitcase that afternoon, it suddenly struck her as made for this night, and this night alone. She slid into it, touched up her makeup, and pulled her fingers through her loose waves. A final check in the mirror confirmed she was ready, and she hurried down the hall, reaching the staircase just as Alex slipped into the entryway.

"Alex?" Julia called, catching her at the front door.

Alex turned, startled. "Julia, I didn't realize you were back upstairs. You look fantastic."

Julia blushed, pleased, and twirled on the bottom step. "Thank you. Where are you going?"

Alex's eyes twinkled in the light of chandelier, and she gestured for Julia to follow her out the front door. "Come with me." Together they went down the front walk and stepped into the yard.

"Is something wrong?" Julia asked, concerned.

Alex shook her head, smiling. "Not at all. I just had to get away from the group for a few minutes. Danny's been on call all week, and our schedules haven't overlapped that much, just a few minutes here and there. He thought tonight..." Alex's cell phone rang. "Do you want to meet him?" she asked Julia.

"I'd love that," Julia replied.

Alex answered the call, and Danny's face came into focus on the screen.

"Hey, Sweetheart," he said, and Julia could sense his affection even through speakerphone.

"Hi."

Julia gave them space on the lawn to exchange greetings and updates from their time apart. After a few minutes, she waved Julia over.

"Danny, I want you to meet Julia."

Julia stepped into the frame. Danny was handsome, she saw, with a strong jawline and dark features. His green eyes looked tired, but lit up as Alex talked about the things they'd been doing. He had loosened his tie, and his hair was untidy as if he had run his hands through it one too many times in agitation.

"Well, it's great to see you Julia," he said warmly. "It sounds like you've made quite an impression on my wife."

"She was my happy accident," Julia exclaimed. "She saved me a real headache in La Spezia, and," she looked at Alex, "she's been helping me with some pretty bad heartache here as well."

Alex smiled.

"Yeah, she's a keeper." Danny said. "Which means you've got to send her back to me in a few days. I hope we get to meet in person someday."

Julia chuckled. "I'd like that."

"Well, I hope you enjoy the festival tonight," he said.

"Thank you, we will. It was great to meet you." Julia stepped back to the front stoop to give Alex privacy to finish the call. A moment later, Alex joined her. "I like him." she said.

Alex smiled at the phone in her hand. "Me too," she laughed. She hesitated, looking out over the yard. "Do you remember what I told you the first night we arrived? That Danny didn't care about my travel because he was always working?

"Yes."

Alex sighed. "Well, the truth is, I have never really imagined traveling with Danny. It was the thing I did after Sam died and the thing I did with Harriet. I always miss him when I'm gone, but I never really imagined him being here. He works so much and never minds my going away for short bursts. So, I was really content to have this to myself."

Julia waited. "But?" she asked finally.

"But something changed on this trip." Alex looked down, a soft smile playing across her face. "Maybe it was hearing you romanticize it. Maybe it was just time. I could see him here. I wanted him here. I want to share this with him."

Julia turned to Alex, surprised. "But you said you love solo travel?"

"I do," Alex confirmed, looking at Julia with misty eyes, "but life moves forward. It's time to move with it."

Julia dropped her eyes, emotion tight in her throat. "Agreed," she whispered.

A commotion in the entryway behind them broke the spell of the moment, and the front door opened as the rest of the tour group joined them in front of the house. Their chatter died away as Harriet handed out short taper candles set in plastic holders to catch the melted wax. Soon each woman glowed in her own pool of gentle candlelight. Julia looked around, seeing in each face the stories, wisdom, understanding, and kindness shown to her all week.

"Shall we?" Harriet invited, gesturing them forward down the driveway and past the namesake tree.

And so, on their last night, fully together for the first time, the women left Olive Haven to walk to Porto Venere.

CHAPTER 21

As the tangle of colorful buildings grew closer, the crowds on the streets grew thicker, so that by the time they entered the shadows of the narrow back roads winding down to the harbor, the women were surrounded on all sides by a throng of people bearing candles toward the water. They were pushed along, a river of shimmering candlelight waiting to spill into the marina, while music played and spectators shouted well wishes from the balconies and rooftops overhead. Priests in holiday regalia offered prayers and burned incense in front of San Lorenzo Church. The clouds of smoke, a perfumed haze, drifted over the procession as it snaked by.

Julia tried to commit each part of the scene to memory as they wound through the glowing streets. The women laughed and chatted around her, and her heart swelled to be part of something bigger than herself. The morning may have been about heartbreak and lost opportunities, but tonight was about a shared sense of renewal and growth. The group hummed with positive energy.

They reached the harbor, and the crowd spread out along

IN THE SHADE OF OLIVE TREES

the water's edge. The sun hung low on the horizon. Deep purples and blues already colored the sky over Porto Venere as they turned to face the city. The road in front of the harbor shops had been closed, and musicians and dancers performed in the street, eliciting cheers and sing-alongs from the masses gathered.

Through the throng came Bernardo, a small, dark-haired little girl sitting high on his shoulders as he wove his family through the crowd. He swung her down as he reached the group, tossing her to Harriet who spun her around in a tight embrace before setting her down. Bernardo's wife broke through the crowd a moment later, holding the hand of the older daughter. She kissed Harriet on both cheeks, then knelt down to help prepare the little girls' boats. Bernardo stood over them protectively.

"Can you imagine having your family here like that some-day?" Julia leaned over and whispered to Alex.

"Yeah," Alex smiled. "Can you?"

Julia nodded slowly. "This might be the first time I've really felt like that's worth wanting again."

A local festival volunteer wandered from group to group demonstrating how to prepare the boats. He opened the folds carefully revealing the flat bottom onto which he dropped hot wax, then pressed the base of his candle. When it had cooled seconds later, the candle stood upright in the center of the vessel.

"When it's time," he said, "you put your boat in the water, and send it off. When the candle burns down to nothing... poof, your message goes to heaven."

They found positions along a small dock. Sitting on the edge, they dangled their feet in the water as they listened to the music and watched the last rays of sunlight play on the waves lapping against the shore.

Aster came and sat beside Julia. She pulled the boat from

inside her jacket. "At your suggestion," she said quietly, "I've made a few additions of my own."

Julia smiled and took the folded paper. "Then when the time comes, you can help me send it off," she said.

"Did Julia help you make a boat today?" Maeve asked, coming down the dock and looking at the paper between them.

"Not exactly," Julia said quickly, fending off further explanation. "I just offered her some space in mine."

A thundering drumroll echoed over the city from the fortress on top of the hill. The crowds began to hush around them. Somewhere on a microphone, announcements were made in Italian. Then, up on the hillside, a pinprick of light began to move along the rocky ledges of the cliffs guarding the town. Along the way it stopped, and a second pinprick grew in the twilight. Then from the fortress emerged a third. Soon, there were a dozen runners trailing along the hillside and down the slanting roads to the sea. In their wake blazed a trail of torches. It was mesmerizing to watch. The coast and hillsides of Porto Venere glowed gold with luminaries. The crowd around them applauded.

Dusk continued to fall.

"It's time to prepare the boats!" Harriet announced.

Julia pulled the pointed ends, opening the flat bottom inside. In handwriting she didn't recognize she saw a new quote written:

"Don't cling to your self-righteous suffering, let it go. Nothing is too good to be true, let yourself be forgiven. To the degree you insist that you must suffer, you insist on the suffering of others as well."

"I saw your quote," said Aster, approaching Julia with her candle. "I thought I'd stay with your poetry theme. May I?" She tipped hot wax onto her words, blurring the middle lines. "Now yours," she said.

Julia tipped wax into the boat then stood her candle in the middle of it. She held it in place while it set.

The sun disappeared below the horizon, and the hillside glittered in the light of thousands of individual torches. Luminaries lined the streets leading away from the water, piercing the shadows of the buildings hulking over them. On balconies, in windows, even along rooftops, lanterns and candles and torchlight outlined the facade of Porto Venere.

Another peel of drums moved people into place at the edge of the water. Then, one by one, the boats were launched into the sea. They drifted in the surf, and within minutes, the harbor sparkled with dozens of candlelit paper boats.

Julia set the boat gently on the water. "Go ahead," she told Aster.

Aster reached down and gave it a soft push away from the dock. It floated out among the others into the harbor. In the growing twilight, Julia quickly lost track of which it was.

"I'm not sure where it is anymore," Aster admitted.

"Me either," Julia smiled. "I think that's the point."

A priest in a heavily embroidered stole came down to the water and stood barefoot in the shallows. He swung incense over the waves and said a prayer. The surrounding crowd murmured amen as they continued to watch the drifting of the boats in measured silence.

Harriet came up behind Julia, placing a hand lightly on her shoulder. "How does it feel?" she asked softly. "Lighter?"

"Can your heart feel both lighter and fuller at the same time?" Julia asked.

Harriet cocked her head and smiled. "I think it can," she said.

"Then I think it feels like that." They watched the candles dance on the waves. "At the start of the trip," Julia continued, "I was haunted by Will's absence. He had my heart, but Italy has stolen it back."

"That I understand." Harried nodded. "As I've told you, after Jack, it was Porto Venere that first felt like home again."

Julia turned to face Harriet. "Well, as much as I'd like to stay as you did, I hope I can at least hold that space open again, waiting for the next thing to fill it."

"I know you'll find it," Harriet assured her. "Just remember, there are times to plan for it and times to be spontaneous."

"Thank you, Harriet," Julia said, swallowing tears.

Harriet pulled her into a hug. They held tightly to each other in the candlelight. A murmur went through the crowd as the last of the boats were launched. They turned back to the water where hundreds of candles now flickered across the harbor. The sight took Julia's breath away.

Alex came up between them, throwing an arm over each of their shoulders. "This is going to be tough to top next year," she told Harriet playfully.

"Oh, I don't know," Harriet said. "Maybe we'll try something other than Italy. I could take a week away. There's always the Fringe, or we could run with the bulls if you'd like."

Alex looked at her seriously. "You'd run with the bulls?"

"I'd at least cheer you on from the sidelines." Harriet smirked.

"I've never known you to sit on the sidelines of anything," Alex teased.

"I suppose not. You help keep me young that way." Harriet put an arm around Alex's waist, and Alex dropped her head onto her shoulder. They stood and watched the boats drift.

"I almost forgot," Alex said suddenly, turning to Julia. "We have something for you."

"For me?"

Harriet reached into her bag and pulled out a small box wrapped in dark green paper and tied with gold ribbon.

"A small gift to take back with you so that when things get tough, and you're in the thick of the hard work that is moving on, you remember the peace you had here and hopefully draw on some of the perspective you found as well," she said, holding it out to Julia.

Julia took the package and unwrapped it carefully, revealing a small, square jewelry box covered in blue velvet.

"Alex, Harriet, I…" She turned the box in her hands, overcome with emotion.

"Don't cry yet, you haven't even opened it," said Alex with fake exasperation.

Julia took a deep breath, opened the lid, and gasped. Nestled inside was a thin gold band, inlaid with a dark stripe of wood.

"Italian gold," Harriet explained, "and olive wood, to remember us by. Alex mentioned you weren't fond of buying your own jewelry."

Julia took the ring from the box. It shimmered in the surrounding candlelight as she moved to slide it onto her finger. She paused, looking down at her hand. The thin, light stripe around her left ring finger was gone. She choked on a sob of pure relief and release. The tears fell, but she smiled. When she got on the plane, she never would have imagined finding a reason to shed happy tears. She slid the ring onto her right hand instead, admiring it in the fading light.

"I have nothing to give you in return. It's too…" Julia said. "I've done nothing to deserve this."

Alex pulled the three of them together in a group hug, stopping any further objections. Harriet laughed.

"Do you like it?" she asked.

"It's absolutely perfect," Julia breathed.

On the farthest edges of the regatta, the first boats were starting to flicker out as their candles dwindled to nothing. A group of musicians on the shoreline struck up the first chords of an Andrea Bocelli classic as more boats began to sputter and disappear into the darkness. Julia, Alex, and Harriet turned toward the water to watch the remainder of the boats drift away. The music swelled, and the water sparkled with firelight. The rest of the women joined them in a huddle, arms around each other, eyes shining with tears and wonder.

As the last boat disappeared in the harbor, a tremendous cheer went up from the crowd, and the band burst into an upbeat, traditional song that immediately had the throngs of people singing along. The women joined the festivities dancing their way along the main road as the procession slowly began to form in reverse, winding back the way it had come toward San Lorenzo where the devout of Porto Venere would hold a candlelit mass.

Past the church, up the hill, and out of the city proper, the music faded and the road darkened. The women laughed and talked merrily as they walked back toward Olive Haven one last time. As they came around the bend in the road and caught sight of the villa, however, the chatter died away. The driveway from the road to the house had been lined in luminaria lighting the pathway to the front door, and a candle burned on every windowsill of the house. But the star of the show was the olive tree. Tiny candles not only ringed its base, but also were tucked into the knots and crevices of the gnarled trunk and hanging in small jars from the branches.

Whereas the scene in the harbor had felt expansive, the olive tree now felt incredibly intimate, and they approached it in silence. Flutes of prosecco stood bubbling on the bench, and Harriet passed them around to the women. She took the final glass for herself and raised it.

"Rumi said, 'If light is in your heart, you will find your way home.' So it is, perhaps, appropriate that we spend our last night here celebrating this Festival of Lights. I hope that your hearts have been filled this week by the lights of Porto Venere and by each other. And I hope that upon returning home, you find your hearts are lighter from the time we have spent together. To hearts full of light, and light hearts full of joy. *Saluti!*"

There was a gentle tinkling of glasses, and then quiet conversations as the women enjoyed one final nightcap together.

Julia looked around at the villa bathed in amber, the candles flickering above her, and the soft glow reflected in the gold band on her finger. The wood stripe stood out in sharp relief in the flickering candlelight and shifting shadow. She closed her eyes, sipped her wine, and memorized the moment. It was more than she ever hoped to find.

A soft tap on her shoulder broke the spell. Lucy stood next to her, eyes shining in the candlelight. She smiled and held open her arms.

Julia gave her a gentle hug. "Lucy," she smiled. "Do you think Rome can stack up to a night like tonight?"

"Oh, I'm sure it has its charms," Lucy chuckled. "What about you? Where will you go from here?"

"This is the end for me. I have one night left in Florence, but it's kind of just a technicality. By the time I get off the train and check into my hotel, I'll probably just grab a quick bite and get to bed early."

"Very good, then. Well, I'm going to bed, but I hope it's safe travels for you heading home," Lucy said. "It was such a pleasure to get to know you. I'm so glad you and Harriet stumbled upon each other."

"Me too," Julia said. "And I hope you have a fabulous time with your son." She kissed the older woman on the cheek and watched Lucy's silhouette return to the house.

Her thoughts drifted back to Florence. It seemed a lifetime ago that she was there. She remembered the dance,

Allegretto's, and the Duomo piazza. She thought about how the specter of Will had tainted the whole evening and how far away he seemed from it now. She looked up at the sparkling branches of the olive tree and felt peace.

"No goodbyes tonight," Alex said, coming up beside her. "We've still got tomorrow."

"Deal," Julia agreed. It would be impossible to say goodbye tonight. Even tomorrow, she couldn't imagine finding the words. They'd ride the train together to Florence, make their way through the station, and then... Julia tried to picture leaving through the doors of the station alone. Tonight was perfect. She could not have written a better ending. And yet, something still felt unfinished. All at once, an idea started to form.

"Alex?" she asked, "what exactly are your plans in Florence tomorrow?"

Alex shrugged. "We don't usually make plans. Once I meet Harriet at the hotel, we'll just decide where to go from there." She looked at Julia curiously. "Why do you ask?"

Julia smiled that fate would hand her one final opportunity. "Because if you're up for it," she threw Alex a puckish glance, "I've got just one more thing I want to take care of before heading home."

CHAPTER 22

J ulia spent the next morning in a repetitive loop of goodbyes. Lucy left first before most of the house was awake. She would travel with Harriet who would ride with her as far as Florence. From there Lucy would board the train to Rome, and Harriet would stay to spend a final night with Alex.

After breakfast, the rest of the women taxied to the harbor for the ferry to La Spezia. They said goodbye to Bernardo at the dock and loaded the boat, positioning themselves along the railing to wave as they slipped back from the pier and away from Porto Venere. Julia tried not to let her emotions take over as the colorful harbor front disappeared from view. She would undeniably miss it.

Arriving in La Spezia, they wandered slowly through the town, stopping in gift shops and foccerias, licking dripping cones of gelato one last time and putting off further inevitabilities as long as possible. At the station ninety minutes later, they shared another round of farewells as Beth, Elise, and Margo, who had flights out of Milan, headed west to Genoa for their connection. There were more hugs and tears, promises to stay in touch, and last-minute photos as they walked to their platform, boarded the train, and pulled out of the station. Maeve and Aster followed Julia and Alex to their own platform for the train headed east to Florence.

As they wound through the Italian countryside, Julia watched the scenery streak by, remembering the first train ride and the first conversation with Alex. Everything else had bloomed from that moment, and now here they were again, zipping back toward Florence with one final night to take care of unfinished business. She was overwhelmed with gratitude for their friendship. She looked up and found Alex watching her.

"Are you disappointed," Alex asked, "that you didn't do everything that you'd planned?"

Julia shook her head. "No," she said with certainty. "I plan for a living, so it was hard to imagine what I could gain by leaving so much to chance." She twisted her new gold band thoughtfully. "But I wouldn't trade Olive Haven for anything. It wasn't my dream trip, but only because I couldn't have known how to dream it."

The train slowed as it approached the station. The cream stone walls and red roofs of Florence rose up suddenly around them. Maeve and Aster, lost in quiet conversation, broke away to watch the scene unfold out the window.

"What will you do tonight?" Julia asked.

Aster looked at her sister. "We agreed I have about six days' worth of sightseeing to make up for," she said. "We extended our trip a few days, and Maeve is going to play tour guide."

Julia nodded, her heart warming to see Aster making an effort at the hard work of moving on. At this point, she knew that work well. "You'd be welcome to join us for dinner," she offered.

"A very kind invitation," said Maeve, "but I think we'll just see where the evening carries us."

The train lurched to a halt, and they stood to collect their things. Out on the platform, Julia pulled Aster aside to say goodbye. "How do you feel?" Julia asked.

"I should probably be asking you the same."

"I feel better than I did when I arrived," admitted Julia, "and more ready to face the life waiting for me at home. I hope you feel the same."

A whistle blew across the station, and a swarm of people sidestepped around them, rushing off to connections and final destinations.

"If my story is a burden to you, then I'm sorry," Aster offered.

Julia shook her head. "If telling it makes your going home easier, then I'm not." She pulled Aster into an embrace.

Maeve rolled two suitcases along the platform. She pushed them towards Aster as she approached, freeing herself up to hug Julia as well. "It was fun, kiddo," she said warmly. "Thanks for bringing this one around." She put an arm around Aster. "Ready?"

Aster nodded. "*Arrivaderci!*"

They wheeled their suitcases into the heart of the station, quickly getting swept along in the crowd.

"*Ciao,*" Julia called after them, but they were already gone.

Alex brought her suitcase beside Julia. "Well," she said, "since you couldn't be convinced to change your reservation to our hotel, should you go get checked in before we reconvene this evening?"

"Yeah," Julia agreed. She turned to Alex, and they stared at each other for a long moment. The teeming train station continued to swirl around them, but they stood frozen on the platform, neither wanting to be the first to leave.

Alex laughed, and looked away quickly. "It's not goodbye

yet." Her voiced wobbled slightly. "We'll see you in a couple of hours." She spun her suitcase around in front of her, and headed towards the exit on the right. "Later," she called over her shoulder.

"*Ciao,*" Julia called after her, hesitating a moment longer. Alex waved a hand casually over her shoulder but did not turn around. Julia watched her disappear into the crowd, then gathered her things, and headed to the exit on the left.

The streets in front of Stazione Santa Maria Novella were no less chaotic upon her return than they had been at her departure, but Julia felt no rising panic this time as she navigated through the crowd, crossed in front of the bus depot, and headed down the sloping boulevard past the calls of the vendors and the sunbathers on the lawn in front of the Santa Maria Novella Cathedral. She closed her eyes, letting the sounds and smells take over. She was met with a heady rush of déjà vu. Mopeds whizzed by on her left; busses filed onto the boulevard on her right. Garlic and sweet cigar smoke wafted on the breeze. It was a far cry from the tranquility of Olive Haven.

Out of convenience and familiarity, she had booked the same accommodations for her final night's stay, and she followed the Arno River back toward the Uffizi Gallery. Giuseppe looked up from the desk as she entered the small lobby a second time.

"*Signorina Giulia!*" he declared. "You've returned to us. Look at you; you're glowing."

"It's all that Mediterranean sun," Julia said, blushing. "It's good for the soul."

"*Si, signorina.* You had a marvelous time?"

Julia rolled her suitcase to the marble counter, remembering how it had felt to leave in a panic during the strike, marveling at everything that had happened since then.

"Even better than I could have planned it."

Giuseppe smiled. "And your favorite part?"

Julia thought it over, her fingers absentmindedly tracing the gold and olive band on her finger. "There was this villa with an ancient olive tree," she started.

Giuseppe nodded knowingly, clacking at the computer keyboard. "But of course, this is the tree of peace."

"And I definitely needed some of that."

He looked up, grinning, and handed her a set of keys. "Up the stairs in the middle. I will take you."

"That's okay," Julia begged off. "I remember. Thank you, Giuseppe."

She left the lobby and climbed the stairs, hesitating at the middle door before turning the key and stepping inside.

It was exactly as she remembered.

Late afternoon sunshine streamed through the floor to ceiling windows framed in clean white curtains; the mountain of jewel tone pillows sat stacked against the delicate headboard. An enormous arrangement of lavender scented the breeze, and the smaller arrangement in the bathroom, she was delighted to discover, was accented with a sprig of silver olive leaves. The only thing missing was the heaviness of her grief, and while she felt a twinge of apprehension about going home to face the aftermath of her heartbreak, it no longer consumed her.

She opened her suitcase, rummaging through the dirty laundry piles, until she found the floor length, yellow sundress buried at the bottom. She laid it out on the bed, smoothing out the wrinkles, and stood back to consider it properly. Satisfied, she retrieved one of the plush towels from the armoire and went to take a shower.

At seven o'clock, Julia, dressed in the yellow dress with a loose braid hanging over her right shoulder, came down the steps and crossed the lobby. Giuseppe was just locking up the cabinets behind the counter.

"Oh, it's déjà vu. Where do you go tonight to grace Florence with your presence looking so beautiful?" he asked.

Julia smiled, twirling for him.

"It's a night to make better memories," she exclaimed.

Giuseppe laughed. "In *bocca al lupo!*" he called behind her as she danced out the door.

On the corner, the old man selling roses held out a pink flower on a short stem to her as she passed, and she stopped and tucked it behind her ear. She bought two white roses from his basket and turned up the side street away from the river and toward the hulking dome of the cathedral.

The city glowed around her as limestone buildings and terracotta roofs flamed in the evening sun. Stepping into the piazza, the palatial form of the Duomo hulked before her. Evening tourists huddled around its base while musicians tuned in its quiet corners. It all felt familiar, yet with a heart now healing, it all felt vibrant and new as well.

She crossed the piazza to Allegretto's in the corner and found Harriet and Alex waiting, engaged in lively conversation. They turned, smiling, to Julia as she approached.

"You look terrific," Harriet said, stepping forward to kiss her on each cheek.

Julia blushed. "Thank you, and thank you both for taking part of your last night to meet me. I've probably monopolized enough of your time for one vacation. As the tiniest token of my thanks," she held out a rose to each of them, "these are for you."

"They're beautiful," said Harriet. "*Grazie.* Now, Alex said there was something you needed help taking care of?"

"There is," Julia said sheepishly. "When we first met on the plane, you talked about going back to make better memories where you had made mistakes," she said. Harriet nodded. "Well, I was hoping that before we left, we'd make a better one right here."

"What do we have to do?" Alex asked gamely.

"Just have dinner," Julia said. "There," she pointed at the twinkling lights of Allegretto's. "My treat."

Alex and Harriet exchanged a look and shrugged. "It would be our pleasure," Harriet said.

They took seats at a table overlooking the piazza. The waiter brought crusty bread and tart red wine, and they laughed and conversed about the week, about plans at home, about Aaron and Ellie, about what else Harriet had planned for the retreats that fall. They tucked into piles of pasta, and Alex called Danny, putting him on speakerphone in the center of the table to be peppered with questions from Julia and Harriet.

Music started in the piazza. Wine flowed. Three plates of tiramisu took the place of empty pasta bowls, and Harriet got weepy talking about Alex and how much it meant to have her there. Alex looked away embarrassed, wiping tears of her own. Julia gave them a moment of privacy at the table and walked across the piazza where the group of musicians were starting their second set of the night.

She stopped a few feet in front of the table as she returned, holding out a hand to Harriet and Alex. "There's just one more thing," she said as the first, sad strains of the violin reverberated off the stones around them.

"What?" Alex regarded her hand suspiciously.

"A dance," Julia said.

"In the middle of the piazza?" Alex glanced past Julia to the tourists mingling around the Duomo.

Realization broke on Harriet's face. "A redo?" she asked, raising an eyebrow.

Julia merely smiled.

"Okay," Harriet smiled in return, pushing back her chair and accepting an outstretched hand.

"You're going to dance to this?" Alex said skeptically, glancing from Harriet to Julia. "Why?"

Julia shrugged. "Why not? I called you twenty-four hours after we met and let you convince me to come meet you in Porto Venere, where I didn't have a reservation or know another soul, and now you're questioning whether a dance is a good idea?"

Alex stood up and made her way around the table, chuckling. "Well yeah, considering you said yes to that, I think it's only fair to question your judgment."

The violin hung on a single, suspended note.

"Do you know this song?" asked Julia.

"No," admitted Alex, taking Julia's other hand.

Julia looked between them, heart soaring, as the violin set off on its whirling counter melody.

"Then hold on!"

EPILOGUE

From her room at the front of the villa, Julia looked
out the window over the grounds and the hulking,
twisted form of the ancient olive tree. Surrounded
by glass paned hurricane lamps and resplendent in twinkling
fairy lights, the tree was the star of the show for at least
another fifteen minutes.

Already, small pockets of guests clustered around two
dozen mismatched chairs pulled from the kitchen, terrace,
and a few neighboring houses and arranged in untidy
columns facing towards the villa and the base of the tree.

Julia made out the familiar shapes of Aaron and Harriet
conversing casually near the stone path leading through the
gardens. Their laughter tinkled lightly on the evening breeze
that rustled the sheer, linen curtains that barely concealed
her position at the window. She closed her eyes, took a deep
breath, and smiled. It was more than she ever could have
hoped for.

If she had canceled the trip altogether, if she had decided
not to change her train ticket, if she refused the invitation to

stay at Olive Haven, everything would have been different. And while it would have been impossible to predict that everything about that first trip would culminate in this moment, it was equally impossible to imagine being anywhere else.

A knock on the door behind her redirected Julia's attention, and she stepped back from the window, catching her reflection in the full-length mirror on the back of the door as she turned. The ivory column of silk was fitted to perfection with a deeply cut neckline and an open back. It cascaded elegantly around her to the floor where the train pooled at her feet. Delicate gold beading along the straps sparkled in the lamplight, winking along with diamond tear drops that dangled from each ear and a solitary pendant suspended on a fragile gold chain.

Her heart skipped at the beauty of the dress and the perfection of the moment. How impossible it would have seemed three years ago when she stood, brokenhearted, in this same room for the first time, to find herself back here in a wedding dress. How impossible it seemed now, even having lived it. Fate, it seemed, continued to pull her to Olive Haven. She took a steadying breath, realizing her final private moment of the evening had passed.

"Come in," she called as lightly as she could manage.

The door opened a crack, and Ellie poked her head into the room. She lit up, eyes instantly full of tears at the sight of Julia in front of the mirror.

"Oh Julia," she said, coming into the room and closing the door quietly behind her. She laid a black garment bag on the bed. "You look...exquisite."

Julia smiled. "Thank you, Ellie." She stepped across the room and met her with an embrace.

A hug that lasted mere moments contained three years'

worth of emotion. A three-word phrase conveyed three years of gratitude.

Ellie, who had picked Julia up from the airport, listened patiently to every detail of her time at Olive Haven, welcomed her into the guest room of her home, and gamely went apartment hunting with her in the weeks after the trip. Ellie, who had rented the moving van and led the expedition back into the condo to box up the rest of Julia's possessions, stayed in the new apartment the very first night when Julia thought that being alone might break her, came back five months later when the birth of Will's daughter unexpectedly did. Ellie, who had counseled and cautioned and encouraged as Julia had tentatively ventured back into dating, consoled the first time a new flame flickered out, prayed on the night Julia called to talk about Nathan, that he really was everything that Julia wanted him to be.

When it turned out he was, Ellie was the first person Julia asked to stand by her side.

The two women separated, and Julia dabbed gently at the tears that threatened to spill onto the unblemished dress.

Ellie sniffed and wiped at her own eyes. "There goes my mascara," she laughed as she unzipped the garment bag revealing a sheath of emerald silk. She looked at Julia. "It's almost time."

"I'm ready," Julia said calmly.

"Then I better be too," Ellie picked up the dress by the hanger and headed towards the bathroom. "Give me just a minute."

Julia turned back toward the window. The majority of the guests were settling in around the tree. Harriet had left Aaron with their father on the garden path, and as she watched, Danny emerged from the house to join them holding the hand of a toddling little boy in a pint-sized tuxedo. His son. Alex's son. Jack.

Danny shook hands with her family in greeting, and they settled into murmured conversation.

A second knock on the door turned Julia's attention back to the room just as Ellie emerged from the bathroom. Though she had retouched her makeup, she dabbed again at the corners of her eyes as she caught sight of Julia at the window.

"I'll get the door," she said shakily, looking away quickly.

"Is it going to be this way all night?" Julia laughed.

Ellie shrugged. "Probably, I won't apologize." She opened the door a crack, peeking into the hallway. "Get in here," she said affectionately, throwing open the door to reveal Alex in matching green silk.

"Sorry, we had a baby bowtie emergency," Alex said, stepping into the room.

"Words I never imagined coming out of your mouth," Julia laughed.

"Me either," Alex breathed with a soft chuckle. She regarded Julia and sighed. "You're stunning, Jules." Alex had easily adopted the friendly moniker after spending a weekend with Aaron and Ellie. "How does it feel?"

"It feels...right," Julia said assuredly.

"Good," Alex said, looking out the window over Julia's shoulder, "because he's here."

Julia's heart lurched, and she spun around to face the window.

"You can't just stand there!" Ellie exclaimed. "He'll see you."

The three women ducked to the side, peering carefully around the frame out to the road where Nathan walked up the driveway and towards the olive tree with Bernardo in tow.

~

A FRIEND OF DANNY'S, *that's how the suggestion had originally been made. On a trip out to Denver to meet baby Jack, Alex had casually mentioned that, if Julia wanted a break from perpetual crying and endless dirty diapers, Danny had a friend, Nathan, who was a year removed from a serious relationship and looking to date again. He was a physical therapist who liked to hike and was a tennis star in college. He had a golden retriever named Elton. He played poker with six guys from the hospital once a month, and Danny claimed Nathan lost more often than he won because he was too honest to keep a poker face. He was a bit of a foodie and happened to have two tickets to the Denver Food and Wine Expo that same weekend. Alex had called it a perfect coincidence, and given that their entire friendship was based on its own happy accident, Julia couldn't help but feel a touch of fate hovering around the meeting.*

They spent Friday night walking around the Mile High Convention Center with plastic wine glasses and small plates of food, an evening that ended with a nightcap at Rocky Mountain Tap House and a kiss on the cheek before she got into her Uber.

Then Alex had done Julia the favor of inviting him over to grill and watch football with Danny on Sunday afternoon. Julia had studied his easy-going nature with Danny, awkwardness with Jack, thoughtfulness in offering to run out for cheese and buns for the burgers when Alex realized she'd missed them on her shopping list when Jack had melted down in the produce section.

At the end of the game, when Danny offered to take Jack upstairs for his bath and Alex nonchalantly slipped away a few minutes later to check on his progress, Julia found herself, heart pounding, alone with Nathan in the kitchen silently finishing the dishes. She drained the water and wiped out the sink while he dried the last of the plates and tucked things into cupboards. He turned, leaning on the counter, and watched her at the sink.

"What are you thinking?" he asked after a moment.

Julia swallowed hard. "I'm afraid I just met the perfect guy a thousand miles away from home," she admitted. She looked up at him, surprised to see a smile play around the corners of his mouth. "What are you thinking?" she asked quietly.

"I'm afraid a thousand miles will make you think we shouldn't even try."

Try they had, and sixteen months later, they'd flown five thousand miles more to promise forever.

~

JULIA WATCHED as Nathan crossed under the sparkling branches of the olive tree. Too far away to see his face, Julia still knew what she'd find. Soft, amber eyes framed in tortoise shell glasses. A strong jaw studded with stubble. Dark hair swept back from his forehead.

His trim fit tuxedo jacket stretched across strong shoulders, and his mother straightened his bowtie as he reached the front row of chairs. His gold cufflinks glinted in the light of the sunset.

It was time.

Julia, Ellie, and Alex stepped back from the window.

"Should we go down?" asked Alex.

Ellie's eyes shone with tears again. "I'm sorry," she laughed. "I thought I'd hold it together better than this."

"You were much better the first time," Julia said casually.

Ellie looked at her stunned. "I didn't think we'd talk about…" she trailed off.

Julia shrugged. "Why not? It feels different, don't you think?" She smiled.

"One hundred times better," Ellie agreed, dropping a kiss on Julia's head and picking up a small bouquet off the top of the chest of drawers. She moved to the door. "Here we go."

Throwing open the door with a dramatic flair revealed Harriet, hand raised, about to knock.

"Harriet!" Julia exclaimed.

Harriet beamed, and her hand went from the door to her heart. "Julia," she breathed in a rush. "Look at you. You're stunning. Everyone's ready. Your parents are just downstairs. Is there anything else at all you need?"

Julia felt emotion welling in her throat. "Could I steal you for just a moment before we go down?" asked Julia.

"Of course." Harriet glanced at Alex, who shrugged and slipped past her in the doorway following Ellie downstairs. She closed the door and turned to face Julia. "Is something wrong?" Harriet asked. "I've seen Nathan. He's absolutely jubilant. This is the real deal, Julia. You found it."

Julia smiled. "I know. I'm not worried. In fact, it's like I've never done this before at all. Everything about it is different. Everything about it feels right."

"Then what is it?"

"It's not about Nathan or the wedding. I just…" Her voice caught and she looked away quickly to keep the tears from spilling.

Harriet stepped forward and took her hands. "Julia?"

"Once, when I was too hurt to see it, we sat under the olive tree and you dreamed that a day like this would happen for me."

"Your 800-year-old olive tree," said Harriet quietly, running a thumb over the gold and olive wood band on Julia's right ring finger. "I remember."

"It might sound funny, but I can't help but feel like I have you to thank for all of this."

Harriet shook her head. "You put the pieces back together yourself. You opened your heart again, and this time you found the right one."

"Still," Julia pressed, "if it wasn't you in that seat on the plane, if it wasn't your invitation and Olive Haven and that time we spent together..." she trailed off. "You weren't wrong then, when you said Will did me a favor. I'm a better woman walking down the aisle today than I was back then, Harriet, and there's a better man waiting for me. So, thank you."

Harriet squeezed her hands. "I'm one hundred percent certain you could have figured it all out without me," she said warmly. She paused and smiled. "That said, while I've played witness to dozens of women's stories, it's entirely delightful to find myself continuing to play a part in yours." She folded Julia into a hug. "You are so loved, by Nathan, your family, Alex...and me."

"I love you, too," Julia replied, her voice cracking.

From out on the lawn, a string quartet struck up the opening lines of a lilting sonata. Julia took a deep breath.

"It's time," Harriet said, pulling back. "You're ready."

Julia smiled. "I know."

Harriet opened the door, hurrying into the hallway and down to the entryway to alert the others that the bride was on her way.

Julia turned to the window one final time. The sky was painted in pinks and violets, accented by thin wisps of gilded clouds. The olive tree sparkled, awash in the golden light of sunset and the lights strung through its branches and nestled around its base.

The guests were seated.

Nathan was waiting.

Once, in a not-so-distant past, Julia had sat alone beneath the same tree trying to wrestle with her feelings of heartache. Once Harriet had told her the hard truths of moving on. Once they had gathered in candlelight to toast light hearts finding the way home. Once she and Alex sat beneath the branches sipping white wine, sharing stories of heartbreak.

She hated olives, Alex had said, but she loved that tree. The shade of the olive tree was the best place to rest.

Looking out the window, Julia loved it too.

And tonight, beneath the olive tree, waited the rest of her life.

ACKNOWLEDGMENTS

In writing a story about a tribe of women, I was fortunate to be supported by my own tribe of women who provided feedback, encouragement, questions, and edits.

To Sarah Kasprowicz, the first person who ever suggested I had any writing talent. Your support of my eleven-year-old ramblings lit a fire that sustained me through the fits and spurts of stories started, stopped, abandoned and forgotten. More than twenty years later, your insights and feedback continue to be invaluable, and no doubt helped shape and refine this narrative. Most importantly, your unwavering encouragement helped me believe that this story was worthy of being shared.

To the friends who graciously read around the typos and plot holes of my first drafts. Barb, who got to read it by pure chance. Cait, who carried it around to read in her free time. Kiett, who became its biggest fan. Kim, who promised she liked it. Nicole, who is certain her copy of the rough draft will be worth millions someday. Sarah W, who might still be reading it. Sheila, who read it through the toughest of circumstances. Thank you all for the time and care you showed the manuscript and me.

To Grandma Jean, who knows the value of travel, generosity, and a backup plan. Your "second act" inspired generous hearts and love of adventure in my characters.

To Amber Rami, who let me be the first author she photographed and was incredibly gracious with her time and talent.

To my editor, Jenn Wallace. Five minutes into our first conversation, I believed you knew my book almost better than I did. Your patience, professionalism, and perspective have made this a better novel and me a better writer.

To the team at Olive Street Publishing. I am so proud to have published with a company that amplifies women's voices and women's stories. Thank you for your guidance and support every step of the way.

I would be remiss not to thank my family, who never doubted I would publish something and eagerly asked about this story, even when they knew I would not let any of them see it. It takes a special kind of belief to support and encourage something that you know next to nothing about.

Finally, to Josh. No one believed in me writing this book more than you did, even after you found out all the husbands were dead. You listened to, commiserated over, and championed every single page and iteration of this story and never let me believe I was not good enough to see it through. You are my great love story.

ABOUT THE AUTHOR

Kate Laack is a high school English teacher, theater director, and author. She earned degrees in English and secondary education from the University of Wisconsin – La Crosse, where she also got her start in publishing on the editorial board of the university newspaper, *The Racquet*. Her freelance work has appeared on *Thought Catalog*, *McSweeney's Internet Tendency*, *The Comedy Show Show*, and numerous blogs and professional publications. Kate lives in Pine Island, Minnesota with her husband Josh in a home they built with their own four hands. *In the Shade of Olive Trees* is her first novel.

CPSIA information can be obtained
at www.ICGtesting.com
Printed in the USA
BVHW041947231122
652684BV00001B/34